Praise for the
Alpha Pack Series

"With *Primal Law*, J. D. Tyler has created a whole squad of yummy shifter heroes, who readers will fall head over heels for. Heroine Kira Locke is courageous and intelligent, with her own intriguing paranormal talents, while Jax Law is a sexy alpha-male werewolf who is both heroic and just dominant enough to give a girl wicked ideas. I can't wait for Tyler's next Alpha Pack adventure!"

　　—*New York Times* bestselling author Angela Knight

"What do you get when you combine top secret military teams and werewolves? Try Tyler's sizzling new supernatural series featuring the Alpha Pack—a specialized team of wolf shifters with Psy powers. In this launch book, readers are introduced to the various team members, with the primary focus on Jaxon Law. Tyler has set up an intriguing premise for her series, which promises plenty of action, treachery, and scorchingly hot sex."　　　　　　　—*Romantic Times*

"Sizzling and interesting, *Primal Law* pays homage to Lora Leigh's Breed series while forging its own paths. The characters are likable, and the work speeds along."
　　　　　　　　　　　　　　　　—Fresh Fiction

"*Primal Law* is riveting and carnal . . . full of testosterone-laden men, hot action, and unforgettable passion! In other words, a truly addicting series!"
　　　　　　　　　　　—Reader to Reader Reviews

"In a genre where the paranormal is intense, J. D. Tyler may just be a force to be reckoned with. The book kept me riveted from start to finish." —Night Owl Reviews

The Alpha Pack Novels

Primal Law
Savage Awakening

Savage
AWAKENING

AN ALPHA PACK NOVEL

J. D. TYLER

A SIGNET ECLIPSE BOOK

SIGNET ECLIPSE
Published by New American Library, a division of
Penguin Group (USA) Inc., 375 Hudson Street,
New York, New York 10014, USA
Penguin Group (Canada), 90 Eglinton Avenue East, Suite 700, Toronto,
Ontario M4P 2Y3, Canada (a division of Pearson Penguin Canada Inc.)
Penguin Books Ltd., 80 Strand, London WC2R 0RL, England
Penguin Ireland, 25 St. Stephen's Green, Dublin 2,
Ireland (a division of Penguin Books Ltd.)
Penguin Group (Australia), 250 Camberwell Road, Camberwell, Victoria 3124,
Australia (a division of Pearson Australia Group Pty. Ltd.)
Penguin Books India Pvt. Ltd., 11 Community Centre, Panchsheel Park,
New Delhi - 110 017, India
Penguin Group (NZ), 67 Apollo Drive, Rosedale, Auckland 0632,
New Zealand (a division of Pearson New Zealand Ltd.)
Penguin Books (South Africa) (Pty.) Ltd., 24 Sturdee Avenue,
Rosebank, Johannesburg 2196, South Africa

Penguin Books Ltd., Registered Offices:
80 Strand, London WC2R 0RL, England

First published by Signet Eclipse, an imprint of New American Library,
a division of Penguin Group (USA) Inc.

First Printing, April 2012
10 9 8 7 6 5 4 3 2 1

Copyright © Jo Davis, 2012
All rights reserved

SIGNET ECLIPSE and logo are trademarks of Penguin Group (USA) Inc.

Printed in the United States of America

To my dad, Bryan Davis. My steady rock when times are tough, my wise counselor, my hero. When I needed a wonderful father, God knew exactly the right man to bless me with. I love you so very much.

ACKNOWLEDGMENTS

A special thank-you to all of my family, friends, and my two awesome teenagers, who have stood by my side this past year. I couldn't have made it without you, and I love you all.

One

Aric Savage gripped the chains as the silver-barbed lash tore into his back with unmerciful precision. Fire licked over the flayed skin, soaked deep to burn his guts, steal his breath.

Still, he found the strength to snarl his rage between strokes, his wolf clawing desperately to be free. To rip Orson Chappell's minions to shreds, starting with the bastard currently wielding the whip and then moving on to Beryl, his malicious bitch of a stepsister. The pair of them were an open sore on the world's ass. He'd take great pleasure in tearing out their throats, but not before making them scream as they'd done to him. And then he'd track down the big boss himself. Drag him from under the rock where he was hiding and butcher him, too.

Slowly. Painfully, so that the fucker squealed like a piglet as Aric's wolf devoured him alive.

Here, Piggy, Piggy, let me in!

Not by the hair of my chinny-chin-chin!

No problem, asshole. I'll just incinerate your door, come right in, and watch you piss your pants as I unleash my beast—

Another blow fell, shattering the inner dialogue as liquid agony scored him from shoulder to hip.

"Ahhh! Fuck . . . fuck this . . . b-bastards . . ."

With every stroke, it became harder to retain his hold on sanity. Beryl's efforts were beginning to pay off. After weeks of this hellish trip into Psycholand, the unbelievable pain, he was close to the breaking point.

He'd never dreamed there were so many methods of brutal torture. Or that he'd be forced to sample every fuckin' one of them.

He wasn't aware the whipping had stopped until a hand cupped his chin and thrust his head up. Beryl's flat, soulless eyes bored into his, searching for weakness, for the knowledge that stepbrother dearest was finally a broken husk. A gibbering pile of shit.

"Sorry to disappoint, bitch," he whispered, his throat raw and aching. "I'm still in here." His mind might not be gone just yet, but screaming had stripped his voice during a session with Beryl's handy silver knife. If he should get out of here, he might never recover, in more ways than one.

"Good. I'd be terribly put out if you gave up too quickly." One corner of her mouth curved up. "As it is, you amuse me. So tenacious, my fierce brother."

Her touch made his skin crawl, but he didn't have the strength to jerk his chin out of her grasp. Even if she did set him free, he had nothing left. Despite his longing for vengeance, he didn't have the strength to let loose his raging wolf, let alone summon his gifts of fire or telekinesis. Pathetic.

"I'm surprised Chappell lets you play with his test subjects," he taunted.

A flash of something that might've been unease interrupted the deadness in her eyes, then was gone. "That isn't your concern."

He huffed a laugh that was more like a strangled rasp. "He doesn't know." This kept getting better.

"What?" There. Again the flicker of alarm.

Despite the pain assailing his battered body, he sneered. "Chappell doesn't know what you're doing to me down here, screwing with one of his lab rats. Wonder what he'd do to his pet witch if he found out?"

Flicking a lock of long auburn hair that was a shade darker than his own over her shoulder, she affected a look of complete disinterest. "He has more important concerns than one shifter."

"I'll just bet."

"Whether you're here or in the lab doesn't make a difference to you, anyway." Giving his face a hard squeeze, she shoved, snapping his head to the side. "You'll be just as dead when I'm done with you."

He didn't bother to answer. He knew his chances of escaping from either place dimmed with each day. Spinning on her heel, she turned and left, the gloom beyond his small patch of light swallowing her form and the click of her boots until he was once again alone with his grim thoughts.

How was Beryl involved in all of this? And why the special torture reserved for the older stepbrother she'd barely bothered to know, and vice versa? Why the all-consuming hatred?

True, she'd always been a self-absorbed bitch. From the day Aric's mother had remarried and his stepdaddy had brought that strange, sullen teenaged nightmare home to play house, Aric had done his best to steer clear of her. Not always successfully, either. Joining the Navy SEALs, getting out of that pressure cooker of a house, had been a blessing.

Right up until his unit had been attacked by rogue wolf shifters in the mountains of Afghanistan and his world had been completely fucked. Forever.

If he was honest, he would have to admit that he hadn't been happy since he'd lost his humanity. He loved his brothers on the Alpha Pack team, but when that last op had gone south, they'd given him up fast enough, hadn't they? *Jax gave me up. To save his mate.* When the chips were down, Aric was alone. As always. No one had come for him, and no one would. His throat tightened with emotion, burned with the tears he would never allow to fall. Maybe he was better off dead.

But he couldn't bring himself to give up. No, he wanted to live long enough to slaughter every single person responsible for his being in this hellhole, suffering this endless goddamned agony.

General George Patton had it right. He was going to strut through the valley of the shadow of death—and he'd be the meanest motherfucker there. Make them all pay.

Then, and only then, would he willingly let the Reaper take him.

Rowan Chase jerked the wheel in a hard left, brought the car skidding to a stop in a filthy, garbage-strewn alley between two run-down buildings, killed the ignition, and was out before her rookie partner, Daniel Albright, even got his seat belt unbuckled.

One glance at the situation told her things had already gone FUBAR—fucked up beyond all recognition.

A crowd of about twenty Hispanic men of varying ages surrounded two guys rolling on the ground, the edgy group shouting obscenities, egging the fight on. Quickly, her brain assessed the struggling pair, taking in the information rapid-fire. One stocky male, six feet, about two hundred twenty pounds. The smaller one younger, slender, five-seven, about one sixty. She recognized him as Emilio Herrera. Both wore the East Side Lobos' colors. Family fight. Over what? Drugs, a girl, or some imagined slur? Who knew?

Sunlight glinted off a sliver of metal between the combatants, and blood blossomed on the smaller guy's shirt. *Knife. Shit.* Rowan unclipped her holster as she jogged toward them, adrenaline rushing through her veins.

"LAPD!" she shouted, her pistol clearing leather. "Break it the fuck up!"

"Get back! Give us some room!" Danny bellowed.

Danny was green but he was a good officer. She trusted him to control the agitated crowd while she dealt with the fight—and trust was imperative. A second unit was on the way, but that didn't mean it would arrive in time to prevent disaster.

The pair were oblivious at first, the younger man completely focused on defending himself against his assailant. The stocky man was clearly the aggressor, his rage palpable. He was the one she needed to reach.

"I said break it up! Now!"

Switchblade in his meaty fist, straddling the younger man, the stocky one turned his head to glance at her, a snarl on his face. She sucked in a breath, recognizing him. Luis Garcia. She should've known. He was a dangerous bastard with a long rap sheet full of violence. Worse, he was unpredictable, his mind fried from a lifetime of drug abuse.

"Little *puta* stole my shit," he slurred, spittle flying.

"I didn't!" Emilio cried, holding up his hands. "I don't do the powder, you know that! *La familia* knows that!"

"You took it and I'm gonna gut you like a—"

"No, you're not," Rowan ordered, using her most authoritative voice. She held her pistol at her side, pointed at the asphalt. "Put the blade down and come talk to me. We'll sort it out."

"Shut up, *lesbiana*. You think you have bigger *cojones* than Luis, *si*? Perhaps you do." He gave a nasty laugh.

Rowan let the insult roll off. She'd been called worse. "Emilio is telling the truth, Garcia. I know him and I swear to you he wouldn't take your blow." *Now, your car? He'd steal that in a heartbeat, but not your coke.* "I wouldn't lie to my own people. Put the knife down."

To her right, the Lobos' leader pushed through the crowd, apparently late on the scene. Salazar Romero was tall, muscular, and menacing, with long black hair and a soul patch, arms covered with tats. "Don't be stupid. Listen to *mamacita*, Luis. She's street. One of us, you feel me? Her word is good enough for me, so it's good enough for the Lobos."

Finally, a break in the ice. The bigger man visibly wavered, his grip on his quarry loosening. He tried to stare Salazar down, but looked away first, like the dog he was. But that didn't mean the danger was over. Rowan's stance remained tense as Garcia let the knife fall from his hand, let go of Emilio's shirt.

"Climb off him and stand," she directed. "Slowly."

Garcia let go a string of muttered curses, but did as he was told. On his feet, he stepped away from the bleeding man and turned toward her, shaking his head. Still cursing. Gesturing and swinging his arms as he became more agitated. She didn't like his body language. The man was going to lose it again.

"Kneel, hands behind your head."

His head snapped up. "You said we was gonna talk!"

"First, kneel, hands be—"

"Fuck you, bitch!"

Rowan knew what Garcia was going to do, even as he dropped his right arm, reached behind him to grab something at the small of his back. She reacted a split second faster, brought up her weapon and leveled it at his chest, shouting, "Drop it!"

But he brought the gun around, swung the muzzle toward her, his intent clear. She was hardly aware of her finger pressing the trigger, and the deafening explosion was over before her brain registered the noise.

Garcia jerked backward, eyes widening in surprise. A bloom of scarlet began to spread across his chest as his knees buckled and he crumpled to the ground. Weapon still trained on his fallen form, she walked over and kicked the man's gun from his outstretched hand. Wary, she crouched next to his head and placed two fingers on his neck.

"Dead?" Danny asked.

"Yeah." She heaved a shaky breath and stood, surveying the few people that were left.

Most of them had gotten the hell out of there when Garcia drew down and his act of stupidity proved fatal.

Emilio was still sitting a few feet away, a hand pressed to his bloodied side, grimacing in pain. Salazar and a couple of his lieutenants were with him, praising the kid for facing down crazy Garcia, as though the kid had taken him out himself. The little car thief's street cred had just risen substantially, along with plenty of temptation for a rival gang to add him to their hit list.

And the cycle never ended.

Rowan holstered her weapon, feeling sick. *Oh, God. I killed one of my own. Right here on my home turf, among the people I'm supposed to keep safe. Could I have handled this differently? How?*

"Chase!"

Startled, she blinked at Danny, who was right in her face, hand on her shoulder. "What?"

"Whatever shit is going through your head right now, stop," he said in a low voice. "You gave him every chance to give up. Hell, you almost waited a hair too long to draw down and pull the trigger. It was a righteous shooting. No one is going to dispute that."

"The baby cop is right, *mamacita*," Salazar said in a loud voice. "Luis was broken, man. He acted on his own to jump Emilio, and the Lobos wash their hands of him. There will be no retribution."

Broken, meaning Salazar had recently demoted him. She supposed she should feel relieved that Luis had already become a problem they wanted erased, or her East Side upbringing might not mean squat. Suddenly aware of several sets of eyes boring into her, studying her reaction, she clamped her mouth firmly shut and gave a curt nod.

Salazar waved a hand at his remaining followers. *"Vamanos!"*

No retribution. Staring at their retreating backs, she couldn't work up the gratitude. Eleven years on the force and she'd drawn her weapon less than a dozen times. Never fired it outside the shooting range, before today.

And today, she'd killed a man. No matter his failings, Luis Garcia had a wife and six kids who depended on him. Her breakfast threatened to make a reappearance, but she managed to keep it down.

"Chase?"

Rowan turned, blinking at Captain Connolly. She couldn't seem to shake the fog that had wrapped itself around her brain. "Sir."

"What happened here?" he asked matter-of-factly. His weathered face was calm, his blue eyes patient.

Quickly, she gave their supervisor the rundown, in detail. Danny backed her up, and the captain nodded.

"All right. Looks like a clean shooting, but you know what happens next," he said kindly.

She did. Although she'd never had to fire her weapon, much less kill a suspect, other officers had over the years. They all knew the drill. She exhaled a deep breath. "I guess I'm on leave."

"I'm afraid so." Connolly squeezed her shoulder. "At least until the investigation is over. It'll probably be just a formality in this case, but it still sucks. We've got things covered here. Head on back to the station, take care of your paperwork. Make sure all your i's are dotted and the t's crossed. Then surrender your weapon and go home. I'll call you."

"What about Albright?" She gestured to her partner.

"I'll temporarily reassign him pending the closing of the investigation."

"Yes, sir." Damn, she hated losing a good rookie to another officer. Even if Internal Affairs closed the matter quickly, she'd have to fight to get him back.

"Take it easy," Danny said, trying to be reassuring. "Everything will be fine."

"Sure. Take care, and I'll see you."

She walked away, aware of eyes at her back, measuring. Wondering whether she'd be the department's new head case, waiting to see if this would be what finally sent her careening over the edge. First the loss of her younger brother, and now this.

Climbing into the patrol car, she forced herself to start the ignition and calmly drive away when all she wanted to do was sit there and fall apart. Later, she promised herself. She'd pick up a six-pack of beer on the way home and let go where no one could see.

For now, "compartmentalize" was the word of the day and the only way to get through it.

Three hours later, Rowan finished the last of her mountain of paperwork, surrendered her pistol, and headed out the door, thankfully unnoticed except for a couple of buddies who'd heard the news and stopped her to deliver brief pep talks. She felt decidedly naked without the comforting, familiar weight of a weapon at her side and just wanted to get the hell out of there before more of her comrades noticed and wanted to get the lowdown firsthand.

She hurried to her truck and fired it up just as her cell phone vibrated on her hip. With a sigh, she left the vehicle in park, retrieved the device, and checked the caller ID. This one she had to take. "Hello."

"Hey, it's me."

In spite of herself, she smiled. "Hi, me. What's

cookin'?" Her friend, FBI special agent Dean Campbell, never spoke either of their names on the phone. Paranoia was more than in his job description—it was embedded in his DNA.

"Plenty. I've got those Dodgers tickets you wanted," he said cheerfully. "Meet me for a burger, usual place?"

Her smile vanished and the blood drained from her face. Her mouth opened a couple of times before she could find her voice. "I'll be there in half an hour. I need to go home and change first."

"On my way. I'll get us a table."

Punching the OFF button, she tossed the phone in the seat next to her and peeled out. *Oh, God.* Finally, after months of a fruitless, agonizing search for answers and a maze of dead ends, the call she'd been praying for had come. And for a while longer, she had to bleed just a little more inside, not knowing whether this was the end or the beginning.

Not knowing if Micah really was dead, as the government claimed, or if he was alive somewhere, waiting to be rescued.

And if her brother was alive, what the fuck was going on?

The questions and possible answers whirled in her brain all the way to her apartment, and didn't let up as she hurriedly stripped out of her uniform and changed into jean shorts, a tank top, and tennis shoes. She couldn't stand another second of this torture now that the end was in sight. The drive to Willy's had never seemed so long, yet she made it there in under fifteen. The bar and burger joint wasn't crowded this time of afternoon, so she was able to get a pretty good parking spot on the side of the building.

Jogging around to the front, she pushed inside and spotted Dean sitting in a booth near the back. He waved and she went to meet him, returning his quick hug before sliding into the seat opposite his.

Mustering a smile, she crossed her arms on the table. "You look good, my friend." He always did. Dean was in his mid-thirties, with honey blond hair, big brown eyes, and a killer smile. The whole package stopped traffic. It was a shame she felt nothing more than mild attraction for the man, and vice versa, because it had been *way* too long since she'd had any sort of an intimate relationship.

"Back atcha." Sitting back, he eyed her in speculation. "I already heard through the grapevine about the shooting. How are you holding up?"

"Jeez, that was fast," she muttered. "I'm okay."

"You sure?"

"No."

He patted her hand, his gaze softening. "That's normal. You'll be all right, trust me. Especially after I give you something else to occupy your mind." Reaching into his pocket, he withdrew a legal-sized white envelope and slid it across the table.

Swallowing hard, she eyed it. "My *tickets*?"

The agent glanced around, but there was no one nearby to listen. Still, he spoke in a low voice. "Read that, memorize it, then destroy it."

Turning the envelope over she glanced at her friend. "What's inside?"

"Directions to a place that doesn't officially exist." He paused. "A compound in Wyoming, situated deep in the Shoshone National Forest. Top secret, black ops."

"Unless you know the right people to squeeze."

A corner of his mouth lifted. "Exactly."

Taking a deep breath, she asked the one question burning in her heart. "Is my brother alive?"

"I don't know," he said, tapping the envelope. "But those are the ones who will."

So close, but still no answer. Yet. She fought back the tears that would do neither herself nor Micah any good. "You risked everything to get this information for me. I don't know how to thank you."

"By not getting yourself killed." He wasn't joking.

"I'll put that on the list right after finishing with IA, taking personal leave, packing, and hitting the road."

"Call me when you leave town, and keep in touch."

"I will," she promised.

"You hungry? I'm buying."

To Rowan's surprise, her stomach snarled. Funny how a sliver of hope could revive a person's appetite. "I could eat, but it's on me. And if this lead takes me to the truth about what happened to Micah, there's a steak dinner in it for you when I return. It's the least I can do."

"Only if you bring Micah with you," he said softly.

Damn it, she would *not* cry.

"It's a deal."

Understandably, their meal was quite a bit more subdued than usual. Rowan was far too preoccupied to make a good companion, but that was the beauty of true friendship; neither of them had to say a word to be comfortable. They had each other's backs.

While they ate, her thoughts drifted to this mysterious compound and what kind of operation she would find. Not to mention the reception she'd receive, especially when they learned of her mission.

But she wouldn't leave there without finding out, once and for all, what had happened to her brother. She and Micah had always shared a mental connection that most people would scoff at, and certainly wouldn't understand. They weren't twins, but she felt strongly that she would *know* in her heart if and when he died. He was alive. Had to be.

No, this wasn't the end at all, but just the beginning. She'd find her brother if it was the last thing she ever did.

And then she'd make reservations for three at the finest restaurant in L.A.

With every mile that took her closer to her destination, Rowan's anxiety grew by leaps and bounds. The gorgeous backdrop of the Shoshone National Forest, resplendent in full summer greenery, hardly registered as she steered her truck up the winding road.

Gripping the wheel, she eyed the left-hand side of the road, looking for the obscure turn outlined in the directions she'd memorized and then burned three weeks ago. Three miles later she found it. Or hoped she had.

Turning, she braked in front of a metal gate. It was simple, the kind any landowner might use, along with the black and white NO TRESPASSING sign nailed to a post next to the chain and padlock. Neither posed a deterrent to her bolt cutters or her determination.

Leaving the truck running, she grabbed the cutters and made short work of the chain, then unwrapped it, letting it hang from the gate. *In for a penny.* If she was in the right place, she'd soon have a lot more to worry about than a measly charge of trespassing on government property.

After swinging the gate open enough to drive the vehicle through, she returned to the truck and did just that. Then she got out and closed the gate again, wrapping the chain around it so that, hopefully, nothing would appear out of the ordinary to a casual passerby. So far, so good. She continued on her way.

A couple of miles deeper into the forest, the second barrier was an unpleasant surprise, and a formidable obstacle. She could have screamed in frustration.

The chain-link fence was about ten feet tall and topped with razor wire. This gate was much more sophisticated, at least two feet taller than the fence on either side, and automated, with a pass code box on the driver's side. On top of the security box, a camera lens stared her in the face like an all-knowing eye.

"Shit."

She didn't have the code. And after several minutes of punching a green CALL button and then waiting, it became evident that no one planned to answer her summons. The operatives inside were probably having a good laugh. Maybe they thought she'd get bored and go on her merry way.

They thought wrong.

Calmly, she reached for her purse, never happier that the captain had returned her weapon. Extracting the Glock from within and squinting, she pointed the gun at the camera lens. "Knock-knock, assholes."

And fired, sending a shower of glass and metal raining all over the drive.

That ought to get their fucking attention. Best to meet them head-on. Stepping away from the truck, she tucked the gun into the waistband of her jeans and walked over to inspect the gate. State-of-the-art stuff, a real fortress. What was this place and how was Micah involved? She wasn't leaving until they enlightened her.

A shuffle sounded to her left. And low growling.

Turning, she cursed softly, eyes widening. Guard dogs? Several of them, on *her* side of the fence, fanning out to surround her, heads down, ears flat, fangs bared. Moving almost silently through the sun-dappled forest.

But no, these weren't dogs. They were . . .

Wolves! And one really large black *panther*?

She blinked rapidly as they approached and backed slowly toward her truck, thinking she must be seeing things. Wolves were now common in the Shoshone, thanks to wildlife rescue efforts. But she'd heard that wolves went out of their way to avoid humans. Right? Just not *these* wolves.

And what about the big cat? Black panthers didn't even technically exist!

Tell that to this one.

"Stay," she called, holding out a shaking hand. "Nice doggies. I'm not going to hurt you."

A loud snarl came from behind her, and a glance nearly stopped her heart. One wolf had moved behind her, blocking her escape to the truck. She was completely surrounded. Her pulse beat a terrified tattoo in her throat as she gripped the butt of her gun, easing the weapon from the waist of her jeans.

Just then, the images of three of the wolves and the cat began to shimmer. Sort of like heat waves on hot pavement. Their bodies began to re-form, the fur retracting. Canine and feline limbs becoming arms and legs. *What the shit?* Staring, she told herself she was *not* seeing a group of sexy, naked men standing among the rest of the wolves and wearing a range of emotions on their faces, from amusement to grim resignation.

A dark-haired god of a man—wolf, whatever—strolled forward. "I'm Nick Westfall, commander of the Alpha Pack team. And you're in a shitload of trouble, Miss Chase."

How did he know her name? Rowan couldn't catch her breath to reply, even if she could've formed a response. Her vision blurred and the tough woman raised in an East L.A. barrio did something she'd never done in her life. Not even when she'd been informed of Micah's "death."

She fainted dead away.

Two

Rowan came awake with a start and blinked at her surroundings in confusion. Immediately her brain cataloged the soft, comfortable bed she was lying in, and the modestly furnished bedroom. For a few moments she struggled to make sense of where she was and why—and then the memory returned.

As she sat up, a slight pain lanced the back of her head and she winced, probing the area with her fingers. Under her hair at the back of her skull lurked a lump that throbbed when she pressed a little too hard, but it wasn't too bad. Anyhow, that seemed to be the least of her worries.

She'd come to this place—if she was indeed inside the compound—seeking answers about Micah and had seen . . . what, exactly? Then she'd fainted like a rookie observing her first autopsy. With her gun in hand.

Her gun that was now missing.

Looking to the nightstand, she reached out and opened the drawer. Empty, except for a sheet of paper typed with a list of what appeared to be phone extensions. Sliding the drawer shut, she took another survey of the room. Her purse rested on the top of the otherwise bare dresser. The black duffel bag she'd brought, stuffed with several changes of clothes and underwear, sat on the floor in front of it. She doubted very much that she'd find her weapon stashed in either one.

Pushing herself up from the bed, she wobbled over to investigate. The rest of her belongings seemed to be intact, but as expected, the gun was missing. That they'd taken it was no surprise, but being without protection was unsettling. Damn it, she felt naked without it.

Naked. Oh, God. She'd seen several wolves and a panther become hot men not wearing a stitch. Hadn't she? Or maybe everything she'd been through in the last few months had finally sent her over the edge. Bye-bye sanity, hello blissful insanity. Maybe she'd been institutionalized and this was her jail cell, disguised as a normal room. Any minute a nurse would be by with medication that would send her back to the land of happiness and light.

"Oh, good, you're awake!"

Turning, Rowan blinked at the attractive woman standing in the bedroom doorway wearing a white doctor's coat over a green blouse and black pants. "Shit, I *did* go crazy," she murmured.

"Excuse me?"

She waved a hand at the woman's attire. "Which are you, my nurse or my psychiatrist? Because I'm pretty sure I've suffered a break from reality and you're my keeper."

The brunette laughed good-naturedly, and pushed a

lock of long, curly hair from her face, tucking it behind one ear. "I'm Dr. Mackenzie Grant, but no, I'm not *your* doctor, warden, or anything else. I'm just here to make sure you're all right. You took a nasty bump to your head when you passed out."

"Right. When I checked out because I saw . . . or thought I saw . . ." Frowning, she trailed off.

The doctor cleared her throat. "Yes, well. Nick will want to talk with you about that, I'm sure."

"Nick Westfall," she recalled. "Your commander."

"Not *my* commander, exactly, but yes. He's the head honcho around here. He leads the Alpha Pack team."

"Who are wolves and cats in disguise."

The other woman's gaze was sympathetic. "I'm sorry, I really can't talk about—"

Rowan gave a laugh that was half-hysterical, dripping with sarcasm. "Of course not."

"Nick will tell you everything he feels you need to know, but after that we can talk all you want."

The doc was loyal, at least. She could respect that. "When does he want to see me?"

"As soon as you're feeling up to it. I can take you to his office now if you'd like, Miss Chase."

"Call me Rowan. Wait, how did you know my name?" She cast a suspicious look at her purse. Had these people gone through her things?

"Nick told us."

That's right—Westfall had called her by name the moment they met. "And how did *he* know? Did someone alert him that I was on my way?" Rowan frowned. Dean wouldn't have betrayed her, she was certain. "Never mind. I'm sure that's another one of those things he'll have to tell me. And believe me, Dr. Grant, he'd better."

"Mackenzie or Mac is fine," the woman said amiably, ignoring Rowan's last remark. "Are you ready?"

"Sure, lead the way."

Glancing at her purse and bag again, she opted to leave them behind. She wasn't carrying much cash, and only a couple of credit cards. No, if these people had planned to keep her stuff they would've taken the rest along with her gun. She followed the doctor from the bedroom, through a furnished living room, to the door, and out into a carpeted hallway lined with more doors, all numbered. Quickening her pace, she fell into step beside the other woman.

"So, this area is what? Like a dorm?" she guessed.

Mackenzie nodded. "Yes, but unlike dorms, the residence wings are fully equipped apartments, and we aren't required to share quarters. Privacy is a highly valued commodity in a busy place where so many of us live and work, and it's usually in short supply."

"It's nicer than I expected," Rowan admitted, admiring the dark green carpet and cream-colored walls adorned with sconces that reminded her of the inside of a nice hotel. "On the drive here, I envisioned something much more stark and unfriendly. You know, what with it being a top secret compound and all that."

"Which begs the question of how you found out about us." The doc cut her a curious stare.

Rowan smirked. "I guess that's something your illustrious leader can tell you if he wants—after he and I have a little chat."

"Touché," Mackenzie said with a laugh.

As they walked, a glint of silver at the vee of the other woman's blouse caught Rowan's eye. A round disk about the size of a silver dollar hung there, suspended on a sturdy chain. It struck her as being a bit heavy, like a piece of jewelry more suited to a man. But what did she know? She was a cop, not a fashion critic.

"That's a gorgeous pendant," she said, waving a hand at the doc's chest.

Mackenzie started and glanced down at the item as though she'd forgotten it was there. "Thanks."

She peered closer. "Is that a . . . pentagram?"

"Yes, it is." But the doc didn't offer anything further.

Tough. Cops liked answers. "Cool. Are you Wiccan?"

"No." A hint of annoyance crept into the doc's tone, and her words became clipped as she tucked the disk under her blouse again. "The necklace was a gift."

Subject closed, at least for now. But Rowan sensed a story there and sooner or later she'd ferret out the mystery. Investigating, prying answers from people who didn't want to give them, was in her blood. For the time being, she let it go.

She had bigger fish to fry.

Mackenzie led her through a maze of corridors, and Rowan made sure to catalog every turn in her brain. The information would come in handy whether she stayed or had to get the fuck out of here fast.

Finally the doc halted in front of a closed door and nodded. "This is Nick's office. Don't be intimidated— he's not as mean as he looks."

"That's okay, because I'm *meaner* than I look." She wasn't kidding, but Mackenzie smiled anyway, giving Rowan's arm a squeeze.

"I'll check on you later."

"Thanks." Rowan watched the woman start back the way they'd come, then turned her attention to the door. Heaving a fortifying breath, she gave three sharp raps and waited until she heard the man's deep voice call out for her to come in before turning the knob and stepping inside.

The interior of Westfall's office was much the same as her room—comfortable but nothing too fancy. A big desk equipped with a laptop and a cordless phone fit the space nicely, leaving room for a couple of stuffed chairs across from it. But the man himself quickly captured her attention as he rose and offered her his hand, his expression unreadable.

"Miss Chase."

"Rowan, please."

"Nick." They shook hands and then he sat, gesturing for her to do the same.

"Who told you I was coming here?" she asked, careful not to sound defensive right off the bat. It wouldn't do to piss off the man who might have the answers she needed.

"No one." He held her gaze, his deep blue eyes seeming to look right into her soul.

She wondered what he saw there. "Then when I arrived, how did you know my name?"

The handsome dark-haired man appeared to consider his reply carefully before he finally spoke. "I'm a PreCog."

"Come again?"

"I'm a PreCog. I sometimes see events before they happen."

Rowan stared at him, wondering which one of them

was nuts. Maybe Luis Garcia really had shot her and she was lying in some hospital in a coma, dreaming all of this.

She cleared her throat. "On top of being a wolf-man? Right. Sure you are. Listen, it doesn't make two shits to me who ratted me out or what delusions of grandeur you're suffering from. I just came here to—"

"Find out what happened to Micah," he interrupted softly.

That rattled her for a couple of seconds, but she shook it off. "Not impressed. I'm sure the person who told you I was coming also told you why." Leaning forward, she felt the slow boil of anger begin on hearing this stranger speak her brother's name in such a familiar way. Her fingers dug into the arms of her chair. "So let's just cut all the dancing around the subject. If Micah's alive, tell me where he is and why in God's name I was told he was dead. If he *is* dead, help me get his body home."

Those last words emerged from her lips as though she was being strangled, stopping short of uttering the inane phrase about needing closure. There would *never* be closure if Micah truly was gone, the bleeding hole in her heart never filled.

"It's not that simple."

Months of alternating between grief and frustration with getting the runaround had frazzled her temper, and it snapped. "What the hell do you mean? He's either dead or alive!" she shouted. "Which one is it?"

"I don't know!"

His thundering tone echoed in the enclosed space, leaving a stunned silence in its wake. She blinked at

Nick's miserable expression, the slump of his big shoulders. "He's missing?"

"Off the record, yes."

"That Navy guy, General Jarrod Grant, said . . . The government lied to me," she whispered. "They said Micah was killed during training maneuvers and that his body couldn't be recovered. I buried an empty fucking box while that bastard Grant handed me an American flag and told me how sorry he was. And all the time I was grieving, my brother was out there somewhere, possibly alive, waiting to be rescued. Maybe still is."

The horrible reality blew her mind. The lack of her brother's body had disturbed her all along, and deep down she'd thought—prayed—that the report of his "death" had been a mistake. But to find out the whole thing was an outright *lie*? Rage churned, too big for her skin, threatening to tear her apart.

"For what it's worth, I *am* sorry," he said sincerely. "I would have preferred to tell you the truth, but I was overruled."

"By whom? General Grant?"

"Yes."

She wanted her gun back. Then she'd shoot someone. All she needed was the correct target.

"What *is* the truth? Was my brother really in the SEALs when he disappeared?"

"No. By then he was working here, as a member of the Alpha Pack team."

"But in the beginning, he was with the Navy, right?" That's what he'd *told* her, all those years. Now she wondered how well she'd known her brother.

"Yes, he was, just like many of my men before this

compound opened about five years ago. There was a different team leader then, and I replaced him a little over six months ago. *After* he, Micah, and several other Pack members were allegedly killed." His gaze bored into her.

She studied him for a minute, thinking. "The general. Would he be any relation to Mackenzie Grant?"

Nick nodded. "Jarrod Grant is Mac's father . . . and my main contact with the military. We sort of work together."

"Wow, you're all just one big happy family, huh?"

He ignored her sarcasm. "Most of the time, though we have our squabbles now and then."

She stood and paced a little, stopped and stared out the window over his head. The rage had subsided to a bearable level, but the slow burn of anger remained. Along with a big side helping of frustration. "Why didn't you know?"

"Excuse me?"

She looked down at him to see him frowning at her in question. "You claim to be psychic, right? Why didn't you know what was going to happen to my brother and stop it?"

His expression became sympathetic. "I'm not psychic; I'm a PreCog. Big difference, because the visions I receive as a PreCog are only a small part of psychic ability. Anyway, I was a special agent with the FBI at the time Micah and the others vanished. I didn't know the team members seven months ago, but even if I had there's no guarantee I would've seen the event in time to avert it, or at all. I'm not omniscient."

"So you pick up what you can, like spotty cable television reception?"

One corner of his mouth curled up. "Something like that."

It was a really nice mouth, too. Sexy. The big bastard was probably an animal in the sack. Though like Dean, the buttoned-down sort wasn't really her type. Shutting off that line of thinking, she focused on her mission, crossing her arms over her chest. "Okay, the twenty questions routine is wearing me out, and when I'm tired I get cranky. Fill in the blanks for me, starting with what the hell my brother's job here entails, what he was doing when he disappeared, and what you think happened."

Nick took a long time to answer. But when he did, his voice was low and patient. "Like most of the team, Micah's a wolf shifter. Almost six years ago, when he and several of the others were part of a Navy SEAL team stationed in the mountains of Afghanistan, they were attacked by rogue werewolves."

He gave her a few seconds to digest that tidbit, and she took the time. "All right. I'm a cop, and we deal in facts. I *saw* men turn into wolves—and one into a panther. I think maybe I'm in a coma and dreaming, but I'll go with it."

The man chuckled, shaking his head. "No, you're very much awake, though before long you'll wish you weren't." He paused. "As the survivors recovered from the attack in a military hospital, physicians discovered anomalies in their blood work. It wasn't long before the first man shifted into a wolf right in his hospital bed, and chaos ensued."

"I can imagine." What a wild tale. But still, she had seen the results with her own two eyes.

"Studies were conducted on the men, and it was

found that each of them not only could shift into a wolf but had various special abilities."

"Like the one you claim as a PreCog?"

He didn't comment on her apparent continuing doubt. "Exactly. But each man's is different. One is a Telepath; one's a Firestarter . . ." He trailed off, a look of sadness shadowing his face before he went on. "It turned out they'd possessed these tendencies since childhood, but after they became shifters, the power of their gifts had increased many times over."

"Assuming I can buy what you're saying, what is Micah's so-called gift?" She couldn't wait to hear this.

"He was—or is—a Dreamwalker. The team and the doctors here told me that your brother could literally visit people's dreams to communicate."

Rowan's legs grew weak and she sat down in the chair again, hard. Instantly, she was transported back to when she and Micah were children. Growing up, she'd had dreams in which she talked with her brother about whatever, and she distinctly recalled several occasions where they'd compared notes and discovered they'd had the same dream. But a lot of people had those. Didn't they?

No, they didn't. Not the same dream at the same time. What if . . .

Her mind whirled with the implications, and the truth was wrenched from her gut. "I haven't dreamed about my brother in almost a year."

"That doesn't mean he's dead," Nick said gently.

"Unlike what I was told by your colleague, General Grant," she snapped, swiping impatiently at a stray tear.

"That was done against my better judgment."

"And yet you didn't rectify his lie."

"I wanted something solid to give Micah's family first," he said firmly. "Grant was right in not giving the relatives false hope, and he didn't want the questions that listing them as 'missing' would prompt. I just don't agree we should've claimed they were dead without the bodies to prove it."

She could almost feel her insides crumbling under the weight of all she'd learned. Especially about the brother she loved more than her own life. If he could walk in dreams, and yet hadn't visited hers in months, chances were he really was gone. Despite Grant's lie.

"Fortunately, I do have something I can share with you."

Shaken out of her downward spiral, she snapped her gaze to his. "I'm listening."

"A few weeks ago my team conducted a rescue op at a facility where some nasty experiments were being performed on shifters and humans. While there, one of my men swore he caught Micah's scent."

"His *scent*?"

"Yeah. Wolves have an excellent sense of smell. We can discern the signature of each individual scent and never forget it."

"Sure you can." Jesus Christ in a tutu. "So, was it Micah's? Do you have any other evidence?"

"Actually, we do. One of the shifters we rescued told us that a man named Micah, who'd been kept in a nearby cage, had been moved just a few days before we busted into the place. We have reason to believe—"

"Hang on. Are you telling me whoever took my brother put him in a fucking *cage*, then treated him like a goddamned animal for whatever twisted reason?"

Nick sighed, looking weary. "Yeah, that's what I'm saying. The man also fits your brother's description."

"What are those assholes doing to my little brother?" she asked, her voice low and dangerous.

To his credit, Nick didn't mince words. "We've learned that a company by the name of NewLife Technology, headed by Orson Chappell, has a secret project. Their goal is to take shifter DNA and genetic strands, combine them with humans', and morph them into a new, invincible breed of soldiers."

"In layman's terms?"

"They're trying to create super-shifters with Psy abilities, and they hope to mass-produce them like an automobile factory would produce cars. If they succeed, humanity as we know it is history." He scowled. "Chappell is murdering people in the process, too. You can bet his reasons have nothing to do with bettering this country or saving lives, but involve his own power and greed."

Rowan gaped at him, trying to assimilate this new information. The seconds ticked by as the man watched her. "And how is that different from what you're doing here? Because from where I sit, I've been lied to and cheated out of the only family I have left. How do I know you haven't turned the story completely around, that you're not the bad guys?"

"That's a fair question. But let me ask you this—why would we have greeted you as shifters instead of humans when we could've kept that part of us a secret? We could have met you with a show of force, turned you away, and you never would've found out about us or what's going on with Micah."

"But you didn't make me leave, and you all showed me one of your secrets."

"Exactly."

And they hadn't harmed her in any way. They'd shown her their collective underbelly, so to speak, and hadn't attacked. All at once it hit her. "You wanted to gain my trust. To show me you're the good guys."

He smiled. "Well, I don't know about *good*. But as my men are fond of saying, we're not the guys you have to worry about."

Okay, that seemed logical. But none of it was very comforting.

Suddenly she was so damned tired. Her mind couldn't handle any more. "This is all so messed up," she muttered, shoving a strand of hair out of her face.

Dark humor colored his reply. "No argument there."

"So what does your Alpha Pack team do?"

"We're enforcers of a sort. We take care of paranormal problems that pop up all over the world."

She couldn't help it—a laugh escaped that was absent of humor and a lot on edge. "Pop up? Like the measles? What are we talking here, ghosties and ghoulies?"

"Yes. And much worse."

The man said that with a straight face, too. "Okay, I'll bite. Like what?"

"Vampires, rogue shifters of all kinds, witches, demons. You name it. If some being in the paranormal community is wreaking havoc, we get called out to either capture it or eliminate it. Some of them we bring here to undergo rehabilitation. You'll meet the rest of our residents soon enough." He shrugged, as though dealing with these creatures was an everyday occurrence.

"And I suppose you can prove everything you're telling me?"

"I can, though I can sense you're already starting to believe me whether you want to or not."

"I still want solid proof." She noted he didn't seem concerned by this, which meant one of two things: he knew she wouldn't be here long enough for it to be an issue, or he really could produce the evidence she wanted. Either way was troubling. "What about you? You said that you've only known these guys for a few months, so how did you become a wolf? Were you attacked, too?"

"No. I was born a shifter."

Another surprise, which she couldn't keep off her face. "That's . . . neat. Was your family—"

"My family is not up for discussion," he said coolly.

Whoa, the drop in temperature could've given her frostbite. Message received. "Hey, my bad. You can't blame me for being curious after hearing all of this. No hard feelings?"

The man relaxed some, and nodded. "Not at all."

She hesitated. "Assuming I can ever, in a zillion years, swallow that you guys battle mythical creatures, why enlighten me? Why not just tell me Micah is dead and send me on my way?"

"I could have," he acknowledged. "But you'd already learned of our compound and I saw right away you're not the type of person to be put off once you're on the hunt. We're similar that way, you and I."

"True enough."

"Besides, your journey led you here for another reason besides finding your brother. One every bit as important."

"What— Oh. More psychic stuff, huh?"

"PreCog, and yes."

"Whatever." She resisted the urge to roll her eyes. Barely. But she couldn't help but be curious about his mysterious claim. "What other reason would there be?"

He looked uncomfortable for a second, then shook his head. "Can't tell you that. As a rule, I try not to influence others' life decisions, which means I don't interfere with free will."

"Well, thanks, Great and Powerful Oz," she deadpanned. "That's real helpful. Now what?"

"We have a new lead," he revealed, studying her intently. "One that might take us to Micah and another of our teammates, Aric Savage, who was captured by this same group a few weeks ago during an op gone bad."

"That's the best news I've heard all year—the part about the lead, not the screwup." A thrill of excitement fired her cop's blood. "So, what's the plan? When do we leave?"

"The plan is, *Alpha Pack* is going in to hopefully capture as many of the organization as possible, and rescue our men along with anyone else being held. *You* are staying here."

Her spine straightened. "No damned way. I'm a cop, remember? I can't get furry and I don't have any cool supernatural talents, but it sounds to me like you guys need all the help you can get, what with losing your team members right and left."

"You may be a cop, but in my world you're a civilian. I can't be responsible for getting you killed. What am I supposed to tell your brother when I bring him back and he learns that I allowed you to get hurt, or worse?"

Made sense when he put it like that. The Pack's boss man didn't want to take the heat if something happened to her.

"All right," she said nonchalantly. "I can live with that. I wouldn't want you to feel guilty if I got my ass shredded."

Nick's piercing blue eyes narrowed in suspicion. "Why do I get the feeling I've been played?"

For the first time since meeting the Pack's boss, she smiled. "I'd say you didn't need to be a fuckin' psychic to know that."

As the door to his office closed behind Rowan Chase, Nick sat back in his chair and plowed a hand through his short hair with a weary sigh. The arrival of Micah's sister was a complication he didn't need right now. But he couldn't deny that she was going to be very important to the team.

And to one man in particular.

A knock interrupted his thoughts and he glanced up to see the newest addition to Alpha Pack open the door and poke his head inside.

"Got a minute?"

"Sure, come on in."

Kalen Black strolled inside and stood in front of Nick's desk with his booted feet spread, arms crossed over his chest. As always, Nick fought not to stare at Goth-boy dressed in his usual black ensemble, but for better or worse, the young man commanded attention wherever he went.

Jet-black rock-star hair fell in messy layers around his face and to the shoulders of his battered leather duster. Underneath, he wore a mesh T-shirt and jeans tucked into calf-high boots adorned with silver buckles. Black-tipped nails graced the strong fingers digging into his biceps, and striking kohl-rimmed eyes the color of emeralds gazed back at Nick unflinchingly.

Their resident Sorcerer/Necromancer, who was also a panther shifter, was no attention seeker, though. A graduate of the School of Hard Knocks, Kalen simply didn't give a damn what anyone thought of him. The kid possessed the most raw power of any being Nick had ever run across. And made him feel really goddamned old, which was the sad truth.

If the team knew just *how* old, they'd never believe it.

"The woman, Miss Chase," Kalen prompted. "I'm assuming she's related to the Pack member with the same last name?"

"Rowan is Micah's sister," Nick confirmed. "But since neither of us knew Micah I'm guessing you're not really here to talk about the missing wolf or his sibling."

The Sorcerer's neutral expression darkened. Slowly, he lowered himself into one of the chairs opposite Nick, rested his elbows on his knees, and put his face in his hands. That was when Nick noticed that the silver pentagram pendant the younger man wore around his neck, was never without, was missing.

A shiver of dread shot through his veins, and he straightened. He'd learned to never ignore the faint beginnings of a vision. "Where's your necklace?" he asked sharply.

Kalen's head came up, his face etched with resignation. "Someone needed it more than I did."

The sense of dread grew roots and began to flourish. "You gave it to Mackenzie? Damn it, kid—"

"That's not up for discussion," Kalen said firmly, holding up a hand. "I'm just here to let you know I'm leaving."

"You're *what*?"

"Look, I appreciate everything you've done for me. Nobody else except my grandmother ever gave a shit about me, or even cared enough to give me a chance to do something with my life. But you were different," the Sorcerer said quietly. "That means more to me than you'll ever know, but it's time for me to hit the road."

Nick studied Kalen for several long moments. The slump of the man's shoulders, the tightening around his mouth and the weariness in his eyes told Nick that his newest recruit didn't want to go but felt he must. "No. Not acceptable."

The other man blinked. "I can't stay. You don't understand."

"So fill me in on the problem and we'll deal with it."

"I don't think it's going to be that simple." A sad laugh escaped his lips. "As if anything would be where I'm concerned."

"Tell me, son," he urged, injecting all the warmth and confidence into his voice that he could muster. After a long moment, the younger man nodded.

"My pentagram was given to me by my grandmother," he began, gazing at his boots. "She once told me it had been crafted centuries ago by a master Sorcerer, and spelled as a protection against even the most powerful evil. I was never sure about any of that until recently, but it was a gift from her and so it was special to me."

Nick frowned. "Then why did you give it to Mac?"

"Because she needs the protection and it's the strongest—the *only*—talisman I have to give."

"Why does she need protection? Does this have to do with the attack?" A couple of weeks ago, Kalen and Mackenzie had gone into town separately and had run into trouble in the form of one of those nasty winged creatures with the big mouth full of sharp teeth, like the one he had locked in the basement cell. The two of them had nearly been killed by the damned thing, and would've been if Kalen hadn't gained the upper hand and dispatched it to hell.

"Yeah. Remember, it scratched her and bit me. What I didn't tell you is Mackenzie started hearing a voice. A sinister one telling her to do all sorts of bad shit." His expression was bleak. "I tried everything, every spell I knew, but I couldn't get rid of it. The bastard, whoever he is, was driving her crazy. Literally."

Nick stood and made his way around the desk, parking his butt on the edge and telling himself not to lambast the younger man for keeping this from him for so long. What mattered now was getting answers. He waited.

"So I put the pentagram around Mackenzie's neck and told her never to take it off. Seems to be working."

"Okay, so if she's fine, why do you feel the need to leave?"

"Because now the bastard is in *my* head," Kalen said miserably. "He's a very distinct, intelligent being. Those big-mouthed ghoul fuckers work for him."

Nick stared at him, stunned. "He admitted this?"

"Yes, and that's not all. He said he knew that by driving Mac out of her mind, he'd force me to give her the pendant, leaving me vulnerable to his machinations. I'm the one he wanted all along. He somehow knows way too much about me, wants to use me—and I'm afraid he's slowly winning the battle."

The dread that had taken root morphed into fear. What entity was such a great physical force in the universe that it could manipulate a Sorcerer who had few equals?

There were only two possible beings on that list, and either of them taking control of Kalen would spell disaster for everyone. *And why? What is his ultimate goal?*

First, they had to contain the threat.

"Kalen," he said, "I can't let you leave. Do you understand what I'm saying?"

The Sorcerer stared at him for a long moment, then swallowed hard. "If I go, you'll hunt me down and kill me."

"If you go rogue and fight us, yes. I'll have no other choice. But if you stay, we'll monitor you and do all we can to free you of *his* influence, whoever he is."

"Then I guess I have no other *choice* but to stay," he said bitterly.

"There's always a choice."

"What's going to happen to me?" Green eyes pinned Nick, begging for the truth.

The vision that had been threatening finally exploded in Nick's brain. His head fell back as the office vanished and he found himself racked with pain, kneeling in the middle of a field as cold rain lashed down like needles and lightning split the sky, then zipped down to scorch the ground.

All around him, his men battled unearthly creatures from hell and beyond. Losing ground with every passing minute. Facing their doom.

And on a high pinnacle stood the Sorcerer with his staff, soaking wet. Screaming to the heavens for help that would not come.

A detonation shook the ground and all was lost in a maelstrom of wind and rain. Of blood and tears. The world fell away.

"Nick!"

Dead. Was he dead?

"Nicky!"

Nick's eyes snapped open and he gasped, sucking air into his lungs. Kalen was crouched on the floor in front of him, shaking his shoulders, face panicked. "I'm okay," he croaked.

"Are you sure?"

"Yeah." *No.*

"Jesus," Kalen breathed. Standing, he took a step back. "You scared the crap out of me."

"Sorry, kid." He took a few steadying breaths.

"Nick, am I going to die?" he asked softly.

Oh, God. Don't you understand I wouldn't tell you even if I could? "We all die sometime. But I know what you mean, and I honestly can't tell you because I didn't see that."

Technically, it was true.

"Am I going to hurt any of my friends? Innocents?"

"I don't know."

Seconds passed in heavy silence.

"All right." Kalen sighed. "I'll stay."

"Good. Keep me posted on any developments with the creature. In the meantime, be ready to roll. I have a feeling that lead on where Aric and Micah are being held just may pan out, and soon."

"Will do."

With that, the Sorcerer walked out and left Nick alone.

So alone. As he'd been for the past two and a half centuries.

Three

The fierce arguing reached Aric's ears long before the combatants came into view. A woman's and a man's voices. No, two or three men. Beryl and who else? He couldn't make out their angry words over the roaring in his ears and the pounding in his head, and decided it didn't matter, anyway. There wasn't much left of him but a slab of meat hanging in chains, and the wicked stepsister would carve up the rest soon enough.

Was there anyone on the planet who gave a damn what happened to him?

He wasn't a guy normally given to loads of introspection, but there was nothing to do in this hellhole but think. The longer he remained their special guest, the more the twin demons of doubt and fear eroded his confidence, unraveled the threads holding together his sanity.

But maybe losing his mind wouldn't be a bad deal.

As footsteps neared him, he lifted his chin slightly to peer at the group through the fall of his long, dirty red hair. He wished he hadn't, because even more than Beryl, the sight of three men, two in lab coats and one meathead that was obviously the hired muscle, chilled his soul the way nothing else could have.

Except for their heated conversation.

". . . better be glad I'm not making a phone call," one of the men said coldly. He was average in height and looks, brown hair. Outside of this place, nobody would give him a second glance.

"Do it, Bowman," Beryl retorted with a self-satisfied smirk. "And see who he blames. You're the employee, not me. You'll face his wrath for letting a test subject get away."

Dr. Gene Bowman of NewLife Technology. The former supervisor of Jaxon Law's new mate, Kira Locke. Sweat rolled down Aric's face.

Bowman remained unmoved. "If you honestly think spreading your legs for some demon is going to protect you from any fallout from what you've done, you're sadly deluded. This project is much bigger and more significant than your petty games. What we're on the verge of accomplishing is huge, and he'll let nothing get in the way—especially not a slutty, mediocre witch who's easily replaced in his bed."

Aric missed Beryl's pissed-off retort. His brain was too busy reeling at the overload of information. *Demon?* Was that a slur against Orson Chappell, or had Bowman meant "demon" in the literal sense? Anything was possible—including the idea that Chappell was *not* the head of the snake, something Nick and the team had feared. Whoever the head slimeball might be, Beryl was sleeping with him.

Bowman turned to the muscleman and the other

guy in the lab coat. "Get him down from there and take him to the lab for prep."

Before that moment, he'd only *thought* he'd known fear.

The taller doctor and the meathead released his wrists, allowing him to drop. Arms dead from little circulation, limp as cooked noodles, he face-planted on the dirty concrete floor with his legs still attached to the wall, spread-eagle.

It was the single most degrading moment of his life.

Then the doc and the muscle guy hauled him up, easy as pie considering all the weight he'd lost, one taking him under the arms, one getting his ankles. Carried faceup, naked body on display and nobody caring, his carcass no better than a number to write down in their sordid files.

After an ascent in an elevator, he tried to keep track of the twists and turns they made, but he was simply too exhausted. Disheartened. Several minutes later, he found himself in a stark space that distinctly resembled an operating room.

It was then he noticed the drain in the tiled floor.

When they placed him on his back on a steel table, he began to struggle, attempted to call his fire or his wolf. Anything. But the "gifts" he usually cursed had deserted him when they counted most, and his rebellion was short-lived. A needle slid into the crook of his right arm and a cold burn seeped through the limb, stretched icy fingers across his chest. Suddenly he had trouble breathing, whether from the medication or sheer panic he didn't know.

The freeze slowly crept across his stomach, to his groin and legs. With the cold was the realization that he couldn't move at all—though his mind remained aware.

Bowman's hated, innocuous face appeared over him, smiling faintly. "Console yourself with the thought that this is for the greater triumph of mankind. Now relax." To the other doctor, he said, "Note that the experimentation on number five fifty-two has commenced."

"Wh-what're you doin' to me?" he slurred. His tongue felt heavy as a wet blanket, his thoughts growing sluggish. He peered at a bright light overhead and it quadrupled, as did the faces above him.

No one answered his question. His legs were spread and fastened with restraints, and so were his wrists at his sides.

A scalpel appeared in Bowman's hand as he continued to dictate the procedure and findings to someone Aric couldn't see. "Subject is malnourished and dehydrated, with cuts and lesions in the late stages of infection over forty percent of his body. Taking samples of the subject's DNA and semen to determine their viability to our cause."

Semen? What the fuck?

"Percentage of probability of scheduling subject five fifty-two for termination?" a robotlike voice intoned.

"Will advise."

"Thank you, doctor."

Yeah? Fuck you very much, doc.

Focused on his task, Bowman answered with only a grunt as he lowered the scalpel to the center of Aric's chest, just a millimeter south of his sternum. Aric's instinct was to struggle, try to yank on his bonds, get his hands free and torch them all, but again, absolutely nothing happened. He could only watch as the small blade sliced gradually into his skin, parting the surface like hot butter. There was pressure but no pain, an odd and frightening thing when a maniac had total access to his body and he couldn't do a damned thing to stop the asshole.

The pressure increased, the knife digging deeper. So deep he swore the doc was cutting straight to his heart. Maybe he was. Apparently satisfied with this cut, the doc removed the now-bloodied knife, laid it on a nearby tray and held out his hand for a new instrument. A large pair of what Aric thought of as oversized tweezers were slapped into Bowman's palm and he pried apart the sliced flesh, inserting the points. A strange tugging sensation in his chest, now accompanied by some pain, took his breath away.

Bowman lifted the tweezers. Aric's eyes widened to see a piece of his own tissue dangling from the instrument. If he'd been capable, he would've gotten violently sick. As it was, the procedure was repeated twice more while Aric tried desperately to think of anything but what they were doing to him. The medication didn't prevent him from closing his eyes, but he couldn't stop watching.

The last sample of flesh was handed to an assistant. "Log in and test the heart tissue samples from test subject five fifty-two. I want to know if his DNA and gene strands are compatible to merge with human subject two twenty-nine."

"Yes, doctor." The assistant disappeared.

And something chilling occurred to Aric—the fact that Bowman hadn't bothered to put him to sleep, was openly discussing the procedure when he and his bosses *knew* that Alpha Pack was onto them, meant that Aric wasn't supposed to survive.

When they were done using his body, they *would* kill him.

Bowman continued, moving down to stand next to Aric's spread legs. "Now obtaining semen sample from five fifty-two."

The scalpel was handed back to Bowman, and Aric's brain reeled in horror as the doctor's latex-covered hand lifted his testicles. Only when the knife descended did he realize that the numbing agent must be wearing off. *Fucking bastards!*

The pain was extraordinary, both bone-cold and white-hot, like nothing he'd ever felt. Not even when he'd been attacked and turned into a wolf. In spite of the paralyzing medication, his back arched off the table.

And the red wolf howled again and again, but only in his mind.

"Hello! Can I help you?"

Rowan turned to the speaker with a half-formed reply in the affirmative . . . which promptly died on her lips. Standing right in front of her was a tall, lithe, impossibly gorgeous man dressed in skinny jeans and a snug navy T-shirt.

And, yeah. The guy had long, flowing sapphire blue hair she would've thought had been colored by Miss Clairol—if it weren't for the matching wings.

"Well, fuck me sideways," she blurted.

Golden eyes sparkled with humor. "An interesting idea. May I at least have your name first?"

That surprised a laugh from her, and she held out her hand. "Rowan Chase, LAPD. You?"

The man, or whatever, took her hand but instead of giving it a firm shake, turned it over and placed a kiss on her palm. "Some call me Blue, but my real name is Sariel, and I'm a former prince of the Seelie court. Now I'm an assistant in Block R, where I help Kira Locke oversee the rehabilitation of displaced and injured otherworldly creatures."

Her skin tingled where his lips had touched and she slowly withdrew her hand, blinking at him. O-kay. "Seelie? What the heck is that?"

"I'm Fae," he said proudly. "Or faery if you prefer."

She eyed him from his glorious head to his feet, which sported a snazzy pair of Doc Martens. While the gorgeous slice of man looked like he belonged on a Paris runway, he *so* didn't look like any fairy in her book. But hey, whatever floated his boat. "Fae it is."

"What is L-A-P-D?" he asked, spelling the letters carefully, as though they were foreign to him.

"That stands for 'Los Angeles Police Department.' I'm a cop, here on personal business."

Excitement lit his face. "Oh! I've seen those on the television, capturing and shooting bad guys," he said, making a gun with his thumb and forefinger.

His enthusiasm would've been cute if it hadn't been for the vision of Luis Garcia dead on the dirty ground that still stalked her brain. "It's not all fun and games," she replied shortly. "Those people on the tube are actors and the shows rarely get it right."

His smile fell. "I'm sorry. It's just that I'm still learning so much about your world and have so far left to go that when I recognize something familiar . . ."

"Hey, no sweat." Now she felt bad for ruining his fun.

Shrugging, he went on. "Anyway, you must be an extremely worthy female of your kind to have such an important job."

"Tell that to the media and the general public."

"What?" His brow wrinkled.

"Nothing." She couldn't believe she was having this conversation—*any* conversation—with a blue-haired dude wearing wings. "Say, where does a hungry person get something to eat around here?"

Sariel brightened again and offered her his arm. "In the dining room, and you're in luck because it's time for the evening meal. I'll escort you."

"Sounds good. I could eat roadkill right about now." Taking the man's arm, she saw him wrinkle his nose and couldn't help but laugh. "Relax, that's just a saying. I don't eat dead animals off the pavement."

"Good to know!" His relief was palpable.

Sariel led her back through the maze the way she'd come, but when they reached the hallway where her room was located, he made a turn in a new direction. After a few moments, they ended up in a big dining room, as promised. Like the rest of this place, the room was designed to create a homey feel.

Several large tables took up the space, which was made to house a number of people yet provide for more intimate conversation than it would have with just one huge table. In the center of each table were platters of food, served family style. And around the tables were quite a few men and a sprinkling of women. Most of whom had stopped talking and were checking out the newbie. Rowan looked around for Mackenzie, hoping for a familiar face, but didn't see her.

"Hey, Blue," someone called. "Who's your friend?"

"This is Rowan Chase," Sariel announced, either ignoring the slight awkwardness or unaware of it. "Apparently she's our guest for a while. Come on."

He tugged her to a nearby table where a small blond woman sat with a handsome, dark-haired, goateed man and two other guys she'd seen at the gate. At least now they were dressed. The body language of the blonde and the goateed man, the way they sat close, the big brute leaning into her, made Rowan think they were together. Rowan sat next to Sariel, across from the others, eyeing the steak and baked potatoes in the middle of the table.

Her stomach growled, hopefully unheard due to the talking that had resumed around them. The goateed guy pushed the plates closer to her side and nodded.

"Dig in."

"Thanks." Reaching for the big fork on the steak platter, she dished up a piece, put it on her plate, then stabbed a potato.

"I'm Jaxon Law, by the way," he said, and then gestured to the blonde burrowed into his side. "This is my mate, Kira Locke."

Mate? Okay. Wolves mated, right? Did they get married, too? She didn't see any rings on their fingers.

She addressed the other woman. "You must be the one who works with Sariel rehabilitating, um . . ."

Kira smiled. "Basically, we help any creature or intelligent being when they become lost or hurt and are brought to us. Right now we have a gremlin, a basilisk, two rescued shifters, and a wolf who's—" She cut off the last part of what she was about to say at a quick shake of Jaxon's head. What was that about? "Anyway, Nick is going to provide funds for us to build a rehab center on the grounds for that special purpose."

"That's really neat," she said, and meant it. "I don't have a nurturing bone in my body when it comes to taking care of sick people, so I can only imagine how hard it must be to nurse something that most folks don't know exists."

"We're learning as we go," Sariel put in. "We have doctors here, and Kira at least has an advantage because of her training in the medical field, especially in genetics, and she's good with the patients. It's not as if running a center like this has ever been done before, and certainly not in my realm, where they simply cast out anyone who's different." A shadow crossed his features, but he shook it off. "Still, the work is rewarding when we get good results."

After a round of enthusiasm from the group about the project, a man with black hair a bit longer than Jaxon's spoke up from beside him. "I'm Zander Cole, or just Zan. This is Ryon Hunter." He waved at a blond man on his other side, this guy appearing a little younger than his friends.

Ryon smiled, open and friendly. "Hello."

"It's nice to meet you all." The jury was still out on the truth of that statement, but it was the polite response. Now she was eager to get to the heart of her visit. "I suppose by now you've been told I'm Micah's sister. Do any of you know him?"

Guarded expressions met her question as she took a bite of tender meat. Too bad worry for Micah took the enjoyment right out of her meal, as it had with every aspect of her life since she was informed he'd died.

Jaxon spoke first, indicating himself and his two friends. "The three of us were in the SEALs with him. Then we joined Alpha Pack together, along with Aric and Raven, who aren't . . . with us at the moment." He paused, apparently reluctant to embellish.

Rowan glanced around the group. "It's okay. Your boss already filled me in on what this place really is and what you guys do for a living. I'm a cop and I'm used to dealing in facts, so I'm not sure I totally believe all this stuff about conspiracies and otherworldly creatures. But I'm getting there." She shot a pointed look at Sariel for emphasis. When she did, she noticed that he hadn't made a move to touch any of the food, but she didn't have time to wonder why.

"Kind of hard not to believe it when it's shoved in your face, huh?" Kira said in sympathy. "A.J. over there was the same way not too long ago. He's a former police officer, so maybe you two will have some things in common." She gestured to a man who sat across the room with a huge bald guy. Jaxon wrapped an arm around Kira's waist and kissed the top of her head.

Rowan shrugged. "Maybe."

Jaxon brought the topic back to Micah. "About your brother, all of us thought he and several other Pack members were dead because that's what we were told, same as you. We were devastated. When Nick came on board, he knew that the bodies were missing, but he was pretty much ordered not to say anything. We're no happier about that than you must be, but we don't blame him. Nick didn't know for sure whether they really were dead—only what he was told."

Rowan shook her head. "I'll admit I was angry with your boss at first, but I don't blame him, either. I just want the truth, and to find my brother. Even if he's gone," she added hoarsely. Her appetite fled.

Reaching across the table, Zan laid a hand over hers. "That's all we want as well. Micah was—is—a brother to us. Now that we're pretty sure he's being held somewhere, alive, nothing is going to stop us from getting him back. And the other guys, too, if they're out there."

Heat enveloped her hand, traveled up her arm to her heart. The agony in her chest lessened, and she wondered if this was Zan's gift—easing people's pain.

"We know Savage is," Ryon put in.

"Yeah, the snarky son of a bitch." Jaxon's words held no real heat, and his tone was sad, his eyes brimming with guilt. "It's my fault he's not here."

"Oh, sweetie," Kira breathed, hugging him tight. "You've got to stop blaming yourself. Aric's being taken was Chappell's doing, not yours."

Confused, Rowan waited for someone to enlighten her. Zan obliged.

"Jaxon's gift, other than his wolf, of course, is that he's a Timebender. He can literally bend time backward, but by no more than a few minutes. A few weeks ago on a rescue op, Kira was killed and—"

"No offense, but she's looking pretty good to me," Rowan interrupted, studying the other woman.

Zan continued while Jaxon stared at his plate. "That's because Jax bent time back and saved her. But that caused Aric to be taken prisoner by Chappell's minions instead."

"Uh-huh." Her cop's brain balked at this one. She pinned Jaxon with a steely look that had made many a suspect squirm. "Show me."

"What?"

She waved a hand. "If you can bend time, show me. Back up to when I walked in with the angel here."

"Fae," Sariel corrected.

"Whatever."

Jax gave a wry chuckle. "I can't. Wouldn't do any good."

"Why not?"

"Because you wouldn't remember if I did. How do you know I didn't perform it already, and we're simply repeating the same conversation?"

She stared at him a few seconds, trying to process this, then snorted. "Damn, what a mindfuck." The men laughed, and she supposed the joke was on her. Undaunted, however, and determined to get some sort of proof of these gifts Nick told her about, she addressed Zan. "So what's your talent? Bet you can't prove it, either."

"I'm a Healer," he said, arching a black brow. "And actually, I can. Ryon, give me your hand."

The blond held it out. "Man, just don't leave a scar."

Zan turned his friend's hand palm up, then reached into his pants, extracting a pocketknife. "This will make a cleaner cut than the steak knife."

Rowan's eyes widened. "Wait a minute. I didn't mean—"

"Just watch." With a grin, Zan flipped open the blade. Quickly, he made a swipe across Ryon's palm. A thin line oozed red, but not too badly. "Do you see that? His hand is bleeding, right?"

"It is," she agreed. "I think you're both crazy."

Without answering, Zan laid his palm on top of Ryon's, aligning their fingers.

"Um, guys, that's a good way to pass HIV or hepatitis," she warned. Her cruiser was stocked with latex gloves in case she ran across someone with blood on them while on duty, which happened more often than one might think. Blood-borne illnesses were always a concern in her line of work.

Ryon winked. "It would be, if we were still able to catch human diseases."

Before she could respond to that nonsense, Zan lifted his hand, turning it so she could see their palms.

"Now you both have blood on you. So?"

Zan took his cloth napkin and dipped it into a nearby water glass. Then he used the napkin to wipe Ryon's palm clean and held the man's hand closer to her. "Care to inspect it?"

Leaning over, she peered hard at the skin. His *perfectly unmarred* skin. She grabbed Ryon's wrist and rubbed his palm with the pads of her fingers. No mark at all!

"I'll be damned!" Releasing Ryon, she sat back in her chair and looked away from the small group as the total impact of everything she'd seen and heard in her short time here hit her full force.

Really hit. Micah was part of a paranormal black ops team, and the nonhuman type of evil truly did exist. As an LAPD cop, she faced danger every day, but even that couldn't begin to compare to the world she'd stumbled upon and was now up to her neck in trying to grasp.

I wear a badge, carry a gun, and until today I walked around confident that I knew who the bad guys were and was sure of my ability to handle them. Then I find out I'm an insignificant bug on the stalk of the universe. Monster food.

Dinner forgotten, overwhelmed, she rested her elbows on the table and buried her face in her hands. She was in no way prepared for this. How the hell was she supposed to help Micah?

A gentle hand rubbed her back and she started, sitting up to glance at Sariel. His expression was warm, understanding. No one except Dean had bothered to comfort her in years, and the small kindness almost did her in. But she wouldn't cry. She never did.

"It will be all right," the Fae man said, smiling faintly. "Trust me."

"What, so you're a PreCog like Nick?"

"No. But you're not without your own gifts and I have a feeling they will serve you well in your quest."

"You mean I have some sort of talent, like Micah?" He nodded and she perked up some at the idea. She thought of the Dreamwalking thing Nick had told her about. "Cool. What's my gift? How do you know?"

"Humans are so impatient." He sighed, then shook his head. "How I know isn't important, and it wouldn't be as effective for you if I *told* you the nature of your gift. You must experience it for yourself to accept and use it."

"Great. I want answers and I get Yoda for a side-kick," she muttered.

"Who?" Sariel looked baffled and the rest of the group chuckled.

"I think she's going to fit right in," Ryon said.

Before anyone could comment, a Goth guy walked in who commanded not only Rowan's attention but that of everybody in the dining area. He walked like a graceful cat and looked like a cross between a rock star and a gunslinger. Even among these men, he was unique. And no wonder—this was the man she'd seen shift to human from panther form.

"Who's that?" she whispered to Sariel.

"Kalen Black," he answered in a low voice. "One of the new recruits, but extremely powerful. He's a Sorcerer and Necromancer."

"Jesus."

Kalen rapped on the table to get their attention. "Hey, Nick wants to see the Pack in the meeting room, pronto. The intercom's not working, so he sent me to round up you guys."

The guy named A.J. glanced up hopefully. "Me, too?"

"Sorry, man, not yet."

Too green, Rowan thought. Outwardly disappointed at being excluded, A.J. heaved a breath and went back to eating. The bald man with him, however, wiped his mouth with a napkin and stood. As did Jaxon, Zan, and Ryon.

Jaxon shot an intense stare at Kalen. "We going wheels-up?"

"Yep, after sundown. He's got the details on where we'll find our two missing guys, and hopefully a bunch of Chappell's scumbags, too." Kalen's green gaze found Rowan briefly. He nodded an acknowledgment of her presence, then looked at his friends. "Let's go."

"Wait," she called to them. "I want to sit in on this meeting."

"No can do," Jax said over his shoulder.

"This is my brother we're talking about! You can't just—"

"That's exactly why we can—because he's your family and you're way too emotional. And if Nick wants you to know more, he'll tell you."

"I'm getting damned tired of that answer!" They

filed out, ignoring her, and she pounded a fist on the table. Frustrated, she glared at Kira. "Tell me this gets easier."

"Dealing with a bunch of overbearing alpha males?" The blonde snorted. "Right."

"That's what I was afraid of. Same macho attitude, different location."

Fine. They'd left her no choice but to resort to desperate measures. If the Pack thought they were leaving in the night without her, they were in for a big surprise.

Rowan crouched in a dark corner of the huge hangar, waiting. Despite her training as an officer and the dark jeans and shirt she wore, there was a better than average chance that she would get caught. She was only human, armed with nothing but stealth and maybe some luck. The team, with their super-senses, might very well detect her presence and make her stay behind, something she couldn't allow to happen.

Using one of the compound's SUVs as cover, she peered around the back end and studied the hulking shapes of several vehicles in the dim light coming from a wall fixture far across the vast space. Among them she counted two private jets, three SUVs, a couple of motorcycles, and several cars and trucks that she suspected were owned by the team members. The crowning glory was the three big Hueys at the far end, situated under a roof hatch that would open to allow them to take off.

The main problems were not knowing which mode of transportation they'd take, and how she'd manage to stow away and hide.

From the corner of her eye, she saw a faint glow.

Startled, she whipped her head around to watch as a ball of neon blue light grew brighter, larger. Edging backward, she gaped as the ball shimmered into the form of a man—or rather, Sariel.

Crouching, he grinned at her, his beautiful wings spread. "Hello."

"All right, that's going to take some getting used to. What are you doing here?"

"Establishing myself as your partner in crime, of course."

She appreciated the irony, considering. "Hey, that's nice of you, but I don't want you to get in hot water with Nick."

The man looked alarmed. "He would wish me to *bathe* with him as punishment for assisting you?"

"No." Rowan choked, not quite stifling a laugh. "'Hot water' means to get in trouble."

"Oh." He waved a hand. "That doesn't concern me. What can he do to *me*, after all?"

She studied him thoughtfully. "True. But why do you want to help me?"

Amber eyes returned her gaze in the darkness, turned sad. "Because if I had anyone who loved me as much as you love your Micah, I'd want her to come for me."

Aw, shit. Sudden moisture stung her eyes and she blinked it away rapidly. Reaching out, she touched his face. This gentle being's words and that simple act forged the beginnings of a real friendship. She felt it to her soul. "That's a good enough reason for me. So, how can you get me past the wolf squad?"

"Simple. I'm going to cloak your presence and you'll accompany them without them even knowing!"

"How?"

He shrugged. "An easy invisibility spell that even the youngest of Fae children can perform. Causes quite a ruckus around the palace, I can tell you."

Picturing it made her snicker. Good thing human kids couldn't do that trick. "Okay. If you work your magic on me, how long will it last?"

"The farther you travel from the source—me—the weaker the spell will become until it fades altogether and you're revealed. No matter where you are, though, it will only last a few hours at most."

"I'm impressed." She thought about it. "I think that'll work. By the time it wears off it'll be too late for them to bring me back here. I hope."

"That's the idea."

Staring at her intently, Sariel laid a hand on top of her head and uttered a soft incantation in a language she didn't understand. After a few seconds he released her, apparently happy. "Is that all?" she asked.

"Yes. I can see and hear you, but nobody else will for a while."

At that moment, the hangar door slid open with a loud screech and multiple male voices echoed in the cavernous space. The moment of truth was at hand, and she would have been lying if she'd said she wasn't nervous. The noises of the men preparing to leave, opening more doors and gathering equipment, reached her ears. Hesitating, she glanced at her new friend.

"Go on," he urged. "Before it's too late."

"You sure this will work?" A stupid question to ask a magical fairy, maybe, but understandable.

"Positive. Go!"

Pushing to her feet, she gave Sariel a nervous smile. "Thanks. See you soon."

"And with any luck I'll get to meet this brother of yours."

Emotion clogged her throat, so she opted not to answer. Instead, she heaved a deep breath, stepped around the back of the SUV, and began to walk slowly toward the group that was gathered next to two of the Hueys, busy holstering guns and strapping on knives. Part of her was relieved to see some good old-fashioned artillery in the midst of all the crazy I'm-not-human crap. The other part was worried that Sariel was wrong about the spell working around these guys.

But no one noticed as she walked right up to the group. What a freaky trip. Damn, she'd love to use this trick on the guys back at the station.

Nick slung a pack over his shoulder. "Kalen, you and Hammer ride with me." The Sorcerer and the bald man, who she guessed to be Hammer, answered in the affirmative. Jaxon, Zan, and Ryon headed for the second copter.

Four pilots climbed into the copters, a pilot and a copilot for each. Since they hadn't been introduced earlier as team members, and weren't armed, she figured they might be hired as needed per mission. This would leave the rest of the team free to deal with whatever they were facing.

Rowan hovered as the two groups of three separated and began to board the copters. Just as she took a step, Nick whirled and gazed in her direction with a frown. Heart pounding, she froze. He searched, and at one point his eyes actually met hers, causing the spit to dry up in her mouth. How the hell could he sense someone there when the others hadn't?

After a few nerve-racking moments the boss turned

and climbed aboard his waiting Huey. Rowan hurried to scramble into the other one. No way was she taking a chance on some psychic dude ferreting her out before she was ready.

The men got settled. Spotting an empty jump seat at the back, she sat down and tried to calm her fears. Not for herself, but for what she might find when she saw her brother.

A hum sounded overhead—the roof hatch opening. The Hueys geared up for takeoff, shuddered, and lifted, the noise deafening.

She was in this op for the long haul now.

No turning back.

Four

*H*elp me. God, please.
     Or just let me die.

Aric curled into the fetal position on the grimy concrete floor of his cage and tried to breathe through the agony. But the pain wrapped around his ribs, squeezed his lungs, so that drawing in air was nearly impossible. Every inch of his body throbbed, and his balls burned and ached where Bowman had taken what didn't belong to him. But all his equipment down there was still accounted for, not that it would matter soon.

Never had he wished for death. That was before he'd been treated worse than an animal, before he'd experienced the worst of humanity and had it driven home that if his team didn't find him, and soon, this was the end of his life.

I want to go out on my own terms. Not bound and stripped for parts until there's nothing left and they stick a needle in my arm.

He opened his bleary eyes, squinted, and then

winced as even the dim light coming from the adjoining lab pierced his brain like a laser. Twisting his head, he saw nothing but bars all around and above him, a miniature prison not even tall enough to stand in. *It's a damned dog kennel.* If he'd been capable of laughing, he would've. Reaching out, he skimmed a shaking hand along the floor, cursing that he was too weak to raise his fucking arm. If he could barely move, he sure as hell wouldn't have the strength to do himself in.

Goddamn, he couldn't believe he was being forced to consider that kind of shit. Pissed, he used every ounce of strength to push himself to a sitting position. It took several minutes and when it was finally accomplished, he leaned his bare back against the bars—an act that probably took off several strips of skin.

"Fuck!" Pitching forward, he tumbled away from the bars, panting.

Silver. The bastards had used motherfucking silver bars to line the cage. Why the metal had burned him, however, was baffling; simply coming into contact with silver wasn't supposed to hurt in his human form. Being stabbed or shot with it? Sure. So this went down as one more torment to face, the fact that even if he regained the power to shift or use his other gifts, he couldn't bust out.

He couldn't take this much longer. He and his wolf were already going out of their collective minds at being held against their will. Hunched over, he concentrated on calming himself. Taking in air, exhaling. As he did, awful smells began to invade his battered senses.

Urine. Feces. Unwashed bodies and the stale, untouched crap that doubled as food. The stench turned his stomach and he concentrated on not being sick. That would only make things worse and—

Another smell seeped into his consciousness and Aric slowly raised his head. *I know that scent. Oh, my God.*

"Micah," he whispered. Then louder. "Micah?"

No answer. For the first time, Aric took stock of the area outside his own prison. His cage was one of many in a row against the wall, and several other figures lay crumpled in theirs much as he'd been when he'd awakened, naked and hopeless. Closing his eyes, he inhaled through his nose, desperately shutting out all but the one scent he wanted to discern, following the trail to the end.

Behind him. Somewhere close. Scooting around to face the opposite direction took forever and left him panting, aching as though he'd been beaten with hammers. But he had to learn the answer to the question that had haunted the Pack since they'd discovered their brother might be alive—where was Micah?

And the answer was right in the next cage. His old friend lay on the dirty floor, curled into himself as though that would keep the monsters at bay. Micah's brown hair, once a rich sable color worn to his collar, was now filthy and matted, so long it pooled on the concrete around his head. Strands hung over his angular face and his eyes were closed. The man's breathing was ragged, the horrible rattle in his lungs attesting to his lack of medical care. That fact plus a plate of uneaten dry dog food by the barred door—fuck those assholes for giving his friend that shit—and Micah's pronounced ribs, hip bones, and concave stomach, told the story of just how critical his situation had become.

His friend was on the brink of death, and Aric could only sit and do nothing.

The urge to reach through the bars, offer comfort, was overwhelming. It hit him that this was likely part of the reason the metal was made of silver, to keep the "test subjects" from having any sort of positive contact, to kill all hope, and it made his blood boil with rage.

"Micah? We're gonna get the fuck out of here, soon as the Pack comes," he whispered. "And they *will* come. You hear me?"

His friend didn't stir.

Aric lowered his head. And for the first time he could recall, tears dripped off his chin to mix with the filth on the floor.

Talk was scarce on the helicopter, given the noise. Rowan would've felt a little better with a few more details about where they were going and the plan of action on arrival, but that would have to wait. For now, she sat and eyed her group, still amazed that they were oblivious to her presence.

Guess there's something to be said for magic after all.

Which brought to mind the gift Sariel said she possessed. Days ago, she'd have dismissed the idea as insane. Now? She'd seen so much in the short time since she'd arrived at the compound, it was mind-blowing. She wasn't crazy, so that left only one other option.

And she was beginning to believe.

Micah was a Dreamwalker, Nick had claimed. She and her brother had shared dreams since their childhood. Were they able to do that because they shared the same gift? How could she find out?

A headache began to form, so she stopped thinking about anything but getting to her brother. Nothing else was as important.

The Huey began its descent and she checked her watch. Almost two hours they'd been in the air, and it seemed like eons. In minutes the copter touched down and the men prepared to disembark, some checking weapons. All of them, she suspected, qualified as a weapon themselves.

Rowan filed out behind the men, standing off to the side to avoid bumping into anyone as they gathered. Checking out their surroundings, she noted they'd landed in a field bordered by woods on all sides and majestic mountains in the distance, all of it against the vast, beautiful backdrop of a full moon and a zillion stars.

"This is a change," Jaxon commented. "Chappell usually prefers to set up his clandestine operations in or near major cities."

Nick agreed. "Don't know why he thought moving one of his sites to Bumfuck, Colorado, would draw less attention from the locals. Took a while for our government contacts to sniff this one out, but his tactic eventually backfired."

"Still think we should've gone in hot," Ryon said anxiously. "I don't like giving the goons time to find out we're here. Those Hueys can be heard for miles."

His comment earned him a smack in the back of the head from the bald guy, Hammer. "Idiot. You forgetting last time we went in guns blazing? They were waiting for us, which is how things went to hell and they snatched Aric."

The blond's expression was suddenly haunted. "They'll be ready for us, anyway. The ghosts around us, some of their victims, I think, are urging us to be careful."

Rowan stared at him. *Ryon's "gift" is communicating with the dead? The others get to do all sorts of cool stuff and this poor guy gets stuck with being followed around by a bunch of stiffs? Jesus, that sucks.*

"This time we go in quiet," Nick reiterated. "Remember, watch for traps or any signs of an ambush. Detain any personnel who are on duty and liberate all prisoners. Grant has ground transportation waiting close to the target to assist with the victims who need urgent care. Let's go—and be careful. We can't afford another screwup."

As they moved out, she jogged behind the group, thinking not only of Micah but also of the other man, Aric. The Pack was devastated over the loss of all their men in the past few years, but Aric's capture was recent, salt poured into a reopened wound. The guys spoke of him with equal parts aggravation and reverence, and she wondered what he'd be like. For some reason beyond the obvious one that he was their friend who was in danger, she hoped she would have the chance to know him.

She was so engrossed in her musings, she failed to see a fallen log the others had cleared easily. Cursing, she jumped at the last second and almost did a face plant in the undergrowth. Then she nearly ran right into Zan's back when Nick, in the lead, brought the group to an abrupt halt.

"Wait!" Nick cocked his head. "I could've sworn I heard a woman's voice."

"I heard it, too," Zan said, looking around. "Sounded like she said 'shit.'"

Rowan repeated the word, in her head. Damn it, Sariel's spell must be wearing off. But if it just would last until they reached their destination, Nick might not send her back to the helicopter.

"Maybe it was one of Ryon's spirits?" Jax suggested.

"I'm not sure, but I guess anything's possible," Ryon speculated. "They can sometimes gather enough energy to make themselves heard."

After a few tense moments, Nick led them on. Though she was a police officer and in great physical shape, it was a miracle that she kept up, since their night vision and endurance far surpassed hers. By the time the boss slowed and signaled his men to crouch, she was drenched in sweat. The others weren't even winded.

Squatting at the end of the line beside Zan, she caught her breath and peered through the trees at the building illuminated by moonlight. Not just any building, she realized, but an old abandoned church, as evidenced by crumbling walls, sagging roof, and the weeds dotting what once must've been a pretty lawn, the tallest of them sprouting almost to the bottom edge of the broken stained-glass windows.

"What a fuckin' disgrace," Hammer hissed. "Using a house of God for the sick shit they're doing."

The others muttered their wholehearted agreement.

"Where are they hiding their cars?" Jax mused. "The lot is empty."

"Who cares? Let's kick some ass."

"Damned straight."

Spirits ran high. She felt the adrenaline, the excitement among the Pack, not so different from when she and her fellow officers worked a dangerous call. But in that moment, she sensed a tangible bond among these men that ran deeper than what she had with her peers. These men truly were brothers in all but birth, their bond forged by blood, tears, and struggle.

Moving soundlessly, they left cover, splitting into two groups. Nick led Hammer and Kalen directly to the front, while Jax headed around to the back, followed by Zan and Ryon. For no particular reason other than a gut feeling, because subjects who fled a scene typically hauled ass out the back way, Rowan opted to go with Jax's team. What she expected was runners, maybe armed, perhaps a round or two popped off.

What she wasn't expecting was a full-out war.

The back of the church erupted in a collective roar, black shadows detaching themselves from the doorway and several open windows. As prepared as the team believed themselves to be, it was immediately clear they were outnumbered—and facing something horribly familiar.

"Not *those* fucking bastards," Zan hissed, bringing up his hand cannon.

"And this time they've got help." With that, Jax shifted into a big gray wolf and ran to meet the enemy, leaving his clothes and human weapons in a pile on the ground.

Rowan didn't have a spare second to marvel at seeing a man shift into his animal for the first time. Fear for her new comrades propelled her forward and she dove for Jax's discarded gun as Zan opened fire on a creature hell itself must've birthed.

Like its buddies, the thing had leathery black wings, a stout, hairy body, and a greenish wrinkled and cracked face not even a mother could love. Saliva dripped from razor-sharp teeth in its gaping mouth, and it rushed Zan, obviously intent on tearing the man to shreds.

Zan's shots barely slowed the beast, and it closed the gap, fast. In one fluid motion, Rowan raised her gun, sighted its head, and fired. The beast's skull exploded, and it dropped in midstride, sliding to a halt at Zan's boots.

"Shit!" His face reflected the terror of his close call. Then he seemed to realize it wasn't his shot that had brought the thing down, and he glanced around in confusion before rejoining the battle and assisting his friends.

A surge of adrenaline flooded her veins. This invisibility stuff came in handy; too bad she couldn't use it on the force. She took advantage now, though, picking off the ghouls left and right, doing her best to keep the ones closest to the men from reaching them. The Pack was too busy to investigate the source and the beasts were too stupid.

But her luck was bound to run out. When one of the ugly bastards swung his head in her direction, yellow eyes meeting hers and blazing with hatred, she knew Sariel's spell had finally worn off. In mute horror, she raised her gun, got off a shot as it charged. And missed.

The beast closed the distance with dizzying speed. Just before it reached her, however, a silver ball of fur came from the left and launched itself at the creature. A wolf collided with the ghoul and they both went to the ground, the canine snarling, going for his enemy's throat. He missed and the ghoul raked his side with knifelike claws, ripping through his coat. The wolf cried out, twisted, and resumed his attack. On they battled, and Rowan couldn't get a good shot at the beast without risking the wolf.

Glancing anxiously at the rest of the fight, she saw Zan and the big gray wolf she knew to be Jax still engaged in the fight across the yard. That meant the wolf who'd saved her ass was Ryon—and he was losing.

Just as he managed to sink his teeth into the ghoul's throat, the thing tore him free and threw him aside. He sailed through the air, hit a tree hard, and slid to the ground, unmoving. The creep returned its attention to Rowan and she could've sworn it smiled.

She aimed, but before she could fire, Nick ran around the side of the building, Kalen and Hammer hot on his heels. The Sorcerer took in the situation and slid to a stop. A big staff appeared out of thin air and he gripped it in his right hand as he knelt, arms straight out from his sides, head back.

Closing his eyes, he began a chant in a language Rowan thought might be Latin. Instantly, everyone froze in place, even Rowan. She could move only her eyes, and she noted that the battle stopped in the middle of some macabre, deadly dance. That weirded her out, but not nearly as much as what came next.

The beasts began to . . . enlarge. Just inflate, like they were oversized tires that someone was airing up. Their yellow eyes rounded in fear and one managed a whimper—

And then they exploded in a shower of greenish black matter. God, it stunk. If Rowan had been able, she would've gagged.

Head back, Kalen closed his left fist tightly, shook it. His comrades were freed, including Rowan, and she dropped to her knees. The Sorcerer slumped forward, supporting himself with the staff, breathing hard. Nick hurried to his Pack mate, steadying him.

"My panther couldn't have fought those things," Kalen said hoarsely. "Too many of them. I did the first thing that came to mind."

"You did good, kid," Nick praised, clamping a hand on his shoulder. "You okay?"

He nodded. "I'm fine, just need a sec."

Jax shifted back to human form and began pulling on his clothes. "No wonder. Must take a helluva load of power to blow up one of those bastards, much less a whole army of them all at once."

"You could say that." Kalen tried to make it a joke, but nobody was laughing.

"Oh, God," Zan whispered. "Ryon!"

Following Zan's gaze, the others saw where their friend lay crumpled on the ground several yards away. Zan reached him first, dropping to his knees. Once again in human form, Ryon was sprawled on his side. White-blond hair feathered around his handsome face and his eyes were closed. Four ragged gashes, bleeding heavily, marred his left side, and he was peppered with cuts and bruises.

Zan took his shoulders and spoke to Jax. "Help me roll him onto his back."

Once this was accomplished, someone tossed Ryon's shirt over his package for her sake, Rowan figured. Cursing herself, she watched as Zan placed both hands over the wounds on his friend's side.

"If it wasn't for me, he'd be okay," she said softly.

"No," Jax said sharply, glancing up at her. "If you hadn't been here, those bastards would've torn all three of us apart before Kalen got to us. Because they couldn't see you at first, you took out a lot of them and saved our bacon."

Nick's gaze was like twin blue lasers as he looked at her. "Is that true?"

She just shrugged. No way was she gonna take credit when Ryon had ended up hurt, or worse. "I missed my last shot and that fucker got him. That's all I know."

"Who cloaked you?"

She saw no benefit in trying to hide the answer from a psychic. "Sariel. But he had his reasons and his heart was in the right place, so if there's any punishment to be dealt, it's mine."

Something like respect flashed across Nick's face and was quickly replaced by a neutral expression. He nodded, turning back to his fallen man. Zan's hands were now enveloped by a greenish glow that spread outward and appeared to sink into the gashes. Gradually, as Rowan stared in astonishment, the torn flesh began to knit together until the wounds vanished.

"Lacerated spleen," Zan rasped. "Give me a couple more minutes."

Minutes. To heal a serious internal injury. Half the population wouldn't believe in Zan's talent, and the other half would line up at his door if they knew. For her part, she saw the truth with her own eyes. That's all she needed.

Ryon blinked, his lashes fluttering. He stared up at his companions, awareness of what had happened dawning slowly. "God, I thought I was done. Are those damned things dead?"

Zan patted his shoulder. "Yep. Kalen turned them into birthday balloons and popped 'em."

"Gross."

"Come on, let's get your clothes on and then I'll take you back to the helicopter."

"Uh-uh. If our friends are in there, I'm not missing out on the reunion. Just help me up." He paused. "The spirits are upset, urging us to hurry."

Zan and Nick pulled Ryon to his feet. Rowan returned Jax's gun to him, then turned away while Ryon dressed, too eaten with guilt to appreciate the sight of his fine naked body. He'd sacrificed himself for her—a stranger—without a second thought and nearly died for his trouble.

As a cop, putting herself on the line for people she didn't know was what she did. Why did it bother her to be on the receiving end?

When everyone was ready, Nick gestured toward the back door. "Let's stay together this time and follow the ghosts' advice to get a move on. I'm sensing it won't be long before reinforcements show up."

They headed for the back stoop and filed inside cautiously, Rowan in the middle of the line. She couldn't see as well in the gloom as they likely could, but her sense of smell didn't need to be equal to theirs to guess what waited for them. The stench clogged her lungs, and fear for Micah seized her heart.

"Holy Christ," Kalen gasped from somewhere in front. "I know Chappell and his docs don't care about how they hurt others with their experiments, but how can they stand to work in this awful smell?"

"Probably just used to it," Nick said.

Someone found a light switch and flipped it on. The group stood in the area that used to house the pews but now was a large, mostly empty room. A utility table and folding chairs were placed near one wall, and four camping cots topped with sleeping bags and pillows were in different corners.

"Where did the scientists go?" she wondered aloud.

Nick answered. "They're either hiding while waiting for more backup, or went into the nearest town for a while and have no clue we're here. This way."

A set of double doors at the rear of the room took them into a hallway leading to what had once been classrooms where various groups had held their Bible studies. Now many of the rooms were full of computers and lab equipment. Methodically, the men checked each room along the way for booby traps, locating five trip wires attached to explosives, which they carefully disarmed.

At the end of the hallway, the smell, unbelievably, got worse. Nick eased the last door open, looked down, and pointed. Jax got busy dismantling the last trip wire, and then they were in. Jax flipped on the light, and they rushed inside—straight into a nightmare.

"Aw, fuck me," Hammer moaned.

Rowan stared, unable to process what she was seeing. Cages lined two walls of what might've once been a storage room, currently being used as a prison. And inside the small cages were men. Filthy, naked men too large for the restrictive space, lying curled on their sides. Some staring and unresponsive to their arrival, some unconscious.

There. A man with long, tangled brown hair. Could it be . . . ?

She was moving before she realized it. "Micah?" Reaching the cage, she dropped to her knees—and the air left her lungs. She'd know her brother anywhere, no matter how changed his appearance. She rattled the door and cried out. "Somebody find a key! Micah!"

Zan knelt beside her and sniffed the air. "By God, it *is* him!" He touched the bars and quickly drew his hand back with a curse. "Silver, and this stuff burns. We're going to need gloves," he called out.

"Aric's over here," Jax shouted.

Ryon jingled a key ring. "These were hanging on the wall. We'll just have to try them and see if any fit." He tossed it to Zan, then walked over to a workbench, grabbed an old rag, and brought it over. "No gloves. Use this."

First Zan tried the keys one by one until at last one fit the lock. He turned it, careful not to brush the silver bars again, then used the rag to open the door before handing the ring to Ryon by the correct key. "Hopefully this is a master that'll open the others."

Ryon moved off, but Rowan's attention was solely on the still form of her brother. When Zan started to move forward, she pushed him back. "Let me. I'm strong enough to move a person and there's no sense in you getting burned."

Not waiting for the man's answer, she got down into a low crouch, inching her upper half into the cage. Resolutely tamping down the rage at Micah's horrid condition, she grabbed him under his arms and began to drag him backward. When she had his shoulders out, Zan helped and together they laid him on the floor between them.

The physical mess that had once been a gorgeous man broke her heart. His once lean, athletic build was emaciated, his collarbones and every one of his ribs visible. His hair was matted and greasy, and his bearded face . . .

She sucked in a breath, tears pricking her eyes. All their lives, Micah had turned heads everywhere he went because of his nearly blinding beauty, which shone from both within and without. Someone had taken great pains to destroy that wonderful light. The left side of his face from the bridge of his nose, down his cheek, and curling under his jaw, was a puckered expanse of scar tissue that his uneven beard had not grown over. It appeared healed, and looked very much like the perpetrator had poured something hot over that side of his face.

"I'll kill them all." She didn't realize she'd said that aloud until Zan spoke.

"You'll have to stand in line." Zan's serious gaze met hers.

She looked back to her brother. "You're going to be all right now. I love you."

"Come on, honey. Move back and let us help him."

Normally she would've torn the man a new one for calling her "honey" while ordering her away from the one person who meant the most to her. It was a testament to how shell-shocked she was that she didn't argue, but simply stood and watched Zan perform what healing he could on Micah's scar-riddled body.

Elation at finding him alive warred with helplessness. She was a human out of her depth in a game of monsters, as ineffectual as a fly on a dragon's ass. The other activity in the space near her finally registered and she glanced around to observe the others, busy removing four more victims from their cramped prisons.

Immediately her attention was snagged by Jaxon bent over one of the men, his expression one of pure anguish.

"Aric, I'm sorry. So sorry," he repeated. "I had to save my mate, but you have to believe I didn't mean for this to happen. Please—"

"Jax?" Aric's voice was hoarse, and he swallowed as though talking was extremely painful.

"Yes?"

"Shut the fuck up before you give me an aneurysm."

Ryon covered Aric's lower half with a blanket, grinning. "You haven't lost your charm, I see."

"Fuck you, too, twerp."

Jax choked out a half laugh, half sob and fell quiet, but he didn't let go of his friend's hand. Curious, Rowan edged closer to get a better look at Aric . . . and the air left her lungs. This time for an entirely different reason.

The man was, quite simply, beautiful.

He was tall and lean, with a broad, muscular chest. A stunning Celtic tattoo swirled over his left pectoral and over his shoulder, the head of a howling wolf set in the center of the design. Long, dark auburn hair that must have fallen halfway down his back pooled around his head. His face was chiseled, with high cheekbones and full, sensual lips. A nice, square masculine jaw that weeks of not being able to shave couldn't hide saved his countenance from being too pretty, and piercing green eyes held more than a little cynicism, like life had taken a giant dump in his front yard one too many times.

He looked like a proud man, she thought. Gazing at the ceiling, muscles tense, tight lines bracketing his fine mouth. He hated being vulnerable in front of his Pack, hated to need anyone. Even them. How she knew this she couldn't say, but she did. Something about him drew her, and she almost smiled at the image of the proverbial moth and flame. Would have if the situation hadn't been so serious.

Then his head turned and those green eyes found hers. Pain and exhaustion shadowed their depths, but his spark of stubbornness refused to give in. Slowly, his lips tilted up. "Well, I must be dead after all," he said softly. "If this is heaven, sign me up, angel."

His dark lashes swept closed and his body went slack. She tried to recall the last time a man had said anything to her that was so . . . poetic, and sort of suggestive. Her brain came up pathetically empty.

Shaken, Rowan stared at the unconscious man for a few seconds, then returned to her brother's side, telling herself she needed to stay with him. She'd never run from anyone or anything in her life.

And she sure wasn't about to start with a smart-mouthed, redheaded wolf shifter with killer green eyes. She could handle him.

No sweat.

Five

Aric awoke to the scent of clean sheets and antiseptic. He was lying on something soft, his body cocooned by warmth. A bed, cushioning his hurts.

For a while he lay still, wondering how that could be. He struggled to recall, and foggy images crept in.

Torture. His body invaded. Despair. Discovering Micah. Jax, his brothers, suddenly there—along with a stunning woman. Then he must've passed out.

Was he safe, then? His eyelids didn't want to cooperate, but he finally coaxed them open. When his bleary vision cleared, he could've wept. This was the compound's infirmary. After weeks of hell, he was home.

A wave of emotions threatened to drown him, but he fought it down. No sense to bawl like a damned baby now that he was tucked firmly in the bosom of his Pack. Compared to Micah, he wasn't even in such bad shape. He lifted one hand to his face and realized someone, probably a nurse, had shaved off the itchy beard. That made him feel somewhat better.

"Hey, how's my favorite redhead?" Mackenzie slipped into his room, shutting the door behind her, and came to stand by his bed. The woman had that pleasant doctor expression down pat—friendly and encouraging her patient to spill his guts.

"Ready to party." Christ, he sounded like his throat had been scrubbed with a Brillo pad. "Get your dancin' shoes on and we'll paint the town."

"Sarcastic as always, I see." Taking his wrist between her thumb and forefinger, she did a quick check of his pulse.

"The day I'm not, that's when you really need to worry."

A half smile curved her lips as she released his wrist. "True. But with a minimum of snark, tell me truthfully how you're doing."

Wasn't easy managing a shrug while lying down, but he pulled it off. "I'm alive, healing. I'm good. When can I get sprung?"

"Aric."

"I'm thinking I'll just go chill in my room and—"

"Aric." Pulling up a chair, she laid a hand on his forearm. "This is me you're talking to. It's not the scars on the outside that concern me."

He snorted a laugh, ignoring the twinge of pain it caused all over. "Yeah, and this is *me* you're talking to, so you know I don't do the feelings and head-shrinking crap. Besides, no one wants to know."

"I do," she stressed.

"You get paid to care," he snapped. "You're a doctor."

Mac's eyes widened as she was taken aback, but she quickly composed herself. "I'm your friend, too, and

I know you well enough to get when you're deflecting. I also know you don't take well to lazing around, so if you want to be cleared for duty again, you *will* open up."

His gut clenched. "You wouldn't."

"Try me."

"Damn it, Mac." Fisting his hands at his sides, he stared at the IV stuck in the back of his right one. A minute ticked by, two, while he struggled with how to put his damned feelings into words. "I'm not going to freeze up on the next op, if that's what everyone's worried about."

"Okay. What *will* you do?"

"Rip them all to fucking pieces and torch the remains. What else?"

Her expression softened. "Now we're getting somewhere."

"Why? Because I'm letting out healthy anger or some such shit?" He rolled his eyes. "I'm stating a fact—they'll pay."

"Anger can be healthy if it's directed at the right target."

"What the hell is that supposed to mean? What other target would I . . ." Then he got it. Shit. "You think I still blame Jax for what happened to me?"

"Do you?" She leaned forward, her gaze pinning him to the bed.

"What? No!" But the lie almost strangled him.

"But you did at one time," she pointed out. "You said 'still.'"

Looking away, he thought about it. In captivity, he'd thought about the choice Jax had made, saving his mate's life instead of his brother's. About being hauled into that helicopter, the horror of realizing there was a very good chance he'd never see the Pack again. The endless torture, and yes, in his darkest hour, hating Jax. Cursing him for what he'd done.

But wasn't that justice for what you've done to him and the team?

Taking a couple of calming breaths, he was able to tell Mac what she wanted to hear. Not necessarily the unvarnished truth. "I hated him, for a while. Or thought I did. But the second I saw him—was it last night?"

"Yes."

"When I saw him last night, and he was so torn up over it . . . I knew it wasn't Jax I hated." *Liar.* He swallowed and went on with difficulty. "It was Chappell and his whole operation. If it weren't for them, humans and shifters wouldn't be suffering the terrible things being done to them. It's Chappell's doing, and his minions', and they're the ones who deserve to pay. I'll live for the day that happens." Okay, that last part was true, but his heart still held a load of pain and inner conflict with regard to the choice Jax had made. Regardless of how much he'd deserved it.

She studied him a long moment before replying. "All right. You're saying the right things, but I'll want to schedule a couple more visits in my office before I release you as fit to work." She held up a hand to stave off his protest. "I have to make certain your head is together before you get back in the field. An operative harboring suppressed rage makes mistakes, and mistakes get innocents killed. You're too good a Pack member not to understand that."

"Fine." He sighed. "But I don't have to be thrilled about it."

This earned him a full-fledged smile. "No, you don't. Rest and I'll check on you later."

Persistent woman. Aric contemplated Mac long after she left, mostly because he had nothing else to do. She was lovely and wonderful, and a genuinely nice person. Not for the first time, he found himself wishing she "did it" for him. He was damned sick of being alone. But even if there'd been an attraction on his part, it might've been too late.

Mac was wearing Kalen's pentagram. Interesting. Maybe he'd ask her about that later.

Aric began to fidget, plucking at the sheets and picking at the bothersome tape holding his IV in place. He really needed to talk to Nick about getting televisions installed in the infirmary rooms. Even the crappiest of hospitals had TVs, for God's sake.

He'd just decided to close his eyes and try to take a nap when the door opened again. At first he couldn't place the woman who walked in and couldn't imagine why a stranger would be at the compound, much less visiting him. She was tall, probably only three or four inches shorter than his six-foot, two-inch height. She wore her shoulder-length sable hair pulled back into a ponytail, and her angular face was fresh-scrubbed, very attractive though she wore no makeup.

As she turned to close the door, he couldn't help but notice that her jeans fit her long thighs and rounded rear end like a glove. Not too tight but emphasizing the junk in the trunk that made his mouth water. Manna from heaven to an unrepentant ass man like himself.

Turning to face him, she approached his bedside, curiosity—and maybe fatigue—in big, chocolate brown eyes that were shadowed underneath as though she'd had little sleep. Tired or not, she carried herself with her spine straight, shoulders back and head up. Totally in control of herself and any situation she encountered, assessing him openly.

"I saw you last night," he realized out loud. "In the lab, when my team came."

She held out a hand. "I'm Rowan Chase, Micah's older sister."

"Aric Savage." Automatically he started to raise his right arm, but the tug on his hand reminded him of the IV, so he gave her his left one instead.

The instant their fingers curled around each other's, a jolt shot down his arm and through his chest at the contact. *What the hell?* His visitor looked as surprised as he did by the zing of electricity, quickly snatching her hand back and wiping the palm on her jeans as if he had a contagious disease. Inside, his wolf paced restlessly, distressed at the broken contact. Aric covered his confusion with the obvious question.

"How's Micah?"

A small smile tinged with sadness graced her lush mouth. "Alive, but he's got a long road ahead for recovery. He's—" She cleared her throat, obviously restraining her emotions. "He's not healing all that fast, not like I've been told a shifter should. I don't think he's fighting too hard."

That answered a couple of questions. One, she knew what they were. Which meant Nick had probably filled her in. Two, Rowan loved her brother very much.

"Listen, I know for a fact that Micah loves you more than anything," he told her. "Once he realizes he's been rescued, and that you're here, nothing will stop him from getting well."

"You sound so certain." Her voice held so much hope.

"I am."

He studied her closely, and she returned the favor right back. She wasn't the most model-gorgeous woman he'd ever met, but there was something about her that attracted him. She radiated inner strength and a spine of steel, but her sharp features were softened by a hint of vulnerability that made him want to take her in his arms and not let go. A new awareness crept in, and it took a few seconds before he recognized what it was.

Rowan's scent.

It didn't jolt him as her touch had done, but rather, filled his senses slowly, like the aroma of a lit candle finally reaching him from across the room. *An ocean breeze and tropical flowers.* That was the beautiful essence of her, and it sank into every cell of his body, calling to him—and to his wolf—as nothing else ever had.

Underneath the sheet, his cock swelled rapidly, filling until the damned thing was rock hard and aching. *Aw, hell.* He raised one knee a little, hoping she didn't notice his problem. He wasn't easily embarrassed or made uncomfortable, because he just didn't give a fuck what most people thought. But this sudden, overpowering need he felt to press his naked skin to hers, to be inside not just any woman, but *her*, baffled him. And scared him a little.

"Sounds like you know my brother well," she said.

"We were in the SEALs together, and later joined the Pack. I guess when you practically live with guys for years, you sometimes know them better than their own families do."

Stark pain crossed her face. "Too true."

"Shit, I'm sorry," he said, frowning. "I didn't mean to imply I know Micah better than you do."

"No, it's okay. I'm sure in many respects you do." Pausing, she looked down, absently regarding his IV. "Micah never told me he left the SEALs and joined Alpha Pack. I'm assuming you were all forbidden from telling your families where you were and what you were actually doing?"

"Under Terry Noble's leadership, yes. Nick urges us to be careful what we say to our families and old friends outside this place, but he's not quite as rigid as Terry was. He trusts our judgment."

Pinning him with her gaze again, she asked, "What do you tell your family?"

"Nothing," he said shortly. "I don't have a family anymore. My mother is dead."

Beryl, the bitch, and his stepfather didn't count. He didn't give a damn where the old bastard was now or what had happened to him, and the next time he met up with Beryl, he'd tear out her throat.

"I'm so sorry."

"Me, too." He tried a reassuring smile. "It was a long time ago. I shipped off to the Navy and she died after my first deployment."

He hadn't been able to leave home fast enough after she'd married the asshole. Had waited years for his freedom, then joined the service and never saw her again. The pain and guilt never healed.

Rowan didn't seem to know how else to respond, and settled on steering the topic to her brother again. "You were held captive with Micah."

So here it was—the real reason for her visit. He'd

wondered when she'd get around to it. "Yeah, but I didn't know he was there until right before we were rescued."

"Did he say anything to you about what they did to him?" Anxiety laced every word.

"He wasn't conscious by the time I was placed in the cage next to him," he said carefully. "Until he wakes up, we can only speculate on what he went through."

"But they were experimenting on people in that awful place."

"Yes."

"You, too?"

Nope, not going there. "Look, I don't have the answers you want. I wish I did—then maybe I could help him."

For the first time, her posture slumped. "That's all I want, too. I'd just hoped . . . well, never mind. You've obviously been through the wringer and I've kept you awake. Thanks for talking with me."

"Anytime."

She turned to go and he realized he meant that—he'd like to be there if she needed him. In fact, he didn't want her to go at all, but there wasn't a good way to encourage her to stay without sounding like a creeper, what with being a stranger and Micah being so sick.

Before she reached the door, she looked at him over her shoulder. "I hope you're feeling better and out of here fast."

"I feel better already," he replied softly. He held her gaze to make sure she got the message.

A quick smile, and she was gone.

Aric sagged into the pillows with a heavy sigh. "Jesus, what's wrong with me?"

Already he hated her being away from him. Where he couldn't get to know her. Touch her.

Fuck her against the wall.

Hadn't something similar happened to Jax when he'd met Kira?

"Oh, shit."

No. That was *not* what was wrong with him! His neglected libido was reacting to an unattached female, nothing more. Wait—was she single? He hadn't seen a ring, but that didn't mean there wasn't a boyfriend.

His wolf snarled, totally pissed off at the notion that there might be another male in her life. Someone waiting for her, wherever she was from. His lungs constricted, it became hard to breathe, and he knew one thing for sure.

He. Was. Fucked.

Closing the door behind her, Rowan leaned against the wall, allowing her composure to crumble. The man— Aric—was every bit as delicious as she'd thought when she saw him last night. More so, with the beard gone. Deep auburn hair falling around that sexy-as-sin face, startling green eyes that had seen too much. Intelligence sharp as the blade of a knife. He was—

"What the hell am I thinking?"

Micah was deathly ill, and he needed her at his side. She had to help him pull through. That was why she went to see Aric, to find out if he had any insight into what had happened to her brother. Not to moon over the wolf like a teenager.

Wolf. Crap, was she actually starting to accept all of this? Looked like she had no choice, really. Hard to refute what was right in front of your face, and last night had been the clincher. Thanks to a crash course, her thinking about the world and the creatures in it was already changing.

Pushing away from the wall, she walked two doors down to Micah's room and padded inside. The silence was eerie, life evidenced only by the beep of a monitor and the rise and fall of her brother's chest. Pulling up a chair, she sat and gazed into his now clean-shaven, but still ruined, face, willing him to open his eyes.

Heart aching, she rested her arm on the bed and stroked his hair. During the long, lonely night, she'd attempted to brush it, thinking the action might stimulate him somehow, but the locks were such a snarled mess it would take a haircut and several washings, plus a good conditioner, to have it looking decent again.

"You'll feel better when your hair is clean," she whispered to him. "You'll see. We're gonna make sure you eat well, take lots of vitamins. When you're stronger, we'll work out together and I'll beat you at the hundred-yard dash like I always have. Right?"

The man slept on, and she had to wonder if he was dreaming. If she gave in to exhaustion and drifted off, would she be able to reach him? Faced with days ahead of watching him lie there like a corpse, she was desperate enough to try anything.

As it turned out, she didn't have to coax her tired brain to cooperate. Her head felt so heavy, she needed to rest it on the bed next to his shoulder, just for a little while. The instant she did, sleep claimed her.

A loud keening noise burst into her awareness and quickly ramped into a hideous, drawn-out scream.

Rowan bolted upright, pulse pounding, hand automatically reaching for the gun that still hadn't been returned to her. A glance at Micah cleared the cobwebs in a hurry.

Her brother's body was taut as a bowstring, dark head back, eyes screwed shut as he gripped the sheets, screaming as though he was being skewered and sliced into little pieces.

"Oh, my God! Micah!" Without thinking, she laid a palm on his chest, hoping to calm him. Instead, he began to thrash. "Honey, it's me, Rowan!"

At that, he flung himself sideways off the bed. Where he got the strength she had no clue, but she made a desperate grab for him and was taken to the tiled floor so hard the air left her lungs in a rush. They landed in a jumble of limbs and his IV line, and the rolling thing that held the bag of fluid crashed to the ground as well. He fought like a wildcat—or a terrified wolf—as she pushed him facedown and lay across his back in an attempt to subdue him.

"Micah, stop!"

"No! Ahhhhh!"

He was completely out of his head. Fighting his tormentors. He bucked wildly, shouting, trying to get the leverage to dislodge her.

"Someone help me!" she yelled.

Even in his horrible condition, Micah's well of strength was incredible. Drawing up his knees, he flung himself backward. Rowan was along for the ride and the back of her head slammed into the floor, pain blasting through her skull. Her vision grayed out, but she saw Micah looming over her, lips pulled back in a feral snarl, his normally brown eyes gone black. His nose began to elongate into a snout, fur sprouting around his face.

He's going to kill me.

"Micah, no!" she cried, shoving at his chest.

The door crashed open and Micah's weight suddenly disappeared. The sounds of fierce growling and snapping, furniture being shoved, reached her ears, the unmistakable fury of two canines battling it out. Sitting up, she clutched the back of her head and gaped at a pair of wolves—one brown and one red—fighting for dominance.

They were a blur of speed and motion. The brown wolf rolled, dodged, but the red one advanced, teeth bared, backing him into a corner. The brown wolf was smaller, his coat dull and matted when it should've been as full and lustrous as that of his red and cream counterpart. The brown, she guessed, was Micah.

As evidenced when he toppled over and passed out . . . and then changed back to human form. The red wolf approached his fallen companion, sniffed, and whined softly. Then his fur slowly retracted, limbs reshaped, and became a human male crouching where the wolf had been.

A very naked male. Aric.

Later, she would appreciate the memory of the view. At the moment, she stood on shaky legs as he did the same, scooping her brother into his arms and carrying him to the bed. A woman she hadn't met before, who by the white coat she presumed was a doctor, and a young male nurse, hurried to help Aric get Micah into another gown and settled once more. The nurse fussed with the IV while the doctor checked his vitals, listened to his heart and lungs.

Aric righted an overturned visitor's chair and pushed her into it. "Are you okay?" His tone was quiet and concerned, and he brushed away her hand to examine the back of her head. Fingers probed gently at a lump forming there, and she winced. "You're going to have a bit of a headache, and you were already about to drop. Why don't you go to your room and lie down for a while?"

Her throat tightened with fear. Misery. "I can't. He needs me."

"He needs you to stay well," Aric countered. "He doesn't know you're here right now and a few hours' sleep will only help you."

"That wasn't my brother," she whispered.

"I know, honey." His knuckles grazed her cheek.

The small act of caring was nearly her undoing. And suddenly, a man calling her "honey" wasn't so bad either, coming from this man. Hanging her head, she struggled to hold back the flood of tears that threatened to spill.

"Go ahead and cry if it'll make you feel better."

She gave a watery, humorless laugh. "You know, I was shocked and grief-stricken when that asshole told me Micah had been killed. But now I don't feel a whole lot different, except I might be losing my mind."

"No way," he teased gently. "The limit on crazy is one sibling per family."

This time, her laugh had a bit more heart. But only just. She turned to look at him, kneeling by her chair, handsome face full of nothing but concern. Against her will, her eyes did a quick tour south, but in his position, with the arm of the chair blocking her view, she could see only see his sculpted upper half. His chest was broad with a nice sprinkling of dark hair and two bronzed male nipples puckered from the air-conditioning.

God, he was beautiful. And it had been too long.

Shaking herself, she looked away and fell back on her cop persona. "Normally I arrest people for walking around like that."

Ignoring the doctor's *humph* of agreement, he snickered. "Encounter a lot of streakers, do you?"

"Some. Especially around Halloween."

"Hey, here it's Halloween *all* the freakin' time." He waggled his brows. "What a bonus."

Glancing up from her patient, the doc grumbled, "Put on some damned clothes, Savage."

"You're just jealous 'cause mine's bigger than yours," he shot back. "*Mel.*"

The glare the other woman leveled at him told Rowan how much she appreciated that nickname.

"It's Melina, dickhead." To Rowan, in a marginally nicer tone, she said, "Dr. Melina Mallory. I already know you're Rowan, Micah's sister. Believe me, we're going to take really good care of him."

"Thank you." She looked at Aric. "And thanks to you, too, for intervening when Micah lost it. I think he would've hurt me."

"Not you, the demons in his head. He wasn't seeing you at all."

Not a comfort. Recalling the incident, she thought of something. "How did he have the strength to lunge out of bed like that? I mean, I've subdued plenty of perps who were high on all sorts of drugs, and although the shit in their systems can make them seem almost superhuman, I can usually take them down.

Physically, I was nowhere near my brother's match, weak as he should be."

"There are a couple of good reasons for that," Dr. Mallory said, coming around Micah's bed to stand in front of Rowan. "One, even at his weakest, like now, he'll still be stronger than several human men if he feels threatened. The other reason is that the drugs those barbarians gave him to keep him sedated are working their way out of his system. His awareness is returning, and with it, the real concerns begin."

"His mental state, and reaching him."

"Exactly." The doctor patted her on the arm. "I won't kid you. Getting him well isn't going to be easy, but he will make it. I'm going to make sure of it. Now follow the obnoxious redhead's advice and get some rest. I'll ring your quarters if there's any change."

She sighed. "Okay. But just for a while."

Dr. Mallory frowned at Aric, her gaze dipping to the bloody hole in his hand where he'd yanked out his IV. "And you! Get your ass back in bed! Noah, take him and get him settled," she ordered. The cute nurse turned from straightening the room and hurried over to Aric.

"But—"

"Now, or I'll keep you indefinitely," she warned.

Rowan thought it was sort of funny, the stern but diminutive doctor with the cap of short dark hair, ordering around a shifter who could take her apart. But Aric caved, though from his scowl, he wasn't happy.

"Damn it, fine." He squeezed Rowan's hand. "I'll check on you whenever Attila springs me."

"Oh, that's not necessary—"

"It is. Trust me."

With that, he stood and headed out, Noah draping a gown around his shoulders and blocking what surely would've been a nice view of his butt. When the door closed, Rowan shook her head and looked at Dr. Mallory to see a bemused expression on her face.

"What was that all about?" Rowan wondered aloud.

"I don't think he knows," the other woman said cryptically. "But he will."

Whatever that meant. "I take it Aric's not usually the warm and cuddly type?"

"Not by half. But he was definitely different with you." This seemed to please the doc to no end, a smile softening her harsh features.

"I don't know why," she said with a shrug. "We just met and I'm not all that cuddly myself."

"Go, get some rest."

"What if he gets upset again?" She studied her sleeping brother, biting her lip with worry.

"I gave him something in his IV to keep him calm. It's nothing like the crap those so-called scientists were giving him before," she assured Rowan. "But it will help him adjust as he comes back to us."

After a long moment, she gave in. "All right. I'll be back later."

"He's in good hands."

Rowan rose and left before she changed her mind. Passing Aric's hospital room, she thought for one second about stopping by to make sure he was as well as he seemed to think. An inner voice, however, urged her to keep going. No matter how drawn to the man she felt.

Aric Savage was like no man she'd ever met.

She couldn't help but think that might be a very good thing.

Six

"I'm going out of my fucking mind," Aric muttered, pushing the buzzer thing. Wasn't that supposed to bring the pipsqueak running? What was his name? Oh, yeah—Noah. "Stop the damned Ark, Noah. The wolf wants off."

No response.

"O-kay, that's it. I'm outta here."

Working at the tape on the back of his hand, he picked up one corner. Then, holding the tube in place, he pulled the strip off carefully, wadded up the tape, and stuck it on the nightstand. Last, he slid the IV out, wincing at the slight discomfort. A little blood beaded from the hole, but nothing like last night when he'd ripped out the whole thing trying to get to Rowan.

Thinking about the incident, he felt his gut clench. Never had he felt anything like the rage that had overtaken him yesterday when he'd seen Micah in wolf form, pinning his sister to the floor with madness in his eyes. The need to protect her had consumed him. He'd wanted to kill the other wolf for threatening what was his.

Ours.

Even now, his wolf paced restlessly, demanding he seek her out. Rub his scent all over her skin so the others would know she was theirs and stay the fuck away. Then he'd pin her down, plunge his aching cock into her tight, sweet heat, let his fangs drop, and—

Sink them deep into that soft vee of her neck and shoulder.

Claim her?

"No," he breathed, shocked at his own thoughts. "*Hell*, no."

Nothing like that had ever crossed his mind before, so why now? With this woman he barely knew? Though she didn't seem like a complete stranger, being Micah's sister and all. The man had talked about his tough cop sibling quite a bit over the years.

A cop. That was another reason not to get involved with the woman. Nothing against the guys and gals in blue. Quite the contrary; he had nothing but the highest respect for the dangers they faced every day to keep the streets safe for humans. They were dedicated, married to their jobs.

And that was just one of the many obstacles he faced by simply glancing in Rowan's direction. No mate of his would be allowed to place herself in jeopardy for others. Not that he wanted a mate because he didn't.

There. Issue solved.

A pathetic whine came from deep within his wolf's soul and he scowled, pushing himself off the bed. He didn't need this shit. *He* was in control, not the beast with its pathetic urges.

Which was why, gown flapping against his naked ass, he strode directly to Micah's room and checked to see if Rowan was inside. She wasn't, and his anxiety level rose another notch. Where was she? Why hadn't she come by to see him today? Okay, she didn't know him. But it would've been nice, since he *had* saved her pretty butt.

Taking a few seconds to make sure Micah was resting peacefully, he turned and stalked through the halls of the infirmary. Instantly, Noah blocked his path, eyes wide.

"Wait! Where are you going? You have to get back in bed!"

"If I get in bed it's gonna be my own. I'm leaving, which I would've told you in person if you'd bothered to answer the damned buzzer."

The nurse frowned. "I was busy taking care of Mr. Chase. You can't go or Dr. Mallory is going to chew my ass."

"Then she'll need a lot of salt."

"Huh?"

"Move out of the way, squirt."

"No. You can't—"

"Move, *now*." Annoyed, Aric let his wolf loose, just a little. Enough to allow a partial change into half-man, half-wolf form. A sight he knew for a fact was scary as hell by the way the guy screeched and jumped aside, hand over his heart.

Much better. Stalking off, he let himself return to normal—if there was such a thing—and headed into one of the main hallways leading to the living quarters. God, he couldn't wait to take a shower. That was the first order of business after weeks of captivity and being forced to endure his own filth. The nurses had shaved him and given him a sponge bath, but that couldn't compare with the real thing.

Thankfully, he didn't encounter anyone and reached his door without incident or argument. Standing outside the door to his quarters, however, he had a bad moment when he realized he'd been gone so long, had endured so much, he couldn't quite recall the security code to get inside.

Such a simple, mundane action. One he wouldn't take for granted again.

Reaching out, he let his fingers trace over the keypad. After a couple of incorrect entries, the sequence came back to him and he was inside, breathing deeply and looking around.

The apartment wasn't the same as he'd left it—the place was spotless. He was sure there'd been newspapers, beer bottles, food wrappers, and a few issues of *Big Tits-N-Asses* scattered everywhere. He could've sworn he was in the wrong place, except the code worked.

Every surface gleamed and the scent of lemon polish hung in the air. The counter separating the bar from the kitchen had been straightened up and cleaned, and so had the counters in the kitchen itself.

Moving into the kitchen, he inspected the fridge. The milk inside, as well as sandwich meat and an assortment of condiments, was fresh. There was a covered casserole dish, too, and he suspected one of the women had baked it for his return.

And yeah, there must be lint in his eyes. He sniffed and cursed simultaneously, glad nobody was here to witness his homecoming. Closing the fridge, he turned and padded toward the bedroom, stripping off the awful gown as he went. He tossed the thing on the floor and made a beeline straight for the shower.

His bathroom sparkled as well, and he winced, thinking of the layer of grunge his friends must've tackled to help him out. He turned on the water, gave it a minute to heat, and then stepped inside into heaven.

Hot streams of water sluiced over the top of his head, wet his hair, and ran down his body. Massaged tired, abused muscles. He groaned in sheer bliss and stood under the spray for several minutes, and it hit him that he hadn't even realized until that moment how bone-cold he'd been.

After shampooing his hair twice, he squeezed some men's shower gel into his palm, sudsing his face, neck, chest, stomach. Legs and feet. He saved the glory trail for last, following it down between his thighs to soap his balls.

"Ahhh, yes."

Too goddamned long. Felt so freakin' good to rub the slippery suds along his sac, roll them around. Thank God his balls weren't sore anymore. His cock took interest in playtime, lengthening to curve toward his belly and beg for attention. He took his sweet time, washing his balls, rinsing. Then he poured a generous amount of the liquid soap—unarguably the greatest invention *ever*—along his cock and took the eager member in hand.

Hissing, he gripped his shaft tighter, shivering at the pleasure flowing through his belly. He began to pump, down to the tight sac, up again to the plump head, flushed purple with need. Good, but . . .

The intensity was missing. The *Oh, my God* factor

that made him strain to hold back from coming and sent waves of fire through his body. Concentrating, he fisted himself almost brutally, reaching for the pinnacle that remained elusive.

To his complete astonishment, his erection began to wilt.

"What the—? No fucking way!"

Leaning against the tiled wall, he gaped at his flagging dick, trying to imagine what had gone wrong. He and the rest of the Pack had the highest libidos he'd ever seen and required release on a regular basis— something they took care of with occasional trips to Las Vegas. Aric had been denied any sort of sexual contact—well, he wasn't about to jack himself in front of his stepsister or her cohorts even if he'd been able—so he should've been ready to blow the second he touched himself.

This was *so* not right. Thinking hard, he called to mind the last whore he'd fucked in Sin City. Problem was, she wasn't all that memorable, though he'd been in ecstasy at the time. No, only one woman interested him in the least. A gross understatement.

Rowan's face, her tall, strong body and luscious ass, invaded his mind. Arousal slammed into his gut like a sledgehammer and his cock stiffened instantly. A growl of satisfaction rumbled in his chest as he began to stroke himself, fantasizing that she was here with him. As eager to taste him as he was to slide the head between her lips. Deeper, inching all of his meat down her slender throat.

"Oh, fuck."

That's what he'd do. Fuck that lush mouth of hers, slow and easy. Grip her thick sable hair, guide himself in and out, increasing the pace until he was giving all she could take. Fast and furious as she slurped him down.

"Shit, yes!"

His balls drew up, ribbons of electricity zinging through his groin, his thighs. Orgasm bore down on him like a freight train and his cock erupted, creamy streams of come arching into the spray of water to swirl down the drain. Shuddering, he milked the last of it and slumped.

Lord, he was tired. The exhaustion from his ordeal, followed by a refreshing shower and a great orgasm, left him hardly able to stand. Quickly, he finished and got out, drying off and toweling his long hair to get out all the moisture he could.

He fished under the sink for the blow dryer, took a brush, and went to work on getting out weeks' worth of tangles. Maybe someday he'd just hack all of it off short. He liked his long hair—and so did the women, they said—but taking care of it was a bitch. He had to blow it dry because he hated sleeping with wet hair.

As he did, he winced at his reflection in the mirror. He'd lost weight; no surprise there. His chest still sported a few bruises, but he wondered about his back since he'd yet to look. Once the long mass was reasonably dry, he put away the dryer and, taking a deep breath, turned his back to the mirror. Moving his hair out of the way, he peered over his shoulder and studied his reflection—and cursed.

His skin looked like a fucking road map.

Angry, puckered pink lines crisscrossed the entire area from his shoulder blades to his ass. The silver barbs in Beryl's favorite whip had performed just the way she'd known they would on a shifter, taking twice as long to heal and leaving terrible scars when a regular whip wouldn't have.

He would be carrying these reminders of captivity for the rest of his life. However long, or short, that might be. If it took his last breath, he'd find a way to make Beryl, Chappell, and whoever was calling the shots suffer. Scream as he'd done.

As he walked out of the bathroom, a wave of dizziness nearly toppled him. He braced himself with one hand on the wall until the rocking stopped, and suddenly hoped he could make it to the bed. He was that tired.

Lurching the last few feet, he fell onto the mattress and let his body sink into the softness. He didn't have the energy to pull back the covers, but didn't care. He was home. His eyes drifted shut and his last thought was that it was kind of warm in the room.

And then sleep claimed him, and he no longer cared about that, either.

Aric knew he was dreaming.

Dreams were like that sometimes. The subconscious mind knew you were in bed, cozy and slumbering away, but the spirit was willing to go along and see where the adventure led.

His inner twenty-one-year-old *loved* Las Vegas. Had ever since he'd become legal and had first set foot in the city, a lifetime ago, it seemed. He'd never forget the lights at night, the city in constant motion, strangely alluring, like a gaudy lady getting a bit older, wearing too much makeup and jewelry, laughing a little too loud. Yet when she beckoned, a young man couldn't help but follow.

It made perfect sense that he found himself standing on the street downtown, gazing at the light show on the awning overhead. Crowds of people bustled in and out of Fitzgeralds, the Golden Nugget, the Horseshoe, and Union Plaza. Others strolled toward the main drag, on their way to hop buses to the Strip, to partake of shows or other pleasures.

Aric knew what sort of pleasures he sought—and they didn't involve gambling away his hard-earned cash or going to one of the adult shows. Not when he could participate in a private show of his own.

He started walking, thinking maybe he'd grab one of the flyers from the newspaper box that didn't really contain news at all but ads outlining the various escort establishments and the experienced women a man could find there. His wolf, however, growled in anger at the idea.

What the hell? It's my dream, damn it! I can do what or who I please.

Determined to ignore his furry counterpart, he reached for the handle on one of the stands.

"Will you find what you're looking for in there?"

Straightening at the familiar voice, he turned and blinked at Rowan. She stood a few feet away, wearing a pair of snug brown leather pants and a cropped black top that showed a tantalizing slice of her tanned abs. Shiny, rich brown hair tumbled around her shoulders and her bold mouth and cheekbones were accented with a hint of makeup. Truthfully, she didn't need any, but the total effect had his cock hardening in his jeans.

The woman was stunning.

"I'd thought so," he replied, stepping closer. "But now I have serious doubts."

"Because I showed up?" Her tone was amused, teasing.

"Why did you? How are you here, with me?"

Her expression became thoughtful. "I don't know. I wasn't looking for you."

"Then who?"

"Micah. I'd hoped to find him in our dreams, like we used to do as kids. I wanted to reach out to him, try to bring him back." She frowned. "I tried so hard, but it didn't work."

"Did Nick tell you everything?"

"About all of you, what the team does, and Micah's gift, yes."

"Are you a Dreamwalker, too?" The idea fascinated him.

"I don't know." She regarded him with hope. "If you and I both remember this dream, then maybe I am. I could still reach him."

"I hope so," he said sincerely. "But I'm sure he'll start making progress soon. The doctors at the compound are the best."

"Thanks."

He gestured to her eye-catching outfit. "If you weren't expecting to find me, what's with the leather? Assuming that's not the way you'd dress to meet your brother."

Glancing briefly down at herself, she looked up again and smiled. "I had on jeans and a T-shirt, but when I saw you—poof! New clothes. Dreams are great, huh?"

Cocking his head, he felt a slow grin spread across his face. "You changed for me?"

She shrugged. "That's a woman's prerogative, isn't it?"

"Sure. It's just that when we met, you didn't strike me as the type to go out of your way to impress a man by wearing snazzy clothes and makeup."

A hand fisted on one hip and her eyes narrowed. "Why, because I'm a cop? Because even if I can't do something cool like turn into a wolf, I could still probably get you in a choke hold and take you down like a petty thief?"

He laughed. God, she was beautiful, especially when she was annoyed. How could he ever have believed she wasn't the most gorgeous woman he'd ever seen? "No. Okay, maybe," he admitted, holding up his hands in mock surrender. "At ease, officer. I try to take people at face value when I meet them, that's all. You struck me as being a very earthy and honest, no-frills lady. I liked that."

"But you don't like this?"

"Of course I do, honey. I'm a guy." Well, damn, that didn't sound like much of a compliment. He sucked at this. "But on *you* it looks extra hot. *Smokin'*." There. Better.

"Then I guess you don't need that paper to find the fantasy you were searching for."

Lips turned up in a catlike smile, she closed the distance between them and reached up, running a nail down the side of his face. Down his neck, and his chest. His cock pulsed painfully behind his zipper as he stared at her, asking himself if he'd won the lottery or been plunged into hell.

"I can't." Taking her wrist in a gentle grip, he removed her hand.

"Why not?"

"For one, you're the sister of my good friend, who will kick my ass when he gets better and finds out I took advantage of her."

"Funny, I don't see it that way. Maybe *I'm* taking advantage of *you*." She pressed her front to his, her warmth, her ocean-and-flowers scent making him light-headed.

"Rowan, we just met." The argument sounded weak. His wolf agreed.

"You wouldn't have said that was a problem with any of those women," she said, gesturing to the news dispenser.

"You're not like them." *No, she's worth one hundred of them. More.*

"You don't think so?"

"No."

She appeared pleased by this. "Good. Just because it's been way too long and I have a need to scratch an itch with one man in particular doesn't make me a slut. Well, much." Her free hand wormed underneath the edge of his T-shirt, smoothed over his flat belly. Crept lower, to the button of his jeans.

Scratch an itch? Why didn't he like the sound of that? In the past, that's exactly the term he would've used, but with Rowan . . . it didn't seem like the right description. He did like one part of what she'd said, though.

"You've been thinking of being with me?" *Please say yes.*

"Every minute of going on two days, since we rescued you guys." Her intense gaze held him immobile. "I'm drawn to you and I don't understand it."

"Sexually?"

"Yes. But it feels like more, too. Do we have to analyze it here and now?"

"God, no! This is our dream, and we can do what we want."

"Anything?"

"Tell me want you want."

"You."

She brought her mouth to his, and Jesus, her lips were soft. Kissable. One of her arms slid around his neck while the other hand pressed to his crotch. Rubbed the hard rod straining to get free. Groaning, he deepened the kiss, desperate for a taste. So good, better than he'd hoped. Their tongues tangled, bodies ground together, fanning the flames of desire.

Breaking the kiss, she panted, gripping his shirt in one fist. "You want to hear my fantasy?"

"Like you can't believe."

"I want you to take me in there," she said, pointing at the entrance to the Golden Nugget. "And I want you to fuck me right on top of a blackjack table."

Aric almost choked. "Holy shit! You're not serious. Are you?"

"Why not? It's only a dream."

That was a suggestion he wasn't about to refuse. Grabbing her hand, he dragged her toward the casino as she laughed joyously in a low, husky voice. The sound sent a thrill down his spine, so sexy he almost came in his jeans. Jogging, he pulled her down an aisle of slot machines, looking for the tables. Any table would be fine for him, but Rowan wanted a blackjack table and she'd have it if he had to search forever.

In a semisecluded alcove off the main gaming room

were some tables. An unoccupied blackjack table was
there waiting, as if he'd wished it into existence. Weird.
But not as strange as the other gamblers' being faceless,
sort of blurry, like his brain couldn't conjure individual
features, so they were simply avatars. He pulled Rowan
up to the table and positioned her, back against the
edge.

"Stay just like that. I'm going to enjoy peeling off
every inch of that getup."

"What if I want to undress you?"

"You'll get your turn." He winked. "In the next
dream."

"You're sure there'll be a next one?"

"A guy can hope."

Taking the hem of her shirt, he pulled the material
over her head and tossed it away. Her full breasts were
almost spilling over a lacy black bra, and he resisted
the urge to lick his lips. Instead he flicked the front
clasp and parted the cups, revealing a gorgeous pair of
breasts tipped by dusky nipples that perked under his
attention. Especially when he rolled them between his
fingers, plucking them to firm peaks.

Bracing her hands on the table's edge, she arched
her back with a moan of pleasure. Moving between her
spread thighs, he leaned into her, cupping one pretty
globe and flicking the nipple with his tongue. The
sweet flavor of her skin burst on his taste buds, pure
delight—to him and his wolf. The beast in him growled,
wanting more. All she would give.

Kneeling, he grasped the waistband of her leathers
and paused, looking up to be sure this was truly all
right. If not, he'd stop. He'd be left with a serious case
of blue balls, but he would never force a woman. The

wicked twinkle in her eyes and a slight nod was all the green light he needed.

Unbuttoning and unzipping the pants, he began to peel them down, half expecting to see a scrap of lacy black undies to match the bra. A neat thatch of dark curls greeted him instead, and lust almost sent him over. His blood ran hot, the fire within stoked to boiling.

"Figured they'd only get in the way," she said in a husky voice, as though reading his mind.

A witty reply lodged in his throat as he uncovered long, toned thighs and those muscular buttocks. By the time he pulled off her boots and finished with the pants, he was damned near salivating. Rowan was more than perfection.

"You're a goddess."

She laid a hand on top of his head as he urged her legs to a wider stance. The scent of her sex combined with her unique ocean fragrance was ambrosia, enough to drive him wild. Gently, he parted her folds and tasted the little clit. She squirmed, tightened her grip on his head, encouraging him to take more.

Glad to oblige, he laved her slit, giving her as much pleasure as he knew how, getting her nice and wet. Then he tongue-fucked the slick channel, playing with the nub of her clit at the same time, until she yanked on his hair.

"Please! I need you in me."

Pushing to his feet, he wiped his mouth and grinned. "Anything the lady wants."

"I want to not feel like a lady right now," she retorted, beckoning him with a finger.

"I think I can deliver." At last he freed his erection,

shoving his jeans down his hips. "Up on the table you go, on your back."

He helped her up, and after she was lying down, he hooked his arms under her knees and pulled her forward, until her bottom was off the edge and being supported by him. Knees shaking with anticipation, he draped her legs over his shoulders, lifting her rear. The head of his leaking cock was pointed at the dewy mound he couldn't wait to bury himself inside.

Inching in slowly, his gasp joined hers. If any woman had felt so fine hugging his cock, he couldn't remember it. Her velvet heat encased him like a glove made for him. He sank into her slowly, watching in fascination as his length disappeared. When he was fully seated he basked in the sensation, until she bucked her hips and arched her back.

"Oh, God. Fuck me, Aric," she demanded. "Fuck me like you mean it!"

That's all it took to break his control. Withdrawing slowly, he then slammed home, shaking the table and causing his lover to cry out in bliss. He pulled out faster, slammed in. Out and in, and soon he was plunging into her pussy like a piston, reaching the point of no return faster than he wanted.

But it was good. So fucking good, he couldn't stop the come that shot from his balls as he shouted, filling her up. Spasming again and again, riding the waves of her climax as well as his own. Her head tossed from side to side, fingernails digging into the green surface of the blackjack table. When the last of the waves subsided and she went limp, he carefully withdrew and offered her a hand to sit up.

"You were amazing," he praised, kissing her lips.

"Not too shabby yourself." She flicked his bottom lip with her tongue. "Too bad it wasn't real."

Her words sent an unexpected blade into his heart. "What?"

"Dream," she reminded him. "Not real."

"Sure felt real to me." He didn't miss the bereft note in his voice, but hoped she hadn't noticed.

Turning away, he saw that the rest of the casino had vanished. Blinking, he spun back to Rowan—but she wasn't there anymore, either. Shit!

"Rowan? Hey!"

Confused, he started to run . . . and stepped off into empty air.

Fell.

And jolted awake, safe in his own bed. Pulse thrumming in his throat, he glanced around, seeing that nothing had changed. His bedroom. His things.

"God, it *did* seem real."

His body certainly thought it was, too. A glance at his lap and the sheet confirmed they were drenched in come, his erection still at half-mast. Some dream. Only, what if it wasn't?

Running a hand down his sweaty face, he became aware of how very hot it was in the room. Or maybe the room was fine and he was the one overheated, after the mind-blowing encounter he'd just had. Whichever, the temperature was unbearable, so he got up and ran a cold shower.

He washed, and stood under the spray until he no longer felt like he was about to spontaneously combust, then got out and dried off. Better. But was his face still a little warm? He couldn't tell, and was too tired to think about the dream or anything else right now. But he had to change the sheets.

Stumbling to the bed, he stripped off the dirty bedding, balled it up, and tossed it into a corner. He stared at the mattress, bare except for the fitted pad, and decided he just couldn't be bothered to deal with making it up. Later.

He took only a couple of seconds to yank on a clean pair of boxers and flopped across the bed.

This time, when he slept, it was deep and dark.

And dreamless.

Seven

Rowan awoke from her nap gradually, her body still humming from the awesome dream she'd had, with Aric in the starring role.

Tentatively, she touched between her legs and even found herself moist with her own come. When in the hell had she ever had such a vivid dream of sex with a man? Never. Hadn't known it was possible, not to that degree of detail.

She could still smell him on her skin, musky and male. She envisioned exactly how he'd pierced her with those striking green eyes as he'd eaten her out, and the satisfaction on his face as he'd fucked her into next week, that glorious auburn hair falling over his chest and the swirling tattoo.

As she'd told him, too bad it wasn't real.

Surely it wasn't. She was no Dreamwalker, at least not one of much talent if she couldn't find her brother and reach out to him in his mental prison. If she couldn't help anyone, what good was a gift? Better to stick with what she knew and could see. Guns and bullets, flesh and blood. And yes, monsters of all kinds. What was tangible could be dealt with.

Which was why she was so lost in regard to Micah.

She'd left him alone too long. It wasn't easy to get moving, since the nap hadn't really been restful and her head still hurt some. If he was calm and his vitals were good, she might turn in early tonight and get a fresh start in the morning.

Cleaning up quickly, she decided to wear the same jeans she'd had on, and a different shirt. Ready, she slipped into the hallway and became aware of some sort of commotion at the end. Already headed that way, she made out a small group of people standing outside a door. Dr. Mallory was knocking, and raising her voice for whoever was inside to answer it. She didn't sound happy.

Rowan's footsteps slowed as she approached. Nick stood to the left of the doctor, Jax on the right. Mallory waved a hand at Nick in agitation.

"Use your pass code. I need in there to see if that stubborn idiot has set his recovery back by leaving the infirmary too soon."

"Micah left?" Rowan blurted, alarmed. "How?"

The doctor glanced at her, shaking her head. "Not your brother. Aric."

"Oh." Instead of relief, a sense of fear invaded, shaking her to the core. Aric being in trouble was no more acceptable than if it had been Micah. Helplessly, she watched as Nick blocked the keypad with his body and punched in the code. Then the group streamed inside, calling for their friend.

After hesitating, Rowan trailed them. Nobody had

ordered her to stay out, and Aric was already becoming a friend, of sorts. She hoped he would be, anyway, and she didn't want anything bad to happen to him.

Rowan recognized the layout and guessed all the apartments must be pretty much the same. They hurried through the living room and down the short hallway to his bedroom. She heard Nick and Jax calling their friend's name, and then cursing just as she stepped inside. Oddly, Aric was lying on the bare mattress, curled on his side, wearing only a pair of boxers.

Nick was kneeling on the bed, shaking Aric's shoulder. "Aric, wake up! Shit, what's wrong with him?"

"Let me take his pulse," the doctor said briskly. "Move."

Both men wasted no time getting out of her way, though they paced anxiously. Rowan moved closer, hand over her mouth as Mallory dropped his wrist, shaking her head.

"It's too fast, and he's hotter than hell." Removing a white strip from her pocket, she peeled off the back and stuck it to his forehead. Within moments she got a reading and removed the strip as Aric remained unaware. "One-oh-six."

"That's impossible," she breathed.

Mallory answered. "Not for Aric. Remember, he's not human, and he's a Firestarter on top of that. His normal temp is around one-oh-two, but this is too high. He needs to wake up."

Firestarter? God. "What's wrong with him?"

"That's the million-dollar question." She fixed Rowan with a strange look, then turned back to her patient.

That was twice now with the look. What was up with that woman?

"Nothin' wrong with me," Aric muttered, opening his eyes to frown at the group. "Can't a man get some sleep? Think I've earned it, for fuck's sake."

"We're worried about you, asshole." Jax crossed his arms over his chest.

"Really?" Aric's voice dripped with nasty sarcasm as he sat up and came fully awake, shoving hair from his face. "See, now I've an entirely different take on how much you're *worried* about whether I'm dead or alive. My viewpoint was from the inside of a helicopter as it took off and I was carried away to be tortured for weeks!"

Jax's face paled and he looked like he'd been punched. "You don't know how sorry I am about that," he rasped. "But I only had one chance to save my mate, and I took it. You're both alive, and—"

"But my survival wasn't a certainty, was it?" Aric asked in a deceptively quiet voice. Like he was a time bomb about to blow. "I was left to be picked apart by vultures, especially Beryl, the bitch. She always—" The man cut himself off and clamped his lips shut, stark torment replacing the anger of seconds ago.

The cop in Rowan went on alert, and she wondered what he'd been about to say. What he might be hiding about the "bitch" in question.

Nick, too, studied him for a few tense moments, but didn't pursue the subject of Aric's torture or the woman responsible. "We came for you as soon as we had a location. You had to know we would."

"But whether I'd be alive—did you know for sure?"

"I felt you would be, yes."

"What a comfort."

"I'm so sorry," Jax told him in anguish.

Rowan's chest hurt. Friends who were as close as brothers shouldn't be tearing one another apart over terrible events that neither would likely do differently if given a second chance. Aric was hurting, but not for a second did she believe he would've sacrificed Jaxon's mate to save himself. As for Jax and the others, she'd made some tough decisions herself, and no doubt Luis Garcia's survivors blamed her for making the only one she could at the time.

"Thought I was getting a handle on this." Aric gave a bitter chuckle. "Guess that was before I was put to the test, huh?"

"Aric—"

"Don't concern yourself. I'll get over it. So if you'd all kindly show yourselves out, I'd appreciate it."

The doctor was having none of that. "No can do. You were so lethargic we had trouble waking you and your temp is one-oh-six, which is a bit high even considering your specialized system. You're coming back with me for a more thorough checkup, and that's nonnegotiable."

"I don't need—"

"You're not the physician. I am," she said sternly. "You can come peacefully or I can call in reinforcements, but you're coming."

Her ultimatum hung in the air, Aric trying hard to glare her down. He didn't have a prayer. Rowan thought the doc would make an excellent police lieutenant or captain—one icy stare and most of the guys' balls would freeze and fall off.

"Fine, whatever," the angry redhead snapped, bouncing off the bed. His small show of defiance was ruined, however, when his legs wobbled and Nick grabbed his arm to steady him. Cheeks flushing, Aric shook off the help and crossed the room, yanked open the door to his walk-in closet and disappeared inside.

Nick blew out a breath and massaged his temples. "That went well."

"That boy is his own worst enemy," Dr. Mallory observed.

"This *boy* is thirty-five years old and has the hearing of a dog," Aric called from the closet. "Oh, wait—I *am* a dog. Shit." A humorless chuckle floated from inside.

His friends exchanged exasperated glances, but nobody wanted to touch that one. Rustling was heard and a couple of minutes later their friend emerged dressed in low-slung jeans and a loose T-shirt. When he met Rowan's gaze, the hard edges of his expression softened, and if she hadn't known better, she would've said he looked like he had a secret. One he'd like to share.

Or a naughty one they already had.

She wasn't a blushing kind of woman, but her face heated as the memory of the wicked dream chose that moment to taunt her. Stupid, because there was no way he'd had the same—

"Doc, are you sure I have to come in right now?" he asked, never taking his eyes off Rowan. His lips curved in a predatory smile. "I'm feeling a sudden urge to pop down to Vegas and play a little . . . blackjack."

Oh, crap! Her eyes widened and she saw immediately that he knew she fully understood his meaning. *But it wasn't real! It can't be if two people connect only in their minds! Right?*

The doc's brows drew together. "What?"

Aric ignored the woman, keeping his attention on

Rowan. "Come on. I'll walk you to the infirmary so you can see Micah and I can put up with the doc poking on me."

Realizing she was still gaping at him like a landed trout, and that his friends were glancing between them trying to figure out the private exchange, she schooled her expression and gave Aric a polite response.

"That would be nice, thanks."

The party filed out of Aric's quarters. Nick and Jax promised to visit Micah later, and left to attend to other business. Dr. Mallory issued firm orders for Aric not to waste time and get to the infirmary stat, and then stalked ahead at a rapid clip, leaving them alone.

"I can't decide whether I like that woman or not," Rowan said, mostly to herself.

"Melina's a good person," Aric said thoughtfully as they walked together. "But she was changed by the massacre as much as the rest of us. Our leader, Terry Noble, was her mate."

A wave of sympathy washed over her. "Now I feel horrible."

"Don't. Melina wouldn't thank you for showing an ounce of pity, so it's best to be real around her."

"Like it's best with you?"

That visibly took him aback for a second, but then he agreed. "Yeah. She and I are a lot alike in that respect. I don't do pity. We're both prickly, too."

"You might make a good couple." The idea of Aric making up half of a good couple with anyone made her want to hurt someone. Weird.

He snorted. "Hell, no. I'm not interested in a woman who has bigger balls than me."

"What, you have a problem with strong, career-minded women who don't take shit off anybody? Who could maybe kick your ass?" She heard the defensive tone in her voice, and he must've as well.

"Hey, back up. I see where you're going with that and you're wrong," he said earnestly. "I'm not one of those guys who gets his fragile ego wounded when he runs up against a female who can hold her own with any man. That's not it at all. I'm talking about chemistry, and I'm not attracted to *anyone*—man or woman—who struts around acting like they're the shit. Does that make sense?"

She thought a second. "Okay, I can buy that."

"Gee, thanks."

She smiled at his affronted tone. "Seriously, I'm with you there. I work with people like that, and while it doesn't mean they're bad, I just don't relate to them. But I try to remember there are reasons people present themselves a certain way, and sometimes they're covering deep hurt."

"So *could* you kick my ass?" His lips quirked.

"Definitely, as long as it's a fair fight."

"Really? Criminals fight fair?" he teased.

"You know what I mean. You couldn't let your wolf loose or turn me into ash."

"Or toss you across the room without touching you. I'm a Telekinetic, too."

"Good grief, anything else?"

"Nope, that's all."

"Well, thank God for small favors."

She found herself enjoying this interplay between them. He seemed to be, too.

"So let me get this straight," he said with mock seriousness. "You can go a round or three with me *and* win, as long as I don't use my full abilities. I have to hold back. Hmm, hardly seems fair to me."

"I prefer to think of it as choosing our weapons. I choose the ones we were born with—unless you'd like for me to even the odds by using a gun loaded with silver bullets."

He laughed and slung an arm around her shoulders. "Okay, you win. Name the time and place."

"Do you guys have someplace where you work out?" The heat from his side seared into her, and his male scent tantalized. Lord, being held against him felt damned good.

"We have a gym where we train, basically keep our skills in shape. It's across the building not far from our rec room."

"That'll work. It's a date, after the doctor clears you for strenuous activity."

"There's not a thing wrong with my stamina, as you know." His smirk shot warmth straight to her toes.

And with no little discomfort, something she wasn't used to. "I have no idea what you're talking about."

"Oh, come on. Playing dumb doesn't become you, officer." Moving suddenly, he pushed her back against the nearest wall and trapped her with his arms, noses almost touching. "A blackjack table? Really? Naughty, naughty Rowan."

"Rein it in, caveman," she said, glancing up and down the hallway. "Someone might see."

"That's not what you told me a little while ago." Leaning so close his breath fanned against the shell of her ear, he affected a falsetto. "Oooh, fuck me harder, wolf-man."

"That is *not* what I said! Well, not exactly."

"Yes, you beast, do me down and dirty!" His Rowan impression was punctuated by a laugh.

"Stop it!" But the order didn't sound very convincing. Especially when she dissolved into a fit of giggles. God, when the hell was the last time a guy had made her *giggle*? But Aric was darned funny, when he wasn't going out of his way to be defensive or snarky.

"Next time say it with a bit more oomph if you expect me to believe it." Looking mighty smug, he pushed away from the wall and began to walk again. "Coming?"

"Already did," she retorted.

Green eyes glittered with amusement. And there was that heat again, searing her to the core. "I like you, officer."

"Good to know. You're pretty okay, too."

"I'll accept that as high praise from you."

"Trust me, it is."

They walked slowly, by mutual consent, and Rowan thought he was as reluctant to reach their destination as she was. The silence was companionable, the discomfort of moments ago banished. She decided to chance a burning question.

"Do you think something is real if it happens only in the mind?" If she'd thought he'd take the opportunity to tease or make some witty retort, she was wrong.

"You're talking about our mutual dream-fantasy."

"Yes, but I also wondered in a broader sense. The idea is scary. Fascinating, too, I'll admit."

"Before I can answer that and have you believe what I say, you have to reconcile your perception of what's real and what isn't. You have to understand that what humans traditionally accept isn't the only reality there is in the universe."

She stared at him, impressed and pleased that he was taking her so seriously. "You're pretty smart."

"Not really. I've just had longer to come to terms with alternate reality."

She thought about what he'd said about the universe. "I guess I have no choice but to believe."

"Nope, no guessing. By now you've seen enough to know whether you do or don't."

"Okay, I do. But I don't want to," she clarified. "My brain still rebels against all of this stuff."

"That's fair. Then I can say yes—there are occasions when what happens in the mind is very real. Even better, I can prove it."

"How?" Her fact-loving self liked this.

"Easy. Here, I'll show you." Grabbing her hand, he veered off course, turning down a different hallway.

"The doc isn't going to like that you didn't get your butt straight there like she said."

"She'll get over it. Besides, this will only take a couple of minutes."

"That's all? A few minutes to make me accept the 'mind over matter' theory?"

"I'll let you be the judge."

The trip was shorter than she would've hoped, because she really liked his big hand enfolding hers. It made her feel like a teenager again, and very few things could perform that miracle these days. In moments, they stood in a room that held a huge rectangular table and a bunch of chairs. A big flat-screen television adorned the wall at one end.

"This is our conference room," he told her. "Nick just splurged on updating it with new furniture and the TV. A vast improvement over the secondhand crap we had in here before."

"Nice. But what can you show me in here?"

"Watch."

Guiding her farther inside, he directed her to stand off to the side, away from the furniture. She observed, puzzled and a little amused as he raised one arm, turning his hand palm up and simply held that position, staring intently at the table and chairs.

Which ever so slowly began to rise.

"Oh, my God!"

Her mouth fell open as they continued upward, like they were being hoisted by invisible ropes and pulleys, damned near to the ceiling. Then down again. When the legs were about six inches off the floor, they dropped the remaining distance with a noisy clatter, less gracefully than they'd gone up.

Aric braced one hand on the back of a stuffed chair, looking a bit pale. "There's your proof. I told you I'm a Telekinetic. I can start fire the same way, though Nick would be kinda pissed if I torched the new goodies."

"I've never seen anything like that in my life," she breathed.

"The mind is a powerful tool. There's so much untapped potential in every single human's brain—that demonstration only scratches the surface." He gazed at her. "Now do you believe in power you can't see?"

She gave a shaky laugh. "Yes. It's very safe to say I do. Who would've thought?"

"I ask myself that question every single day," he said quietly.

"Are you all right? You suddenly don't look well."

"I'm fine."

She frowned, not convinced, and cupped his cheek. "You're still burning up, and now you're pale. That took too much out of you when you're still not recovered from your ordeal. Let's get you to Dr. Mallory."

"Yes, ma'am. You can call her Melina, you know. She doesn't bite too hard."

"I'll keep that in mind."

He was teasing, but the fact that he didn't attempt to argue again about getting checked was worrisome. She figured a stubborn man like Aric had to feel really awful to admit he needed help of any kind. Not that he *had* admitted it, exactly, but still.

Leaving the conference room, they started on their way once more. But halfway to the infirmary, he stumbled. Acting quickly, she grabbed his arm and leaned her body into his until he got himself steadied.

"I'm okay. I'm good."

He wasn't, but she didn't argue. They made it all the way to the infirmary, where the cute nurse, Noah, sat behind a desk and greeted them with a tentative smile.

"Thank God you brought him back!" Noah rose and hurried to help Rowan. "Dr. Mallory has been on the warpath since he went AWOL."

"Well, I'm back. So she can get her panties unbunched and . . ."

Aric's knees folded and his head tilted back as he collapsed. Rowan cursed, she and Noah jumping for him at once and lowering him to the floor. The nurse shouted for help and both doctors, Melina and Mackenzie, came running, along with another male nurse Noah had called Sam, this one substantially bulkier than Noah. She guessed it made sense to have at least one strong man on staff when constantly patching up supernatural soldiers.

The two men lifted Aric, the big one hoisting him under his arms, Noah at his feet, and placed him onto a gurney.

"Roll him into the ER," Dr. Mallory ordered. "I want a complete workup done, and he's not leaving until I find out if he's just still weak from captivity or if it's something more."

They rushed to comply, and Aric was rolled out of sight. Rowan's chest seized at the thought of him in there alone. Well, not by himself, but without anyone to comfort him. Someone who wasn't a doctor or nurse, but a friend. There was nothing she could do for him at the moment, and she hated it.

I'm afraid for him. I can't remember the last time I cared about someone like this who isn't family. Where it hurts inside, thinking of anything bad happening to him. I don't want to give a shit.

But she did.

"He'll be okay," Mackenzie said, giving Rowan's hand a squeeze. "Why don't I walk you down to see your brother? Melina will bring news of Aric when she can."

Rowan blinked away the stupid tears that wanted to form. Crying would help nobody, least of all Micah or Aric. "All right. I was coming to visit Micah, anyway."

"Good girl. One thing you should know, however. He woke up again a little while ago. In fact, that's what delayed us in going after Aric."

"What? Why didn't anyone call me? Did he . . ." Dread halted her words.

"No one notified you because we were busy with him until he drifted back to sleep, and you needed your rest. He'll be in and out all day, most likely. And there won't be a repeat of the incident from before because he's being kept calm with a special sedative that we've developed for shifters."

"Dr. Mallory told me about the drug. How long will he be on it?"

"It's hard to say, but our plan is to wean him off gradually, until he's completely healed from his ordeal."

"Meaning, until he's not a danger to himself or others."

"I'm afraid so." She patted Rowan's arm reassuringly. "Try not to worry. Micah's a strong man to have survived, and with all of us pulling for him, he can't lose."

"Thanks."

"Sure. Let's go see him."

They walked the short distance to Micah's room and went inside. Rowan approached the bed, hating how fragile her brother seemed lying there. It wasn't fair that someone who loved life as much as he did had been reduced to a catastrophic disaster. Rage wrapped in layers of pain, and then drugged so that it all boiled under his skin, ready to break free and level everyone around him.

Lowering herself to the chair beside him, she scooted close and took his hand. "I'm here, little bro. Come back to us, please."

She hadn't expected a response, but his lashes fluttered and she found herself looking into glazed, dull brown eyes.

"S-sis?" he croaked.

She swallowed the cry that almost escaped. The last thing she wanted to do was upset him. "Hey, trouble," she said, a catch in her voice. "It's good to see you awake." And not feral, but she didn't want to remind him if he couldn't remember that detail.

"What . . . where am I?"

"At the Alpha Pack compound. Your team rescued you." She stroked his hair, his confusion tugging at her heart. "You're safe."

He looked confused. "How are you here?"

"It's kind of a long story, so we'll save it for when you're feeling better, okay? I'm here, I'm staying until you're better, and that's all that matters."

"Okay." His expression saddened. "Sis?"

"Yes, sweetie?"

"They . . . hurt me."

"I know about the experiments, the shifters and the supernatural stuff. You don't have to explain."

"No, I mean they *hurt* me."

Ice flooded her veins, and damned near froze her vocal cords. "Are you saying they raped you?"

Shame flooded his face, and a tear traced down his cheek. "Don't let them hurt me anymore. Please . . ."

"Shh. I won't. Nobody's going to let those sleazy bastards near you again," she soothed, wiping away the moisture. "Do you hear?"

"Yeah."

But she wasn't sure how much he actually registered of their exchange, or what he would remember. His lids drifted closed, and in seconds his chest was rising and falling in steady rhythm, the drug doing its job.

"He'll be all right."

Rowan started. She'd forgotten about Mac's presence in the room. "When was someone going to tell me?" she hissed angrily.

To her credit, the doctor didn't pretend to misunderstand. "I planned to counsel him first, let him talk to you about it when—and if—he was ever ready to share. I'll still hold sessions with him, of course, and any details are his to divulge to you. I'd never break a patient's confidence."

"I understand that, but someone should've told me the full extent of his abuse in that horrible place. Is there anything else I should know?"

"Not that I'm aware. For what it's worth, I am sorry. Both about not telling you, and the fact that it happened in the first place," she said sincerely. "Micah is very much loved by his team and all of us here at the compound. We only want the best for him, same as you."

Rowan forced her anger into a tiny box. What had befallen her brother wasn't Mac's fault. "I can see that. Thank you."

"I'll leave you two alone for a while."

The doctor left, closing the door softly.

Leaving Rowan alone with a broken wolf shifter and not a clue how to help him recover.

Aric heard the door to his room swish and he opened his eyes to see Rowan walk in, giving him a tentative smile that softened her features. It was amazing how his heart stuttered in his chest, just being in the same room with her.

"Hey," he croaked.

"Hey yourself." Taking a seat, she patted his arm. "I'll ask the stupid question—how are you feeling?"

"Better, thanks." He still couldn't believe he'd passed out in front of her, and he tried not to let his embarrassment show. But her tantalizing scent hit him hard, shot straight to his cock, and went a long way toward making him forget anything else.

"I'm glad. Did they figure out what's wrong with you?"

"I'm still waiting, but I'm sure it's exhaustion or something from my time in Motel Hell." He shrugged. "No big."

"I don't know how you can be so nonchalant about that," she said, frowning. "It's definitely a big deal for Micah."

"Damn, that's not what I meant at all." Sitting up straighter, he took her hand. "I'd never make light of what he's going through. I hope you know I'm not that much of a jerk."

She blew out a breath. "I do. It's just hard to see him hurting. He's nothing like the man I remember . . . not that I believe I ever really knew him."

"Who was the Micah you knew?" he asked quietly.

She thought for a moment. "Fun-loving, always laughing. He had a great sense of humor, and even though he knew the world wasn't perfect, *his* world was always rose-colored. His glass was always half-full."

"Yeah, that's how I saw him, too. How everyone saw him, as far as I know. Even after we were turned into shifters, he was determined to help all the guys see the good that came from the bad. He had his work cut out with me, because I hated what I'd become."

She squeezed his hand, her expression warm with concern. "Do you still hate it?"

"Not like I used to, and Micah gets a lot of the credit," he said honestly. "He'd spend hours talking to me, spinning what had happened to us into a positive thing. We were alive and more than human, and we could use that to do good, et cetera. He started getting through, too, and then . . ."

Her voice was almost inaudible. "Then he was gone, presumed dead."

"Yes."

She fell silent for a minute, studying their linked hands. "Would you do something for me?"

"Anything." The word was out before he thought, but he realized he meant it. Something about this woman compelled him to want to make her happy, though he didn't know why, except for the fact that she was Micah's sister and he genuinely liked her.

"Tell me what it was really like the day your SEAL team was attacked and turned," she urged, leaning forward to clasp his hand even tighter. "I need to hear the story of what happened to all of you."

Aric blinked at her. He wasn't surprised that she wanted to hear the account, since it had changed her brother's life, but she couldn't possibly have made a more difficult request of him. Hell, he didn't know anyone who'd want to relive those hellish few minutes in Afghanistan. But if he refused to tell her, she'd simply go to one of the other men.

And for some reason, that didn't sit well. Better him than having her turn to someone else.

"All right. I can do that."

"Thank you."

Taking a deep breath, he began. "It was so fucking hot that day, we thought we'd die. Little did we know that half of us *would*, and not from the heat or from facing the enemy we expected to find . . ."

Five and a half years earlier . . .

"Jesus Christ, I'm rank," Raven bitched, scratching at his crotch. "When I finally get to change this underwear, it'll probably walk off."

Micah grinned. "With assistance from the crabs you caught from that woman in the last village."

"Shut up, needledick. She did *not* give me crabs."

Aric and a few of the guys chuckled. Giving one another shit was about the only pastime out here, unless you counted paying a visit to one of the whores available in the dirt-poor villages to relieve the tension. The idea made Aric shudder. *Hell*, no. He'd settle for his fist indefinitely to avoid catching something he couldn't get rid of.

They tramped through the thick undergrowth, using the barrels of their weapons to push aside limbs and foliage. Sweat trickled down his spine and between his ass cheeks, and his shirt stuck to his torso. Tuning out his comrades' continuing banter, he dreamed of home. Of a meal that wasn't prepackaged and didn't taste like dog crap. Of pizza and beer.

God, he could taste the dough and cheese, washed down with a cold one—

"Hold up," Jax whispered, coming to a halt. Tensing, he studied the mountain forest around them, frowning. Somewhere hidden in the greenery, a footstep crunched to their left. Another to their right. And one from behind.

A chill slithered down Aric's spine as they exchanged glances, readied their weapons. They couldn't have reached their target's stronghold already, and this area was supposed to be clear.

Tell that to the bastards who had them surrounded.

Then the forest went silent. Those few heartbeats that followed the utter stillness, those seconds before their lives changed forever, as he locked gazes with Raven, and then Micah, would forever be crystallized in his memory.

Thud, thud, thud.

The ground trembled and the leaves shook. When a deep-throated roar split the air, Aric jumped, pointing the muzzle of his M-16 into the trees, hands steady, heart racing, a bead of sweat dripping off his nose.

"Fuck," Micah whispered. "What the fuck is that?"

It was a horror right out of *Jurassic Park*, the scene he'd never forget as long as he lived. The thing that broke through the foliage to their left stood erect on two legs and was more than seven feet tall. Covered with a thick mat of grayish brown fur, it had a long torso, two arms, muscular shoulders, and a head sporting two upright ears and a long, snarling muzzle full of sharp teeth.

It looked like a creature that was half man, half wolf. He stared, mouth open, finger frozen on the trigger.

How things might have been salvaged, disaster averted, they'd never know. Because their buddy Jones started screaming, pumping bullets into the beast's chest. After that, everything went to hell fast.

The creature staggered backward and then rallied quickly, rushing Jones. With a swipe of a paw the size of a dinner plate, the big bastard ripped out Jones's throat, tossing him aside like a twig. Then it pounced on Raven, biting into the vee of his neck and shoulder as the man screamed.

They opened fire just as several more of the beasts emerged from the forest. It quickly became apparent that while their bullets could wound, it would take something with far more power to kill them. Aric dropped into a crouch and desperately palmed a grenade as his friends fell all around him, waging a battle they couldn't win. The one who'd killed Jones shook Raven like a rag doll, released him, and ran toward Aric.

He let the grenade fly. It hit at the target's feet and exploded, sending the damned thing to hell. But it wasn't enough.

Micah went down, his knife in hand, slitting one's throat. But another jumped on him, and his struggle was short-lived, his screams echoing in Aric's ears. Jax fell next, then their CO, Prescott, Ryon, Zan, Nix, and so many others. All of them, one by one. Dead or dying.

Unsheathing his own knife, Aric spun to face the beast coming up on his flank. "Come on, bitch," he hissed. "Let's dance."

Today he would die. But he'd take this one with him.

Surprising the creature, he rushed in and leapt, burying the blade to the handle in its gullet. As it fell, he whirled, heart pounding with fear. Automatically, he thrust out a hand, employing one of the weapons in his personal arsenal that he had sworn never to risk using unless the situation became dire. No reason to keep it a secret now.

Pouring all his consciousness, every ounce of his energy into his gift, he unleashed his fire. A column of flame shot out from his palm and engulfed the wolf-man. Screeching, the beast dropped to the ground, writhing as it burned.

"Take that, cocksucker!"

Filled with renewed hope, he torched three more wolves. He could do this, and save at least some of his teammates. All wasn't lost.

Until his fire was depleted. Suddenly the flames died and one of the remaining beasts advanced, wearing a sinister expression that could have passed for a grin. He faced it head-on, without flinching, allowing his anger to override the fear that would mean certain death. And if there was any prayer of survival, he'd take it. Moving slowly, he palmed another grenade.

"Come on, you ugly fucker. Come to papa."

Whether it understood, he couldn't have said. But it ran at him, and he braced himself. The beast took him to the ground and his back hit hard as he pulled the grenade's pin. Not a second to lose.

The wolf brought its nose to his, mouth open, breath fetid, fangs dripping with bloody saliva. Seizing his opening, Aric rammed his fist down the beast's throat, pushing his arm as far as it would go. Immediately, the thing gagged and jerked back reflexively, clawing at his shoulder and arm to dislodge him. Pain burned his biceps and forearm as he was shoved backward, but he ignored it, scrambling as far from the beast as he could.

The grenade detonated, spraying fur, blood, and entrails everywhere. Aric lay there, ears ringing, for several long moments before he realized that all sounds had ceased. He raised his head, saw the prone figures of his team, flung everywhere. Some gasping and moaning for help, others mangled beyond recognition.

He tried to crawl toward the pleas, struggled so hard to make it to even one of his fallen brothers.

But he was too fucking weak. His arm burned like it had been dipped in acid, and he peered at it to see several long, deep gashes that had been carved by the wolf-man's teeth. He was losing blood at an alarming rate, becoming light-headed.

Rest. Just for a minute. Then he'd try again.

The next thing he knew, a hand was shaking his shoulder. "Aric? Oh, God! Please don't be dead. Please!"

Cracking his eyes open was hard, but he managed. Zan was crouched over him, gripping Aric's arm—the arm that should've had several deep slices. And now it didn't. The skin was still bloodied, but smooth, as though nothing had happened.

"What the hell?" he rasped.

"Easy," Zan said. His face was pale as milk, the meat of his shoulder torn open from a nasty bite. "You're not the only one with a trick up his sleeve, my friend. I'm a Healer."

Before today, despite his own gift, Aric might've laughed. Now he just sent his friend a weak smile. "Thank fuck. So heal yourself while you're at it."

"Doesn't work that way. Stop talking and rest, okay?"

His brain was growing foggy, his body heavy. He had no choice but to obey. Maybe he would die after all, lost in this little slice of hell, along with his friends.

He might have wished for death back then, had he known that he would carry a piece of that devil's spawn for the rest of his life.

Aric finished his story and reached out, gently wiping Rowan's tears from her pretty face. "I'm so sorry. I did what I could for your brother and the rest, but it wasn't enough. It never will be."

"No, don't say that," she protested. "You fought hard, all of you did. And you killed the last one, giving the survivors the chance to be rescued and begin a new life."

"Such as it is." He winced at the bitterness in his tone.

"Is it really so bad?" she questioned softly. "This career, this life you've built here with your friends?"

He studied her earnest expression, drowned in those brown eyes. She was so close, so beautiful. She smelled so freaking good he wanted to leap from the bed and take her like the beast he was.

More than that, he wanted to know Rowan—on the inside as well as out.

A small smile curved his lips and he answered seriously. "No, I guess it isn't. Especially now."

Slowly, she returned his smile.

They spent the afternoon talking about nothing, really. But despite the circumstances of their meeting, Aric couldn't remember when he'd enjoyed a day more. When she finally left, he could think of only one thing.

When he'd get to see her again.

Eight

Aric flat out refused to spend one more second in that damned uncomfortable infirmary bed. They were torture devices specially designed to make the patient want to get well fast, just so he could get the hell off that stupid mattress that must've been designed for a ten-year-old. His fucking heels hung off the end, unless he hitched his knees to the side.

Instead, he sat in a visitor's chair near the window and gazed out longingly at the forest, itching to go for a good run. He would, too, as soon as Melina got her skinny butt in here and let him out of the loony bin. Two days he'd been here since the doc had made him come back. Now he knew how animals in the zoo must feel, and his wolf growled in agreement.

The door opened and Melina stepped inside.

He jumped to his feet, grinning. "Just the lady I wanted to see. Let me out!"

She didn't return his enthusiasm, but met his eyes

calmly, shoving her hands in the pockets of her lab coat. "Aric, sit down. We need to talk."

"Talk while you sign my release papers."

"I'm being serious."

"Uh-oh." His smile wilted. "What's up?"

"Your temperature, again. By two tenths of a degree."

"That's all? Jesus, doc, you scared me." He plucked at the ugly gown. "Now can I get out of this thing? It's a little breezy and—"

"Aric. Sit down."

Her steely tone could wither the balls right off the toughest of men. Himself included. Swallowing hard, he planted his ass in the vinyl chair again and waited for her to get to the point.

She wasted no time, removing a flat wooden stick from a jar on the counter and moving her rolling stool so that she was situated between his knees. "Open wide."

He did, trying not to gag as she depressed his tongue and shone a light into his mouth. After a few seconds, she removed the stick and tossed it in the trash. For a minute she regarded him in silence. He fought the urge to squirm like a schoolboy in the principal's office.

"Your throat is a little red, though it wasn't yesterday. Is it sore?" she finally asked.

He blinked at her. "I don't know. I hadn't really noticed."

"Swallow."

He did, trying not to wince.

"Does that hurt?"

"No."

"Aric."

"Okay, some."

She sighed. "I'm going to run a culture, but I doubt anything will show up, since shifters don't contract human diseases."

"Then why bother?" He just wanted out.

"Because it could be something we haven't seen before in your kind. Or it could be an indicator of an altogether different issue."

His brow furrowed. "Such as?"

"It could just be that your body is out of whack from the abuse you endured at Chappell's site."

"But you don't think so." This *really* was starting to worry him. "Come on, Melina. It's not like you to beat around the bush."

"No, it isn't. Bear with me another minute." She paused, leaning forward. "Your temperature was normal when you were first rescued. We were worried about your body's condition, but it was fairly good, all things considered. This didn't start until you got home. Specifically, when you met Rowan."

He stared at the doc, his pulse leaping. "What does she have to do with me?"

"Do you feel a pull toward her? Does your wolf?"

Ah, shit.

He affected a smirk. "Are you kidding? The woman's totally hot. And babes in uniform? Damn, there is a God."

"You know what I mean. Do you? What if I were to inform you—and your wolf—that I'd seen her and Zan involved in a deep, passionate kiss, right before they disappeared into the forest?"

"What!" He was on his feet, hands shifting to claws,

fur sprouting before he realized it. His voice emerged in a snarl. "Where is that motherfucker? I'll tear his asshole out through his throat and feast on his carcass!"

He spun, but before he could dash out the door, a firm hand grabbed his biceps. "I didn't say that's what happened. I asked you *what if*? And I believe you answered my question."

As he turned to stare at her, it slowly dawned on him that he'd been baited. The wolf inside him hadn't been able to tolerate the idea of another man touching what belonged to him—

"Oh, fuck me." The fur and claws retracted and he walked to his chair, sat down hard. Slumping, he braced his elbows on his knees and hung his head, staring at his bare feet. "Is this what happened to Jax when he met Kira?"

"I can't discuss that because of confidentiality, but I can tell you that your symptoms are consistent with what we understand so far about the changes a male wolf shifter experiences when he finds his mate."

"But she and I just met! Don't get me wrong, I really like her—but I don't want a mate!" Even as he said this, however, a miserable ache formed in his gut. His wolf paced inside, anxious. Unsettled.

"I have a feeling your wolf doesn't care what his human half wants," she said. Her tone was kinder than normal, which said a lot about the seriousness of his situation. "Am I right?"

"Yeah. He's about to shred me from the inside out." Leaning back in his chair, he stared at the ceiling. "I can't fucking believe this. Any of the other guys would make a better mate for Rowan than I would."

His stomach lurched and he fought not to be sick at

the thought of her with someone else. And not to tear the furniture apart.

"Why's that?"

His laugh was bitter, but he couldn't help it. "I'm not settling-down material, my friend. My family was so freakin' dysfunctional, we made the cast of *Married with Children* look like the damned Cleavers. I know absolute shit about how to make another person happy, or what a family is supposed to be like."

"I don't agree. The men you work with, they're your family," she pointed out. "You're close as brothers, and blood doesn't matter when it comes to the people who really have your back."

That threw him, and he pondered it for a long moment. "Okay, that's true," he said slowly, looking at the doc. "But they're guys. I don't have to worry about being bound to one of them for the rest of our lives."

"Actually, we have no proof that one of you *couldn't* have another man for a mate."

He cleared his throat. "Well, to each his own. I've got nothing against folks finding happiness with their same sex and all, but I happen to know that's definitely *not* my case."

The barest hint of humor softened her face. "Anyway, the point is that you have a family right here, one that obviously means a lot to you, though you do your best to hide your feelings behind a wall of sarcasm. It's not as if you can't learn to be a good, loving mate to your female."

He wasn't so sure about that, but figured it best not to get into that debate. "What happened to Jax . . . will it be the same for me?" His friend had gotten really sick before the couple decided to bond. Aric hated being ill, but he just didn't see how mating would ever work out for the likes of him. What woman needed his shit?

"You're already symptomatic, with the sore throat and fever, which seems to accompany the start of the mating urge. The longer you put off biting your female, taking her as your Bondmate, the sicker you'll become. Of course, if you *do* bite her, then there's a possibility she'll turn into a shifter as well."

"Isn't there a chance I could just wait it out? Get well?"

"Based on what I've seen so far, and what Nick has told me as a born shifter who's lived with his wolf a lot longer than all of you have . . ." She sighed. "It doesn't seem likely."

Deadly calm settled over him. There was no point in stressing about the future when he'd just learned he didn't have one. "Listen to me and listen good," he said in a low voice. "Rowan is not to know what's going on with me. I won't have her pushed into mating with me like Kira was with Jax. You understand? Rowan is a good woman and she doesn't deserve to be saddled with this life, or me."

"Aric, it's not such a bad existence—"

"No. You tell Rowan, or anyone else, about this and I'll leave. For good."

"Nick will know, eventually. No one will have to inform him."

"He's different. But the same rule applies to him."

"Try telling that to Nick," she said drily. "He's not bound by the same oath of confidentiality as I am."

"I'll deal with that when and if he confronts me."

Melina fell silent for a moment, studying him, suddenly looking older than her years. "I honestly hope you reconsider before it's too late." He didn't answer. "Okay, I'm going to get that culture, and when it comes back clear, I'll release you."

"Thanks."

She left to get the kit she needed, and he sat there staring out the window once again. Only he wasn't nearly as excited as before about the prospect of getting out. He was simply trading one prison for another, this time being held hostage by his own body. With a sigh, he slumped in his chair and covered his face with one hand.

I'm going to die. After the hell in Afghanistan. After all those weeks of torture, praying for rescue, and death finds me, anyway—in the form of my mate. Ain't fate a bitch?

Melina returned. "Let's get this done so you can get going."

In less than a minute, she'd swabbed inside his throat with the end of a long stick and taken it away. In fifteen more she was back, announcing that as expected, he had no viruses or bacteria to account for the sore throat and fever. His blood work was fine, too. He was healed from his time in captivity.

"One last thing," she said, leveling him with a firm look. "When you find yourself unable to perform on the team, remove yourself from duty or I *will* have to go to Nick."

"How long do I have before I get to that point?"

"I wish I had a firm answer," she said grimly. "The pace of decline seems to vary. But it will happen, unless you talk to Rowan. Explain to her."

"I can't." God. Losing his team and his place among them would truly be the end of him. When that happened, he would shift and disappear into the Shoshone, let nature take its course.

Melina signed his paperwork, no doubt believing that when push came to shove, he'd change his mind and bite Rowan, risk turning her into a wolf, to save his own hide. The doc was wrong. He wasn't that big an asshole, no matter what people might think.

After she left, Aric pulled his clothes out of the small closet across from the bed and dressed in sweats and an Alice in Chains T-shirt, trying to ignore the slight soreness in his muscles. How long would he be able to hide his condition from his friends? Not long enough, knowing those guys. They were too damned perceptive.

On his way out, he stopped to see Micah despite his hurry to put the infirmary behind him. Easing into the room, he was struck by the awful stillness from the man on the bed. The drugs were doing their job to keep his friend quiet. He'd almost rather see the guy go for his throat again than this. But either way he was suffering.

Aric went to stand by the bed and rested his hand on the side rail, not sure what to do or say. Nothing seemed adequate, so he settled for what he was best at—the blunt truth.

"Hey, man," he told his sleeping friend. "This is a load of bullshit, huh? But I happen to know you're too tough to let this keep you down. Don't let those assholes win, you feel me? Get well for your sister and your team. Everyone is pulling for you. And when you get out of here, we'll go kick some ass."

That was about as good a pep talk as he could manage. Especially with his sudden emotions threatening to strangle him. Damn it, he might not even be around by the time Micah recovered. But his friend didn't need to know.

"I'll be back, buddy," he promised.

He started out, waving to Noah and the bigger nurse, and kept going, trying to decide what to do. He probably should inform Nick he'd been sprung, but he didn't want to see the boss just yet. The man was too weird with that PreCog shit, and if he didn't already know what was up with Aric, being alone with him might prompt a vision. Or something. No need for him to find out sooner than necessary.

He wasn't hungry, either, and didn't feel like watching TV. The last thing he wanted was to be alone in his room. That left the gym. Might be a good idea to get some exercise while he still could. Blow off some frustration.

Liking this idea, he jogged straight there, glad when he arrived that he wasn't the least bit winded. So what if he was a little sweaty and warm? That wasn't too remarkable when he'd been running. Slowing, he walked inside and took a look to see who was hanging around.

Jax and Zan were sparring on the mats, going at it like two warring gladiators instead of best friends. They appeared to be enjoying themselves. Hammer was doing bench presses, working on the stomach that already boasted an eight-pack, being spotted by Ryon. But it was the sweet thing doing sit-ups in one corner that got his undivided attention.

Rowan wore black spandex workout pants and a matching sports bra, both of which showed off her sleek, toned body and generous breasts. She was no small, scrawny woman like Kira. No, sir, she was built like a brick shithouse, every muscular, kick-ass inch. He practically drooled watching her abs scrunch and her hips flex every time she sat up.

Damn, she's just about perfect. How could I have ever thought I was attracted to Jax's mate?

He'd been observing for at least a couple of minutes before she noticed and eased up one last time, then reached for a hand towel at her side. She wiped her face and then tossed it down, elbows on her knees.

"Are you spying on me?" Good-natured humor laced her tone.

"Nope, flat-out ogling. Spying implies I have something to hide." He almost winced at his choice of words.

"*Everybody* has something to hide, Savage." She arched a brow.

Yeah, including himself. Just not the way she might think. "I guess you're right about that."

"The doc cleared you to be out running around?"

"Do you see a posse chasing me this time?" he pointed out.

"No." She grinned. "How about going a round on the mats, then? I still want my sparring match and none of those guys would cooperate." She flicked a hand at the others and made a disgusted face.

Damn, she was sexy. The thought of *any* of his friends laying a hand on her, even for an innocent wrestling match, had him smothering a growl. "Probably didn't want to hurt a woman."

"I'm not some helpless female," she said with a hint of challenge.

"We're not regular guys, though. But in the spirit of fun, I'll take you on."

"Human to human?"

"Of course. I wouldn't want things to be more un-even than they already are."

She shot him an evil little smile, and the glint in her brown eyes gave him pause. "Let's do it."

He offered her a hand up and she took it, getting to her feet with a bounce. Together, they walked over to the mats and Aric yelled at the two combatants. "Give it a rest, knuckleheads. The cop wants to kick my ass." He said the last with a touch of sarcasm, as if to imply she'd need a lot of luck.

All four of his buddies hooted with laughter, Jax and Zan pushing to their feet and getting out of the way, wiping sweat from their faces. A round of encourage-ment ensued as the jerks gathered, for Rowan to smear him all over the floor.

"Yeah, yeah. Root for the girl, see if I care." Kicking off his shoes, he walked to the center of the mat and bounced on his toes, motioning Rowan forward. "Come on, sweetcakes, let's see what you've got."

"You can't *have* what I've got, Red."

"Ooh, can't I?" He was thinking of their mutual dream, and saw that she got his meaning.

Though his friends didn't know the full story behind their exchange, it caused them to hoot even more, but Aric ignored them. He focused on Rowan as they cir-cled each other, each sizing up the opponent. He had no doubt the woman was tough, given her occupation, but he was confident of his ability to best her. Even if he held back, which he refused to do out of principle, he was a former SEAL. A highly trained operative. She just didn't have his skill.

He waited for Rowan to make the first move, his strategy for learning hers while holding his close to the vest to start. As he expected, she took a few jabs with her fist, feinting left and right, feeling him out. Grinning, he thought she looked too frickin' gorgeous, eyes narrowed, all serious about their match, completely oblivious to the whistles and catcalls from the cheap seats.

Jesus, look at that rack jiggle in that tiny sports bra.

Which was why he was totally unprepared when his opponent shifted her stance, and in a move worthy of the Karate Kid, delivered a high kick to his jaw that fucking knocked him into the middle of next week. The blow reverberated through his skull and he felt himself falling backward, then hitting the mat with an undignified grunt. The loud consensus from his so-called friends was "Holy shit!" and he agreed.

"Not fair," he mumbled.

Her faces appeared over him. All three of them. "Which part? My foot in your face, or the loss of your pride?"

"Both." Blinking, he tried to get all the tripled figures to merge again while the idiots around him almost choked on their laughter. "Shut up, needledicks." The order didn't help.

"Beaten by a woman," Zan observed with a snort.

"By a *cop*. Got his butt served up, too!"

"That's 'cause he was too busy ogling the package to see the dynamite!"

The four bumped knuckles and Aric sat up, glaring at the group. "Who wants to take her on next? Nobody? That's what I thought. Losers."

"Are you all right?" Rowan asked.

"I'm great." To prove it, he stood. His brain swam, but damned if anyone would guess.

"Why don't we go again, and this time keep your attention where it should be." she suggested, flicking her ponytail over one shoulder.

Fuck if she didn't make him half-hard! Thankfully, the loose sweats hid his problem. "Whenever you're ready, officer."

Determined to save face, he concentrated on her stance, how her muscles bunched. Anticipated her move before she stepped into his body and pushed, trying to unbalance him and get a foot hooked behind his ankle. Instead, he grabbed her hands and using her momentum as leverage, pressed the outside of his left knee to the inside of her right leg and twisted his upper body to the left. She was thrown off balance and easily overpowered in this type of hand-to-hand contest. He put her on the mat, but hung on to one hand to lessen the impact when she hit. No matter their deal not to pull their punches, he wasn't capable of unleashing his full strength on his mate.

Oh, God.

"Way to go, dude," Ryon said, and the others echoed the sentiment. "Go for the best of three."

Suddenly all he wanted was to be alone with her, away from all these curious eyes. "Nah," he said, giving her a hand up. He focused on Rowan, who dusted off her seat. "How about we go for a run?"

She brightened. "Sounds good. Then I won't have to let you win again."

The guys laughed and Aric rolled his eyes. "Whatever. Come on, let's ditch the idiots."

He let their comments and speculation roll off as they put their shoes back on. They were whispering, but he heard. Already, they wondered what was up. None of their biz. Aric led her from the gym. In the corridor, he absently rubbed his jaw.

"Is it bruising?"

Meeting her gaze, he saw the concern in her eyes, and he'd have been lying to himself if he pretended not to like it. "Maybe some, but it'll heal pretty fast."

"I'm sorry. I only meant to take advantage of catching you off guard, not really cause any damage."

"You played by the rules we set, that's all. Stop fussing."

"Okay." She sighed. "I'm not typically a worrier. Seems I've done nothing but worry since I've been here, though."

"You've had good reason."

"That's the understatement of the universe. I never dreamed any of this existed," she said, waving her arms to indicate the compound and its inhabitants. "It's a bit much, even for an L.A. cop, and I've seen some weird shit."

Then and there, he knew he'd made the right decision. He could never add to her stress, tie her to this life or the dangers in it. She could not find out about the mating bond waiting to be forged between them, and he would never claim his mate.

The truth stabbed his gut, but he didn't let his despair show. All his life he'd been good at hiding his sorrow behind a mask, and he just had to keep it up until she left for L.A.

"As strange as that?" he asked, pointing to the end of the hallway.

Rowan stopped dead at the sight of Kira and her furry little friend coming their way. "What the freaking hell *is* that thing?"

Aric chuckled. "That's Chup-Chup, or just Chup for short. Kira named him after the noise he makes when he's happy. We're not really sure what he is, so we call him a gremlin."

"He looks like something from a Steven Spielberg movie."

"I suppose."

As Kira approached them and stopped, the gremlin turned rounded eyes to Rowan and Aric, scuttling behind Kira and clutching at the leg of her jeans with tiny paws.

"Cute!" Rowan said, smiling. "Does he bite?"

"Only when he's afraid," Kira replied. "Want to meet him?"

"I'd love to."

"Okay." Bending, she picked up her charge, who immediately nestled into her arms with a contented *chup*. From the safety of his perch, Chup peered at Rowan curiously. Kira spoke softly. "Reach out, nice and slow, and let him smell you. Like you would with a strange dog."

Rowan did, curling her fingers inward to present the creature with the back of her hand. Aric thought that was pretty smart, to reduce the risk of losing a finger if the little thing got scared. He'd bitten Jax once, and according to his friend it had hurt like hell.

Chup stretched forward as far as he dared, clinging to Kira for safety. Then he sniffed for a few seconds and, apparently liking his new acquaintance, rooted under her hand with his head, making his demand clear.

"Someone wants a scratch," Rowan cooed. Chup ate up the attention like honey, purring and making his funny noises. She looked at Aric. "Want to try?"

Shrugging, he offered the back of his hand for sniffing, and swiftly got a low growl in response. "I think he still doesn't much care for men," he said, dropping his arm.

Kira nodded. "It's taken him a long time to warm up to Jax. Could be he was abused by a male figure, but I guess we'll never know."

"Poor guy. Who would do something like that to you?"

The gremlin knew how to work it, for sure. He went back to purring and Aric swore the creature knew exactly what he was doing. He possessed more intelligence than the average dog, in his opinion.

"Well, I need to find Jax," Kira said. "I'll catch up with you guys later."

"He's in the gym." Aric hitched a thumb in the direction from which they'd come. "Go get your man."

"Thanks." With a wink, the blonde hurried to find her mate.

Aric turned to watch her go, and a wave of sadness swept over him. His mate might hurry to him one day, if only he'd—

"Aric?"

He shook himself. "Sorry. Ready to go for that run?"

"After you."

His route took them through the rec room, where Kalen and A.J. were playing a game on the Wii. Seeing the sorcerer without his pentagram pendant, he wondered again why it was now hanging around Mackenzie's neck. Next chance he got, he'd ask Nick or one of the guys. Seemed he'd missed a few things while he was a guest in the motel from hell.

They exited through the door that opened straight to the outside, to the grassy lawn and a field beyond that. He pointed. "We play football, soccer, and other sports out here when we need to blow off some steam. You should see a bunch of shifters and a Fae prince out here playing ball and trying not to cheat. Funniest damned thing ever."

"I'll bet." She laughed, as though imagining it. "I want to get a game going sometime, if the others are up for it."

"Oh, they will be. You've never met a more competitive group of people than the ones living here."

"I'm starting to get that idea. Which way are we going?"

"There are several great trails, but my favorite one starts over there," he said, pointing to the far end of the cleared land, where the forest began. "I know I said we'd jog, but I wouldn't mind walking if you want. Easier to talk and enjoy the view."

"Sure." She looked around. "I'd hate to miss out. It's beautiful here."

"Yes, it is." The only beautiful sight he noticed was right beside him as they made for the trailhead.

Their footsteps, the wind through the trees, and the calls of various birds were the only sounds for a few minutes. He felt so at ease in her presence, as though his heart had been raw for the past thirty-five years and he hadn't known it until they'd met, and she'd soothed the ache. Too bad a new one had taken its place, but he wouldn't think about that right now.

"Tell me about being a cop," he prompted. "Do you love what you do?"

Her expression lit up. "God, yes. I can't imagine not being on the force. Every day is different, always a challenge. And then there's my friends, they're like my brothers. I guess you can understand that."

"I can." The new ache grew to a sharp pain that tore his insides. "What made you decide to follow that career path?"

"That's an easy one. I grew up in the East Side barrio, in one of the most run-down slums in L.A. My mother was a legal immigrant from Mexico and my father, to use the term loosely, was poor white trash. It was the match from hell, and he took off when I was five and my brother was three. Never saw him again, but at least we were free from his rages."

"I can understand the relief," he said, thinking of his stepfather. "Sorry. Go on."

"In the years before he left, the cops were always at our house. Some weeks, they came every day to break up the fighting, haul his ass to jail if necessary. But they were always so kind to me and Micah, even gave us each a teddy bear once, to hold when we were scared. Eventually, they knew us by name, and even after Dad was long gone, they'd stop by and make sure we were okay. I never forgot that. One of them is still on the force, though he's almost ready to retire. How do I explain?" She paused. "The people of the barrio are mine to protect. Does that make sense?"

"Perfectly," he assured her. "You're paying it forward."

"I guess so."

She would never want to leave her home, her people. Not for him. He was doing the right thing. Which made his heart hurt, because he was starting to see what a truly special person she was.

He cleared his throat, which was more sore than it had been earlier. Crap. "Is your mother still living?"

"No. She passed away a couple of years ago from cancer," Rowan said wistfully. "But she was content. I'd saved enough to help her buy a nice little house several years ago, and she got to enjoy it for a time. When she died, I sold it and stayed in the barrio."

He frowned. "Why? Wouldn't you have been safer going to live in your mom's house?"

"Maybe, maybe not. I'm well-known in the barrio. Living there, where I work, gives me street cred, and if I move out, the gangbangers I try to keep in line would see that as a betrayal. Like I thought I was too good for them. They wouldn't trust me anymore, and that could be more hazardous to my health than living there in the first place."

"You're *their* cop. That makes sense." But he hated it. She shouldn't live in such a dangerous neighborhood.

She eyed him in speculation. "What about you? What happened to your family?"

"What makes you think anything happened to them?" The question put him on edge.

"You told me that your mother had died, remember? After you left for the Navy."

"Oh. Right." He'd forgotten about that.

"It's sad that you weren't able to be with her when she passed away. Was it sudden?"

He took a deep breath. "She slipped and hit her head in the bathtub. It was ruled an accident."

"You say that like you don't believe it."

"Part of me thought my stepfather was responsible, but I couldn't prove it."

"Where is he now?"

"Don't know. In hell, if the world is lucky."

"Do you have any siblings?"

"You're starting to sound like a cop."

"Is it such a hard question?"

"Damn it, Rowan, I—"

Whatever he'd been about to say was forgotten as a large shadow suddenly blocked the sun coming through the trees overhead, and there was a sharp flapping sound. Like someone snapping a heavy canvas. He'd heard that before—

"Get down!" he shouted, shoving her to the ground. They sprawled in the undergrowth by the side of the trail, Aric on top of her, as two sets of claws scored his back. "Ahh, fuck!"

He rolled to the side, had just enough time to see the look of sheer horror on Rowan's face as she turned her head to witness the creature that was circling around for another attack. Coming in fast.

Placing his body between his mate and the ghoul bearing down on them, Aric let his wolf free. The change flowed over him, limbs reshaping, feet and hands to paws, his nose becoming a muzzle full of teeth, bared to protect what was his.

But not fucking fast enough.

Before he could work free of his clothes, the bastard hit him full force and they went sliding, tumbling together over the rough ground in a tangle of fur and leathery wings. Dirt and brush flying.

Rowan's scream rang in his ears as the creature's gaping jaws opened wide, showing yellowed, knifelike teeth dripping with saliva.

And those jaws clamped onto his side, teeth sinking deep.

Nine

Rowan stared in terror as the giant batlike creature dropped from the sky, just like the ones they'd battled at the old church in Colorado. It was a hideous thing with a wide face and a pushed-in snout, leathery wings snapping as it dove for Aric.

How the huge creature moved so fast was almost incomprehensible. She had a mere two heartbeats to see that Aric was shifting into his wolf for the fight. That the change wasn't going to happen in time for him to get free of his clothes, and she needed to help him.

Then the bastard hit Aric like a cannonball, and the pair exploded, tumbling over the earth. The wolf ended up under the beast, paws scrabbling for purchase, turning his head to snap at his enemy. But the thing was holding him down, ripping away his shirt and pants, opening its gaping mouth to reveal teeth like sabers.

She screamed as the creature sank its teeth into the red wolf's side. The wolf's agonized cry split the air, the beast shaking him like a rag doll. Then he twisted his body in the creature's hold and clamped his jaws around one of the thing's smaller front legs. Held on.

He even shifted to human form, sent a blast of fire into the beast's face, but it wouldn't let go. Aric couldn't hold his human form, and from his grimace she guessed it was because of the pain. It slammed the wolf hard into the ground. And again. She realized it was trying to kill Aric—and it would succeed if she didn't do something fast.

That got her moving. She cast about, searching for anything she could use as a weapon. Her eyes fell on a large tree limb a short distance away, and she half crawled, half stumbled toward it. The limb was about four feet long and weighed a little too much for her to handle easily, but she had no choice.

Hefting the limb with the jagged, broken end facing forward, she held it like a javelin and ran, resisting the urge to yell. She didn't want to alert the creature to her attack before she could strike. But it was completely focused on annihilating its prey, giving her a slight advantage. Using all her strength, she rammed the sharp end of the limb into its back, right between the wings.

The creature straightened and threw its head back, the throaty roar shaking the treetops. Her tactic worked; it released the wolf, which fell to the ground, panting, blood pouring from his side. But then the beast yanked the limb from its back and hurled it away. Turned and pinned her with hate-filled eyes.

"Oh, God," she whispered. The blood drained from her face.

It had to stand seven and a half feet tall on its hind legs, and looked like something straight out of a horror movie. Not just its physical appearance, but the eerie intelligence in those eyes. This wasn't some mindless beast. It was here to kill—and it would enjoy the bloodshed. Human or not, there was no mistaking that look.

It stalked forward and she began to back up. But there was nowhere to go. She would never be able to outrun the bastard, and even if she could, she'd never escape when it took to the air.

I don't want to die. Not like this!

The creature lowered itself to all fours, and started to gallop straight for her. A scream stuck in her throat, and she froze to the spot. Waited to be torn apart.

But a red blur raced in from the side and launched itself through the air. The red wolf barreled into the creature, knocking it off balance and sending them both to the earth. On top this time, Aric had the advantage as he got behind the short, grasping arms and their sharp claws and went for the beast's neck. But just briefly. The creature rolled, switching their positions again, trying to dislodge the wolf, to crush him into the ground.

The wolf was tough, but unless the tide turned, the beast would kill him.

Rowan ran for the discarded tree limb and was about to use it on the creature again when help arrived. A black panther and several wolves burst from the trees and raced across the ground to where Aric struggled. The panther leapt, teeth bared, claws extended, striking the beast square in the chest and knocking it over backward.

Strong cat jaws ripped at the creature's throat as Aric's teammates converged, tearing into every available spot. Sensing its doom, the beast fought harder, but to no avail. Its struggles slowed, and in minutes, stopped altogether. The red wolf and the panther held on the longest, clearly reluctant to let go until they were absolutely certain their enemy was dead.

A gorgeous white wolf shimmered, became Nick. "Aric! Kalen! It's over. The damned thing is dead."

The panther released its prey and took a few steps back. As it morphed into Kalen, the young man turned his head, and still crouching, spat into the grass. "God-damn, that fucker tastes like a pile of shit. What the hell are those things, anyway? That's the second one that's showed up around here in the past few weeks, except the one that attacked me and Mac was close to town."

"Wish we knew," Jax said, having shifted, too. "Better yet, who commands them and how did this one know where to find us?"

"Maybe this one being way out here is a coincidence?" Ryon suggested.

"I don't believe in coincidences."

Everyone looked at Aric, who'd spoken last. He was lying on his good side, one hand over the deep puncture wounds spread across his ribs. Nick loped over, followed by Rowan and the others.

"Christ, can't you stay out of trouble?" Nick said gruffly.

"Doesn't look like it." Sweat rolled down his temples, into his auburn hair.

Zan knelt beside him, studied the wounds. "I can heal this."

"No, don't drain yourself. I'll be fine in a couple of days." His eyes were becoming glazed, unfocused.

"Shut up and be still."

Whether Aric stopped protesting because he was told to or because he didn't have the strength any longer, Rowan didn't know. She suspected the latter, as prickly as he could be. If Aric wasn't arguing, that was a testament to how badly he'd been hurt.

Zan placed his palms over the oozing punctures and closed his eyes. A green glow began to pulse around his hands, increasing in brightness until it was white and almost blinding. This was like his healing Ryon at the church, but on a much grander scale. This was life and death, and every second counted.

Gradually, the light faded. Zan slumped backward and Nick caught him, eased him to the ground. The flesh on Aric's side was bloodied, but appeared totally intact. The redhead sat up with Jax's help and someone else tossed his shredded shirt and sweats into his lap. Moving carefully, he discarded the shirt as useless, stood and pulled on his sweats. They weren't in much better shape, but he'd be covered until they returned to the compound.

Aric looked at Nick. "How did you know we were in trouble? Did you get a vision?"

"No."

"Well, the bastard came in from the air, so I'm guessing he didn't sound the perimeter alarm."

"After you were kidnapped, Kalen used a spell to place some powerful wards over our property for a twenty-mile radius. Anything supernatural or human that breaches the wards and doesn't belong here is supposed to alert him, and it worked. He yelled for us and we came as fast as we could."

"Wow," Aric said, obviously impressed. "That's some strong mojo you've got. Saved our butts, too. Thanks, man."

Kalen waved off the praise. "Just glad it paid off."

He nudged the dead creature with one toe. "This one was alone, like the one a couple of weeks ago. Gotta wonder why."

"Maybe he was a scout?" Ryon suggested.

Nick cursed. "I'm getting nothing on this guy, no vibes at all. If that's the case and he was looking for something or someone in particular, we need to dispose of all traces of the body." He shot Kalen a meaningful look, and Kalen's expression grew bleak. She wondered what the silent exchange was about.

"Whatever he was doing, that's not a bad idea," Rowan put in, staring at the awful thing. "He gives me the creeps."

"I'll take care of it," Kalen said. "But first . . ."

Waving a hand at his team, he spoke a couple of quiet words that, again, sounded like Latin. Instantly, the men were clothed. That's when Rowan realized Kalen was the only one who was clothed when he shifted back to human form. Handy.

"Having a Sorcerer on your side must be nice," she muttered. "Are you sure you don't want a job with the LAPD? I can put in a good word."

"He's taken," Nick quipped.

Grinning, Kalen turned toward the carcass, but before he had a chance to dispose of it, a voice called out from above.

"Wait!"

Shielding her eyes, Rowan looked toward the sky to see Sariel approaching. Gliding down, he landed on his feet with a graceful stretch of his azure wings, his golden eyes riveted to the creature's body. Approaching slowly, he stopped a short distance from it and crouched, studying it, his expression grim.

"Gods," he whispered. "This can't be."

Those four words went through the group like a bolt of lightning. The tension level shot through the roof as the guys glanced at one another.

"Sariel," Aric said, "if you know what this thing is, enlighten us."

Resting his elbows on his jean-clad knees, the Fae prince addressed the group at large. "First, tell me if this is what attacked your team months ago."

"Fuck yeah," Zan replied hoarsely. "There were a dozen of them or more, and the bastards cut through us like a hot knife through butter."

Micah and Aric—along with Zan and Jax—had almost died in that attack. Rowan shivered.

"One came after me and Mac two weeks ago when we were in town," Kalen added. "And there were lots of them at the church in Colorado, too."

Sariel shook his head, sapphire hair falling into haunted eyes. "More than a dozen? Even one shouldn't be possible, not in this world. These creatures are the Sluagh, and this is what happens when a member of the Seelie court turns to evil. They're cast out and land in the Fae Underworld, where their former beauty is twisted into this," he said sadly, gesturing to the deceased Sluagh.

Aric, incredulous, found his voice. "So, if you were to go over to the dark side, you'd become like that thing?"

"Yes. Well, partly." He sighed, but didn't explain what he meant by "partly." "Once the Sluagh are completely transformed, they are little more than drones who exist to cause mayhem. This makes them very popular for members of the born Unseelie court to use as sentinels, or watchdogs, to send out and do their terrible bidding. Spying, kidnapping the Seelie, murder—the list is endless. Once they're set on a mission, the Sluagh are relentless until the task is accomplished."

"Or they die trying," Nick said.

"Eagerly. They're single-minded, not stupid, and they know no fear, which makes them the perfect tool."

"You said they shouldn't be in this world, and yet they seem to be all over the place," Nick observed. "Explain."

Sariel pushed to his feet and stepped away from the body. "The barrier, or the 'hedge' as we call it, between the Fae realm and yours is inaccessible to the Sluagh. Or has been, until recent months, it would seem. Their presence here means that they were assisted through the barrier, and there's only one being powerful enough to accomplish that feat."

"And that would be?" Hammer asked.

"Malik, king of the Unseelie." Sariel gave a bitter laugh. "My sire."

"Nick, my God," Kalen breathed.

There—that weird vibe passed between the two men again. This time a couple of the guys noticed, but before anyone could ask about what had Kalen so upset, Sariel continued.

The Fae prince hung his head, speaking quietly. "Their being in your world means so much, I wish I'd realized sooner that these were the creatures you'd all spoken of. They are the thread that ties everything together."

"Hang on," Aric said. "We have one of these in the basement, in Block T. You haven't seen it?"

"No. I knew of a creature being held, but I wasn't

allowed down there. If I had seen it, I would've been able to relate this information to you all sooner." Sariel paused. "It's no longer there. I was told it perished while you were gone."

Nick confirmed this. "That's right. The creature seemed to have some intelligence, which is why we were holding it. But it wouldn't communicate or eat, and finally it died."

Rowan couldn't find it in herself to be real sorry that it had croaked. The thought of literally having a monster under your bed was a bit too much.

"I'm forming a picture here, and it's one I don't like." Aric stared hard at the Fae, who continued his thoughts on the subject.

"Where the Sluagh are present, so is Malik. Since he's the only one who could've brought them to this world, they'll do his bidding, and his alone. And as badly as my father might want to destroy me, he wouldn't bring an army of Sluagh here just for that. He wouldn't need that much help."

Nick glanced around at his men. "Then it's safe to assume Malik was behind the ambush on Alpha Pack more than six months ago, as well as placing them on guard at the old church where we found Micah and Aric and the other prisoners. He even sent this scout, perhaps to find us, if not Sariel. It's much worse than we thought—Orson Chappell isn't the head of the project to create a legion of super-shifters. He's working for Malik or, more likely, is under his control."

"That would be my guess," Sariel replied grimly. "And if it's true, no one on earth is safe."

"Nick, tell them the rest," Kalen said quietly, looking away. "They need to know."

Nick was silent for a moment as the team stared at them. Finally he nodded. "You're right. We'd have to fill them in sooner or later, so it might as well be now." He faced the group, his voice low. "The short version of it is, since Mac and Kalen were attacked in town by that Sluagh, Kalen's been hearing a voice in his head. The being, or whatever, is trying to control him. He's fighting it, and has been successful so far, but . . ." He shook his head.

The danger to them all slowly sank in.

Jax pushed a hand through his spiky black hair. "If Malik can gain control of a Sorcerer, he'll have the ultimate weapon."

"The two of them together would be nearly unstoppable." This from Zan, who studied Kalen thoughtfully.

"I can leave," Kalen offered sadly. "I told Nick the other day I was going, but he talked me out of it."

"He was right." Ryon shook his head. "We're not throwing you to the wolves, pardon the expression. You're one of us now, and the Pack sticks together."

"Exactly," Jax said. The rest echoed his sentiment, and Kalen looked touched.

Rowan also knew that it was safer to keep Kalen here, where he could be watched. Though nobody said so, the others had to know it, too.

"Okay, how do we toast Malik's ass?" Typical Aric.

"If my sire has a weakness, I don't know what it is. But I'll keep searching."

"We'll help however we can." Aric sighed. "Though most of us know shit about the Fae. Maybe some of us can research online?"

Sariel rolled his eyes. "Kira is teaching me to become 'tech-savvy,' as you guys call it. Don't believe everything you read on the Internet. Most of it is garbage."

"Kalen," Nick called. "Can you place another ward over the property, one that acts as a cloak, making it appear as though there's nothing here but forest?"

The Sorcerer shrugged. "Sure, that's easy. The question is, will it fool Malik and his ghouls?"

"For a while, perhaps," Sariel mused. "It can't hurt to try."

With a nod, Kalen held out his right hand and his staff appeared in his palm. On the top was a glowing ball of light, blue on the edges and white in the center. Rowan recalled that when he performed magic at the church, he'd knelt. This time he remained standing, booted feet shoulder width apart. Head back, he raised the staff and began to chant.

She peered at the sky, not seeing anything unusual. But she felt something like static electricity, the hair on her arms and on her head crackling as though it were being rubbed with an inflated balloon, like she used to do as a kid. Returning her attention to Kalen, she couldn't help but be awed. To be able to command the elements, bend them to your will to do magic, must be such a rush. And he looked damned cool doing it, too.

"What're you staring at?" a voice growled softly in her ear.

She turned her head to find herself looking into Aric's annoyed face. "Just watching him use his magic staff thingy. It's just as awesome as the first time I saw him do it." His breath puffed against her neck, making her break out in chill bumps.

"Yeah? Bet his magical staff can't do what mine can." His lips turned up and his green gaze lit with mischief.

Her brows rose. "My, you must be feeling better. Is that why you really wanted to go for a walk? So you could ravish me in the woods?"

"Wouldn't you like to know?"

"Actually, I would."

"It's done," Kalen said, breaking into their exchange. "If the wards fail, we'll know soon enough. Now for the body."

Another incantation, and the Sluagh's carcass slowly withered, like a raisin in the sun. Then it began to crumble, and finally disintegrated all together.

Hammer shuddered. "Man, it grosses me the fuck out when he does that."

"On that note, I want everyone to get inside the compound and restrict their roaming for a while," Nick ordered in a stern tone. The predictable groans ensued. "Sorry, but it's for our safety. If you must go out, do it as a group. No running or going into town alone, and no groups smaller than four."

"Crap."

"Damn, that sucks."

Rowan could tell nobody really blamed Nick, though. Leaders did what they must to protect their teams, and Westfall was no exception. She and Aric lagged behind the others as they trooped back to the compound, but kept them in sight. As they entered the building, Nick turned and pointed a finger at the red-head.

"I'm not going to make you go to the infirmary, but I want you to rest. That's an order."

"Yes, Dad."

"Cocky shit. Don't push it." With that, Nick walked off, his men snickering.

"Damn, now what? There's nothing to *do* in this place," Aric bitched.

"Are you kidding? You almost got eaten by an evil Unseelie pet and you're *bored*?" Grabbing his hand, she began to pull him toward his room. "Come on."

"Where are we going?"

"Three guesses."

"Somewhere I *won't* be bored?"

"Ding-ding, got it in one." She pulled him along, not surprised when he saw where she was taking him and dug in his heels.

"Wait a sec—my room? I'm not a kid and I'm not going to be put down for a nap."

"Who says we're going to sleep? Unless you were all talk out there . . ."

That got his undivided attention. His dumbstruck expression was priceless. "You . . . I just . . ."

"You're just what? Fine with the teasing, but not with real intimacy? Spontaneity?"

"Hey, I did pretty good with that when we were in Vegas," he asserted, puffing his chest out a little.

"That was nothing but a dream."

"Was it? No, I believe it was more and I think you do, too."

Did she? "Maybe you're right, but I still have a hard time buying stuff I can't see. Now, those fucking Sluagh things, and the awesome stuff Kalen did? Hard to refute what's in your face."

"Kalen!" He made a face. "What's the Goth kid got that I don't?"

"A really big staff?" She giggled as his mouth fell open.

"All right, that's it! Big staff, my ass," he muttered, punching in the code to his door. It opened with a pop and he pushed inside, pulling her into his living room. Then he whirled and snaked an arm around her waist, pressing her flush to his body.

Her laughter abruptly died as he crushed his mouth to hers. *Oh, shit, yes!* A man—*this* man—making her fantasies come true, in the flesh. God, it had been much too long since she'd been held in a man's arms, and never in a pair as strong as Aric's. She'd never been kissed as deeply by a man who tasted as delicious, whose masculine scent drove her so completely insane. His hard cock pressed into her pubic bone at the base, the length extending almost to her belly button. She moaned, grinding against him, wanting that searing heat to slide inside her, pumping to her core.

"Shower," he murmured into her lips. "I need to get that creature's stench off me, but I don't want to let you go. I'm a selfish bastard."

"I can handle that." Anything, as long as she didn't have to give up this heat, the promise of being with her wolf.

My wolf.

Why would she think that? He wasn't hers, but she wouldn't pass up the chance to be with him while she was here. Ignoring the pang in her chest at the thought that she would eventually leave for L.A., she let him lead her into the bathroom. Like hers, it wasn't fancy, but was more spacious than she would've thought, adorned with nice brass accents and updated tile. Aric had added his own touches, his rugs and towels in rust and brown colors, the pattern giving it sort of a South-western feel, like the rest of his apartment.

"Did you grow up in the South?" she asked as he stripped off the tattered sweats. "I can't quite place your accent."

"I'm a Texas boy—Houston, but I've been gone for so long I've lost most of the drawl. Strip, honey."

She did, pulling off her sports bra, loving how his eyes widened as he took in her freed breasts. "I'll bet you were raised on Southern rock."

"Huh?" His eyes somehow made it to her face.

"You know, Lynyrd Skynyrd, beer, and tailgate par-ties?"

"Oh, sure. What good Texan isn't?"

Drinking in his naked body, she lost the thread of their conversation. She'd seen him in the buff before, but not when he was all hers. Not when they were about to get wet and naughty. The man was over six feet of lean, cut muscle. Long, burnished hair flowed over his tattooed chest, down his back in a luxurious fall she wanted to drown in. His penis was hard, jutting proudly from its nest of dark curls, arching toward his stomach like a comma. He wasn't the least bit shy about it, and she found that confidence incredibly sexy.

Pulling open the glass door to the shower stall, he turned on the water and stuck his hand under it to test the temperature. When he deemed it satisfactory, he stepped inside and held out a hand. Though she could manage just fine, she took it, strangely touched by the gesture. None of her former lovers had ever cared about showering together, and certainly none had been very solicitous.

And that described Aric to a T as a lover, she soon

learned. Kind and caring. Thoughtful. Such a contrast from his public persona, especially with his friends.

Shutting the stall door behind her, she stepped into his arms. He pulled her close again and she reveled in the sensation of his naked skin against hers. His tight rear end felt damned fine in her palms, perfectly round and smooth. His lips descended, warm and soft, the kiss every bit as deep as before but gentler. Searching. His tongue licked the roof of her mouth, behind her teeth, probed everywhere as though he had to learn every ridge.

Then his hand worked between them, fingers combing through her curls to find the nub of her clit. She widened her stance, encouraging his touch. He played, stroked and teased, sending little tingles to her limbs, revving her long-neglected libido into overdrive. Unable to resist, she wormed her hand between them as well and cupped his heavy sac, testing its weight.

He broke the kiss, groaning. "Fuck, yes, baby. Explore all you want. That's yours."

She liked that idea, a helluva lot. "This is all for me? Nobody else?"

"No one but you."

He sounded very serious, but it had to be a line. They'd met only days ago, not nearly enough time for any attachments to form. Right? It had to be a statement born of lust, nothing else.

The unwanted image of another woman pleasuring her wolf came to the fore, and she ruthlessly squashed it. He might not be hers, but she wouldn't allow reality to intrude on the here and now.

He spread his legs wider, making it clear he was a man of his word. She could do what she wanted and he'd enjoy every second. Carefully, she knelt and grasped the base of his cock with one hand and steadied herself by holding on to his thigh with the other. Looking up, she admired how the water cascaded over his head, wetting his hair, and streamed down his chest and stomach, poured off his cock and balls. He was like some water god come to life especially for her, and she wouldn't waste a moment.

Testing the seeping head of his penis with her tongue, she was surprised and happy to find that his flavor was sweet, unlike the salty bitterness of past lovers. Giving head wasn't her favorite thing, but for Aric she could change her mind.

She sucked on the spongy crown, smiling inwardly at the way he melted under her ministrations, making incomprehensible noises that might've been endearments. Or curses. Who knew? All she cared about was rendering the man incapable of speech. At least any that made sense.

She took him down her throat, loving that his entire length seemed to fit like a hand in a glove when this wasn't typically her forte. He was warm and slick, and she laved every vein and contour, eating him like a stick of candy. The man was putty in her hands and mouth, so she upped the ante, increasing the suction on his cock. A hand fisted in her hair and he increased his rhythm until his hips were snapping like a piston, fucking her face like there was no tomorrow.

She opened to him, squeezing his balls, hoping to make him lose control. Her efforts met with resounding success. After giving a series of quick thrusts, his body tensed, balls drawing up tight.

"Shit! Coming!"

He tried to pull out, but she held fast to her prize. Surrendering to her wishes, he came with a shout, his seed spurting hot and thick onto her tongue, down her throat. She drank him greedily, not wanting to miss a drop, though it wasn't easy. The man was loaded with cream and maybe hadn't enjoyed this in quite a while. Or so she hoped.

When he slumped against the tile, she licked away the last drops, then let him slip from her lips and smiled up into his sated face. "Damn, you taste good, my wolf."

"What?" He blinked at her as though startled.

"You taste good," she repeated.

"Oh. Thanks." Helping her up, he smiled. "I'd love to return the favor."

"You can, but I did that because I wanted to. I enjoyed it, very much."

He looked rather proud of that. "So did I, as if you couldn't tell. You're amazing, sweetheart."

She basked in his praise as he grabbed a bottle of shampoo and squeezed some into her palm, then his own. They lathered up, took turns rinsing, then soaped their bodies as well. She had fun sudsing his chest and back, not to mention his groin, making him laugh at her playfulness. He soaped her, too, paying special attention to her breasts, tweaking the nipples to hard peaks. Then he soaped between her legs, making sure to rub the sensitive slit so that she squirmed with arousal.

By the time Aric turned off the shower and handed her a towel, she was a ball of frustrated, excited desire. She needed the edge taken off, and fast.

They dried off and then Aric got out a blow dryer, saying that his hair was so long, it was a miserable, cold, damp mop if he let it dry naturally. Rowan itched to get her hands on his mane, and he relinquished the dryer and brush with a minimum of fuss. She had him sit stark naked on the toilet seat facing away from her, and tackled the glorious tresses with relish. As it dried, the mass was silky and shiny, and he practically purred with pleasure at the attention.

When it was sufficiently dry, she did her own, which didn't take nearly as much time, then switched off the dryer. "Have you always worn your hair long?" she asked, rolling up the cord and replacing the dryer in the cabinet.

"Except for my years in the Navy, I have. Drives the women crazy."

"Conceited much?"

"Nah, not me. Truthfully, I just like it this way. It feeds my inner rock star wannabe."

She laughed. "Sling an electric guitar over your hips and the image will be complete. Love it."

"See? Works every time."

"You're incorrigible."

"Would you want me any other way?"

"I doubt you'd wear 'sweet and innocent' very well, so no."

Standing, he crowded her against the sink, a position she liked a lot. "Good, because I've never been anything but a really bad boy," he said, cupping her cheeks.

His tongue teased the seam of her lips, slipped inside to play for a few seconds. Then he pulled away and took her hand, making straight for the bed. She crawled into the middle, laughing when he flipped her over as if she weighed nothing and fake-tackled her, covering her body with his. She spread her legs to accommodate him and he settled his weight comfortably, taking care not to squash her into the mattress. She loved the solid feel of him, his clean, crisp scent.

She especially loved how his hair fell around them like a fiery silk curtain. Unable to resist, she twirled a lock around one finger.

"I think you just want me because of my hair." His grin was teasing.

"Oh, that's not all. Trust me. But I'm not going to list your assets no matter how much you fish, because your ego is inflated enough already."

"Not my ego," he said with a wicked gleam in his eyes, grinding the proof into her belly. "You walked right into that one."

"So I did."

With her fingertip she traced the gorgeous scrolled tattoo that spilled over his left shoulder and onto his chest. The snarling wolf's head in the center was more of an outline than a detailed picture, a silhouette.

"You like?"

"It's stunning," she answered honestly. "When the others shifted to human form, I've noticed that except for Kalen, Hammer, and Nick, each of you has one somewhere on your body. Even Micah has one."

His expression darkened a bit. "Yeah, all of us who were attacked and changed years ago, in Afghanistan. We did it when we joined the Alpha Pack, as sort of a memorial to the life we'd lost, and the one we were beginning."

"That's sad," she said softly.

"To us, it was a tribute of sorts. A way to say 'fuck it'

and move on." Leaning in, he nibbled her neck. "Let's not talk anymore. For now."

"Okay, for now— Oh!"

His teeth scraped along her vulnerable skin, and she felt his canines, sharp and dangerous. God, that was sort of kinky. And a huge turn-on. Suddenly she wanted very much for him to sink his teeth into her neck, though she wasn't sure why. He didn't, and her disappointment was lost in anticipation as he continued downward, pausing to capture a pert nipple in his teeth.

She squirmed, buried her fingers in his hair and tugged. He chuckled, sucking and teasing the nub, giving the tiniest shock of pain with the pleasure, then repeated his attentions on the other. Then he kissed a line down the middle of her stomach, pausing where her patch of neat curls began.

Pushing her thighs apart, he rubbed her slit with two fingers. Spread the moisture, looking his fill. The hunger on his handsome face made her feel wanton. Sexy. Excited. So many things she was unaccustomed to in her life. In her job, where she certainly felt anything but womanly. This was different, and extraordinary.

Just like the wolf.

Bending, he tasted her, and a growl of male approval rumbled in his chest. "So sweet, like I knew you'd be."

"But our dream—"

"Can't compare to this."

He was right. No fantasy, even one shared, could compare to flesh and blood. To the warm, strong man whose tongue was working magic, laving slowly, sending the most delightful shivers to every nerve ending. Then he worked between her folds, licking her core. Taking his time, driving her insane. Finally, she pulled at him, almost frantic.

"I need you inside me! Protection?"

"Don't need it," he said huskily, moving up her body to position himself. "Shifters can't catch or pass human diseases, including STDs. And I can't knock you up, either, unless we mate."

"Knock me up?" She wrinkled her nose. "Such a romantic."

"Shh, where were we? Oh, yes—right here."

"But what do you mean by ma—"

He silenced her question with a searing kiss, easing the head inside, blowing her thoughts to dust. Then he slid deep, his girth stretching her but not enough to hurt, filling her more completely than any man ever had.

Having him inside, fucking her with that huge, naked cock . . . it was electric. She'd never allowed a partner to do it bare, and God, what she'd been missing! She clung to him, palms spread on his back, noticed that he seemed too warm. But she lost herself in loving the play of hard muscles under skin that wasn't quite smooth. Ridges? Yes, he had tiny lines, and she recalled the whip marks on his back, evidence of his torture during captivity. She wanted to kiss each scar and make it disappear.

Strangely, the imperfections made her feel closer to him, more connected. For all his strength and special abilities, he wasn't invincible.

He was a man. An incredible man.

His thrusts gained in power and he held on tight,

growling in obvious enjoyment as she licked the salty
skin of his chest, nipped at his collarbone. She pulled
back a bit to watch his face, eyes closed, lips slightly
parted, steeped in bliss. His canines were elongated,
the sharp tips just showing below his upper lip, and he
made such a sexy picture, it drove her to the edge.

"Oh!" she breathed. "I'm going to come!"

"Do it, baby," he rasped. "Come on my cock!"

The last of her control snapped and the orgasm
swept her in a rush of heady ecstasy. She clutched him
tightly, crying out as he shouted, emptying his hot
seed. Filling her to overflowing. When their spasms
died, he eased to the side, slipping out of her, and gathered her close. With a contented sigh, she rested her
head on his chest and wrapped an arm around his
middle.

"You were awesome," she praised.

"Thanks. So were you, sweetheart."

She frowned. "You're really warm and your voice is
raspy. Are you still running a temperature?"

"Maybe a little." He gave her shoulders a squeeze.
"I'm fine, though. Melina said it would pass."

"I thought shifters didn't get sick?"

"I said we don't catch or pass human illnesses. It's
probably just my body still healing from my stay at
Motel Hell."

Something in his tone gave her pause. She'd swear
he was lying, but she couldn't prove it. She tried a different question. "You also said you couldn't get me
pregnant unless we were mated. How do you know for
sure? I placed a lot of trust in you."

"I know, and I'm grateful." He kissed the top of her
head. "The scientists here at the Institute have been

studying us for years now. And Nick is a born wolf shifter, so he brought a lot of knowledge with him when he came."

"How does mating work with your kind, exactly?"

"Um, from what I'm told, you bite your intended mate and, assuming you're *true* Bondmates, you're stuck together for life and you can never be with anyone else." She felt his shrug. "Though I wouldn't know."

Weird. She'd felt a strong urge for him to bite her when they were making love. Somehow it didn't seem like a good idea to tell him that now, if ever. He seemed sort of reticent on the subject.

Well, duh. The man was a free and easy wolf. He probably didn't want a female permanently attached to his side.

"Aric?"

"Yeah?"

"I would never try to tie you down. Just so you know."

Underneath her, his body tensed. Then slowly relaxed. "Sure. I mean, you're going to leave when Micah is better. You have a life in L.A. waiting for you. But there's no reason why we can't have some fun before you go."

A vicious stab of pain lanced through her heart.

"Yes, exactly. This is just sex. I just wanted to put that out there. So we don't get our wires crossed or anything."

"Sure, that's understandable," he said softly. "Sleep and we'll go see your brother later."

"Okay."

But the sandman didn't come. Rowan remained awake long after her lover's breathing had evened out.

Just sex. She'd go home, eventually. Returning to her own boring life would be for the best. A life that didn't include shifters, Fae princes, Sorcerers, gremlins, or evil Unseelies and their pet Sluaghs.

This place was like frickin' Disneyland on meth. She'd be glad to see all of this madness in her rearview mirror.

Really.

Ten

Aric placed a hand at the small of Rowan's back and guided her into Micah's room. After their much-needed nap, they'd awakened semirecovered from the excitement of the Sluagh's attack, not to mention the incredible life-reaffirming lovemaking that followed. No, not lovemaking.

This is just sex.

The straightforward, no-nonsense way she'd said it had stabbed him in the gut. God, he was still bleeding inside. The fact that he'd been right about her not wanting to be tied to him and the loony bin that doubled as his life was cold comfort. He was playing with fire, literally.

And then he'd have to let her go.

"Micah?" Rowan walked over to take the chair by the bed, and wrapped her fingers around her brother's.

Aric went to stand behind her and settled his hands on her shoulders. A gesture of comfort, and God knew she needed it. Micah's eyes were open, muddy and lifeless. He stared into space, either unaware of their presence or too lost in his own hell to acknowledge them.

You caused this, a vicious voice in his head snarled. *If you'd only warned Jax about Beryl, this wouldn't have happened. And half the team wouldn't be either missing or dead.*

The truth was killing him. He would have to confess to his team, and to Rowan. Sooner or later.

"Hey, little brother. It's great to see you awake again." She swallowed hard, making a visible effort to be cheerful for Micah's sake. "I'm getting to know your friends, and they've all been super to me. You've had tons of visitors and we're all relieved you're going to be okay. You know you're safe, right? It's okay to be quiet, but we're here if you want to talk and . . ."

She chattered on, but Aric stopped listening. Jesus, it was beyond painful. Seeing Micah like this, completely catatonic. But he was far from an empty shell. Aric sensed the rage boiling under the surface of the younger man's skin, the sadness choking off all speech. Yet as terrible as this was, it gave him hope. Where there were still emotions, there was hope.

If those emotions died, so would Micah.

"Do you think it's the medication?"

It took Aric a moment to realize Rowan was addressing him instead of her brother. "I believe so. My wolf senses his emotions, and it seems they're being suppressed right now." He stroked her hair. "It's for his own good, just until he can handle reality."

Nobody wanted a repeat of the awful scene from the other day.

"Did you hear that?" she asked her brother, her determination unwavering. "We know you're in there, listening. You're not a quitter, never have been. Let us all help you."

"No," Micah whispered.

Both he and Rowan leaned forward to hear what else he might say, and she reached up to grip Aric's hand. The man didn't speak again. Instead, his eyes welled with tears that spilled down his face, even as he stared into nothingness.

Rowan made a sound of distress and moved as close to him as she could, wrapped an arm around his shoulders and tucked his head under her chin. Rocked and held him tight, talking to him quietly. The blank expression never changed, despite the emotion behind the tears.

Aric had never wanted to run so badly, ever.

Twenty minutes crawled by with excruciating slowness, and finally Rowan eased her brother onto the pillow again. He was asleep, no doubt having worn himself out being full of the despair he couldn't express.

Aric took her arm. "Come on, sweetheart. You can come back later." Reluctantly, she allowed him to escort her out. "Hungry for dinner?"

"Not yet. Walk with me?"

"Where to?"

"Anywhere."

He understood—anywhere but here. He took her hand and they walked together out into the hallway. The more distance they put between themselves and the infirmary, the more the stiffness left her posture.

"He's going to recover, you know," Aric told her firmly. "Physically he's much better already, and Mac will take him the rest of the way. She's really good at what she does."

"I know. He's got great friends, too, to see him through." She squeezed his hand.

Guilt clogged his throat, but he managed to speak around the terrible knot. "We'll all do everything in our power to make sure he gets well."

"I know." She gave him a small smile. "Alpha Pack may battle monsters, but what you do here is about so much more than that. You guys help the innocent, whether they're human or not."

"I hadn't really thought of it like that, but I guess it's true. Though Kira and Sariel, with the help of the doctors and nurses on staff, do the hard work of rehabbing all sorts of supernatural beings through their project."

"Block R. They've told me some about it."

"Did they tell you Nick approved construction of a new building for their program?"

"Kira mentioned it the first day I was here, but just briefly."

"They're going to expand and give it a better name, and they plan to make it a haven for displaced paranormals as well as sick ones."

"That's a neat thing for them to do." She paused. "Is there really a basilisk here?"

"Kira told you that?"

"Yes. She also started to say something about a wolf, but Jax stopped her from saying more."

"Oh. Well, the wolf is a sore subject," he said, unable to keep the emotion from his voice. "His name is Raven, and he was one of our team members when Micah, Jax, Ryon, Zan, and I were in the SEALs. He was turned along with us. The difference is, he never came back from his shifted form. He's feral."

"God, that's horrible," she breathed. "They're trying to reach him?"

"They have been, for almost six years. They're hoping that with the opening of the new center and hiring an expert or two, they'll finally succeed."

Rowan's expression was so compassionate it made him ache. Why couldn't this woman be his?

"I hope so, too. What about the basilisk?"

"Actually, he's a basilisk shifter, and his name is Belial. He's quite a handful, tries to seduce everyone in sight to get what he wants. Of course, he doesn't get anywhere because we've all got his number. No one trusts him, with good reason."

"Can't they kill if a person looks them in the eye?"

"No, that's Internet bullshit. But when he shifts, he goes from a regular-looking tall, lean guy to a snake the size of a fucking sedan. His fangs are each about a foot long, and he could swallow a full-grown man whole if he wanted. He doesn't need more abilities than those."

"Jesus, no kidding."

"They haven't let him out much just yet, but Kira's lobbying for leniency so he can prove himself."

"He might prove useful in the fight against Sariel's father and those Sluagh things."

Aric shrugged. "We'll see."

Their trek led to the rec room, where Rowan stopped. "I suppose skipping through the woods is out of the question. What a waste of great scenery."

"Yeah, unless we want to take two others with us. Kinda cramps the style." He pulled her toward the sofa. "Want to play a game on the Wii?"

"What are we, twelve?" she joked.

"Mentally, that fits most of us around here. Keeps us sane. Anyway, I love video games. I used to spend hours in my room with my old PlayStation, just to stay away from my stepsister . . ." He trailed off, immediately cursing his stupid mistake. Of course, she caught his blunder, eyes narrowing.

"So you have a stepsister. You told me you didn't have any family left."

"I . . . Well, my mother remarried when I was in high school, but I don't consider my stepfather or his daughter to be my family. Far from it," he said bitterly. "Bruce was a world-class asshole and his precious girl was a witch, and I mean that literally. She still is, and a dangerous one."

Rowan paused, and he could almost see those dots connecting at warp speed. Why did the woman have to be such a goddamned smart cop? Then again, maybe a tiny part of him wanted to confess to someone who'd understand.

"Do you know where your stepfather and stepsister are these days? What they're doing?"

"Not my dear old stepdad. But his daughter?" He shook his head, stomach clenching. "I wasn't so lucky on that score. Beryl turned up in my life a few months ago, like the proverbial bad penny."

"She found you here, came to see you?"

"Worse. She showed up on Jax's arm . . . as his girlfriend."

Rowan's eyes rounded. Yep, she got it.

A low snarl sounded from behind them. "You goddamned son of a bitch."

Oh, fuck. This is gonna be bad.

Heaving a deep breath, he stood and turned. Faced an extremely and justifiably pissed-off Jax, who stood in the door to the rec room, fists clenched, blue eyes sparking with rage. Aric held up his palms.

"Jax—"

"Beryl is your fucking stepsister?" he choked. "You knew. For months, that bitch and her evil cohorts were planning to annihilate us, you *knew*. And said *nothing*!"

"I can explain—"

The man crossed the room in three strides and leapt over the back of the sofa, slamming into Aric like a bull out of a chute. Aric flew backward, crashing on top of the coffee table, which shattered into pieces. They hit the floor and he felt a painful stab in his back, probably a shard of wood, as Jax took a handful of his shirt and unloaded on him with a fist that packed the punch of a jackhammer.

Pain exploded in his face, reverberated through his skull. He wondered whether his jaw had been broken, but the blows powered into his head, scattering all thoughts but one—he deserved this. Had it coming for ages. He and Jax had scrapped before, but this time he didn't fight back, simply took what the man dished out.

His lip split, and blood ran down the back of his throat. Rowan was yelling for help, but Jax was unfazed. His sole mission was to pummel Aric into dust. Then, out of one swelling eye, he saw Nick, Zan, and Hammer appear behind Jax. They grabbed him, pulled him off, though it took all three of them to do it. Jax's face was a mask of fury as he struggled to come at Aric again.

"Jaxon, cool it!" Nick yelled. "Knock it off!"

Hammer got their friend's arms pinned at his back. "Jesus, man, what the hell?"

Rowan crouched beside Aric, helped him sit up. "Are you all right?"

Wiping the blood off his lower lip, he winced. "Feel like I was hit by a truck, but yeah."

"I should fucking kill you," Jax yelled.

"Maybe you should," he agreed. That admission seemed to give Jax pause, though he was still plenty angry.

So was Nick. "Anyone care to tell me what's going on in here? Why the hell are two of my best men going at it like junkyard dogs?"

Jaxon pointed an accusing finger. "Ask him who Beryl is to him! Ask him!"

The other three men looked at him in silent question. He didn't want to do this, but since he had no choice, he preferred to be on his feet. He stood, with some assistance, and his heart sank. Every single one of the team including the newest, A.J. and Kalen, were waiting for an explanation. Those who'd been around the longest, during Beryl's time as Jax's girlfriend and the disastrous aftermath, were wearing hard expressions.

Steeling himself, he told the long-denied truth. "Beryl is my stepsister," he said. "But I've never claimed her as family."

Zan gaped at him. "Why would you keep this from us? Even if you don't consider her your sister, why didn't you tell us?"

Jax lunged again, but was held back. "You should've warned us—me—about her true nature. But you never said a word."

He tried to make them understand. "Looking back,

yes, I should have. I was suspicious of Beryl's motives, but I talked to her and she swore you guys made each other happy. I didn't think she could've changed so much from the selfish bitch I'd known when her father married my mother and they moved in with us. But, Jax, you thought you were in love with her, remember? You wouldn't have believed me."

"You never gave me the chance!"

"You thought she was fantastic. Anything I said would've hurt our friendship." He hated the desperate tone of his own voice. The fear.

"You could've at least mentioned her tie to you, if nothing else," Ryon put in. "That's messed up, man."

"She begged me not to, and she did a great job of faking sincerity. She said she didn't want the animosity between us to interfere with the love she'd found with Jax. I *wanted* to believe her, and that's why I didn't say anything. And after the ambush, the guilt was too much and I didn't know how to come clean. Please, try to understand—"

"What I understand is that you should be dead," Jax replied coldly. "It should be *you*."

Jerking out of his friends' grasp, he spun and stalked out of the room. Aric's heart died in his chest, crumbled to ashes. Jax was right.

He had to get the fuck out of here. Whirling, he stumbled blindly for the exit and pushed outside, ignoring Nick's shout to stop, Rowan's entreaty to stay, that his friend didn't mean it. He shut them all out and walked quickly, stripping off his shirt, kicking off his boots and unzipping his jeans. Then he jogged across the lawn, picking up speed until he was running.

He shifted without breaking stride, streaking for the

forest. For freedom. If he ran far enough, fast enough, maybe he could outrun his teammates' voices. The lost souls of Terry, Jonas, Nix, and Ari, accusing.

Do you think we're out here waiting in despair, just like Micah? Being torn apart, piece by bloody piece, driven out of our minds? Praying for death?

It should be you.

Aric kept running. With no thought of ever going back.

"Aric, wait!" Rowan called. "He didn't mean it!"

Her lover vanished through the outside door like a demon from hell was after him. The stark, naked agony on his face was something she'd never forget. After a moment's hesitation, she jogged to the door and, searching, saw him shift and bolt for the woods. No way could she hope to catch him.

Turning back to Aric's shell-shocked friends, she threw her hands up in frustration. "Well, aren't you going after him? I sure as hell can't catch him!"

"Fuck!" Nick burst out, shoving a hand through his dark hair. "Okay, leave Jax alone for now and let's go."

They filed out, and Rowan jogged in the other direction, intent on doing everything *but* leaving Jax in peace. Christ, this place had as much drama going on as they frequently did at the department. One major screwup and too much testosterone in a small space did not make for a harmonious environment.

She spotted her target's retreating back at the end of the hallway and hurried to catch up. Grabbing his biceps, she jerked hard, which probably wasn't the smartest move. He faced her with his lips pulled back in a menacing snarl, canines elongated and ready to rip

something—or someone—to shreds. A glance at his
hands showed that the backs had sprouted fur, his nails
morphed into sharp claws that could kill in a split second.

And in that millisecond she thought about retreating
with an apology—until she recalled Aric's face, devoid
of all hope.

She let every ounce of venom seep into her voice.
"How could you? That man has been your loyal friend
for years, ever since you guys were in the military, and
you just shit on him?"

"He fucked up and cost us half the team," Jax yelled.

"You've never fucked up?" she countered fiercely.
"You've never done anything that cost the team? How
about trusting the witch and bringing her here to start
with?"

Bull's-eye. For a couple of seconds, she really
thought he'd strangle her. The man was big and truly
scary, with his spiky black hair, goatee, and the tats
running down one arm. But the feral light in his eyes
dimmed, the merest fraction.

"If he'd told any of us—"

"Well, he didn't, and there's nothing anybody can
do about it now. Yes, he screwed up, but he did it out
of love for you, with the best of intentions. You heard
him—he truly wanted to believe that she loved you
and he didn't want anything to get in the way of your
happiness. Be honest. What would you have said to
him if he'd bad-mouthed her back then?"

"I would've . . ." His protest trailed off, lost most of
its heat. "I would've been pissed, and told him that he
was full of crap. But we still might've caught on to her,
if he'd just started the ball rolling."

"Maybe, maybe not." Taking a chance, she grasped his shoulder, like she would a fellow officer. In friendship and gentle admonishment. "Jax, you just told a good man, a friend who's had your back for years, that he should be dead. And he believed you."

The words hung between them, awful with their weight.

"You did what?"

Both of them looked to Kira, who stood a few feet away staring at her mate as though she didn't know him at all. She marched up to them, pinning him with a glare that made the tough wolf take a step back.

"Jax, who are you guys talking about?"

"Aric," he said, his defensive tone suffering a quick demise at her incredulous expression. "I overheard him telling Rowan that Beryl is his stepsister! He kept that from me, from *all* of us. Don't you understand what that means?"

"Yes. It means your friend makes mistakes like everyone else," she snapped. "Don't you understand how bad he must've felt all these months, how he probably has been beating himself up already? And then you came along and kicked him when he was down."

The silence ticked away and Jax hung his head, pinching his nose. "God. What have I done?"

Kira took her mate's hand. "Go after him. He's not going to listen to anyone but you now."

"I'll make it right," he promised hoarsely. The man wrapped his woman tightly in his arms, kissed her hard on the lips, and then headed off.

Rowan watched him go. "I didn't think this day could get worse, but that'll teach me to assume."

To her surprise, Kira gave her a quick hug. "They'll

get things settled and it'll be okay. This isn't the first time those two have gone for each other's throats and it won't be the last."

"I'm not sure that's a comfort."

"Alpha wolves. What can you do?"

Rowan was sure she had no clue.

Aric's legs burned. His lungs were on fire, but he didn't stop. For a while, he wasn't conscious of where he was going, but in the back of his mind he must've known. The trees eventually thinned and he found himself racing toward a place where the earth met the sky. Nothing more than a sheer drop. At the last second, he skidded to a halt and stared over the edge of the deep ravine, breath sawing in and out, sides heaving.

What I understand is that you should be dead. It should be you.

His past had finally caught up with a vengeance. Life or death. Was there a choice, really?

It could all be over so quickly. Even a shifter wouldn't survive a hundred-foot drop onto the rough terrain below. Wouldn't that be kinder than dying by slow degrees, longing for a mate he couldn't claim?

Exhausted, he lowered himself onto his belly and crawled to the lip, resting his muzzle on his paws. Rocks and dirt skittered over, into the abyss. The sun had disappeared behind the horizon, leaving the bottom of the ravine shadowed in blues and grays, cloaked from sight. All was still, the earth holding its breath. Waiting.

One leap. Inches separating him from the end of guilt. Of pain.

For months, he'd blamed Jax for his own kidnapping, for saving Kira and changing fate. But the inescapable truth was that Aric had gotten exactly what he deserved. No, he'd deserved much worse. He should've suffered Micah's fate and much more.

It should be you.

Standing on four shaking legs, he told himself he could do this. His wolf resisted with a growl, his survival instinct strong. He tensed, muscles bunching—

And was struck hard in the side, shoved, sent rolling from danger. He bolted to his feet and found a huge white wolf positioned squarely between him and his goal. Nick. The wolf's teeth weren't bared, but his body was like stone, his purpose clear—Aric was not getting past him. Or past the others that suddenly trotted up, surrounding them in a semicircle.

Aric shifted to human form, crouched on his knees, arms wrapped around his middle, and sucked in a deep breath. Maybe that way he could hold in the guts that were being ripped from his torso. "Back the fuck off, Nicky."

His commander shifted, and so did Aric's friends—if that's still what they were.

"Can't do that, and you know it," Nick said in his don't-screw-with-me voice. However stern he sounded, worry still bled into his tone.

"You don't interfere with free will, remember?" Aric snapped.

Concern turned to anger as he took a step closer. "I'm making a goddamned exception. Do you honestly believe you're the only one suffering? That you won't leave a giant hole in this team if you do something so stupid?"

That gave him pause. "I—"

"There's a consequence for every action, Aric. These guys are your brothers, and they'd die for you. Do you care so little for them that you'd place their futures in danger because you took the easy way out?"

A chill settled in his chest, despite the rising fever that made him feel like he was about to self-combust. "I never thought about it like that."

"Which is why I'm telling you. Taking your own life will have far-reaching and devastating effects on every single man here, not to mention on others who aren't present. You can't do this. I won't let you." The finality in his voice was both a relief and a burden.

"I'm responsible for what happened to the team," he said hoarsely. "You heard Jax—I should be dead. He was right. It's what I deserve."

"No." A new voice broke in. "I was wrong."

Great. Just what he needed, Jax getting in his face again. Aric eyed the man warily as he approached, noted the shame etched on his face.

"What prompted the change of heart? Don't want me offing myself on your conscience?"

Jax winced. "After I calmed down, I knew I didn't mean what I said to you. And you were right about Beryl—I've got my own load of guilt for trusting her, and I can't lay that on you. I'm sorry as hell for transferring the blame, and I hope you can forgive me."

He stared at his friend for a long moment. "It's not a question of forgiving you. It's whether I can get square with my part in that whole fucking mess."

"Still . . ." Jax swallowed hard. "I need to hear it."

"I forgive you, man." God, he had to tell them the rest. "But it's not going to make any difference in the long run."

"Why? What do you mean? You're not still plan-ning to—"

"No. I'll let nature take its course, but I won't hurry the inevitable." Everyone looked puzzled. Except Nick. Steeling himself, he explained. "I've found my mate, but I can't claim her."

A moment of stunned silence followed that announce-ment, and then they all started talking at once, peppering him with questions. Most prevalent were, "Who is she?" and "Why the hell not?"

He held up a hand. "You all might as well know. It's Rowan."

"Holy crap!" Ryon exclaimed.

He headed off more nosy inquiries. "I can't claim her because she's leaving for L.A. again as soon as Micah's better. She loves her job as a cop and I won't take her away from her life. She doesn't want a mate and even if she did, she deserves a better one than me and the dangers that come with living in my world."

"That's such bullshit," Jax said angrily. "It's worked out for Kira and me just fine. Have you even told Rowan what's going on?"

"No, and all of you are going to promise you won't breathe a word. I mean it. This isn't your problem."

"Yes, it is," Zan insisted. "Bro, you'll *die* if you don't claim your mate, and we can't afford to lose you—on the team or as our friend."

Aric looked away, into the gathering darkness. "Maybe not, but it doesn't matter. Promise me."

One by one, they did, though reluctantly. Everyone but Nick, who just returned Aric's glare with a hard one of his own.

"I won't say anything unless I feel I have to."

"Fine." Aric sighed. He supposed that was the best he was going to get.

What a joke. His team had intervened, but he was going to die anyway. He'd let down anyone who'd ever loved him. He didn't deserve to be happy, to have a beautiful mate. He'd only end up hurting her, too.

The sun set completely as they shifted and started the long walk back to the compound. Even among his Pack, he felt alone in the dark.

Aching for what might've been, if only he'd been a better man.

Eleven

Rowan hovered at the window to the rec room, alternating between pacing and peering into the waning evening. As in any workplace, word had gotten around about the fight in no time.

Sariel and a couple of others had found Rowan keeping vigil and had been concerned about what happened. She'd simply told them that the boys had a disagreement and went for a run to work out their frustrations. A vague response, but she figured the team's dirty laundry was their business to air, or not.

"They haven't returned?"

She looked around to see the gorgeous Fae walk in again, his brow furrowed. "Not yet."

"I think this 'disagreement' was more serious than you said, since you've paced there for over two hours."

"You could say that. But it's not my story to tell."

"I understand. I only wanted to check and see if you needed a friend."

"Thanks." She smiled at him. "A person can never have too many of those."

"Oh, I don't know. A handful of really good, loyal ones has always been enough for me." His voice was wistful, his expression distant for a moment.

"Did you leave behind someone special in your world?" she asked gently. His golden eyes were so sad, she could've cried for him. She didn't cry easily.

"My five brothers, and my best friend. They were all on a diplomatic visit to the Vampire Coalition or the Seelie court would never have succeeded in casting me from the realm. Politics, you know?"

"I'm so sorry," she said sincerely. "Your brothers and your friend, they knew that your father is this Unseelie bastard?"

"Yes. They loved me anyway," he said quietly, "as did my late stepfather. Now my oldest brother is king, and none of them ever would've told my secret. I don't know how the court found out."

"Maybe Malik told them, or arranged for someone else to do it?"

"Why would he do that? Raping my mother was, and still is, a crime punishable by death."

"Well, it got you kicked out, didn't it? And now you're without the protection of your kind."

"Which is exactly what he must've wanted." He shook his head, causing the fall of sapphire hair to wave like silk. His wings rustled in agitation. "I've been stupid. I couldn't understand how the court learned Malik sired me, but it never occurred to me that he might have been behind it."

"You haven't seen him since you've been . . . on earth?" It was still hard to say shit like that.

His smile was faint. "The Seelie court as well as the Vampire Coalition exist on earth, just on different planes. But to answer your question, yes. Malik was waiting for me almost the instant I landed in the middle of a busy street in Ireland, on the wrong side of the veil."

She blinked, trying to picture that. "Wings and all?"

"Unfortunately. My appearance caused quite a panic, which alerted Malik to my location. I fled, and barely managed to stay one step ahead of him, hiding in several different places. During all of this, the Alpha Pack team was alerted to my presence and came to apprehend me."

"But not Malik?" She frowned. "Why didn't they grab him?"

"He's much more skilled at cloaking for long periods of time than I am, and I was at a severe disadvantage. From what the team has learned, we now know he's living among humans. I very much doubt his subordinates know exactly what Malik is, or how close they really are to dealing with the devil."

"So he appears to be a normal guy," she mused aloud.

"The Pack hasn't had a distress call to apprehend a seven-foot-tall, ugly-as-a-Sluagh's-ass Unseelie with batlike wings and two large horns protruding from the sides of his head, so I'm guessing yes. He appears normal."

She snorted. "Smart-ass."

"Thank you." He appeared pleased. "I'm learning. Humor is sort of lost on the Seelie."

"Serious bunch, huh?"

"You could say that."

She paused. "Would you know Malik, even if he was cloaked, as you say?"

"The Fae can sense one another from long distances. If I were in a room with a bunch of humans, except one was a Fae in disguise, I could identify which one it was because of the magical field they can't hide from other Fae. The Sorcerer, Kalen, might even be able to do this."

"Would you be able to tell if the Fae is Malik in particular?"

"Yes, because I'm his blood. Same with my brothers."

"Hmm." She regarded her new friend thoughtfully. "Why does this guy have such a hard-on for you? I mean, it's not like you're the king or anything— Damn, I'm sorry. I didn't mean any offense."

"None taken. You make a valid point, but I'm the bastard of a Seelie queen and an Unseelie king. Powerful blood, even though tainted, and our tie makes me the only Fae strong enough to kill him. Not that I would've tried without provocation, but that doesn't matter to him."

"Okay, that makes sense, then." Christ, Sariel was in real trouble with that piece of pond scum for a daddy, who had scores of Sluagh at his beck and call. "Why hasn't he come after you before? You're grown, after all."

"Grown." The prince laughed, the smile doing dazzling things to his face. "I'm nine thousand years old, in human time measurement."

"You—you're lying," she stammered. "Human time?"

"In my world, that's nothing. I'm practically a baby."

She eyed his gorgeous self from head to toe. "You're definitely not an infant."

"Figure of speech. But I'm relatively young in a realm where my kind are ageless. As for Malik, I don't know why he's making a move to kill me now when before he couldn't be bothered. Perhaps he'll care to explain before he butchers me."

"He's not going to do that, because the Pack won't let that happen."

"And speaking of which, they've returned." He flicked a hand toward the window.

In the moonlight, the sight of several wolves and one panther emerging from the forest was eerily beautiful. They were pretty much dragging, though, heads and tails drooping. In the middle of the group was a familiar red wolf, and it seemed the others surrounded him almost protectively. Rowan itched to know what had gone down out there.

As the men neared the back door, they shifted one by one and Kalen immediately waved a hand, doing his thing to clothe their buff bodies. Pity.

"I have a feeling you'll want to talk to Aric," the prince said. "I'll see you later."

"Hey, we'll talk more about your situation. I'm sure the guys will come up with a way to catch Malik, and solve a whole bunch of problems, including yours."

He nodded. "Thank you. That means a lot to me."

She watched him go with a little tug at her heart. She likely wouldn't be around for any of the fireworks when the team finally did take out Malik and his operation. Why did that bother her? When Micah was better, he'd keep her updated. So it wasn't like she'd be losing all of them.

The Pack trooped inside and suddenly she wasn't sure how to position herself, what to do with her hands.

She didn't want to appear as though she'd been waiting anxiously for Aric's return, which was ridiculous
because she'd never been the type to be overly concerned with what others thought. But then, the men
and women she worked with at the station were mostly
that—coworkers with whom she felt totally comfortable. Since meeting Aric and his team, she'd been anything but.

The second Aric's green eyes met hers, she was
thrown off balance. She didn't like feeling out of control, as if something greater than the two of them was
hard at work, drawing her like a magnet to a man who
would make falling for him such a rough ride. She
wasn't the picket fence type. She had a rewarding job—
well, most of the time—and her independence. This
redheaded wolf came with too much baggage. He was
a lot of trouble.

And she found herself crossing to him, intent on
making sure he was all right. She stepped in front of
him, gripping his arms, studying his face. The bruises
and split lip from the beating Jax had given him were
already healing, but there were circles under his eyes.
Heat radiated from his skin. Was he hotter than before?

"What happened?"

"We kissed and made up. It's all good." He smirked,
but the effort at offhandedness didn't quite ring true.
The rest of the Pack filed past them, looking as worn
out as Aric.

"Can't you ever be serious when you're asked a direct question?"

"I don't need a mother, sweetheart. Had one, fumbled the ball. Go figure."

"What I'm feeling right now is anything but

motherly—unless you count the number of times she probably wanted to strangle you! Talk to me, damn it."

The mask slipped away and shattered at his feet. The raw anguish she'd witnessed in the face of Jax's accusations returned full force. "I was gonna throw myself off a cliff, but they stopped me," he said harshly. "And I wish like hell they hadn't. Is that direct enough for you, officer?"

The sneer at her profession, at the fact that she *cared*, irked her. But that wasn't what really set her off. "Do you know what I did before I came here? I killed a man. Shot him right through the heart because he drew his gun on me. His choice, and he's dead because of it, regardless of the fact that if he'd taken one more second to think, if he hadn't been high, he'd still be alive. But I had to act, and was put on mandatory suspension until I was cleared of wrongdoing."

"Your point?"

"Do you honestly think that man wanted to leave his wife and kids with no support? That he wanted to be worm food? He had a miserable life, but it *was* worth something. He threw it and his family away on an impulsive decision he can never undo. Don't make the same mistake."

He stared at her for a couple of seconds, then started clapping. The noise was rude in the empty space, the mask in place again. "Bravo. You have a tissue so I can wipe my tears?"

"You are *such* an asshole!"

She stomped off, left him standing there, his laughter floating at her back. His tactic was so transparent, yet she allowed him to get the best of her anyway. This was exactly what he wanted—to put up a wall she couldn't breach. His attitude was a shield he erected between him and the world, probably always had, and he wielded it like a warrior.

Well, he wasn't going to get away with that. He'd won the battle but not the war. She needed some time to cool off and regain her infamous composure, and then the jerk was toast.

Uh-huh. Five minutes ago he was too much trouble. So why do you care so much, girlfriend?

She was sure she didn't want to know the answer.

Aric sat listlessly on the sofa in his quarters, feet propped on the coffee table, crossed at the ankles. On TV was a rerun of some reality show, the one where young twentysomethings went on dates that were set up by their "friends" to turn out horrible on purpose. Usually, he'd be laughing his ass off and munching on popcorn.

Tonight, he couldn't dredge up a smile.

Do you know what I did before I came here? I killed a man.

"And another when you arrived," he whispered.

But that wasn't fair to Rowan. She had no idea what was happening to him, and never would. He'd instruct Micah and Nick to give her some "official" story that he'd been killed by a Sluagh or something. God, how morose.

Rising, he walked to the living room window and stared into the night. He longed to run again, to just keep going forever, selfish asshole that he was. Rowan had that right. Otherwise, he would've made an attempt to actually listen to what she'd been trying to get into his thick skull. And he would've shown a lot more empathy for what she'd been forced to do.

Killing was never easy. The truth was, it sickened him to take a life. Any life, even one as dangerous and destructive as a Sluagh. Ironic, for a man who'd joined the SEALs and had been a part of a damned good team. He knew very well how Rowan must've felt, doing her job and wishing the outcome had been different.

He owed her an apology.

"Crap," he muttered and stalked to the door.

Covering the short distance to her room in a matter of moments, he knocked loudly, just in case she'd gone to bed. He checked his watch. Ten? That wasn't too late, but then again they'd had an eventful day. What with nearly being eaten and all.

He gave her about thirty seconds, which seemed like an eon, and knocked again. Nothing but silence met his summons and he frowned. Where the heck could she be?

Since it was way past dinner, the rec room was his next stop. Unfortunately, it was empty, too. Frustrated, he headed in the general direction of Nick's office and the conference room. He briefly considered that something urgent might've come up and they hadn't had time to grab him yet, then nixed that idea. If that had happened, Nick would've gotten on the newly repaired PA system.

At the end of the hallway, he spotted Ryon and Zan talking to Nick, and he relaxed a bit. At least the building wasn't as deserted as it appeared.

"Please," Ryon wheedled, sounding like a teenager. "If you come with us, it'll make three, and that's enough."

Nick shook his head. "I said no groups smaller than four, and I'm not going to break my own rule. Besides, that would leave us with only Hammer, Jax, and A.J. in the building to fight if we had any unwelcome visitors."

Ryon kept at his boss. "Kalen put that spell on the building, remember? It'll be fine. Come on, Nicky, we haven't gone into town in forever, and the others are already there. We're missing out on the fun."

The others? "Who went to town?" Aric asked, stopping next to the group and eyeing each of them.

Ryon answered, exasperated. "Kalen, Sariel, Mackenzie, and Rowan. They went to the Cross-eyed Grizzly to blow off some steam. Hard day and all."

"And the way to reward yourself at the end of a 'hard day' is to get drunk and throw up," Nick said drily, rolling his eyes. "I think Bill Cosby did a routine about that once."

Zan snickered. "Lighten up, boss. Nobody's gonna get drunk. Buzzed, maybe."

"I have an idea." Ryon brightened. "Aric can come with us, and that's four. Problem solved."

Aric held up a hand. "Man, I'm beat. I was just looking for Rowan to, um, say I'm sorry for being such a dick earlier." He really didn't feel like going out, as appealing as it sounded to be with Rowan in a casual, fun setting.

"Yeah?" His blond-haired friend got a decidedly evil look in his eyes. "I'd say she's already forgotten all about you *and* your dick, so no worries."

"What's that supposed to mean?"

"Just that she seemed pretty happy to be going out on the arm of a Fae prince who looks like a fuckin' runway model, that's all." He shot Aric a grin.

The picture Ryon had painted made his wolf strain

to shred something and his blood began a slow boil. Rowan and Sariel. Getting cozy at the Grizzly and drinking the night away. Oh, fuck no. That was not going to do.

Quickly, he checked his jeans, T-shirt, and shit-kickers. Not much, but he'd probably look better than the regulars. He doubted most of them bathed. "I'm in. Nicky?"

With a sigh, the boss relented. "I'll go for a while, but I'm not staying all night."

"Woo-hoo!" Ryon pumped his fist.

Aric tried to recall when he'd felt that young, and decided it had been before his stepfather and Beryl had invaded his life. Not something he wanted to think about.

"Hang on. How is Sariel able to be out at a bar?" he asked.

"Kalen helped him out with a cloaking spell." Nick smiled. "You should see them. Those two look like brothers now."

Aric tried to call that image to mind, and failed.

Outside, they piled into one of the SUVs with Nick behind the wheel and Aric in the front passenger seat. Ryon, Christ love him, kept the conversation light-hearted, chattering like a monkey on crack the entire way, as though trying to somehow compensate for the total steaming pile of dung the day had turned out to be.

His friend didn't take a breath until Nick parked outside the Grizzly and shut off the ignition. By then Aric's ears were ringing. Maybe his brain would hemorrhage and he wouldn't have to sit in a bar full of stinky wannabe outdoorsmen for hours. But as soon as he went inside, he knew he wouldn't be that lucky.

It took him about two seconds to spot the foursome against the far wall at a long table. They were laughing, having a great time, obviously doing their part to put the day behind them. Kalen and Sariel each had longnecks. Mac was sipping what looked like a margarita, and Rowan had two shots of gold liquid and lime wedges lined up in front of her. He wasn't surprised to find she'd skipped the margarita and gone straight for the tequila.

As his group approached, Aric's attention was drawn to Sariel. The prince took a drink of his beer, trying to emulate his male companion, and ended up choking. *Guess they don't serve Sam Adams in the Seelie court.* Rowan pounded him on the back, smiling, then hugged his waist, she and Mac making sympathetic noises.

Aric held back a snarl. Even with his wings hidden, his long hair disguised as jet-black, dressed in jeans and a form-fitting black button-down shirt, the male was too damned pretty. And way too sensual, leaning into Rowan's attentions, like a cat arching for a nice petting.

The guy would have to find someone else to scratch his itch.

"Can't hold your booze, huh, Sam?" Aric took the vacant seat next to Rowan. Nick, Zan, and Ryon took up open spots at the end.

Sariel's smile of welcome turned puzzled. "Sam?"

He pointed to the bottle. "Nickname. I was teasing you." Blank stare. "The beer you're drinking is Sam Adams."

"Oh! Yes, well . . ." Sariel's nose wrinkled. "Kalen talked me into ordering this and it tastes horrible. I'm sure *that* would be much better." He pointed to Mac's drink.

"Want to try one?" Rowan asked. "They're smooth and sweet, and taste like limeade. With a kick."

The prince gave his enthusiastic approval and Rowan waved at the server. The girl hurried over, giving the men of their group an appreciative eye before taking their order. Sariel requested his margarita, but the rest, including Aric, went for beers. Zan helped himself to the Fae's abandoned brew as a warm-up. Or cool-down. Whatever.

Looking around first to make sure nobody was listening, Aric addressed Nick. "Are we sure it's safe for him to be out in public?" He gestured to Sariel. "Nice work with the disguise, but his kind can sense him."

Kalen flashed him a look of irritation. "My spell will work. Why don't we try to have a night out and relax for a change? We could all use the break."

Taking a deep breath, he forced himself to unwind. Nobody wanted to hang with a perpetual downer, even if his worries were valid. Deciding to try some small talk, he gestured to Kalen's chest.

"I noticed Mac is wearing your pendant. What's up with that?" He cocked his head. "What haven't you told us about the attack on you and Mac?"

The couple glanced at each other and Nick, and Kalen shrugged. Aric thought his nonchalance was forced.

"It happened while you were being held captive. The pendant is protection against evil and I'm letting Mac wear it for a while, that's all. The encounter with those things shook her up and having it on makes her feel better."

"I think that's a glossed-over answer." Aric narrowed his eyes.

Mac gave a weak smile. "What's the big deal? Like Kalen said, let's just have a nice evening."

Nick changed the subject with discussion about a new laser weapon being developed by Grant and his team in the government. Aric tuned them out. Sitting back, he slung an arm over the back of Rowan's chair and whispered into her ear.

"You went out and didn't invite me to the party? I'm crushed." Actually, he kind of was. But he didn't want her to know.

"Maybe because you pissed me off?" she suggested sweetly.

"Yeah, about that . . . Could we step outside for a minute?"

"I don't know. I'm having a pretty good time right where I am."

The stubborn set of her jaw, the militant flash in those big brown eyes, her shiny hair falling around her shoulders were so freaking sexy. His damned cock went rock hard in his jeans and he had to press the heel of his hand to his crotch to get it to behave. Not that it worked. "Please?"

"Let me think—no."

"Fine, have it your way." Pounding a fist on the table, and causing his friends to jump, he cleared his throat. Their conversation stopped, and he met their curious stares without flinching. "I owe Rowan, and everyone else, an apology. I was a complete dick this afternoon and I'm sorry."

Silence.

And then, from Kalen, "Is that it?"

He scowled. "What else do you want? A dozen roses?"

The Sorcerer snickered. "Not me, but the lady there might feel differently."

He turned to Rowan and found that the ice had thawed, some. But he had a bit more work cut out for him. Mustering every ounce of sincerity, he laid his hand over hers on the tabletop. "I get what you were telling me earlier. I apologize for being a jackass. I do that when things get too intense and I don't want to deal, but that's no excuse for shutting you down when you shared something really painful that you went through. I'm sorry, Ro."

Her eyes softened and she offered a small smile. "Nobody calls me that but Micah."

"Do you mind?"

"No, of course not. Apology accepted."

Whew. "Thanks, honey. Did you get to check on Micah before you guys left?"

"I did. He was awake again, but he didn't say a single word this time. I probably shouldn't have left him."

"No," he said, heading off a fretting session. "You had to get away for a while, and he's in good hands. Melina and the nurses are all watching out for him."

She relaxed some. "You're right. I just can't help but worry."

"Have some fun tonight, then get some sleep. You can see him in the morning."

"All right."

She managed to loosen up, and the conversation lightened considerably. The eight of them ended up having a good time, sharing some laughs. Rowan entertained them with some funny stories of calls she and her partner, Danny, had answered, and the guys took turns sharing some of their humorous predicaments, too.

Aric tried not to wonder if this Danny she spoke so highly of was someone she missed a lot. And failed.

"Want to take that walk now?" she said in his ear.

Nick, who overheard, shook his head. "Groups of four."

"Jesus," Aric bitched. "We'll be right outside. Come on, man, give me a break."

His boss hesitated, then reluctantly gave his assent. "I'm not picking up on anything, but don't be long."

"Sure." Taking a last draw on his beer, he grabbed her hand and pulled her toward the exit. As they stepped onto the wooden porch that ran along the front, he sucked in a lungful of crisp night air. "God, it's good to get out of there. The noise and smoke were getting to me."

"I feel like a sixteen-year-old running off to make out."

"Is that what we're going to do?" he asked hopefully.

His "date" giggled. "Oh, if you're lucky."

"We'll see about that."

Outside was quiet, the *thump-thump* of the country music muffled, thank Christ. There were no bar patrons hanging around, just the normal trickle of one or two coming and going at a time. Aric led her to the corner of the building opposite the parking lot, the side that faced the trees, and pulled her into the darkness, out of sight. Opening his wolf's senses, he inhaled deeply. There were no smells other than the normal ones, earth and foliage and the regular nocturnal animals.

"What are you doing?"

"Making sure we don't get surprised this time."

Pushing her back against the side of the building, he grinned and cupped her face. "I don't plan on being interrupted."

Before she could voice a protest, he crushed his mouth to hers. Licked inside to play with her tongue, loving her sweetness. Tequila and something else potent that was all Rowan. Skimming his palms south, he found the edge of her red crop top and journeyed underneath, finding the lush twin mounds he'd been dying to squeeze all day.

She moaned, arching into his touch, giving him permission to keep going. Her bra was some lacy thing, sort of sheer, and he had fun plucking her nipples through the material, teasing them to taut peaks. Then his fingers found the button of her jeans, making short work of that and the zipper.

His hand slipped inside her panties, sought her silky curls. Brushed through them to find that warm place between her thighs and rub her clit, spreading the moisture.

"Aric . . ." Her voice was breathy. Growing more excited.

"Let's get these jeans out of the way so I can make you feel really good, baby." Grabbing the waistband, he shucked them down along with her panties, leaving them at her calves. Then he spun her to face the building. "Hands on the wall, spread your feet out more."

"Aric, we could get arrested for indecent exposure," she breathed. But she assumed the position.

"Nick will bail us out." Smoothing his palms over her hips and the round globes of her plump ass, he licked his lips. "Spread a little more. There's a good girl. Tell me what you want, honey."

"I—I want you to fuck me." She poked her ass back, inviting him.

"How do you want it? Tell me." With his right hand, he skimmed under the curve of her ass. Took two fingers and parted her folds, and rubbed the slit. Then worked inside to fuck her channel, drive her crazy.

"H-hard and fast. Fuck me like you mean it!"

His wolf rumbled in approval. Anticipation. His canines dropped and his heart sped up as he quickly freed his dripping cock. Brought the head to her entrance and began to push into the velvet heat.

"Shit, yes. You're so hot and tight, baby. You just brace yourself, 'cause I'm gonna give you a ride to remember."

"Do it."

She begged so pretty, he almost came from that, and from the sight of his woman spread for him. Wet and ready for his cock. "Mine."

"Yours! Oh, yes . . . all the way, I need you in me!"

He thrust to the hilt and stilled for a few seconds, gripping her waist. The need to bite her, claim his mate, was never stronger than at that moment. It took all his willpower not to succumb to the blinding, tearing need to bond. To make her his for always.

But he controlled it, barely, and began to take her in unhurried but powerful strokes. The slap of their slick skin drove him crazy, and her channel clasping, squeezing his rod sent him to the edge in minutes.

"I'm not going to last," he warned her.

"Me, either. Please, do me hard!"

He increased the tempo some, but mostly the force, putting even more strength behind the strokes. Enough to send them both into ecstasy, but not enough to harm her.

Her orgasm hit suddenly and she cried out, undulating on his cock, milking him. His own release was explosive and he came endlessly, hard and deep. Just like she'd wanted.

All too soon they were spent and he pulled out carefully, placing a gentle kiss between her shoulder blades. "Thank you, sweetheart. You were incredible."

"So were you." Turning, she gave him a blazing kiss. When he pulled back, he couldn't help but stare, awed by her beauty. And right then, the truth hit him like a bolt—he wasn't just losing his life by not claiming Rowan.

He was losing a special woman, one who would've made him the happiest bastard alive.

If only things had been different.

Twelve

Rowan was sitting by Micah's bed, holding his hand and reading aloud to him from Jim Butcher's latest book about PI wizard Harry Dresden's adventures, when it happened.

"Hey, Ro," a voice croaked.

The book fell from her nerveless fingers and she raised her eyes, looking straight into Micah's. "Oh, my God! You—you're awake! You're back!"

"I'm back? Where'd I go?" He smiled tiredly, looking more than a little confused.

"You were hurt," she answered carefully. "Don't you remember?"

His handsome face scrunched, the scar tissue from the burn pulling on the left side as he thought hard. Thankfully he hadn't noticed it yet, but he would. She wasn't looking forward to his reaction.

"I . . . We were sent out—wait, where am I?"

"At the Alpha Pack compound. You're safe, sweetie. Nick and the others rescued you."

"From where? Who's Nick?" He began to appear alarmed. "You know about Alpha Pack?"

Sensing his mounting anxiety, she stroked his hair. "One thing at a time, honey. Yes, I know about your team and what you guys do. How you eliminate rogue demons and different kinds of creatures, all of it. You can guess how fun that was for a nonbeliever like me." The humor was lost on him.

He took a long moment to digest this, studying his lap. When he finally looked at her again, his expression was one of quiet dread. He spoke with difficulty, his voice raspy from disuse. "We were sent to an abandoned building, to rescue some hostages from vampires, I think. Then it's just a blank. Where's Terry? Is everyone okay?"

Her heart turned over, aching for his loss. "From what I was told, that op was a setup and you were all ambushed. Sweetie, Terry and some of the other guys are most likely dead. I'm so sorry."

"I— What? That doesn't make sense. How . . . Oh, God." He sank into the pillows, seeming so young and vulnerable. Nothing like the tough warrior she knew him to be. He was scared and he had no idea what was going on. She let him process it all.

He went on. "Who is Nick?" he repeated.

"Nick Westfall. He's your new commander. Everyone really respects him and from what I gather, he's fit right in very well in the time he's been here."

"How much time? I mean, he couldn't have replaced Terry in just a few days."

"Micah, the ambush was more than six months ago," she said softly.

"But . . . where have I been? What happened to me?"

Her brother honestly didn't remember. Christ help them all, how were they supposed to get him healed with him blocking the whole thing? But his mind slamming the door on the horror was likely the only reason he was awake and communicative now.

"You were held in several different buildings, labs where this guy Orson Chappell, CEO of NewLife Technology, and his band of merry lunatics are doing experiments on shifters and humans, merging their DNA. Does any of this ring a bell?"

He thought for a time, shook his head. "No." His brown eyes were shadowed, though, and she wondered whether his brain was struggling to keep the events suppressed.

With a sigh, she gave him the rundown of events over the past few months, without going into details about what was done to his body by those insane bastards. It might do more harm than good to tell him what he'd suffered before he was ready to hear it. She'd have to talk to the doctors. When she was finished, he lay there exhausted. Thinking, she could tell.

"So, since I survived, Terry and the others might still be alive somewhere, waiting for rescue," he said hopefully.

"Maybe, but nobody knows. I'm not sure whether it's cruel to hope that's true or not."

Licking his lips, he glanced at the plastic pitcher and cup on the nightstand. "Can I have some water?"

"Sure." She patted his arm. "Be right back."

Taking the pitcher, she found Noah leaning over a counter looking at a chart. "Good news—Micah's awake."

He turned with a bright smile. "That's great! I'll get

him some water and then let the doctors know. Give me a minute."

"Thanks."

She went back to her brother's room to wait. Neither of them spoke until Noah walked in carrying the pitcher.

"Here you go," he said cheerfully. "Micah, it's good to see you awake! We've all been worried, but you're on the road to recovery. You're going to be fine. Don't worry."

"Thanks," he said hoarsely, trying to return a small smile. But the skin on his cheek pulled again, making the effort lopsided. "How are you, kid?"

"I'm good. Just small sips, okay?"

The nurse poured a half cup of water and placed a straw in it, then held it out while Rowan helped her brother sit up. He took more than he was told, faster than he should, and Noah removed the straw, placing the cup on the counter.

"Don't guzzle it or you'll get sick," the nurse warned.

Nodding, Micah reached up to wipe his mouth. His fingers grazed the left corner where the puckered skin began, and Rowan held her breath. Frowning, he let the pads of his fingers explore his cheek, over the rough terrain to the bridge of his nose. Then down where it curved under his jaw. She and Noah shot each other a worried look.

"What the hell is wrong with my face?" he asked, panic creeping into his voice, eyes wide. "What is this?"

Rowan cleared her throat. "You were injured. There's a scar, but it doesn't look too bad."

"I want a mirror."

"I think we should wait—"

"There's no *we*. It's my face and I want a damned mirror!"

Rowan gave Noah a desperate look, and he stammered, "I—I'll get one. And I'll see what's keeping Dr. Grant and Dr. Mallory."

Hurry. Her brother was becoming more agitated, hands fisting in the sheets, glancing around the room, eyes a little wild. She couldn't handle a repeat of when he'd leapt off the bed and attempted to tear out her throat. He didn't even remember doing it, which was scary.

"Micah, calm down. Please. You don't want the doctors to be forced to give you a sedative again, do you?"

"I don't want to sleep. I just want to know what's wrong with me."

But he kept picking at the sheets, at the tape on his hand holding the IV in place. Feeling his scar. After what seemed an eternity, but was probably only a couple of minutes, Mac and Melina walked in, trailed by Noah. All were wearing neutral expressions. Mac was carrying a handheld mirror, the large round type one might find in a beauty shop—or a hospital, when a patient wants to look at an injury.

Mac moved to her brother's bedside and gave him a broad, genuine smile. "It's so good to see you awake. Do you know who I am?"

Rowan knew she was testing how "awake" and "present" he really was, checking for areas of concern.

"Of course I do." He tried again to smile, but couldn't quite manage it. "How are you, Mac? Pretty as ever, I see."

She laughed. "Always the charmer. How long have you been awake?"

He looked to Rowan uncertainly, so she answered. "No more than ten minutes."

"Ah." Mac gestured to Melina. "Well, before we do anything else, Dr. Mallory and Noah are going to check your vitals, make sure you're still physically doing well. Then we'll get to the other stuff, all right?"

"Sure."

"Micah, it's good to see you back in the land of the living," Melina said kindly.

"Thanks. Hey, you cut off your long hair."

Melina's smile was strained. "I did. It just got in the way, so I went into town one day and had it whacked off."

"When we find Terry, he'll want you to grow it back," Micah said softly. "He loves it long."

Everyone fell silent for a moment. Rowan knew he was just trying to offer hope in his own way, and apparently from her expression Melina did, too.

"I know. Thank you." She got down to business. "Okay, just relax."

Rowan moved into a corner by the window, out of the way, and watched. Noah took Micah's blood pressure as Melina shone a light into his eyes, checking the dilation of his pupils. Then she had him squeeze her fingers and checked some other reflexes.

"What's your full name and birth date?"

"Micah Lee Chase. October 4, 1979."

They went through some other simple questions, like when he'd joined Alpha Pack, what his job entailed, who was president of the United States. He answered them all with no more than the normal thoughtful pause in between, passing with flying colors. Until Melina addressed the most recent events.

"Micah, do you remember your rescue, or anything since you were brought here?"

"I . . . No, it's all a blank." His brows furrowed. "Was I ever awake? I must've been, or why would you ask?"

"You awoke several times, but you weren't yourself." Melina paused, but obviously decided not to mince words. "The first time, you shifted into your wolf form, leapt out of the bed and attacked your sister."

"What?" He glanced at Rowan, and the rest of them, stunned. "I would never hurt Ro!"

"Like I said, it wasn't really you," the doctor replied gently. Despite her rigid demeanor, Rowan noted she did have a soft heart when it came to her patients. "You were hurt, in pain and traumatized, and your wolf was only protecting himself and you from further injury."

"I went nuts is what you're saying." Collapsing back, he stared at the ceiling. "I attacked my own sister. This is so fucked up."

Melina pulled up a chair and sat. "Micah, you're going to get better, and we're going to help you. But first we need to know what you remember from the time you were taken up until your rescue."

Again, he appeared to try hard to remember. His frustration was evident as he sighed and buried a hand in his hair. "Not a damned thing. It's all a blank, like one minute I was with the Pack and we were about to hit the building where some vampires were holding hostages, and the next I wake up and Ro is here—six months later? And half of us are maybe dead? God."

Melina appeared shaken. Understandable when one of the men believed dead was her mate. "Yes, and I'm sorry. More than you know. But right now our priority is to get you healed, inside and out."

"I want to see my face," he demanded stubbornly.

After hesitating, Melina agreed. "Okay. Dr. Grant."

Mac handed him the mirror. He took it with the hand not encumbered by the IV and heaved a deep breath. Lifted it and stared for endless moments at his reflection. Then slowly his hand began to tremble. And then shake until his fingers lost their grip and the mirror landed in his lap. Mac retrieved it and gave it over to Noah, who hovered anxiously.

"I'm a freak," he whispered. "I'm a goddamned fugly son of a bitch."

"No! You're not. You're still handsome and—"

"Why? Why would anybody do that to me?"

The explosion Rowan feared didn't come, but the quiet anguish was worse somehow. His chin dipped to his chest and his shoulders started to shake. She hurried forward, nudging Mac aside, gathering her brother in her arms. "I don't know why anyone would hurt such a wonderful, beautiful man as you," she choked out. "I wish I could kill them all for you."

He clung to her as he'd done when they were kids, wrapped his arms around her and hung on. She hated what he'd been through, how thin he'd become. His tears soaked the front of her T-shirt.

"How did it happen? What did they do to me, Ro?"

"Sweetie, I don't think—"

"Tell me."

She cast a look at Melina on the other side of the bed, silently begging for help with the subject. Melina gave a quick nod, indicating that she'd take over. Rowan eased back from Micah and he gave the doctor his attention, wiping his eyes.

"The damage to your face, and the fact that the skin

scarred the way it did, suggests your captors poured hot silver on you."

"So it's going to stay this way?" he asked with a catch in his voice.

"I'd say it's highly probable, yes. There is a chance that with our advances in healing various types of shifters something could eventually be done, but it's beyond our capabilities at this time."

"What else?"

"What do you mean?"

"What else did they do to me? I want to know everything."

"We don't know everything your body was physically put through, and we may never know. Even if your memory returns, you might not be clear on certain things. We have ascertained that you were tortured, extensively. There were also incisions to your torso and groin, indicative of experimentation. What this group hopes to gain is to create a breed of super-shifters."

"Ro filled me in on this Orson Chappell guy and his operation, and that there's a Seelie prince living here now whose father is probably this guy's boss."

"That's right."

There was a heavy silence before her brother spoke again, bitterness creeping in. "Finish. I know there's something else you're chewing on."

"I think," she said slowly, "that some memories are best left to resurface in the patient's own time. When a person is ready, they'll remember."

"You don't think I'm ready?"

"It's early days and you have a long road ahead before you're ready to rejoin the team."

"I'm a head case. I get it. Doesn't matter. I want to

know what I'm up against so I can deal with it, or I'm going to go even more nuts trying to figure out what you're all hiding." His gaze encompassed everyone in the room.

Mac moved close, gripped his hand, and took over from her colleague. "All right. I can see this is going to hurt just as much if we keep it from you." Rowan could see how Mac struggled with the decision to tell him. Even a doctor sometimes didn't know what the best course of action was, psychologist or not.

"Micah . . . you were raped. I'm so sorry."

He stared at her, uncomprehending at first. Then the shock bled in, the expression of a man who'd just watched his house burn down, or witnessed the death of a loved one. In a way, perhaps it was a death of sorts. The demise of any remaining innocence the soul might've clung to all those years, writhing and screaming on the ground.

"Once?" he rasped. "Just once, right?"

Rowan couldn't see what difference once or a bunch of times made to a man who couldn't remember, but it mattered to Micah.

"Tests suggest ongoing sexual abuse. But you're physically healed now," Mac emphasized. "As for mentally, you're going to be all right. We'll get you there."

"You guys keep saying that, like I'm ever going to be normal again." His laugh was painful, on edge.

"You will be. You *are* normal—"

He cut Melina off. "I'll never be anything but fucked up!" His voice rose to a shout and he bolted upright, yanking at his IV. "Why bother with all of this? I'm ugly, tainted inside and out! What the fuck does anything matter?"

"Micah, calm down," Melina ordered. She and Mac grabbed his arms, and Rowan pushed his chest, pinning him to the bed.

"Micah, stop!"

"Fuck you!" he screamed. "Let go of me!"

"Noah," Melina called. "Reach in my right pocket and get that sedative into his IV."

The wide-eyed nurse leapt forward to do as the boss said, retrieving the syringe while the three of them struggled to hold Micah still. Noah hustled to grab the spout attached to the IV tube, yanked the cap off with his teeth, and inserted the needle into the tiny hole. Clear liquid flowed into the line and by the time the last of the medicine went in, Micah's struggles were already becoming weaker. One minute max, and he slumped, eyelids drooping.

"No. Please . . ." Then drifted closed.

He was out. They released him and Rowan studied her brother, overwhelming love and grief clogging her throat. His entire body was lax, his torment washed away, albeit temporarily, by a drug-induced sleep.

This wasn't fair. To Micah, to the missing ones who might still be suffering. None of it. Her brother was such a good man. He didn't deserve this.

Turning, she fled the room. Outside, she leaned against the wall and slapped a hand over her mouth, fighting to win the battle over the tears threatening to spill. She succeeded, but it was a near thing.

The trio inside filed out, and Melina spoke softly to the nurse. He hurried away, and the two women faced her, prepared to give their best rah-rah speech. Rowan wasn't in the mood to listen, but she did, anyway. Micah's welfare was at stake.

"You know he's going to be all right," Mac said. "We won't accept anything less than his full recovery."

"I know, and I appreciate that. But you saw him in there—the only reason he didn't shift again was probably because of the drugs."

"Maybe so, but honestly, he handled the conversation better than I expected. Don't you think?" she asked Melina.

"I agree. It could've been much worse."

"I don't see how, so I'll have to trust you both." She sighed, regaining some control of her raging emotions. "What happens now? Will you continue the sedatives?"

"In low doses," Melina answered, "just to keep him calm and suppress his ability to shift until he's mentally stable. We'll wean him off as he shows real progress in his recovery. And before you ask, there's no telling how long that could be. Months would be my professional guess, but that's a shot in the dark."

"Months. God, I have to go back to L.A. soon. How can I leave him like this?"

"He'll be fine," Mac assured her. "He's got the whole team plus a bunch of staff looking out for him. The guys are in and out of here day and night checking on him, and when they find out he's really awake, he'll have tons of company. He won't be left alone for extended periods of time, I promise."

Damn, having to go was eating her up inside. And if she was honest, not just because of having to leave Micah.

Don't go there.

"Then I guess I'll have to hang on to that until I can get back here to see him."

"When will you go?" Mac asked.

"In a couple of days. I took some vacation time in addition to my mandatory leave from the force, and it's almost gone." Belatedly, she realized they might not have heard why she was on leave from the LAPD. Then again, she hadn't exactly kept it quiet and they didn't ask for the story, so maybe word had gotten around.

"Make sure to say good-bye to us before you leave," Melina said. "That way we can keep an extra close watch on your brother, make certain he's handling your departure. I think he will, but it's only a precaution."

"I'll stop by, no worries. Thanks for all you're doing for him . . ." Damn it, she wouldn't lose it. "Anyway, I'll be back later."

The walls were closing in. She had to get outside for a bit, and didn't want to run into anyone. Not until she had herself under control. She exited through a side door and started walking, making sure to stay close to the building. If she was violating Nick's "group of four" rule, well, he wasn't her boss. It wasn't like she could get fired.

Heading toward the back, she found herself standing at the edge of what Aric had said was the ball field. The grass was somewhat trampled, evidence that they weren't all work and no play. Would Micah be well enough one day soon to join them in a game?

The thought of all he had to overcome was overwhelming to her; she couldn't fathom how he must be feeling. Spinning around, she planned to head into the building again—and ran straight into a solid wall of muscle. A pair of hands steadied her, engulfing her shoulders, and she looked up, half-expecting to see

Aric. Only this man was far too big and tall to be her lover.

"Hammer! I'm sorry. I wasn't paying attention to where I was going." She stepped back, not out of fear or discomfort due to the man's towering size, but simply so she could see him better. She could swear he'd been nowhere around just a second ago.

"That's okay."

His rare smile was blinding and she blinked. The huge bald man was truly stunning, the epitome of a beautiful, gentle giant. Especially with his usual reserve banished by a bright, welcoming smile. He sort of resembled Vin Diesel, only way hotter. And that was saying a lot.

"Did you . . . need something?"

"What?" He seemed startled from some deep thought. "Oh, not really. I spotted you through the window of the rec room and wanted to make sure you weren't alone. I'm not sure if Nick's rule applies this close to the building, but I wanted to, um, keep you company."

The way he said it, kind of shy, was so sweet. The typically reticent man didn't usually have much to say, but his quiet demeanor obviously hid a big heart.

"Thanks, Hammer."

"John."

"I'm sorry?"

"My name. It's John," he said softly.

"Oh, wow. That's a great name," she said, studying him. "Big John. I love it!"

"Thanks." He actually blushed, and suddenly seemed fascinated by his tennis shoes.

"You know, the guys are all betting your name is

something really nerdy or embarrassing. And here you have a strong, solid name that suits you so well." She leaned forward. "But why'd you tell *me*?"

He shrugged. "You're a cop, and you're Micah's sister. I know I can trust you. I feel it here," he said, placing a plate-sized palm over his gut.

She was beyond touched. "Thank you. Your secret is safe with me. After all, we wouldn't want to upset the betting pool, would we?" He laughed quietly. As she watched him, gave the man some thought, the pieces began to fit together. "You joined the team with Nick six months ago."

"Yeah."

"He said you were in the FBI together. You were undercover, weren't you?"

"Yes."

"You were deep inside and you got made, didn't you?" she asked, gauging his reaction to see if she was right. He tensed, looked into her eyes, and she knew before he spoke.

"They made me, the group of terrorists I helped take down. After the job was done and the lot of them were arrested, they figured out I was an agent, learned my real name. Mine got erased, and I didn't bother to pick a new one. If I don't exist, why do I need some name on paper?"

"True. So who coined the nickname Hammer? Or did you make it up?"

"No, Nicky did, by accident. When we first met, he said my fists were as big as the business end of a sledgehammer. The short version stuck."

"Well, that's true, too, but I still prefer John." She winked. "I won't spill it in front of anyone."

"Say, I was wondering . . ."

The big man faltered, and stared over her head into the forest. Not because he saw anything dangerous or interesting out there. He had that look on his face men sometimes did when they were about to—

Uh-oh.

He cleared his throat, and tried again. "I thought maybe, before you head back to Los Angeles, I could, um, take you to dinner sometime? If you wanted. I mean, nothing serious. I just think you're really cool and well, sexy and— Crap, I'm totally messing this up."

Oh, God. How sweet was that? There was just one problem. A big, snarky redheaded one.

"You're not messing anything up," she assured him. Lord, how to let him down without hurting his feelings? "It's just that I've already sort of been seeing someone. Not that it's serious, but I don't think—"

"Damn." He smiled ruefully. "Should've figured, considering how much time you've spent together. But I thought maybe there was an outside chance for me, since he won't claim— Never mind."

"Won't claim what?"

"Nothing. Forget I said anything." Now he seemed anxious to drop the subject.

Sweeping the man with her gaze from head to toe, she came very, very close to accepting his dinner invite. However, wonderful as he seemed, the temptation was fleeting. In fact, the idea of being with a man who wasn't Aric made her stomach hurt. It was an actual physical reaction that was troubling, how her entire being rejected the mere suggestion of getting close to another male.

Oh, God. I don't want any man but Aric.

"I don't really understand what's going on with me and him," she admitted. "I thought it was a simple out-of-town affair, as slutty as that sounds, but now? I don't know. It's more complicated than I thought if I can't go out with someone as great as you."

"It doesn't sound slutty to me. Being alone sucks, you know? Sometimes it's really nice to have someone, even if it's not forever." His expression grew wistful for a moment; then he shook himself. "Anyway, thanks for being honest. I'd thought maybe things were different with you two. At least I know it's not me, and I'd never poach off one of my friends."

"That's good to hear, 'cause I'd hate to rip out your heart and eat it for a snack."

Both of them faced Aric, who'd somehow come upon them without either of them noticing. He seemed mighty pissed, too. As she took in Hammer's smile, she wondered if the big man hadn't heard his friend approach.

"It's all good, Red." He waved a hand at Rowan. "You can't blame a guy for trying to catch a gorgeous, smart, kick-butt woman, can you?"

Aric snorted. "Guess not. Just don't let it happen again."

"No prob. I'll leave you two alone. Rowan, until later." With a wink, he headed toward the building.

"I hope I didn't hurt his feelings," she said, frowning. "He's a fantastic man."

"Just how fantastic is he?" Stepping up, he wrapped both arms around her, pulled her flush against his over-warm body. "As good as this?"

His lips nibbled at hers and his tongue flicked gently, rather than swooping in for the searing, take-charge kiss he usually delivered. This one was no less dominant, but was . . . tender. Sweet and searching. Instead of a bolt of lightning, the tingle spread to her belly and toes like ripples on a beautiful pond, sparkling with light.

One of his hands cupped her cheek, and his thumb stroked her jaw as he deepened the kiss. He ate her mouth slowly, as though savoring her as long as possible, before drawing back. "My room?"

"Let's go." The words were out before she thought twice. The need to be with him was like an irresistible pull, so powerful a force it was useless to fight it. So she didn't try, just for tonight.

Again, she thought of Hammer—no, John—asking her out, and mused over her refusal. Though she'd been tempted, there was really no question that she couldn't have done it. The two men were as different as night and day; one a gentle giant, one all fire and tempest. John was very nice, but . . . the redhead called to her blood, challenged her, excited her as no man ever had.

For all his sarcasm and rough edges, most of it was a front. Aric was kind, and he cared almost too much. His guilt over Beryl had nearly killed him. He was loyal and loved his "brothers." He'd stuck by Rowan through Micah's recovery.

He was spontaneous and fun, too. She thought of their rendezvous outside the Grizzly and her libido heated. No man had ever taken her in public before, or at least in a place where anyone could've happened along. He made her feel alive, and he had a wicked sense of humor.

Aric had wrapped himself around her heart. And refused to let go.

The walk to his quarters was quick, and they burst inside stripping off their clothes. In his bedroom, he pushed her gently onto her back and moved over her like a blanket, alive and real. Her palms skimmed his back, mapped his muscles, his spine. When he brought the head of his cock to her opening and began to push inside, she opened, welcoming him. Sought the connection that was more than just physical, though she didn't know what exactly that might be. It was the same mysterious thing that drew her to him time and again, a force bigger than the both of them.

Then she quit analyzing and let herself go, got lost in the thrust of his body, the way he danced over her gracefully. Stoked the fires higher. Wrapping her legs around his waist, she arched to meet him, taking him in as far as possible, kissing and licking the salty skin of his neck and chest. His chest rumbled, so obviously he liked her attentions. She kept it up, kneading the round globes of his ass as he made love to her.

And there could be no doubt—this was making love.

Right then, her heart trembled under an assault it had never experienced before. Hadn't wanted to know. She wouldn't name it, but it hung there in all its soul-shattering intensity, with the power to heal, to liberate.

Or to decimate.

"Oh, God, baby! I can't stop," he panted. He drove into her, picking up the pace.

"Don't stop! Please, Aric! I need you!"

That sent him over the edge and he buried himself to the hilt, shouting his pleasure. Hot seed bathed her womb as she found her own release, clinging to him. Her lifeline in the storm.

The man she'd soon have to tell good-bye when she left for a city and a cold apartment that would no longer feel like home.

Not since a certain wolf and his family had gotten under her skin. And buried themselves in her heart.

The voice was noxious, like poison in his veins. Carbon monoxide in an enclosed space. A spike driven under a fingernail.

Kalen sat on his bed, head in his hands. Tried to shut out the intruder, but it was getting harder—no, almost impossible—to do. Even Nick with all his strength in foretelling the future couldn't know what Kalen truly suffered. How bad the torment really was. The lure.

Nick had "seen" only a hint but couldn't have guessed that the possible destruction of the entire Alpha Pack team—the world—rested on the shoulders of a young Sorcerer who'd never known love, or loyalty. That the Unseelie beast enjoyed exploiting that weakness. Had no idea that Kalen was losing ground every day in his battle against the darkness.

Because if Nick *knew*, Kalen would be dead already.

Without the pendant he was lost. His wards didn't work on *himself*.

Better him than Mackenzie. He would protect her, no matter the price. With his last breath, when the time came.

And it would come.

Yesss, my boy, the voice purred seductively. *Why do you bother to fight what you know is true? You are mine, and I do not share.*

"Shut up, asshole," Kalen hissed. "You're full of shit."

Am I? Does your pulse not quicken at the image of the ultimate power we'll wield together? Does your cock not harden at the mere sound of my voice?

His groin throbbed, his length pushing against his leathers. Dark need demanded to be satisfied, the lust for mastery. To own all of the world.

Oh, yes, it's such delicious temptation for a boy who's had so little. No one has ever loved you—

"My grandmother loved me!"

And then she left you all alone. Poor mite kicked out of your family at age fourteen, unloved and misunderstood. But I will keep you safe, and we'll rule together.

"God," he rasped. "Help me."

No, young one. There is no help, not for the likes of us. So we must take what others would not give, and make it ours.

"No."

Yes. Prepare, my apprentice. I will come for you soon.

On that day, Kalen had better have a plan for how he was going to defeat Malik.

And the darkness within.

Thirteen

Sweet Jesus, she feels like heaven.

Aric tucked his would-be mate against his side, so close they were almost one body. As she napped with her head on his chest, he let his fingers slip through her sable hair again and again, and replayed their lovemaking in his head. Never had he felt closer to a woman—or anyone, for that matter.

And he had to lose her.

He was so freaking hot, and not in a good way, but he refused to move her just to try to get cooled off. These last few days were all he had left, and he wasn't about to waste a second. Against him, she wiggled a bit, and a light kiss was placed over his heart.

"Mmm."

He smiled at her sleepy moan. "Awake?"

"Barely. So good, bein' lazy like this. Wish it could last forever."

Closing his eyes, he willed down the pain. Hugged her tighter. "Me, too."

"Unfortunately, I have to move." Raising up, she kissed his lips. "Micah woke up earlier, for real."

"Really? That's great," he said with relief. "How is he?"

"As well as can be expected, I guess. Confused. He has no memory of his months in the hands of those bastards, being rescued, none of it."

"Shit. He's blocking?"

"Yeah. It's there, in his subconscious, but the only way he can cope is to shut out all the bad stuff. I'm so afraid of what's going to happen to him when he can't suppress it anymore."

He stroked her cheek, trying to give her a measure of comfort. "The doctors will be there to help him. We all will."

"I know. But the thing is, I have to head out day after tomorrow. I hate leaving him, but I have to go home for a while," she said worriedly. "I need to pay bills, check on the apartment, and see when I can get more vacation time to come back."

The news, though not unexpected, hit him like a fist in the gut. It didn't escape his notice that she hadn't expressed the same reticence to leave *him*, and he cursed himself for being a selfish asshole. "Reality intrudes, huh? Time and the day job wait for no man. Or woman."

"Something like that." She gave him a sad smile. "It's not like I can tell my sergeant that I can't come back to work because my brother is a wolf shifter who was tortured by an evil Unseelie and his shitheads."

"At least not unless you want to find yourself on the wrong end of a psych eval." He kissed her nose. "But he'll be in good hands. It's not like you're abandoning him, so get that guilt out of your head. You'll be back to visit as soon as you can, and he'll understand. When you wear a uniform and are sworn to protect the public, you don't just walk away from your career. Nobody gets that more than we do."

There. He could be objective about letting her go. He *could*.

Some of the shadows left her eyes, making the sacrifice worthwhile. "Thanks for the pep talk. You're good for me."

Then don't go. Please, don't leave me.

"Great. Let's get you up and moving, and we'll go see him. Shower?"

"Race you!"

Leaping up, she sprinted for the bathroom. A broad smile bloomed on his face of its own accord and he didn't even try to win, because he was too busy watching her edible, naked bubble butt jiggle all the way across the room. As far as he was concerned, *he* was the winner.

Once she disappeared, the lure of wet, soapy woman got his ass going. He jumped in the shower to see her face turned to the spray and he grabbed her hips, sliding his hard cock along the crevice of her butt cheeks.

"Ooh, is someone poking fun at me?"

"You bet!"

She giggled and then moaned as he made good on his threat. He made love to her under the cascade of water, slowly, savoring every moment of the glide of his cock inside her, the pleasure bittersweet. This was the last time, because he couldn't touch her again. Not if he hoped to keep his wolf leashed and restrain himself from claiming her. Something she would never want.

No, didn't deserve. She could do much better than being tied to the man responsible for her brother's kidnapping and torture.

Still, his fangs lengthened, instinct almost stronger than human will. Almost. Resisting the urge to sink his teeth into the delicate curve of her neck and shoulder was more painful than ever. Heat sizzled under his skin, baked his insides. But he held strong in his resolve and plunged deep, brought them to orgasm with a rush of heady ecstasy, filling her.

Making it last forever.

Easing out, he cleaned them both and they finished their shower. Toweling off, they got dressed in simple jeans and T-shirts and went to see Micah.

Slipping into Micah's room behind Rowan, Aric saw Ryon, Jax, and Zan already there, standing around his bed. The four of them were talking, and Micah was sitting up, looking tired but smiling—a fact that soothed some of the heartache, but not nearly enough.

How could he seek absolution for a sin Micah wouldn't even recall?

Micah's smile lit his scarred face. Aric managed not to react to the sight of the puckered skin pulling at his cheek and the corner of his mouth. The man would get the wrong idea.

"Aric! Jesus, it's good to see your smart-ass self." He held out a hand and Aric shook it carefully, avoiding the IV.

"It's great to see you sitting up, bullshitting everybody with that trademark charm," he said with a smile that felt strained. Fortunately, his friend didn't notice.

Micah snorted. "Charm? Well, it's not working or the docs would let me out of here."

"Soon. Don't push yourself."

"Hey, we've been here awhile," Jax interrupted.

"We'll go so you guys can visit. Micah, it's great to have you back. You'll be in the game again, kicking demon ass before we know it."

The trio took turns shaking his hand and slapping his back before making a noisy exit. Micah chuckled hoarsely and regarded his sister and Aric, the facade of good humor sliding off his face.

"How are you, really?" Aric asked, taking a seat. Rowan pulled up an extra chair next to him.

"Tired," he admitted. "I feel like I've been dropped on my head. It's like I went to sleep, opened my eyes ten minutes later and all these changes had happened. Half our guys dead or missing."

Resting his elbows on his knees, Aric steeled himself. "You don't know how sorry I am about that, buddy. I trusted someone I shouldn't have, and it was my—"

"Your fault. Yeah, yeah, Jax just fed me the same line of crap." He shook his head, pinning Aric with a determined gaze. "Jax said Beryl was his girlfriend—which I remembered—and she betrayed us all. I don't remember that part. He also said Beryl is your stepsister, but he didn't blame you for her actions. Neither do I. Hell, I don't blame anybody. I just want to get better and get on with rejoining the team."

"You might feel different when you remember what you went through. You might hate me." Whether Micah did or not, Aric hated himself enough for both of them. He'd take that to his grave.

"No. Not gonna happen." His friend raised a hand to his ruined cheek and his brown eyes darkened. "I owe some motherfuckers for this, but not you and Jax. You're my brothers. That's the way it is."

The man was putting up a brave front, and that's exactly what it was, but Aric let it go. No point in dragging down what little confidence his friend was attempting to muster. He cast about for a way to change the uncomfortable subject, but Micah did it for him.

"So, sis, what's the latest from the LAPD? You've got to get back soon, don't you?"

"Actually, that's what I wanted to discuss with you. I have to go back day after tomorrow, take care of my business. I'm not sure when I'll get more vacation time to come back," she said anxiously.

"Listen, don't feel bad about that." He waved a hand in dismissal. "You have a job, Ro. It's not like we're frigging independently wealthy that we've got a choice in whether to work. Go. I've got the whole team and staff to baby my ass."

Rowan laughed, though her expression was still worried. "If you're sure . . ."

"I am. Just say good-bye first."

"You know it," she said softly.

"So what's new in the land of fruits and nuts?"

She snickered at his old reference to California, and launched into some recent tales from the trenches. A drunken streaker they'd arrested one night, a catfight between two women who'd ripped each other's blouses off, and a bank robber whose car wouldn't start after he'd done the deed. There were more, and she had Micah smiling, troubles forgotten for just a little while.

Aric, on the other hand, sat almost gasping for breath, sweat rolling down his spine. His temples. Trying to act as though nothing was wrong.

If he could last two days, it would be a miracle.

*   *   *

That evening, Aric, Rowan, and the rest of the gang were eating dinner in the cafeteria when Nick strode in, obviously a man on a mission if his serious expression was anything to go by. Conversation tapered to a halt as their commander stopped in the middle of the area and addressed everyone.

"I got a call from Jarrod Grant," he announced. "Orson Chappell and Beryl have been located. Finish your dinner and let's meet in the conference room in fifteen. I want A.J. and Rowan in on this, too."

Setting down his fork, Aric wiped his mouth with his napkin and tossed it onto his plate. He hadn't been able to muster much of an appetite anyhow, and this killed it. Glancing at Rowan, he entertained absolutely forbidding her to ride along on this op, but figured that would go over real well. Not. Besides, Nicky had a reason for requesting her involvement. He'd tell them why himself.

Aric waited as Rowan and the others quickly downed their meals, and then they all filed out, making their way to the "war room," as he thought of it. Everyone took seats at the long conference table except Nick, who stood at the head of it holding a small remote control. Once the group was settled, he began.

"Grant sent us footage, courtesy of the military, of a remote cabin in East Texas where Chappell and Beryl are reportedly holed up. There's no evidence that this is a lab facility—it's just a cabin. But it's a very well-guarded one."

"The Sluagh?" Kalen asked.

Nick nodded and pointed the remote at the new flat-screen TV mounted on the wall. "Let's take a look."

The screen came on and showed a video of the front of the cabin, a nice midsized retreat nestled back in the towering pines. It boasted a wide, covered porch that wrapped around the side of the house, and large windows with the curtains drawn. A stone chimney stood on one side, and Aric had no doubt the interior was just as attractive as the outside. Then again, he wouldn't have expected Beryl to stay in a dump, on the run or not.

Nick paused the video. "Okay, see these dark spots in the footage?" He pointed to several shapes that appeared to be shadows or perhaps bad reception in the feed, located on opposite corners of the porch, several along the edge of the trees. "There are more of these shadows on the porch as the camera pans to the side and back. I believe those are the Sluagh being used as sentries, only their true forms don't show on film. I showed this to Sariel and he agrees. Now watch as the video travels to the back of the cabin."

The transition wasn't smooth. Whoever had risked his neck to obtain the vid pointed the lens in the general direction of the cabin as he obviously sneaked around the building, making the view bounce up and down. Then it smoothed out as he reached his destination, giving a nice shot of the rear of the cabin at a forty-five-degree angle.

More shadows dotted the back porch and surrounding area. Nick paused the video, pointing to a window on the left side. "Right here. Look closely and you'll see two figures, a male and a female. The male on the left is taller, white-haired, heavyset. He's been identified as Orson Chappell. The female with the long auburn hair is Beryl. The military believes they're the only two inside."

Aric let out a curse. He and Jax locked eyes, and he knew his friend was both anticipating and dreading the coming confrontation, because he felt the same.

"Nicky, I counted somewhere in the neighborhood of thirty of Malik's ugly-assed pets," Zan said, frowning. "That's just the ones we can see in the vid. How the hell will we destroy them all to even have a prayer of getting inside that cabin?"

"Because we have some points on our side that we haven't before—the element of surprise and the knowledge of what they are, and that they *can* be killed. Our resident faery prince also gave me a very important tidbit that we'll use to our advantage."

Their commander stopped the vid and then pushed another button. A slide appeared on the screen, a hand-drawn illustration of a Sluagh. The rendering was quite good, done in dark pencil, with all of the minute details, right down to the warts. A red circle was drawn on the beast's upper left side, just above the ribs at the spot where the top of a lung would be, if it were human.

"What is this? Sluagh Anatomy 101?" Ryon joked. The tension was broken and the others chuckled. Even Nick managed to lighten up some.

"Exactly. And this is probably the most relevant fact you'll learn about them." He pointed to the center of the red circle. "When the Seelie transform into their evil counterparts, the transition is physically tough on their bodies, as you can see. Their hearts are displaced, which is kind of appropriate when you think about it." More snickers, and Nick's lips curved in a half smile. He tapped the picture. "The heart ends up right here, far to the left of where human and Seelie hearts are located. Like most sentient supernatural creatures, a Sluagh can't survive if this organ is destroyed. He is, for all his strength and nastiness, simply flesh and blood. Take out his heart, and he's dead."

"But that means we have to get close enough to the damned thing to get at it," Aric observed.

"Not true. Shoot it if you can. Stab it if you must. But one way or the other, kill the fuckers," Nick ordered. "Then take Chappell and Beryl alive if at all possible."

A.J. spoke up. "So, Rowan and I get to go? Are you sure you trust humans along on this op, especially green ones?"

"Fair question. A.J., the rest of the Pack should know that you're more than just a former security guard for one of Chappell's buildings." At the newest man's reluctant nod of assent, Nick addressed the group. "A.J. is a former Dallas police detective and was also part of the SWAT team . . . as a sniper. Of everyone in this room, he's the man most likely to pick off a dozen of those bastards before they even realize what's hit them."

All eyes swung toward the good-looking sandy-haired man. His lips pursed and he looked down at the tabletop.

"Dude, that's awesome," Ryon said.

"No, it's not," A.J. snapped, and Ryon blinked in surprise.

Aric wondered what the guy's story could be, why he'd left the force to become a rent-a-cop, but that was a tale for another day.

Nick quickly took the floor again, steering them away from the uncomfortable exchange. "A.J. has agreed to be the Pack's sniper, an area where he can really excel without having to go hand to hand with our nonhuman opponents. He's been practicing at my request and has accepted the position. Does anyone have an objection?"

It was a moot point if the job already belonged to A.J., but Aric knew Nick would listen. As it turned out, the Pack was supportive, agreeing that having a sniper on the team was a good plan. He'd be loaded with silver bullets for added protection.

"Good. This will also help Kalen, letting him save his magic for bigger problems, and believe me, there *will* be some. As for Rowan," Nick went on, "she's an officer, trained in firearms and apprehending criminals, even if she's used to human ones. She can fight, and she's proven herself in battle as far as I'm concerned— and we need every able-bodied soldier we can get. This is of course up to her, and the Pack has to agree."

"I'd be honored to be included," Rowan said eagerly. "Yes."

"Objections?"

Aric expected one in this case, and not surprisingly it came from Hammer. Their friend who was also sweet on Aric's woman. A growl escaped from Aric's throat, but he managed to make it sound like a cough.

"She did fine before," Hammer said worriedly. "But we didn't know she was with us until it was too late. I've got my doubts about bringing a woman into battle, cop or not."

Oh, the big man would have his hands full with his own mate someday, with an antiquated attitude like that. Aric smirked to himself. Sure, he'd had the same urge to protect Rowan, but he knew she wouldn't have it.

"Are you saying you refuse to fight at her side?"

Nick asked sharply. "That what? Her sex will be a distraction in the heat of danger?"

"No," their friend protested with a scowl. "I'm a better warrior than that, and you know it. You asked, is all, and I said my piece."

"Noted. Anyone else?"

"Nope."

"It's cool, boss."

To Aric, it was anything but cool. Being in the minority, he kept his trap shut. For a change.

"Everyone be armed this time, and use your gifts as you can. Let out your wolf—and panther—only if you have to get that close to one of these creatures. Wheels up in one hour."

The meeting was dismissed, and Rowan turned to Aric. "You're upset that I'm going. I can tell."

"I'm overjoyed," he drawled sarcastically. "Does it make a difference? You'll do what you want because you're as stubborn as anyone I've ever met."

"Including you."

"Yep." He tweaked her nose. "Meetcha at the hangar."

He left her standing in the hallway, and he felt kind of shitty about that. But he needed some distance between this woman and his emotions. He had to psych himself for the coming fight, or risk endangering his friends. His mate.

In his quarters, he stood panting, the fever almost unbearable. He had the strength to get through tonight, barely. This would be his last battle.

He'd make it fucking count.

One hour later, he was armed to the teeth as he strolled into the hangar. He headed for the group and glanced around for Rowan, then spotted her coming in after him. As she joined him, he grabbed a gun from the waistband of his leathers and handed it to her, butt first.

"My extra hand cannon, complete with silencer. Figured you'd need one."

"Thanks. I was going to ask, since they confiscated mine when I got here."

"No problem."

Nobody said much else as they loaded into two Hueys, buckled up, and took off for Texas. Time to kick some Unseelie ass.

And catch his bitch of a wicked stepsister.

They crept through the foliage, and Aric blessed the carpet of pine needles for muffling their approach. They were prickly, and the heavy pine scent in the air made his wolf itch to sneeze, but they were useful.

The Pack fanned out, but Aric kept Rowan close. The woods were almost pitch-black, occasional slivers of moonlight providing a path, like the floor lights in a movie theater. The Pack could see much better, but their human companions were vulnerable.

Thankfully, the cabin wasn't far off the isolated county road, so their trek wasn't as long as some they'd been on. Even though they were moving slowly and cautiously, within a half hour the place came into view. Crouching, they froze as a unit. The hulking shapes of more than a dozen Sluagh were posted in the front, on the porch and perimeter combined. Some lumbering around, a few dozing. One in particular was snoring in one corner of the porch, so loudly he could be heard halfway to Dallas if the wind was right. Aric snorted to himself. No matter how evil you were, good help was hard to find.

"Be careful," Nick whispered. "They just *look* stupid. Go in quiet, kill as many as you can before the alarm is raised, and then A.J. will do his thing. Okay, my group, let's take the back."

Nick, Ryon, Jax, and Zan moved off silently, leaving Aric, Rowan, Kalen, and Hammer to cover the front. A.J. hung back in the trees, sniper rifle in hand. They were as ready as they'd ever be.

Aric's group moved forward, and then spread out to pick off the beasts hanging on the outer edges, the ones alone and close to the shadows. Taking a deep breath, Aric took aim at one and fired. Thanks to the silencer, the shot made the barest whisper. It struck the kill zone and the thing slumped to the ground, dead.

The problem proved to be the noise their rather large bodies made when they fell. Hearing the thump and a grunt from its fallen comrade, one Sluagh swung its big head around, searching for the source of the disturbance.

"Come on, you big bastard," Aric said under his breath. "That's right, come on over and see what's going on."

Sniffing the air, the creature ambled toward his spot. A few steps later, it came upon the other's body and lifted its head to let out a roar. Aric fired again, striking this one in the heart as well, and it crumpled.

To his left and right, his group began taking out the rest of them, but their luck couldn't hold. Someone's shot went wide, hitting one beast in the shoulder instead. The creature let out a booming cry that brought the area to life and made his ears ring.

"Fuck."

Time to dance. They rushed the remaining creatures, picking off as many as they could before the numbers overwhelmed them and he, Hammer, and Kalen had to resort to their gifts. Just as he shot a Sluagh to his right, he spun to find two more nearly on him. He threw out a hand, unleashing his fire, grimacing as they burned, squealing.

Not far from him, Kalen was doing a good job of protecting himself and Rowan from the onslaught, using his magic to dry them to husks. Hammer used his gift as a Tracer, teleporting from one place to another in an instant, barely avoiding decapitation. Aric was so distracted seeing him do that in battle, he nearly got himself gutted.

He collided with one of the creatures, causing him to drop his gun. Shit. In desperation, he pushed his body into the other's massive bulk, then forced a rapid half shift, his fingernails becoming razor-sharp claws. Then he drove them through rancid flesh into the beast's heart. It gave a grunt and fell as he yanked them free again.

Another beast rushed him from the side and he threw out a hand, using his gift of telekinesis to stop it cold, lift it. Then he sent it flying backward with the speed of a runaway train. He gave a shout of triumph as it slammed into a tree with a crunch, slid to the ground, and fell still.

Hammer and Kalen were easily dispatching the last of the Sluagh, though the bigger man was bleeding. Seeing that the path to the front door was now clear, Aric ran, vaguely aware of Rowan racing behind him. He paused long enough to give the front door a couple of hard kicks, and it crashed inward.

Sprinting inside, he searched for the witch. The one he longed to see burn for her crimes. He spotted the white-haired man who must be Chappell running for the back of the cabin, and Rowan shouted.

"I'll get him!" She took off, weapon in hand.

"Be careful!" He scanned the room; it appeared to be empty. Until she spoke.

"Did you miss me so much you had to come back for more?"

Right in front of him, Beryl appeared out of thin air. She hadn't changed. Long hair flowed around a face that should have been beautiful, if not for the ever-present coldness in her eyes and the cruel twist to her mouth.

"I'm here to toast your skanky ass," he snarled, taking a step forward.

She laughed huskily. "Good luck with that."

Aric released his fire again, throwing out a hand. But Beryl was just as fast, uttering a word in Latin and raising a palm toward him. His flames were deflected with a roar as crimson light drove them back, the power of the clash tossing him backward. He landed hard, the hit jarring his spine, and lost his hold on the flames.

The red light enveloped him, entering his body like a million volts of electricity. He screamed, couldn't help himself, the pain was so great. Writhed on the floor like a cockroach that had been sprayed, waiting to die and helpless to do a fucking thing about it.

Then a loud boom sounded and he was released from the light's power. Raising his head, he saw Beryl go flying, crash into a wood-and-glass case, the kind that held little knickknacks. Wood crunched and glass showered everywhere. In the entryway, Kalen stood, staff in hand, whispering another chant and sending a second bolt at the witch.

Aric didn't think he'd ever been so happy to see any of his brothers. No doubt, Kalen was one of them.

Beryl shrieked in pain and rage, flying up into the air with superhuman strength and speed. She flew at Kalen, firing a return blast that lifted him off his feet, propelled him back to smash into a wall. He slid to the floor, and the two of them returned blows.

Aric pushed to his feet, moving around behind the witch. He had to help Kalen while her attention was focused on him. Aric tore off his shirt, let loose his wolf. Shifted, kicked free of his pants and shoes, and ran. He leapt, hitting her between the shoulder blades, taking her to the floor. She twisted and he went for her throat, clamped down, fully intending to tear it out.

"Aric!" Nick's voice shouted. "Don't kill her!"

Damn it! He held his position, kept her pinned. Somehow he managed to suppress the need to tear the head off the bitch who'd caused him such pain. Several sets of footsteps approached, his team joining them. Where the fuck was Rowan?

"Aric, let her up," Nick ordered. "And you, witch. Get to your knees, nice and slow."

Aric moved aside, growling, hackles raised. Ready to go against his leader's command and tear her to shreds if she tried anything. "Now, on your feet. Slowly."

The men surrounded her. Kalen was the closest, keeping a wary eye on her. But even he wasn't prepared when she raised a bloodied finger and pressed it to the center of his forehead.

"Abyssus abyssum invocat," she hissed. Then she

withdrew her hand and licked her own blood from her finger, looking quite pleased with herself.

Kalen's eyes drooped for a moment, and he staggered as though about to pass out. Hammer steadied him and the Sorcerer seemed to shake off whatever she'd done. Immediately, he mouthed his own incantation and the witch went rigid, arms going behind her back.

"She's bound," Kalen said in a tired voice. "We can transport her now."

Aric shifted back to human form and went for his pants. Yanking them on, he looked around for Rowan and spotted her emerging from the hallway. "Thank God," he said, striding toward her. Grabbing her, he pulled her against his chest. "I was way past worried about you."

"I'm good. Chappell, though? Not so much." She sighed, pulling back. "Sorry, guys, but he turned and pulled a gun. I returned fire and shot him in the stomach. He's bleeding out in the master bedroom, and he's not gonna make it. If Nick wants to question him, he'd better get back there."

"Shit," Nick spat. Then he glanced at Rowan, shaking his head. "Not your fault, though. I just wish we could've brought him in. Kalen, Hammer, Ryon, watch the witch. The rest of you can come with me."

They trooped to the bedroom. Aric was as curious as the rest of them to get an in-person look at the man who'd caused so much grief to so many shifter and human families. But when they walked in and saw him sprawled on the floor, clutching his stomach and bleeding out onto the carpet, he simply looked like a pathetic old man.

His complexion was papery as he turned to squint at them, panting hard. What he said next shocked everyone.

"I'm glad you caught me," he rasped. "I'm glad it's over."

His pale blue eyes were clear of malice, his words sincere. Aric had heard somewhere that the dead didn't lie, and he thought it might be true in Chappell's case. Jax crouched next to the older man, placed a comforting hand on his shoulder. Then he closed his eyes, and Aric knew the RetroCog was grabbing the threads of Chappell's past. Gathering the visions that would lead to the truth.

Finally Jax opened his eyes and gazed at Chappell. "You were a good man, and you did great things at NewLife, helping families through organ transplant techniques and medical research. You helped thousands."

"Yes. And then the demon came."

"Malik?" Nick asked, his expression intense.

Chappell nodded. "I never knew such evil truly existed." The old man coughed, and blood bubbled to his lips. "But then he came, and I was lost. He takes what he wants by bending you to his will. He's a seducer, the bastard, and he takes pleasure in the twisting of a soul. In making you enjoy it."

The old man was fading fast. Nick spoke quickly.

"Chappell, tell us how to identify Malik—what does he look like?"

The man gave a laugh that rattled in his chest. "He can be anything, or anyone. But I've seen his true self . . ."

Aric doubted that very much. Sariel had passed

along to Nick and the team the description of Malik he'd given to Rowan—that the Unseelie was ugly as sin with horns growing out of his head. Nick was only trying to discern what form Malik had used with the old man.

"Is he ugly," Nick pressed, "like those beasts he uses as his henchmen?"

"You'd think so, wouldn't you? But no, he's as darkly beautiful as Satan himself . . . black hair and eyes like polished onyx. Huge black wings with blue-black feathers, not leathery ones like those pets of his. Not going to find him like that, though. He can't walk down the street like . . . like that."

Nick cursed. "Then we're right back where we started—without one clue what he really looks like."

"I'm betting Sariel's description is the correct one," Aric said. "He would know better than anybody."

"True." Nick looked back to the old man. "Mr. Chappell, can you tell us what identity he's using to pass among humans? What's his name?"

"He's a millionaire," the man gasped with difficulty. "Goes by Evan . . . Kerrigan."

Nick sighed, relief etched on his face. "Thank you. Because of your help, we have a place to start the search."

Zan, who'd been silent, crouched at the old man's other side. "Mr. Chappell, I can heal you. Let me—"

"No, boy." The man refused the offer quietly. "I've hurt too many."

Zan was not one to easily accept letting a man die. Especially one who'd been innocent, and then controlled against his will. "You were lured into Malik's horrible project, your mind taken hostage just like those being experimented on. He used you like a puppet, and you had no say. You deserve a second chance, and we'll keep you safe. Please, before it's too late."

"Son, it was too late for me when the first person died under one of my own fucking knives. Just promise me you'll get him," he whispered, his eyes meeting Nick's.

"You have my word," Nick said grimly. "One day we'll destroy Malik and use his entrails as Christmas tinsel."

"Good enough. Forgive me . . ." The old man's eyes drifted closed. As they watched, he let out a sigh and then breathed no more.

For a moment, no one moved. Aric's throat was tight. That sure hadn't turned out at all like they'd thought. Chappell had been a great man fallen to a demon, and his death had set him free. It was a sobering, eye-opening few minutes.

"I'll call Grant," Nick said at last. "Have him send a cleanup crew and retrieve Chappell's body. He'll spin a story for the man's family and the press."

"Sweep it under the rug," Zan snapped. "He's mighty fucking good at that."

"Yeah, he is." Nick rose, his face weary. "Let's go."

In the living room, Kalen and the others still stood watch over Beryl, who glared icy daggers at them all. Aric shivered despite the heat lapping at his body again. She'd kill every last Pack member if she got loose, or die trying.

Apparently, Kalen's binding spell had worked on her venomous mouth, too, for which Aric was grateful. Keeping a wary eye on her just the same, he walked over to Kalen and then gave his attention to the spot where she'd pressed her finger. The Sorcerer must've already wiped off the blood.

"What was that she said to you, when she touched your forehead?" Aric asked, cocking his head. He wasn't the only one who wanted to know. Their brothers paused in shuffling around the room to hear the answer.

"*Abyssus abyssum invocat*," he said quietly. "It's Latin for 'hell calls hell.'"

Ryon frowned. "That doesn't sound good. What does it mean?"

"It means when Malik calls, he'll expect me to answer. And if I refuse, there will be hell to pay."

Fourteen

The morning Rowan was scheduled to depart for L.A., Nick called her into his office.

He rose to greet her and then gestured to the chair she'd occupied . . . was it only a week ago? The very place where she'd sat and listened to the most astounding things coming out of his sexy mouth and hadn't believed an asinine word. Until she'd witnessed it for herself, again and again.

When they were situated, he got right to the point. "I wanted to give you this," he said. Reaching into his desk drawer, he pulled out a heavy object and slid it across the surface to her. "I should've let you use it during our shootout at the OK Corral."

"My gun." She smiled. "I figured maybe you planned to keep it."

"Nah. I actually meant to return it before now."

"Thanks." She gave him a thoughtful look. "Somehow I don't think getting my weapon back is the only reason I'm here. You could've just passed it to one of the guys if that's all you wanted."

As always, his smile transformed his hardened countenance into a breathtaking one. "I'd say you didn't need to be a psychic to know that."

She laughed, delighted that he had recalled their sparring that day and tossed her words back at her. "Touché. So, what gives, O Great One?"

"You're the only one I'd let get away with calling me that," he said, only half teasing.

"Why did you?"

"Damned if I know. Anyway, I have something sort of serious to discuss."

"Sounds ominous."

"Not really, unless you count battling nasty supernatural creatures as ominous," he quipped.

"I'm not following."

Leaning back in his rolling chair, he tapped a pen on his desk top. "I want you to think about joining the Alpha Pack team when you return."

After that bombshell, she gaped at him, trying to assimilate what he'd said. "You want me on the team? Are you serious?"

"I don't make offers like that lightly. So, yes, I do."

"But you don't have any women in the ranks, as Hammer pointed out before. How will the guys feel about that?"

"What is this, the Dark Ages? And don't forget, you've already proven yourself in battle, *twice*. The team would be lucky to have you."

"I—I don't know what to say."

"That's a first."

"Har-har."

"Just tell me you'll give it serious thought."

The import of his offer slowly seeped in, and she nodded. "I will. No matter what I decide, I'm truly honored that you'd ask. How soon do you want an answer?"

"It's an open-ended offer, but maybe you shouldn't take too long."

A sense of dread skittered in, like a spider under the bed. "Why's that?"

"Just listen to what this tells you." He placed a fist over his heart, gave his chest a tap, and laid his arm on the desk again.

"So, you're saying there's a reason I should take the job? Is that what you're saying?"

"I can't interfere with your decision, you know that. All I can do is present the options. You have to follow your heart's desire. No one can do it for you."

"And what if that's in L.A.?"

"Then it is." His eyes gave away nothing.

She sighed. "I'll think about it. I promise."

"That's all I can ask." He stood, signaling the end of their meeting. Reaching into his pocket, he pulled out a business card and handed it over. "Call me anytime, day or night."

She studied it, saw that it read only NICK WESTFALL and listed his cell phone number. Nothing more. "Thank you." Taking the card and her weapon, she tucked both into her purse and rose, slinging the strap over her shoulder. "I appreciate all you and everyone else are doing to help Micah recover."

"We'll get him there. It'll just take time."

"I know." She took her leave before this got any harder. "So long, for now."

"I'll see you."

She let herself out and walked to her room to collect her duffel bag, which was already packed and waiting on the bed. How had this place come to seem like home in such a short amount of time? How had the people here come to mean so much?

Especially one man in particular.

In her borrowed quarters, she walked to the bedroom. Every fiber of her being ached at the thought of driving away, leaving him behind. She'd never felt this way, like her guts were being twisted in a giant fist. Like for the first time in her life, she was about to royally fuck up perhaps beyond her ability to repair.

Why should she be tormented over saying good-bye to a casual fling?

Because you know he's more than that, and you're scared. Everyone you've ever cared about has disappeared—Mama, Papa. Even Micah. Yes, he was found alive. But he still left you behind years ago to follow his own dream. You've had no one but yourself to rely on for so long, you don't remember what it's like to just let go. To love without fear.

"Do I love him?"

She thought of how he'd made love to her last, with such tenderness. As though she was priceless to him and he wanted to hold her forever. He'd been hot to the touch, too, more so than ever, and she was worried about him. The idea of anything bad happening to Aric filled her with sick dread.

She longed to stay, keep him safe from harm. Hold him when he was ill, when he was happy. Make him smile, even hear him bitch when he was in a pissy mood.

Was that love?

She blinked several times, realized she'd been staring at her duffel for a minute or two. That wasn't a question she could answer now, when she had a dozen details to settle regarding her life in L.A.

You're running.

"So what?"

She could come back, whenever she wanted.

What if he's not waiting when you do? What if there's someone else?

"Shut up."

Slinging the duffel over her shoulder, she made her way out. Her brother was the first stop, and she discovered him barely awake.

"Hey," he said with a sleepy smile. "Why are ya leaving so early?"

"Long drive, bro." Smiling, she sat and took his hand. "I'll have to stop overnight and make the rest of the trip tomorrow."

"Oh. That's right." He frowned. "I wish you didn't have to go all that way alone."

"I'm a cop, remember? Besides, I made it out here fine, worrywart. I'll call you when I get home if that'll make you feel better."

"It will. But I don't have a cell phone anymore. God knows what happened to my old one."

"I'll just call Nick or Aric. I've got their cell numbers."

Too observant for her comfort, Micah eyed her in speculation. "Ro, I don't want to butt in where it's not my biz—"

"Then don't."

"I have to. You're the only sister I have, and if Aric's playing with your feelings I want to know," he said in a cool voice.

"No, he's not," she said quietly. "That's not it." Fresh pain stabbed her middle, but she pushed it down.

"You have feelings for him." A statement, not a question.

"Yeah. But I'm not sure those feelings are *love*. How am I supposed to know if it's the real thing or just a few great nights fucking each other's brains out?"

Her brother grimaced. "Whoa, TMI. I'm gonna need an extra month of therapy for that image alone, thanks so much."

"You're welcome." It was nice to see he still could joke about some things. "So how do I know?"

"By doing exactly what you are—put some distance between you and temptation. If these feelings quickly become nothing more than a fond memory, you move on. Easy."

"And if my guts still feel like they're being turned inside out a week or a month from now?"

He studied her for a long moment. "Has anyone told you about wolf shifters and mates?"

"Yes." She paused. "Jax and Kira are mates. Aric told me more about the subject, too, like how a wolf shifter needs to bite his intended Bondmate, and then they can't live without each other."

He fell silent. Anxiety formed a knot in her chest.

"Micah, Aric and I are not mates. He hasn't made any move whatsoever to claim me . And he's letting me go without a single protest."

"That doesn't sound like the Aric I know, to let something just go that he really wants." He blew out a breath. "But maybe you're right. Ask him, okay? Just put it out there, point-blank, and ask him if he's sensed a bond between you, if he's felt the need to claim you.

If so, that would explain part of the intense pull between you."

"I'm not sure I should. What if he thinks I'm trying
to trap him or something? I don't want to be a clinging
vine."

"Just do it. He'll be straight with you, if he's the
same guy I've known for years."

"All right. Thanks, little bro." She gazed at him, reluctant to go. "I wish I could stay longer."

"Get going. I don't want you driving after dark."

The order sounded paternal, and coming from him
it was funny. Rising, she gave him a fierce hug, and
then kissed his scarred cheek. "I love you."

"And I love you. Now get before you make me all
mushy."

"See you soon."

"Not if I see you first."

Lifting her purse and duffel, she blew him a kiss and
left, trying not to cry. For the most part she succeeded,
except for a couple of stray tears that she swiped fast,
before anyone saw. She found the guys in the rec room,
Ryon and Zan playing Wii games, the others shooting
the shit and watching TV. Kalen noticed her immediately, and looked over his shoulder at her from his spot
on the sofa.

"Hey, you going already?"

"Afraid so." Her gaze went to Aric and her smile
trembled on her lips. He rose from his spot next to
Kalen and walked over slowly. This was going to be
much harder than she'd believed. "Hi."

"Can I help you to your car with that?"

"Sure."

He took her duffel and the guys hugged her good-bye one by one. Even A.J., whom she was sorry she hadn't gotten to know better. There would be time, though, to foster those relationships. Her brother worked there.

And Nick had given her an opportunity to consider. A great one.

They headed outside and walked around the building to her car. Someone had pulled it up to the front and left the keys in the ignition. Some cop she was— she hadn't even realized the keys were missing in the first place.

Aric tossed the bag into the backseat, shut the door, and then opened the driver's door for her. "I'm going to miss you. Until you come back, that is," he said.

Was that a note of sadness in his voice? Or was it wishful thinking on her part?

"Hopefully it won't be too long. A few weeks at most." She touched his face, traced his lips. "I'll miss you, too."

"You'll probably forget all about me the second you get home, back to the force and the people you're devoted to protecting." His lips curved upward and he nibbled her fingers.

Staring into his beautiful green eyes, she knew that wasn't true. What good was that life, the job that used to mean so much, without this man in it? She'd take a few weeks, see if she felt the same longing to be with him.

"Don't count on that happening," she told him. "I could never forget. In fact, it's highly possible you really aren't getting rid of me."

"What . . . what do you mean?"

"I need to ask you something. Will you answer honestly?"

He shrugged, his gaze wary. "Sure."

"I've felt drawn to you. I've mentioned that before. Now that it's time to go, I feel like my insides are being twisted into a thousand knots, and it's because I'm leaving you. Does it . . . do you feel the same way?"

For several heartbeats, he stared at her bleakly. "No," he rasped. "I don't feel anything like that. I'm sorry."

"Oh." The word emerged as though she'd been punched. "I— Okay. Well. That was stupid of me, huh? Take care, Aric. I'll see you when I come back to visit my brother."

"All right. See you."

She slammed the door shut as soon as he stepped back, fired up the car, and pulled away. Started down the drive without looking back. After he disappeared from sight she let the tears flow. She didn't bother to wipe them away.

No way could she accept Nick's offer now. It would hurt too damned much to work with Aric.

With the man she'd somehow stupidly fallen in love with.

And there she had her answer, at a painful price. She loved him, and he didn't feel the same way. Thank God she hadn't made an even bigger idiot of herself by telling him.

The drive stretched ahead, long and lonely as the trip had been days before. When she'd started out, she never dreamed she'd find her brother alive and experience the greatest high because of it.

She also never imagined finding the one man she could love, here in Bumfuck, Wyoming. And that she'd leave forever changed. Heartbroken.

L.A. loomed ahead, a smog-filled hostile sea of strangers where it had once been home.

The tears didn't stop coming for a long, long while.

Aric watched her go, and as the car was swallowed by the trees around the bend, he sank to his knees. Utter, complete devastation blasted through him, wave after wave of pain. More than he could stand.

His mate. He'd lied and hurt her, sent her away.

He'd never see her again. Not in this lifetime.

Sitting back on his heels, he threw his head back and shouted his anguish to the heavens. The shout became a howl as his limbs reshaped. Fur sprouted and his muzzle elongated. In seconds, the shift was complete.

He let his wolf out and ran. Oh, he'd come back. He'd made his brothers a promise, and he'd keep it.

But they'd find out soon enough that he'd only come home to die.

Rowan sat at her tiny dining table and sorted through the mail. Wasn't much, which was sort of surprising, since it seemed she'd been gone a year.

Bill. Crap. Crap. Bill.

The usual. It took her all of ten minutes to look through and organize the envelopes into what to shred and what was important. The plants were next, though they weren't doing too bad, just a little droopy. Then she tidied the living room, fixed herself a Lean Cuisine, which took all of fifteen minutes to consume, and that was stretching it.

And yeah, the walls were closing in. L.A. was definitely not the Shoshone National Forest, with its majestic mountains and thick trees.

Sluaghs, too. Don't forget those.

Well, here in the city they had shit that was just as bad. She'd like to see one of Malik's pets go up against the East Side Lobos. Now *that* would be worth the price of admission.

Antsy, she reached into her purse and extracted her cell phone to charge it, since she hadn't really used it in days. That's when she finally thought to check her messages, and found she had three from Dean. Damn, she'd forgotten all about him and he was probably dying of curiosity, not to mention worried that she hadn't bothered to check in.

After making sure she had enough charge left, she speed-dialed her friend. He answered on the third ring, his attitude typical Dean.

"It's about fucking time. I was starting to think you'd been eaten by a goddamned Yeti."

"Wrong mountains." *Buddy, you'd never believe what we really ran into.* "As you can see, or rather hear, I'm fine."

"Are you home?"

"Safe and sound. Got in a couple of hours ago."

"I'm coming over. Got any beer?"

"I'm tired, Dean. Drove for a day and a half to get here."

"I won't stay long. I just want the story. I assume there *is* one."

She sighed. "There is. Bring the beer. I'm all out."

"Gotcha. One hour, tops."

Saying good-bye, she hung up and settled onto the sofa to wait. She must've fallen asleep, because she'd just started across a clearing toward a beautiful red wolf she was desperate to reach when a pounding shattered the wisp of a dream and she jerked upright.

The sound came again, a knocking at the door. Rubbing her eyes, she stumbled to the door and peered out, then let Dean inside. The big blond man gave her a one-armed hug and then walked into the kitchen, making himself at home as he removed two longnecks from one of the cartons and put the rest away.

"Okay, spill it," he demanded, twisting the top off one brown bottle and handing it over. "Did you find any sign of what happened to Micah?"

She took a long draw, and wiped her lips. "Better." For the first time since leaving the compound, she smiled. "I found him."

"Really? That's great!" Stepping up, he hugged her again and placed a wet kiss on her cheek. "Why the hell didn't you call me? I've been on pins and needles this whole time, worried that you'd hit another dead end and were probably devastated, and—shit, never mind. How is he? Where has he been?"

Leaning against the counter, Rowan rested the cold bottle against her forehead for a moment, gathering her thoughts. Dean was FBI, and he was a good man. She knew she could trust him. But how much would he believe?

"Micah was captured a little more than six months ago, during an op that went bad. Top secret stuff. He was recovered from the facility where he was being held, shortly after I arrived at the compound you told me about. He was in pretty bad shape, but he's on the road to recovery."

She hoped.

He studied her, the silence stretching out. "That's it? After months of watching you grieve, I get the short version?"

"Dean . . ."

"What was this facility where he was being held?"

What to say? "It's one of many places where some-one pretty well-known is conducting illegal human experiments."

"Human?"

Mentally, she cursed her blunder. "As opposed to chimps and rats."

"Oh. What type of experiments?"

"I really can't say."

"Can't or won't? Come on, Rowan. I searched for months to get you a lead on your brother, and I'd never betray your confidence."

Hesitating, she looked into his dear face, read his concern. He was the one best friend she had, and he'd proven himself time and again. What was more, Nick had never forbidden her from saying anything. She needed to spill her guts to someone she trusted. That would be Dean.

"Bring the rest of the beer. We're going to need it."

Clearly intrigued, he fetched the carton. They car-ried their brews into the living room, placed them in the center of the coffee table, and flopped on the sofa.

And then, she proceeded to tell him everything. From her arrival and being met by shifters, to her wrenching departure. How she'd cried half the way home and just wanted to sleep for a fucking year and forget any of it ever happened. Except she couldn't because that's where Micah was, and where he obviously planned to stay.

When she finished, they'd killed all but two beers and Dean was staring at her, wide-eyed, having not said much for the whole story. Except to interject a question or a heartfelt "holy shit" here or there.

"You think I've gone completely off the deep end, don'tcha?" She picked at the label, feeling a bit fuzzy. Too much trauma and too little sleep on the trip back to L.A., throw in some beer on top of a skimpy Lean Cuisine, and it made for one tired, sad cop.

"Christ, I don't know." He pushed his fingers through his short wheat-colored hair, making it poke in every direction. "In all my life, I've never met a more steady, no-bullshit person than you. You've never lied to me. But this . . ."

"I know it's a lot to swallow. But it's true, every word." She learned toward him, anxious for him to believe her. "I need one person on my side I can talk to about all of this, someone who understands me and won't judge. It's always been you. Please don't humor me, or tell me I'm imagining things because of all the stress. I'm not. It's *real*."

She hadn't realized she'd raised her voice until he laid a hand on her knee and spoke softly. "It's all right, my friend. I need proof just as much as you do when it comes to just about anything I'm told. Job hazard, you know? But because we've known each other so long, I trust that you're telling me the truth."

"You'd still like proof, though, wouldn't you?" She managed a small smile.

"I'm an agent." He shrugged, as if that said it all. And it did.

"Thanks for listening, even if you're still skeptical about supernatural stuff."

"You're my best friend, and that's what friends do." Finishing off his beer, he set it on the table and watched her intently. "What will you do about this Aric guy?"

"What can I do? He said he doesn't feel the same pull toward me that I feel for him. Jesus, my guts are churning and I want to jump in the car and drive all nineteen hours straight through to get to him. What kind of stalker does that make me?"

"You're in love. Give yourself a break. And have you considered that maybe he's just scared?"

"Of what? Me? Commitment?"

"Wouldn't be the first man to run, initially. Could be he needs some encouragement. A little push. One thing for sure, you didn't help your quest to snare him by running home like a whipped puppy."

She curled her lip. "First, I wasn't on a *quest* to *snare* a man. I didn't want a boyfriend." Well, that was a lie. But still, she hadn't been actively looking. "And second, I didn't flee the scene like a criminal—I have a *job*. You know, that thing I do that pays the bills?"

"Whoa, don't bite my head off." His shit-eating grin was cute. "Aren't you conveniently forgetting the job offer the team's boss made to you?"

Frustrated, she waved a hand in the air. "Hellooo! Aric is on said team, and he practically shoved me into my car and launched me back to L.A. Unrequited love and work partners don't mix, as you and I well know."

He winced. "Good point. We've both tried that and failed, haven't we? But I think you ought to reconsider, because I get the sneaking feeling he's not as immune to you as you think. Take some time, is all I'm saying. Don't totally rule it out, or you could really regret it."

A recollection of Nick in his office sprang to mind, placing his fist over his heart.

Just listen to what this tells you.

"Okay, I promise I'll give it some more thought."

"Good. Now, what's to eat around here? I'm starved."

Some things never changed. And that was really, really great to know right now.

Familiarity was all she had to cling to.

After Dean left, Rowan got ready for bed and slid under the covers. Almost as soon as her head hit the pillow, she drifted off, sinking into sleep.

Even then, she couldn't stop thinking of Aric. Longing for her wolf.

Reaching across the vast distance, she pictured the field behind the building. Knew that was where she'd find him because she followed the pull. The damned yearning that refused to be denied.

The field appeared, and she found her toes sinking into soft grass. And across the short distance, the man she sought was bathed in moonlight, the glow illuminating his flawless skin, the lean, rippling muscles. He didn't see her, but stood with his head tilted back, dark auburn hair flowing, gazing at the stars. But he must've sensed her, and he spoke in a low voice as she approached.

"Do you believe that's where we go when we die?"

Moving close, she took his hand. It burned with heat but she didn't release him. "I don't know. I've always preferred the idea that we stay closer to earth, guarding the people we love."

He turned to look at her, a sad smile playing on his lips. "Being a creature of the earth, I like that idea better."

"Why would you be standing out here on a beautiful night like tonight and asking something like that?"

"I wasn't, originally. I was really just standing here, hoping you'd use that gift of yours to find me."

Cupping his face, love swelled in her heart against her will. Without her permission.

"And so I did. Make love to me, Aric," she said breathlessly. With him, she wasn't a cop, a protector. She was a woman, stripped to her bare essence, and it felt incredible.

"You don't know how much I want to." Stroking her face with one hand, he seemed to be memorizing her every feature. "But I can't. I have to go, soon, and I—I wanted to tell you good-bye," he whispered.

Fear seized her soul at the way he'd said that. So final. "Where are you going? Is it an op?"

"No, baby."

"Then what? When will you be back?"

"I don't know." He looked away.

He was lying.

"Tell me the truth, damn you! I deserve to know," she cried, grabbing his arm.

Agony lined his handsome face. "Before you left, I lied. I felt it, too, the pull. I never wanted you to go."

"Then why? I thought you didn't want me!"

"Oh, God. Nothing could be further from the truth. But you deserve much more than a loser like me." Before she could protest, he kissed her lips. Tasted with his tongue, delving into the seam as he pulled their naked bodies close. Then it was over and he backed away. Let go.

"Forgive me for what I did to Micah," he choked out. "Don't forget me."

Then he turned and walked resolutely toward the woods, like a man going to the gallows. She cried his name but she began to be drawn backward, the distance widening until she couldn't see him anymore. Fog swirled around her and she sobbed, lost, calling for Aric.

"Aric, no!"

She awoke, trembling, staring into the gloom of her shoebox of a bedroom in her apartment. Raising a shaking hand to her forehead, she rubbed, trying to clear her mind of the awful dream. The terror gnawing at her gut right now, her no-nonsense inner voice whispering *what if it wasn't just a dream?*

Glancing at the digital clock by the bed, she saw the glowing numbers read three fifteen in the morning. She couldn't very well call Nick at this hour and order him to check on a grown man because she'd had a bad dream.

No. She'd get past this. It was some sort of leftover anxiety making itself known now that she was home. She would call, but she'd wait until the morning and talk to Micah. Pump him enough to hear that everything was all right, and no one would have to know about her little meltdown.

Okay, bad plan. Screw that and go with instinct. That's what good cops did.

Switching on the bedside lamp, she stumbled from the room and went in search of her purse. Inside, she found Nick's card right where she'd put it. Then she retrieved her cell phone from its charger and made the call, pulse racing.

She didn't know whether to be relieved when it went to voice mail, but she left a message just the same. "Nick, it's Rowan. I know it's after three in the morning, but I have this bad feeling something's wrong with

Aric. I had this dream and—well, it's stupid, but call me back anyway when you get this message. Doesn't matter what time. 'Bye."

The next call went to Aric's cell. There, too, she got voice mail.

"Aric, it's Rowan. Did you have that dream just now? The one where you said good-bye? Give me a call back as soon as you get this and tell me that was just some freaky trip, or that you didn't have the same dream, and I'll be happy. Please, call me. I—I miss you."

Damn it. She hadn't meant to add that last bit, but it slipped out. Pressing the END CALL button, she padded back to bed, but laid the phone on her nightstand. Short of driving back to Wyoming, she'd done what she could for now.

Closing her eyes, she drifted into fitful sleep. But this time she didn't dream at all.

Fifteen

Somewhere, a bird was chirping.

No, not a bird. But it was insistent, and pulled him back to consciousness. Aric opened his eyes and fumbled for whatever damned thing was making noise, chirping and buzzing on his nightstand. And of course, in his groggy state, knocked the device onto the floor. His cell phone, he realized.

"Fuck."

It was still night, and by the bedside clock, three twenty in the morning. Who the hell would call him at this hour? Leaning over the side of the bed, he groped for the phone. Lost his balance and landed on the carpeted floor with a thud.

A sizzling noise reached his awareness, and slowly it dawned on him that the sound was coming from the floor, where his palms and knees were braced on the carpet. An acrid smell reached his nostrils. What the hell?

Smoke. The carpet, smoldering.

Lunging for the lamp he switched it on and blinked,

clearing his vision. The carpet was singed and blackened where he'd been kneeling.

"Shit!" Unreal. He was about to set his goddamned apartment on fire.

Scrambling into his bathroom, he sat on the tile, panting. He'd never been this freaking hot since he'd developed his gift as a Firestarter. In fact, he was burning up. Literally. Sweat rolled down the sides of his face, down his chest and spine. God, it was so hard to breathe. And his canines ached with the need to claim the woman who was hundreds of miles away, sleeping soundly. Unless that had been her calling?

Before he could check his phone, he had to try to get cooled off. Pushing himself up, he staggered to the shower and turned the water on cold. Climbed inside and leaned against the tile, facing the spray, watching the droplets hit his skin, then hiss and sizzle. At first he relished the cold water. It felt so good.

Then the soothing effect seemed to wear off. He was so hot he could barely draw in air. His knees gave out and he collapsed onto the floor of the shower stall, barely able to raise his head. Without his mate, his so-called gift had finally turned against him.

"Oh, God." *Help me*.

But there would be no reprieve this time. To ease the pain, he imagined Rowan's sexy face, how gorgeous she'd looked as he made love to her. How lost in the pleasure of their bodies joined.

At least he'd gotten to say good-bye, if only in their dreams.

Nick surfaced from sleep, wondering if he'd heard his cell phone—how long ago? He wasn't sure. Middle of the night calls never boded well, and he had a feeling he should check. Wasn't like he'd get more sleep if he ignored it. So he rolled over and grabbed the thing off his nightstand.

One call, from Rowan at three fifteen. It was three twenty-five now. Gut clenching, he turned on the lamp and pressed the button to play her message.

Nick, it's Rowan. I know it's after three in the morning, but I have this bad feeling something's wrong with Aric. I had this dream and—well, it's stupid, but call me back anyway when you get this message. Doesn't matter what time. 'Bye.

Cursing, he jumped out of bed, completely awake now. Foreboding slithered through him and he knew this was no false alarm. Quickly, he threw on a pair of sweats and a T-shirt and stuck his feet in his tennis shoes without bothering with socks. Then he jogged from his quarters down the hallway to Aric's room, pausing only long enough to pound on Jax's door.

The man opened a long minute later, wearing boxers, smoothing his goatee and peering blearily at Nick. "Boss, what the fuck?"

"I think something's wrong with Aric. I need your help."

Jax came awake, eyes wide. "Give me twenty seconds."

"Tell Kira to go get Mac and Melina," he called after Jax.

In no time the RetroCog was back. "Kira's throwing on some clothes. They'll be right behind us. Think we should get Zan?"

"Good idea."

One more stop, and the three of them were running down the hall to Aric's room. Time was of the essence.

He felt the urgency, pressing down. He didn't bother to knock but punched in his override code to access the door. Then he ran, his men behind him.

The sound of the shower relieved him, but only for a moment. There were no splashing noises, like someone taking a shower. Just a steady stream. No other sounds.

Then he yanked open the stall door and saw why. Aric was sprawled naked on the floor, unconscious. Dark auburn hair streamed over his face, stuck to his chest. Steam rose from his body as the water hit, fogging the glass.

"Jesus Christ," Zan cried, jumping in. He turned off the water and placed a palm on his friend's chest. "He's fucking burning up, from the inside out. I can't—God, I can't heal this. His temperature is out of control."

Jax tossed in a large towel. "Wrap that around him. Can you carry him without getting burned?"

"Yeah, I can neutralize the heat, as long as he doesn't burst into flames."

It was a distinct possibility. Nick watched as Zan tucked the towel around Aric's middle, then grasped him under his knees and behind his back, lifting his friend into his arms. Aric's head lolled back, lashes dark against his pale cheeks.

Goddamnit, they were going to lose him—unless they got Rowan here, fast.

They met the women in the corridor, and the group hurried toward the infirmary. When they got there, a rumpled-looking Noah met them, obviously having been dragged from his bed as well. Mac stopped Nick from following Zan into the room where they were getting Aric settled.

"Let us help him. You'd only be in the way right now."

"But he's—"

"I know," she said gently. "Let us do our job."

Blowing out a breath, he relented. "Sure. I'm sorry."

Squeezing his arm, she disappeared into the room. In moments, Zan emerged, having been booted out to wait with the rest of them.

"If that snarky bastard dies," the Healer ground out, "I'm going to play nonstop country music over his grave as punishment. What the fuck is wrong with him, Nicky?"

Everyone felt his pain. The desperation of possibly losing a great soldier. A good friend and fine man. They deserved to know.

"Rowan is his mate, remember? And he let her go without telling her—and more important, without claiming her."

"I can't believe we let the dumb-ass do that," Jax croaked. "He saw what happened to me!"

"He doesn't feel like he deserves Rowan because of what happened to Micah and the team. He didn't say anything about Beryl, and she ended up hurting all of you. Half your number are still missing, and he blames himself for that, too."

Zan punched the wall, leaving a dent. "What a bunch of shit! Nobody blames him! Why can't he wrap his stupid brain around that fact?"

"Now what?" Kira asked.

Nick took his cell phone from the pocket of his sweats. "We get a certain cop here, pronto. I'm sending the jet to L.A. Who wants to pilot?"

"I'll do it," Jax volunteered. "My license is current."

Kira spoke up. "I'll go with you. I'm betting she's going to need another woman to talk to about the mating thing."

"Good idea," Nick said. "Go. I'll tell her to meet you at our landing strip east of the city."

The couple left and Nick went to the waiting area to make the call. Zan followed and sat across from him, silent. Nick waited, not surprised when she answered on the second ring.

"Hello? Nick?"

"It's me. Rowan, listen to me—you were right. Something has happened and I need you here right away."

"Oh, God! It's Aric, right? What's wrong with him?"

"Jax and Kira are on their way in our jet, and they'll explain when they arrive. Pack your stuff and be at the landing strip in two hours. Can you do that?"

"Of course. Give me directions and I'll be there." Her voice had calmed, taking on that cop tone he'd come to know so well.

Right then he knew without a doubt that Rowan would do whatever she could to save Aric. She loved the man. There was hope.

He gave her directions to the strip and hung up, slumping in his seat. He and Zan didn't speak. They just listened to the clock tick on the wall, and prayed that Jax could get Rowan back here in time.

Rowan showered quickly, got out, dressed. Opting for simple, she pulled her hair into a ponytail and went with little makeup, applying only enough so that she didn't look like a corpse at almost six in the morning.

Next she repacked her duffel with clothes for a good

week or more. Then she called Dean and left him a message, telling him what she knew. Which wasn't much.

A call to her sergeant was next, and boy, was that one as fun as a colonoscopy. He wasn't amused to learn that she wasn't coming back on shift this morning as scheduled. His ominous tone as he spoke the words "We'll *talk* when you return" didn't bode well. It hit her that she might not have a job to come back to.

And then it occurred to her that she really didn't care.

The one thing that mattered was Aric, and something terrible had happened. All she could think of was getting to him. After watering her plants, she scooped up the bills from her table and stuck them in her purse. She'd mail them from Wyoming.

Then she was on her way, leaving L.A., and she had the strangest notion that she wouldn't be back. But she'd have to return, wouldn't she? She chewed on that all the way to the strip, and some more as she waited for the jet that would whisk her to Aric.

Finally it appeared, dipped low and came in for a smooth landing. The craft taxied to the end of the runway, and the pilot didn't even bother to shut it off. Instead, the door opened and Jax popped out, jogging over.

"Here, let me help you with that," he said, taking her duffel and slinging it over one shoulder. "Come on. There's not one minute to waste."

She trailed him, panic beginning to eat at the edges of her self-imposed calm. What could have happened? What could be so bad? And why would they come after *her* in the middle of the night? She didn't see how she could help, grateful as she was to be able to get to him quickly. Jax tossed her bag in, and held out a hand to assist her into the plane.

"In you go. Kira rode along with us. She thought you could use some company, and an explanation."

Relief swamped her. "I appreciate that, more than you know."

"Oh, I have some idea." With a kind smile, he climbed in and shut the door, heading for the pilot's seat. "Buckle up."

She took a seat next to the petite blonde and snapped her seat belt in place. Normally she hated takeoffs, but this one barely phased her. She was much too upset to think about the plane ride.

Kira smiled warmly at her, but Rowan could see the worry shadowed in her eyes. "Hey. I thought you could use a friend."

"I could, thank you. You know, I don't have many girlfriends," she mused. "I guess it's because I've worked for so long in a male-oriented environment. Most women don't warm up to me because of it, especially the cops' wives."

"They think you're out to prey on their men?"

Rowan laughed humorlessly. "Something like that."

"Well, they're stupid bitches, then. Anyone can see what a great heart you have."

"Thanks. So tell me, what's wrong with him?"

Kira was silent for a long moment, then met her eyes. "He's sick, Rowan. I mean, *deathly* sick."

"He . . . he could die?"

Kira's eyes filled with tears. "Yeah. I just hope we make it in time."

Rowan felt the blood drain from her face. "With

what? How? He seemed fine when I left him!" But had he, really? Now that she thought about it . . . he hadn't seemed like himself. There was also that fever the doctors had been concerned about.

"You know about wolf shifters' mates, right?"

"Some. The other day, I didn't want to leave Aric. The idea alone made me sick, and it physically hurts to be apart from him. Before I left, Micah told me to ask Aric if he felt the same pull I did. So I asked, and he denied it. Christ, it still hurts."

Kira took her hand. "Honey, Aric lied to you. He felt drawn to you, like you did to him."

"That's what he said in my dream. What does it mean?" She blinked, making the connection at last. Damn, she was dense. "Wait, are you saying we *are* mates?"

"Yes. And he's known it all along."

The truth ripped through her, the pain almost too much. "Why would he lie? Does he not want to be tied to a cop? Or he doesn't want *any* mate?"

"Nothing like that. He doesn't feel worthy of your love, of being your Bondmate."

Rowan stared at her. The light shone through. "Because of Beryl and what happened to Micah and the team."

"Exactly. He feels like he should pay, and to him that means denying his mating. When a wolf shifter doesn't claim his mate within a certain amount of time, he gets sick. Jax got sick because he didn't want to push me into mating before I was ready, the idiot."

"Hey, I heard that!"

"Anyway, what Aric is going through runs deep. He honestly feels he's doing the right thing, and is unworthy."

God, this was messed up. "How does he claim me?"

"He bites you. Pretty simple, or it would be if he was conscious. They'll have to try to rouse him so he can do it."

She didn't want him to die. No matter her remaining doubt about them as a couple, she would not let that happen.

They fell silent for a few minutes. Then Rowan looked at the hand still holding hers and felt the tears well up. "Thank you for being here. It helps."

"You're welcome," Kira said softly. "But there's one more thing you need to know. After you mate, there's a good chance you could turn into a shifter, too."

"Sure, why not?" Her laugh was a little desperate. "I've encountered just about everything else, why not me getting furry?"

"It's not so bad. Actually, it's really fun to run with Jax through the woods while we're in wolf form. And then there's the hot, naked forest sex when we shift back."

This time Rowan's smile was real. "You do make a good point."

"I thought so."

They lapsed into silence and Rowan fidgeted for the rest of the trip. After what seemed forever, the plane was touching down. Scrambling out, she turned to reach for her duffel and Jax waved her off.

"Go on. I'll take this to the room you were in before."

"Thanks. I appreciate you guys coming to get me in the wee hours."

"Not a problem."

Rowan hurried to the infirmary, Kira at her side.

They burst in and Noah jumped up from the desk on seeing Rowan.

"Thank Christ! Come on, the docs are waiting for you."

He hurried her to one of the rooms, a couple of doors down from Micah's, and ushered her inside. Nick, looking haggard, was propped in one corner. The two doctors hovered on either side of the bed, Melina taking Aric's vitals. There were bundles wrapped in towels, one sitting on Aric's chest, others tucked against his sides. Rowan walked over, laid her hand on one bundle. Ice packs.

"He was literally burning up," Melina told her. "Those seem to be helping."

"How is he, really?"

"Not good. Honestly, I don't know if he'll be able to bite you—if you agree to it."

"Of course I do! I lo—" She stopped herself, took a deep breath. "I want him to be the first to hear how I feel. But, yes, I agree."

"Great. Now we need to get some of your blood into his mouth, try to stimulate his instinct to clamp down on you. Give me your finger."

Rowan held out her arm, palm up. Melina snapped on a pair of latex gloves and took a finger-pricking device from the counter. Rowan hated those things. The doctor wiped the tip with alcohol and positioned the instrument, then let it snap. Blood welled and the doc squeezed to get a nice, fat drop, then swiped the drop onto her own latex-protected digit.

"I'm going to put my finger in his mouth, and hope your blood stimulates a response. It's worked before, so hopefully it will again."

"Why not let me put *my* finger in?"

"You can, after I make sure he's not going to become too aggressive. Step one."

"Okay."

Melina used one hand to pry Aric's jaw open. It didn't appear too difficult, as lax as his muscles were. Then the doctor eased the finger with the droplet between his lips, and seemed to be massaging his tongue. Though it was to save his life, a big part of Rowan coiled in anger at the idea of anyone touching her man's tongue, or any other part of him.

After a moment, his jaw moved. His lips closed around the finger and he began to suckle like a babe at his mother's breast—another image she could do without.

"All right, come here and we'll replace my finger with the one I poked. Be sure to squeeze out more blood first."

Rowan did as the doctor said, and slipped her finger inside Aric's mouth as Melina removed her own. It felt weird, his tongue curling around it, hot and wet. Even that small connection was far too intimate with an audience, but she resolutely ignored them. This was for Aric.

With her free hand, she stroked his hair. "Come on, baby," she whispered. "Come back to me, you stubborn man. Why the hell did you do this to yourself? Wake up so I can yell at your stupid ass."

Making a noise in the back of his throat, he sucked a little harder, more eager to get her essence. She doubted he was aware of what he was doing or why, but maybe it would bring him to the surface. A few more minutes passed, however, and he seemed to be tiring again.

"I have an idea," Rowan said to the group. "Scoot him over so I can stretch out next to him. If I envelop him in my scent, maybe that'll bring him around."

"Excellent idea," Mac said. "At this point anything is worth a shot."

Nick assisted the women in moving Aric over just enough for Rowan to lie next to him. She situated herself on her right side, facing him, and stuck her finger back into his mouth. "Now do me a favor and give us some privacy, please? He's going to bite me, or he won't. Either way, we don't need an audience hovering."

Obviously reluctant to give her assent, Melina thought for a few seconds before replying. "All right. But we'll be back to check on you both."

The group filed out and Rowan let out a sigh. "Well, at least we can talk privately. Or how about I talk and you listen? You're going to be a good wolf and bite me, do you understand? And then if you don't want a mate, I'll go back to California and you'll never have to see me again."

A small growl rumbled in his chest, and she took that as a positive sign. Snuggling closer, she nuzzled his cheek and his hair, doing her best to make sure he couldn't escape her scent. This had to work. If it didn't . . .

She would *not* lose him. Not an option.

Resting her head on his shoulder, she began to talk. And talk, until her voice was hoarse.

He floated, twisting in agony. Nightmares of fire and death consumed him.

He'd surfaced now and then, but the pain was too

much. Not just physical, but the awareness of all he'd lost. He was ready to give up, to embrace the end.

And then a sweet flavor burst on his tongue. Delicious. There was something in his mouth, and it carried whatever tasted so good. Candy? No. It was warm, alive.

Flesh. Someone's finger. And . . . blood?

That made no sense. He was a wolf, not a vampire. But wolves liked blood when they ate a rabbit or a deer. This taste wasn't from an animal, though.

As his thoughts became more lucid, he became aware of warmth at his side. Instead of adding to the discomfort of the internal fire that raged, it was a comfort. So was the heady scent teasing his nose. Ocean spray and flowers wrapped around his senses, giving him peace, soothing the agony.

His wolf recognized the owner of that wonderful scent before he did, and whined, needing to get closer. *Mate. Mine.*

Rowan?

Had he said her name aloud? He tried again. "Ro?"

"I'm here, honey." Arms wrapped around him and his face was pushed against her skin.

Jesus, she smelled so good. Felt right against him. He nuzzled the curve of her neck and his canines lengthened. He longed to claim his mate, thought he shouldn't, but couldn't remember why not.

"Bite me, Aric," she whispered. "Make me yours."

Parting his lips, he let his teeth graze along the delicate skin. God help him, he couldn't resist one more second.

He struck, sinking his teeth into her neck. Her ambrosia exploded on his tongue and his body detonated.

Rode wave after wave of ecstasy as his mate screamed her pleasure.

Mine!

His. For always.

"Bite me, Aric," Rowan whispered. "Make me yours."

For a second, she didn't think he would give in. His teeth scraped the curve of her neck and shoulder, and he hesitated. And then he sank his canines deep.

Instant, unbridled, bone-melting joy lit her like a torch, from the inside out. A golden thread wound its way through their souls, binding them together for always. She actually felt it, and saw it in her mind's eye, and knew it was real.

Vaguely, she was aware of screaming. *That's me. God, it's so good!*

Footsteps came running, the door opened. Then they must've quietly slipped away, because as she drifted back down to earth, she opened her eyes and they were alone together.

Withdrawing his fangs, Aric licked the wounds. "Mine," he rasped. "My mate."

"Yes, yours. And you're mine." She hugged him close.

Then his body went slack. At first she was alarmed, but then she realized the horrible heat that had radiated from his body was noticeably lessened. His face was relaxed, but he wore a faint smile, as though he'd just seen heaven. He was simply sleeping.

"Thank you," she said to whatever higher power had saved him. Or maybe he'd saved himself. But she had to thank someone.

And she owed him a butt-chewing when he woke up, for scaring the shit out of them all.

Sunshine. Warm, on his face.

The light didn't burn, and to Aric's surprise, he wasn't hot anymore. In fact, he was damned cozy, with someone snuggled against his side. Prying his eyes open, he let his vision adjust and craned his neck to look down at the woman whose head was resting on his chest, brown hair fanned out. He liked being her pillow, and smiled a little.

But wait—he was supposed to be sick. Dying. How was she here, and he was . . . normal?

Yeah, he felt fine. Tired, but okay. Thinking hard, he cast about for an explanation—and remembered. "Oh, God."

He'd bitten Rowan. Claimed her.

Mine, his wolf rumbled, immensely pleased with himself.

The man, however, was ashamed. How could he have done this? Tied her to the likes of him forever? "Rowan," he said quietly, jostling her gently. "Baby?"

She stirred some. "Mmm?"

"Ro, wake up." He kissed the top of her head, his heart beating a strange tattoo in his chest. He wanted to deny what he'd done, but he felt protective of the bond. Like his soul absolutely would not accept his denying it now.

Stretching, she raised up and gave him a sleepy smile. "You're awake. How do you feel?"

"Pretty good, actually. Better than I should."

"Oh, no. We're having no self-pity in this mating,"

she said firmly. "Grow a pair of balls, wolf, and use them."

His eyes widened. "Are you calling me a pussy?"

"If the vagina fits."

He choked, not sure whether to laugh or be pissed. He went with amusement, as he just didn't have the heart to be mad at his mate. She'd obviously rushed to his side, and saved his sorry ass. "Is that so? I don't care how tough you are, officer. My balls will always be bigger than yours."

"Thank God for that." Her chocolate eyes were soft with emotion. "I'm so happy the bite worked. I hope you're happy, too."

He cupped her face. "I don't deserve to be, but yes, I am."

"See, we've got to work on that 'I don't deserve you' thing. It's self-destructive, and you're wrong. Beryl and Malik are the ones who've orchestrated every step of their plan, no one else. Isn't it time you stopped taking the blame for that bitch's manipulations?"

For the first time, he really thought about that. The truth seeped in, and looking into Rowan's beautiful face, he was freed. From the horror and the guilt. All of it. "Yes, it is. I'm not saying it will be easy, but I'm willing to put it behind me for you."

"For *us*."

"Right. For us."

"Will you talk to Mac? Let her counsel you so you can heal? I want you healthy, honey, inside and out. It's the only way we'll make it."

He could refuse her nothing. "Sure." Something else occurred to him, a big stumbling block. "What about your job? I know how much you love being a cop."

"I do, but . . ." She thought for a moment. "When I left here, I felt like my heart was being ripped out. Yes, a lot of it was the mating pull, but that's not all. This place, with you in it, feels like home. Micah is here, and I know if I stay, eventually I'll be as close to the guys as I am to my own brother."

Anxiety made his pulse pound. "What are you saying?"

"That I want to stay." Tracing his lips, she whispered, "I love you."

This is happiness. I've waited so long.

"All my life I've wanted to hear those words from someone who meant them," he said in a tight voice. "Baby, I love you, too."

Their lips came together and his body ignited—in the best way possible. His cock hardened between them, demanding to get in on the lovin'. "I need to be inside you," he gasped. "I can't wait."

"I don't think you're in any shape to do the actual deed just yet." She smiled when he made a noise of protest. "But I can help with your problem."

Scooting lower on the bed, she pushed the blanket aside to reveal his naked body. A couple of towel-wrapped bags fell on the floor on the other side of the bed, and he vaguely remembered being iced down. Now he relished the good kind of heat and she leaned down and licked the leaking crown of his cock.

"Do you feel naughty?" she murmured. "Getting head from your mate when anyone could walk in?"

"Shit," he moaned. "Please . . ."

"Well, since you beg so nicely."

Her tongue traced circles around the tip, captured the tiny beads that continued to seep out. He was hard as a freaking rock, the shaft red and throbbing. When she slid him into her mouth, down her throat, he thought maybe he'd died after all. She sucked him, putting just the right amount of pressure, laving the ridged underside. His hips canted upward and he buried a hand in her silky hair, urging her on.

"I'm not gonna last, sweetheart," he panted. "Oh, so good."

The tingle started at the base of his spine and his balls tightened. True to his word, he couldn't have stopped if he'd wanted to. There would be more time, all of their lives, to make love any way they wanted.

That thought alone made him lose control. With a shout, he shot hard, pumping his seed endlessly down her throat. She drank him greedily, not spilling a drop, then released him to sit up and wipe her lips, grinning.

"Next time, I want this bad boy inside me," she said in a naughty voice. "As soon as you're on your feet."

"Nothing will keep me away from you. That's a promise."

"One I look forward to you keeping."

They snuggled together again, and Aric focused on healing. For himself, and his mate.

Sixteen

"Aric? Honey?" Rowan called across the rec room to her man, who was busy in a life-or-death battle with Jax on the Wii.

"Yeah?" Her mate continued leaping around like a frog as they played whatever stupid game they'd started almost an hour ago.

"Is the honeymoon over already?" she muttered, scratching her arms.

"What?" He jumped again, and hooted as he scored a point against Jax.

"I'm itching." The more she scratched, the worse it got.

"Stop scratching!"

"I can't!" Damn it, it was everywhere. Her arms, neck, stomach, hands, and feet. "I'm about to lose my mind."

Finally he stopped playing and walked over to her, frowning in concern. "Did you use some of that cream Melina gave you?"

"Yes, and it hasn't helped." She sighed. "I'm going back to our quarters to take another shower."

"I'll go with you." Taking her hand, he called "Later" to Jax and walked back with her. Once there, he punched in the code and let them in. "You want something cold to drink? It might not help, but it would taste good, right?"

Bless him, he really was worried now and was trying to be of help. She gave him a smile and kissed him soundly. "Sure. Some kind of soda would be great."

"Okay. Be right there."

She continued on to the bedroom, started stripping off her clothes. Every fiber of her shirt and jeans seemed to aggravate the problem, and it was annoying as hell. Once naked, she inspected herself in the dresser mirror, and saw nothing out of the ordinary. The only marks visible were the ones from her own fingernails as she'd scratched like a dog with fleas.

Or wolf. Could it be . . . ?

Just then, a sharp pain gripped her stomach. Clutching her middle, she gasped, managing to stifle a cry. Maybe it would pass, and she didn't want to scare Aric. But a second pain followed on the heels of the first, this one radiating to every limb. Her legs folded and she hit the floor with a thud, but that didn't hurt an ounce compared to the knives stabbing her arms and legs.

"Aric!" she cried, tears welling. Curling into the fetal position, she grabbed her stomach.

"Rowan, what— Oh, shit!" The can of soda went rolling as he dropped to his knees and scooped her into his arms. Quickly, he laid her on the bed and started checking her for injuries. "What happened, baby? Where does it hurt?"

"All over," she whimpered. "I—I'm being stabbed."

"Where?"

"Arms and legs. It hurts!"

"I'll call Melina." He started to get up, but she grabbed at him.

"Don't leave me! Just hold me, please," she begged. Never had she been so needy. All she wanted was Aric. "I've never felt anything like this."

"Is the pain better?" he asked anxiously. Sitting on the bed, he moved her into his lap, holding her protectively in the circle of his arms.

"Some. But I'm tingling and I don't feel good. Sort of sick, like I ate something bad."

He fell silent, rubbing her back. When he spoke again, he was much more calm. "Sweetheart, this is exactly the way I felt right before my first shift. And it was about two weeks after I'd been bitten."

"Same as me." As she looked into his face, sweat popped out on her forehead and her fear increased. "I don't know if I can do it," she whispered. "Not if it will always hurt like this."

"It doesn't, baby, I swear. Just the first time." He kissed her, slow and soothing.

"I don't know what to do." She hated the whiny tone in her voice. Hated feeling weak.

"Okay, let's see." He thought for a second. "Try opening your mind to your wolf. Let her in. Do you feel her?"

Closing her eyes, she took a deep breath and concentrated on relaxing. Wasn't easy with the pain still twisting her limbs, but she reached down with her mind. "I sense something. A presence?"

"I'd bet that's her," he said, starting to sound excited. "Do it again, and try not to think so hard."

"Easy for you to say." But she tried, delved deeper. This time, an image of a wolf came to mind. Sable, like Micah, but smaller. She gasped, and the image vanished. "Was that me? I saw a brown wolf!"

He grinned. "You're getting there. You have to call her, and make her obey. Want me to shift? It might help."

"Okay, let's try it."

She watched as Aric rose from the bed and began taking off his clothes. Lord, he was gorgeous and she was the luckiest woman alive. Naked, he knelt on the bed, his green gaze holding hers, auburn hair flowing over his shoulders. His full mouth quirked and his eyes smoldered. The man knew full well she loved what she saw, how he affected her.

He shifted slowly, and she figured that was for her benefit, so she could study the process in a way she never had before. His face reshaped, his nose becoming a muzzle, red hair becoming fur, ears tufting. His arms and legs became canine, his chest rounded. His tail was plush and wagging playfully as the change was completed, tongue lolling.

"You're beautiful," she said, rubbing his head. She laughed as he butted under her hand, obviously wanting a scratch. "I don't know if I can do it . . ."

She'd barely finished that thought when her stomach turned over. The tingling under her skin became a swarm of bees. Inside, her wolf growled, making its presence known at last. She stared at Aric and saw concern. Encouragement, too, as he licked her face.

Then suddenly, she had no choice any longer. She yelped in alarm as the first of the changes jerked her body. A picture of Pinocchio came to mind as her face elongated, particularly her nose. Fortunately, her muzzle seemed the right size when it stopped growing. Then her arms and legs began to thin and fur sprouted. Her hands became paws, her torso reshaped. And something was sticking out of her ass . . . She turned as best as she could to see her brown furry rump, with a tail standing up like a flag. Giving an experimental wag, she found it worked just fine.

A happy bark brought her attention back to Aric. Her mate danced around her on the bed and nipped playfully at her butt. She nipped back at him, but then her attention was caught by her reflection in the dresser mirror.

Oh, my God!

But the words came out as a bark. Looking back at her was a sable wolf, smallish, just like in her vision. Her coat was full and shiny, her face delicate. She'd never been delicate in her life, so this was a nice change. *I make a darned pretty wolf if I do say so!*

You bet you do, beautiful! And you're all mine.

She spun around to face Aric, stunned. *You can hear me?*

Yep. Kira and Jax can communicate like this, or so they've said. I didn't know whether it was true, but apparently we can, too. Cool, huh?

Yes! I can't believe this. I'm a wolf.

Pretty shocking for a big-city cop.

And then some.

Try out your doggie legs? He jumped off the bed and jogged to the door, waiting.

Here goes. She leapt, hit the floor and wound up in a heap. Aric's laugh echoed in her head and she scowled. Or tried to. *Don't laugh at me, buddy. See if you get any tail, so to speak.*

Hey, no need to get cranky.

Trotting over, he pushed his body into hers, encouraging her to get up. She stood on shaky legs and followed as he led her out, down the hall, and into their living room. For a while they simply walked around, letting her get used to the new form and moving on four legs instead of two. She did fairly well, and he began to nip and play again, wanting her to join him.

Throwing herself into the spirit, she nipped back, growling, faking being the baddest wolf. He snarled, showed his huge teeth and she yelped, taking off, jumping the coffee table, scrambling onto the sofa, and leaping over the back of it. He was right behind her as she sprinted in circles around the living room.

Fierce joy overflowed as they ran. She'd never been so free. She loved this man, her wolf, and was loved in return. He caught up and jumped on her, taking her to the floor, but he didn't hurt her. He was very careful, even as they roughhoused. She enjoyed every second, thinking everybody nearby must hear their barking and growling.

Finally, they tired and lay on a rug, panting. Slowly, her mate shifted back and propped his chin in his hand, smiling.

"Okay, your turn. Shift back. Same way you did before, in reverse. Call to your human half."

After the agony of the first impending shift, returning to human form was surprisingly easy. She imagined herself as Rowan, with human features. It worked, and the change happened smoothly, in seconds, leaving her naked and with an armful of horny mate.

"God, you're beautiful." He kissed her hard, and

deep. "I could just eat you up. In fact, I think I will. Roll onto your stomach."

"Bossy."

"You love it."

He had a point. She did as he said, and he spread her legs wide, crawling between them. She felt him lying down, the puff of breath on her sex. They almost made a daisy chain—well, one with only two links. That's all there ever would be.

"I'm gonna eat that sweet pussy," he said, his voice husky. "You want?"

A little jolt went through her at the dirty talk. Their last few times together had been sweet, tender. This was a side of him that called to her on a whole different level, especially now that they were bonded. Nothing was truly dirty as long as it was the two of them, and it fueled her desire all the more.

"Yes, please!"

"Say it," he demanded.

"Please, eat me," she begged, breathless.

"That's my girl. I'll take good care of you."

She moaned as fingers opened her, and his tongue began to lick her core. It did naughty things no normal tongue should be able to do, sliding deep to fuck her. In and out, steadily driving her crazy. Feeling decadent, she spread wider. *Take all of me. Do what you want.*

Oh, I will, sweet baby. Count on it.

He licked her slit, teased the little button. She writhed, needing more, and lifted her hips to send him the message. From his chuckle, he received it.

"You need my cock fucking your pretty pussy, baby?"

"Y-yes! Fuck me, please!"

His lean body covered hers, and the round helmet of his cock slipped between her folds. He pushed deep, thrust all the way to the hilt. Then began a sensual grind that made her nerves sing. The man fucked like he did everything else in his life—with his heart and soul. He worked his rod in her channel, driving them both to the edge.

She couldn't last. Didn't want to.

Her release exploded and she cried out, spasming around his length. He thrust two, three more times, and stiffened, filling her with his seed. His fingers twined in hers and he lay over her back, kissing her neck.

"Beautiful," he murmured. "Thank you, my sweetheart. Love you."

"Love you, too." Lethargy set in and she felt herself melt into the rug.

"My poor tired mate. You've been through a lot today. Let's take a nap, huh?"

"Sounds great."

Vaguely, she was aware of him pulling out, standing. Gathering her into his arms. She rested her cheek against his chest, safe and warm.

She was asleep before he laid her on the bed and tucked her close to his heart.

Hell calls hell.

Go to her, Kalen. She waits.

Kalen dropped the TV remote, heart pounding. He stood, glancing around his apartment in fear, but Malik wasn't there. Not in the flesh, anyway. The Unseelie king couldn't break the wards to get into the compound—or so Kalen hoped.

"Go to who? Never mind, it doesn't matter. Leave me the fuck alone!" he shouted.

Not going to happen. You need me, and I'll not abandon you as everyone else in your life has done.

"I have the Alpha Pack now," he seethed. "They're good to me. They've become my friends. I'll bet *you* don't have any of those."

I have something better—power. You have it, too, my little diamond in the rough. So much raw, untapped power begging to be developed, harnessed, channeled in the proper direction. I can do that for you. All you have to do is surrender to me, your master.

"My *what*? You're a crazy bastard. Not gonna happen," he snarled, tossing the Unseelie's words back.

An amused laugh curled around Kalen, making him shiver. The faint crackle of electricity shimmered in the air around him, like someone balling up cellophane. A ghostly touch, like that of a finger, trailed down his cheek. Continued on, dipped into the vee of his black button-down shirt.

You belong to me now, and you'll do as I order. You have no choice. Do not fight me.

The phantom hand skimmed his stomach, and finally, slipped to his zipper and the aching bulge there. For a moment, he allowed himself to drink in the pleasure. Would it be so bad to be owned by one so powerful, who could make him feel—

Gasping, he jerked backward, away from the forbidden. "No. I don't belong to you!"

Yes, you do, my boy. Every inch of you is mine.

Never had he run up against a being whose power rivaled his own. Never even close. In spite of himself, he was intrigued. Lured. Darkness seeped into his mind and he knew that it was Malik. Tried to push him out. But the dark lord was stronger, and an image began to form, come to life.

Kalen's body, naked. Spread in submission. Hands and mouths, devouring him. Consuming his body and soul. He wanted them to take all of him. Fuck and use him.

Beryl looked up at him from between his thighs. *Give yourself to our master. He alone knows what we truly are, what we need.*

"But, Mackenzie," he began, voice breaking. He was weakening under their onslaught.

You're not together, Beryl said. *You made that clear to her. You belong to Malik now.*

She took his cock between red lips, sucked him down. He wanted someone to claim him, longed to be loved. Malik answered.

I will give you everything you need. Allow me in.

"Yes," spilled from his lips. "Master." The blackness entered his heart, delicious. Like dark molasses. His cock drove into the hot mouth, fucked it with abandon. The wicked pleasure was too much and his orgasm rolled over him. He came with a shout, filling her mouth as she suckled him dry.

As the tremors of release faded, he looked down. Beryl was gone, and his clothes were still in place. His cock was softening, but a quick check revealed there was no come in his jeans. Had she ever been there? Was it just a vision?

Very good, my boy. You will have all the sex your body can stand, all the acceptance you desire. Do you want these things?

"Yes, Master," he whispered, reaching for the pendant that wasn't there. That would never again protect him from the evil that raced like heroin through his veins.

Then see to your first task. Go to the Pack's basement and release Beryl. She has one last task to perform before she leaves us.

"Leaves?" He frowned, trying to clear his head.

Beryl was never meant to remain with us, my pet. She's a tool, nothing more. Release her, then feign horror at what you've done. They must not know you're mine now.

"I'll do as you say."

This was wrong. He knew it, but couldn't find the foothold he needed to fight against such a dark being. Exiting his room, he walked the corridors, searching for the elevator to Block T—which stood for "Termination." The witch would be executed soon, for her part in Malik's heinous crimes, whether she talked or not.

Locating the elevator, he rode it down to the basement and got out. The witch's cell wasn't hard to find, as there weren't many and hers was the only one occupied. She moved to the door and gave him a catlike smile, as though she'd been expecting him.

"Good blow job?"

"So that really was you?"

She shrugged. "No. It was Malik. You already know he can change forms, and he's great at projecting his spirit-self."

"But was it *real*?"

"Who's to say? Malik is the master of the mindfuck. It's as real as you want it to be."

Cold sweat formed on his brow. He couldn't think of that now. He had a task to perform. Quickly, he uttered a spell and the lock popped, then the door slid open on its track. Beryl stepped out and pushed into his chest, thrust her tongue into his mouth, kissing him for several moments before breaking away. "There's more where that came from, later. Right now, I have to see to my task. Take the next elevator so we're not seen together."

He shrugged, but said nothing. Little did the witch know there wouldn't be "later" for her. Either the team would kill her or Malik would. He didn't care which.

As she left, he struggled against that fact—that he didn't care about her life. That wasn't him, but the feelings of empathy weren't there. As though Malik had surgically removed them.

He waited. When the elevator returned, he followed.

"What have I done?" he whispered, leaning against the inside wall. The hated voice answered.

Your task, and you've done it well.

"Fuck you!"

A throaty laugh was the bastard's only reply. Kalen's knees shook as he wiped the sweat from his face. His stomach rolled.

What was Beryl going to do? Whatever happened, it would be his fault. Kalen hoped he could find the strength enough to do the right thing. He had to go against Malik's order and stop Beryl.

God, please help me!

But He had never answered Kalen. Not once, in all his life.

And now he was prey to the one that would.

Aric held Rowan's hand as they walked down the corridor together. A silly thing, but it made him happy. He was all domesticated, a state he hadn't imagined himself in.

"I talked to my friend, Dean," she said. "Told him I resigned from the LAPD."

"What did he say?" He'd managed not to snarl when she'd said her best friend was some guy, and a handsome FBI agent at that. He congratulated himself on his calm tone.

"He wasn't exactly shocked. I'd told him about you. He'd like to come visit sometime."

"Hmm. We'd have to clear that with Nick, but since you said he's the one who learned about the compound in the first place, I'm guessing it won't be a problem. I bet Nick will want to speak with him in person about that, to try to find out where the leak came from."

"True."

Something was eating at him, and he had to get it off his chest. "Ro, you know I'd move to L.A. with you, if that's where you want to be. I mean that."

"I know, and I love you for it." She kissed his cheek. "But my home is here now, with you and the Pack."

He was about to say something else when Sariel came around the corner. The Fae prince stopped and gave them both a blinding smile, rustling his blue wings. Aric thought those were kind of cool, but he'd never say so.

"Congratulations on your mating," he said to them both. "Will you have what humans call a wedding?"

Aric glanced at Rowan, who shrugged. "I don't think either of us has thought about it. But to me we're already married, as shifters."

"True," the faery mused. "It's the same with my kind."

Before Aric could open his mouth, a deafening blast shook the hallway. Aric and Rowan were thrown to the floor, and as he fell, Aric saw the blast catch the prince high in his chest. Sariel flew backward, slamming into the wall with the sickening sound of the wall giving way and the crunch of breaking bones. He slid to the floor and didn't move.

In an instant, Rowan shifted. To his horror, she ran, attacking Beryl from the side. He had no time to wonder what the fuck the witch was doing loose. The bitch spun and sent a bolt of light at his mate, which struck her in the shoulder. His mate spun with a sharp yelp and crumpled.

Rage suffused him, and the shift happened with no conscious thought on his part. He was a killing machine, bent on the one goal of killing the bitch who'd harmed his mate. There would be no more reprieves for Beryl.

She saw him coming, smirked, sent another blast. Aric dodged it and it sailed harmlessly to his side, smashing into the wall behind him. He had one split second of immense satisfaction when her eyes widened and she knew death had finally come to call.

Then he leapt, was on her, sending them both crashing to the floor. Shouts sounded, the cavalry coming, but no one was going to stop him. Beryl grabbed at him, tried to shove him off her, but he lunged.

His big jaws closed on her neck and he sank his teeth deep. Her screech of pain was abruptly ended when he ripped out her throat. *Heal that, you skank.* He hung on until her body stopped twitching, then sat back on his haunches and let out a howl of victory.

This time, she really was dead.

But Rowan—

Shifting back to human form, he wiped his mouth and crawled to the small brown wolf's motionless body. He was hardly aware of the rest of the team pouring into the hallway as he gathered his precious mate into his arms.

"Rowan? Wake up, baby. Open your eyes for me."

"Aric!" Jax shouted. "What the fuck happened?"

"Beryl got loose somehow," he choked out. Tears pricked his eyes. "She hit Sariel. Check on him, please."

His friend went to do just that, and others joined him in tending to the Fae prince. Aric was worried about the guy, but his mate took top priority. She stirred some, and he could feel her breathing, lungs sawing in and out. Relief nearly undid him, but he tried to remain calm. For her.

Then her eyes opened and she blinked slowly. Her pink tongue poked out to tentatively lick his arm, and he laughed with profound joy. "My God, when she blasted you, I thought— Forget that. You're okay. Shift back, honey. For me?"

It took several moments, but at last he had a lapful of gorgeous naked woman. Who just grinned weakly and tried to make a joke out of the whole thing.

"After little things like drug dealers and gangbangers, witches, demons, and all that other shit are going to take some adjustment."

"You crazy woman," he said hoarsely, kissing the top of her head. "Don't do anything like that again."

"Um, I'm on the team now, Red. Job hazard."

"Damn. Well, promise you'll be more careful."

"Avoid magical blasts from the bitch witch. Check."

"Well, not *that* bitch witch. I killed her."

"Good," she said fiercely. "Wait—how's Sariel?"

"Let's help you on with your clothes and I'll check."

Together, they got her dressed. She was still shaky,

but insisted she was fine. He helped her limp over to where everyone surrounded the faery. Everyone but Kalen, who stood several yards away, his head hanging low, looking like he'd lost his best friend.

Aric turned his attention back to the prince. Melina, Mac, and Nick were crouched beside him, Melina holding a compress to his shoulder. Blood the color of a brilliant sapphire soaked the towel, and Aric's own blood ran cold. How the fuck were they supposed to replace Fae blood?

Noah and Sam, the heavyset nurse, came around the corner fast, wheeling a stretcher. Nick and the nurses lifted Sariel on the count of three, placed him on it, and strapped him down.

"Let's go!" Melina shouted. They set off at a rapid clip.

Nick turned to the Pack, leashing a barely controlled rage that Aric had never seen before. "Someone cover the witch's body until we can deal with it."

"I'll dispose of it," Kalen offered quietly. When no one objected, he turned Beryl's body to ash. Then the ashes swirled and vanished.

"Good riddance," someone muttered. Sounded like Jax.

Nick sighed. "Meeting in the conference room. Right fucking now."

Aric felt sick. He should've been faster, blocked the shot meant for the prince. Now all they could do was pray that he would survive.

Before he headed off, Nick paused to look Rowan over. "Maybe you should get checked out?"

"No, no. I'm just sore and I'll be bruised. Nothing that won't heal."

The boss nodded and walked off. The Pack trailed him, no one celebrating Beryl's demise. A good, gentle being they'd come to think of as one of their own was fighting for his life.

In the conference room, someone shut the door behind them. No one bothered to sit as Nick began. "How the fuck did Beryl get out of Block T?" he asked, his voice low and ominously calm.

For a long moment, there was silence.

"I let her out," Kalen admitted, voice catching. "God, I'm so sorry—"

"Why? Did she seduce you, or was it Malik?" There was no question that one of them must've gotten to the Sorcerer.

"Not her. Malik."

You could have heard a pin drop.

Nick's gaze was hard. "He gained control of your mind long enough to make you let her out?"

"Yes, sir," Kalen whispered. "I think Beryl spelled me, back at the house where we caught her. My defenses are . . . crumbling. I can't keep him out for very long at a time."

"Jesus," Aric said with a shudder. He wouldn't want some Unseelie creep fucking around in his brain.

Nick cursed viciously, rubbed his eyes. "Okay. We'll figure this out. At least now we have Malik's human name—Evan Kerrigan. Grant is tracking him down, gathering intel. With any luck we'll have his location and a complete profile soon."

Just then there was a knock, and Mac stepped inside. Her gaze went briefly to Kalen, and Aric saw real agony there, quickly covered as she addressed the group.

"I'm sorry to interrupt, but we knew you'd want

word of Sariel. We believe he'll recover." Sounds of relief went around the room. "But he was already weak-
ened from some health issues stemming from being in
our world, so healing will take time. He's stable,
though, so I wanted to pass the good news along."

"Thank you, Mac." Nick gave her a tired smile.

She returned it and left. Without looking at Kalen
again, who stared with longing at the place where
she'd just been.

Nick spoke to the group again. "All right. I need to
speak to Kalen. We'll adjourn for now and discuss this
mess later."

Nick led a shaken Kalen out, and Aric didn't envy
him the coming meeting. The Sorcerer was in for a long
session, no doubt. Aric wondered what this would
mean for his future in the Pack. He liked the kid. Hoped
like hell things would turn out okay for him.

Selfishly. Because if the Sorcerer turned on the Pack,
gave himself to the control of the Unseelie king . . .

They were screwed, down to the last man.

A hand settled on his shoulder, rubbing him gently.
"What do you say we go for a run, and escape for a
while?" Rowan suggested. "Just you and me?"

"I think that sounds like a fantastic idea."

Smiling, he took her hand and led the way out of the
building, across the field to the trailhead. This once, he
was going to break Nick's rule. Because he needed to
run with his mate. Make love in the sunshine.

Outside, they shifted and took off for the woods.
Letting their wolves loose, they ran for miles before finally slowing near a stream. They padded over and
took a long drink, slaking their thirst. Then he nipped
playfully at her rear end, yipping as she nipped back

and started chasing him. For several minutes they simply allowed themselves to be free, just a pair of wolf mates frolicking in the sun-dappled afternoon, splashing in the water.

God, they needed this time together. To just be. So they took it, playing until Aric shifted, laughing, and gathered his mate into his arms.

"Shift, baby."

She did, and he was suddenly holding an armful of beautiful, naked woman. Skin slick, water droplets clinging to her hair. She smiled at him and his breath caught in his throat. Rowan was everything he'd ever wanted and never allowed himself to believe he deserved.

Until now.

"I love you," he said, cupping her cheek.

Her lips parted and her eyes sparkled as she took his face in her hands. "I love you, too. So damned much."

Then there was no need for words. Scooping her up, he carried his precious burden to a grassy spot beyond the bank and set her down carefully. She held out her arms and he went into them gratefully, pressing her down, covering her sweet body with his. He captured her lips, kissed her senseless while he plucked at a nipple, already pert from their romp in the stream.

"Make love to me," she gasped.

"That's what I'm doing, baby. It's what I'll do for the rest of my life," he whispered.

Then he moved between her legs, pressed his cock into her moist heat. Slid home, and began to move in a slow, sensual rhythm. In and out, making sweet love to his mate.

And that's what it was. Love.

The pressure began to build, spreading that delicious ache through his balls and to every nerve ending. His entire world narrowed to the two of them, connected in a ritual older than time. Only one thing remained that they hadn't done, and it was something he wanted badly.

"Bite me," he panted, increasing his strokes. "Claim me! I'm so close, and I want to come when you do."

"Are you sure?" She hesitated, but he saw the light of excitement in her eyes.

"God, yes!"

Gathering her close, he pressed her face to the curve of his neck and shoulder. Her hot little tongue lapped at the spot for a few seconds—

And then she struck.

Her fangs sunk deeply into his flesh. A moment of bright, searing pain was quickly replaced by a bolt of ecstasy so intense he almost passed out.

"Ahhh!" His shout echoed through the treetops. His balls tightened and his cock exploded, and he came hard enough to see stars. His body shuddered as he emptied himself forever, vaguely aware that she was convulsing around him as well. After a few minutes, he came down to earth, still holding her close.

"Oh my God, that was amazing," he said breathlessly, kissing her soundly. "Can we do that again sometime? Not today, because coming that hard again in the same day might kill me!"

She giggled, burrowing into his chest. "Sure. But only if you promise to bite me first."

"Damn, who knew that biting thing was some sort of super sex stimulant?"

"If the other guys knew, they'd all be out scouring the countryside for their mates."

Grinning, he pulled out carefully and rolled to his back, taking her with him. She snuggled in and rested her head on his chest, making him feel about ten feet tall.

"I hope they all find their mates," he said, squeezing her tight. "Because nothing on earth compares to this."

"I agree. I believe a person can overcome anything, with someone special by her side. Someone made just for her."

"Or him." He kissed the top of her head. "Finding you sure proved that to me."

"I love you, wolf."

"I love you more, my baby."

They remained there in their private glen for a long while. To heck with rules, just for today.

Yes, there was a storm coming. And it threatened to consume them all in its fury.

But for now, he planned to spend every spare second loving his tough, beautiful mate.

Starting right now.

Turn the page for an exciting preview
of the next book in the Alpha Pack series,

BLACK MOON

Coming in December 2012 from Signet Eclipse

K alen Black stood apart from his team, awash in guilt, impotent in his shame.

Right this second the Alpha Pack's beloved resident Fae prince, Sariel, might be dying. On top of that, Beryl had nearly killed Aric's mate before Aric ripped out the witch's throat—and thereby put an end to any information they might have gained from her.

The danger surrounding them all increased daily. Hourly. A traitor walked among Kalen's friends and colleagues, slowly drowning in the darkness clogging his lungs. Overtaking his soul.

And it's all my fucking fault . . . because the traitor is me.

In the aftermath of Beryl's attack, as Aric tended to Rowan and the prince was rushed to the infirmary, Kalen hung his head. He tried to find comfort in the fact that Rowan was all right, but it didn't work. He wanted the earth to swallow him.

Then it got worse.

Nick Westfall, the Pack's commander, ushered everyone into the conference room and demanded, "How the fuck did Beryl get out of Block T?"

"I let her out." His voice caught. "God, I'm so sorry—"

"Why?"

Kalen died a thousand deaths during the questions that followed his confession and the truthful answers he supplied. In Kalen's wretched lifetime he'd suffered abuse and humiliation. Isolation. Starvation. More horrors than most people ever had to face.

But none of those matched the pain of *almost* achieving his dreams of a home, a job, a family of sorts, and, most of all, acceptance among those who were as different as he was. Almost. Before Malik, King of the Unseelie and Sariel's evil sire, had decided that Kalen Black was exactly the sort of powerful ally he needed in his quest to rule the world.

And that he'd begin by taking over the sorcerer's mind. One evil suggestion at a time.

Facing them all, Kalen admitted that Malik had invaded his mind. Manipulated him into doing his bidding and letting Beryl out of her cell, where her goal, or rather Malik's, was apparently for her to kill Sariel. Though the spell wasn't Kalen's fault, and he hadn't known that Beryl would try to murder the Fae prince, it hardly mattered. He was to blame. He should've been stronger.

Even without the protection of his silver pentagram pendant. The one he'd given to Dr. Mackenzie Grant weeks ago and made her swear never to remove.

After Kalen's confession, he barely heard Nick's brief comments to the team reminding them all that Malik was posing as a wealthy human by the name of Evan

Kerrigan. When Mackenzie came into the room to report that it looked like Sariel would survive, he could feel nothing but self-loathing. His gaze settled on the beautiful doctor, hungrily devouring the woman he could never have again, never allow into his mind or heart. The woman he had to protect at all costs from Malik.

From himself.

"Thank you, Mac," Nick said, bringing Kalen back to the present. She returned Nick's smile and left.

Without once looking at me.

Nick went on. "All right. I need to speak to Kalen. We'll adjourn for now and discuss this mess later."

Nick nodded at Kalen, indicating he should follow. He trailed the commander, wondering if he could take the man in a fight. Nick was tall and muscular, strode with his broad shoulders back, head up, all easy grace and confidence. Yeah, this man had both power and skill. Kalen had seen him take on dozens of enraged Sluagh, the huge batlike creatures that were Malik's drones. Just swat them down like they were flies, and spit on their carcasses. Nick didn't need the gift of sorcery; with brute strength alone he could definitely dispose of Kalen.

Not that Kalen *would* defend himself. No, whatever the white wolf chose to dish out, he deserved.

In Nick's office, the man closed the door and walked to his desk, parking his ass on the edge of it. With a sigh, he ran a hand through his short black hair threaded with silver at the temples, and crossed his arms. "Sit down."

Kalen complied without comment and waited.

"Tell me exactly what happened before you were compelled to set Beryl free. Don't leave anything out."

That was not a scene he'd wanted to revisit. Ever.

But the steely look in Nick's deep blue eyes said that Kalen wasn't getting out of telling the truth. He took a deep breath. "I was in my quarters about an hour ago and the bastard started prying into my head again." They both knew he was referring to Malik. "He told me that he'd never abandon me as everyone else in my life has done."

"Smart," Nick said, an edge of disgust to his tone. "He's isolating the vulnerable cub from the pack, playing the caring mentor."

"I'm *not* a cub." His youth was a sore spot. Always had been, ever since he'd been kicked out of his home at the age of fourteen, nine very long years ago. A lifetime. He'd had to scrabble, and suffer, for every morsel that eased the hunger in his belly. For every night not spent in a dirty alley under a cardboard box.

He didn't feel twenty-three—more like a hundred.

"Trust me—you are, despite all the power that Unseelie asshole is attempting to harness in you. I don't say that as an insult," Nick said seriously. "What I mean is that, in you, Malik has found a young Sorcerer on the cusp of becoming all he is meant to be. As strong as you are, Kalen, you're nowhere near as powerful as you'll be in a few years, then in a few decades. It's like when the very first coach that ever saw Michael Jordan in action said, 'My God, that kid is going to be the greatest player in the NBA one day.'"

In spite of himself, Kalen snorted a laugh.

"It's true," Nick went on. "Malik knows you're a rising star and he wants you on his team. I can't let that happen. Do you understand?"

A lump lodged in his throat. "Do you want me to

leave after all? Or are you just going to take me out now and be done with it?"

"Finish telling me how Malik manipulated you earlier."

It didn't escape his notice that Nick hadn't answered the question. "He promised me power, told me all I had to do to get it was surrender to him. I tried to fight it, but he was . . . very seductive."

"In a sexual way?"

Kalen felt sick, and fought it down. "Yeah. The bastard touched me, and suddenly I wanted everything he was selling. God, Nick," he choked out, "what's wrong with me?"

The commander pushed away from his desk and walked over to stand by Kalen's chair, gripping the young Sorcerer's shoulder. "There's not a damned thing wrong with you. Like the rest of us, you're trying to get a foothold on fighting the Unseelie; only for you it's worse because he's taking a personal interest in recruiting you. That means he'll stop at nothing to get what he wants. Creatures like him wield seduction like a weapon."

"I know. Just like I know him messing with me was nothing but a mindfuck, but that doesn't make it better. I'm losing my goddamned mind." Burying his hands in his hair, he held on as though he could keep his scrambled brains inside. "I called him Master, and I liked his approval. No, I craved it, and would've done anything in that moment to please him. So I guess you're right about the cub thing, huh?"

"Jesus Christ." Nick's gaze pierced him to the core. "Then what happened?"

Kalen lowered his hands to his lap, fists clenched.

"He told me to let Beryl out of her cell. He said she had a task to perform before she left, and that she was never meant to stay with us. I didn't know he meant for her to die, but I should have. Then I let her out, took her up to the ground level, where she attacked Sariel. Rowan and Aric went after her, and Aric killed her."

The commander fell silent for so long, fear balled in Kalen's gut. Finally he gathered his courage and asked once more, "Are you going to kill me?"

"If I said yes, would you submit?"

Kalen nodded, the bottom falling out of his stomach. "I would."

"Why?" Nick cocked his head.

"Because you're a PreCog and that means you can sometimes see the future. On top of that you're a good, fair man. So if the future is better without me in it, if my death will keep the Pack and other innocents safe . . ." He couldn't finish.

"On your knees, Sorcerer."

The commander's tone was cold, his blue eyes like the Arctic North. Legs shaking, Kalen slid from his seat and knelt on the stubby carpet. Placed his hands on his jeans-clad thighs and stared at his polished black fingernails, which were digging into his legs painfully. His heart thundered in his chest, threatening to break his sternum.

Then Nick walked around his desk and opened a top drawer. Reached in and lifted out the biggest fucking hand cannon Kalen had ever seen. The spit dried up in his mouth and he watched numbly as the Alpha wolf approached, went to stand behind him.

The hard muzzle of the gun pressed to the back of

his head. So he'd die on his knees, execution-style. Quick and painless.

Oh, God. Take my soul before Malik can claim it, and look after Mackenzie, too. That's all I ask.

"I'm sorry, kid."

Kalen squeezed his eyes shut. Time crawled to a standstill.

The crack of a gunshot split the air.

"Dr. Grant?"

Mackenzie pushed an errant lock of curly dark hair behind her ear and looked up from the paperwork on her desk to see Noah standing there. The cute blond nurse was wearing a pleased expression as he hovered in the doorway to her office.

"What's up?"

"Blue's finally awake," he said. "Blue" was the name a lot of the staff at the compound called the Fae prince, due to his long, gorgeous blue hair and matching wings.

"That's great news!" She smiled at Noah. "Does Dr. Mallory know?" Melina Mallory was her colleague and a damned fine doctor. Mac counted her as a friend, but the woman also ruled the roost in the infirmary as well as in their research on shifters and other paranormal beings.

"She's with him now. All his vitals are looking good—well, at least for what we know about faeries, anyhow. The prince has got some color back in his face, but he's still refusing to eat. I wouldn't be worried—I mean, it's not surprising that a patient wouldn't be hungry after being severely wounded—except Blue hasn't been eating well since he's been here at the compound."

"We need to keep an eye on that," she said worriedly. "If his weight drops so much as another ounce, I want to know."

"You bet," Noah said. Some of his natural cheer returned. "But he's back with us and that's what counts."

"Yes, it is." Standing, she stretched. "Go and tell Sariel I'll check on him in a short while. I've got a couple of things to do first."

"Yes, ma'am!"

With that, the nurse was gone. Mac couldn't help but be fond of the guy. Noah was a bundle of energy, lived at the compound, loved his job, and rarely took any extra time off. He was in his element taking care of wounded Pack members when they were sent out to battle rogue paranormals and were frequently injured. He'd also started working with Kira, rehabbing the innocent creatures like Sariel, who had no one else to care for them and help them adjust in what was, to them, a strange world.

Noah was adorable, and fantastic at what he did.

After straightening her papers, she walked out of her office and down the corridor, past the exam rooms, in the opposite direction of the patient's rooms. She headed toward the lobby of the infirmary, past the receptionist, and into the main hallway leading to the rest of the compound.

Only when she was alone did she reach up to touch the pendant hanging around her neck from its long chain. The weight of the disk was solid, comforting. She could feel the raised ridges that formed the pentagram within the circle and the pendant seemed to warm in her hand. Almost as though it was seeking to reassure her that it would always do what Kalen had said— protect her from all evil.

Including Malik. The Unseelie slime had sent a Sluagh to attack her and Kalen in town a few weeks ago, and Mac had been scratched by the beast. This had somehow allowed Malik a portal into her mind, and the bastard had truly frightened her. Kalen had promptly given his beloved amulet to Mac, his sole possession of any sentimental value. The enchanted protection his grandmother had given to him was now Mac's.

Oh, but Kalen had shared so much more than that. Her footsteps faltered and she halted, remembering.

Breathy moans and tangled sheets. Messy black hair falling over his kohl-rimmed green eyes as he moved over her. Thrusting, possessing.

Making love.

And then it was over and he'd pulled into his isolated shell, claiming there could be nothing between them. He'd given her the pendant, made her promise never to remove it, and then put miles of emotional distance between them. They might as well have been living on different planets, it was so great.

Why?

A loud *crack* startled Mac, making her jump. The noise echoed down the corridor, and as it faded, she realized what the sound had been.

A gunshot.

Heart thundering, she took off in the direction of the noise. Kalen had used his Sorcerer's power to ward the compound against intruders, but perhaps a Sluagh or some other creature had gotten inside. Or maybe one of the creatures from Block R had become feral.

But no, the sound took her past Rehab, past the wings where the living quarters were located. Men from the Pack bolted from their rooms, came from every direction, rushed past her. She ran, at last realizing they were heading for Nick's office. She couldn't imagine what terrible thing could have happened.

Until she saw Nick standing like a statue over Kalen's prone body, a smoking gun in his hand.

Then Mac's eyes rolled up in her head and she saw nothing more.

I'm not shot. Holy fuck, I'm alive.

Kalen stared at the burned spot in the carpet right next to his leg for about five seconds before he slumped to the floor. His body simply refused to cooperate any longer, and he lay there in shock, hardly believing he was breathing.

"I had to know if you'd go through with it," Nick said quietly. "I'm sorry."

"Shit," he croaked.

"Your last thought was for the safety of others, not yourself. You were willing to die for the greater good, and that means Malik hasn't won. You're a good man at the core, and so there's hope."

"Nick, am I fighting this battle just to die anyway?" It was a question he'd asked before, and he received the same answer.

"I don't know."

"And you wouldn't tell me even if you could."

"That's right."

God, what a screwed-up mess. He wasn't sure how he would've responded, but the sound of footsteps, voices raised in concern, floated from the corridor.

Kalen let out a deep sigh, humiliated that the team would witness this and learn about Nick's little "test" of his worthiness.

"Hey, catch her!"

Her? Kalen sat up quickly, just in time to see Zander scoop Mackenzie into his arms and lift her against his chest. Kalen shot to his feet and, before he thought about what he was doing, grabbed the doctor from Zan with a snarl, holding her close. He glared at the man, warning him back.

Zan raised his hands, palms out. "Chill, man. Would you rather I had let her hit the floor?"

With an effort, he calmed himself. Zan was only trying to help. But inside, his panther raged at seeing Mac—*their woman*—in the arms of another male. He'd never felt anything like it in his life. It was confusing as hell.

"No, sorry," he managed. "I'll just—"

"You can put me down."

Anxiously, he looked down into Mac's beautiful face. Large blue eyes fringed with dark lashes stared up at him, blinking away tears. His gut tightened, knowing he'd been the cause of her tears, in more ways than one.

"It wasn't what it looked like, exactly."

"Put me down. Please," she entreated softly.

Reluctantly, he did as she asked, but that didn't stop him from checking her from head to toe. "Are you okay? Are you hurt anywhere?"

"No." She glanced around at the guys who'd assembled there, her cheeks pale as milk. Swallowing hard, she said, "I'm fine. Now tell me what the hell is going on in here."

"Nick gave me a test. I passed. The end."

She scowled at Nick. "What sort of test involves firing a gun at one of your men?"

Nick addressed the group, keeping the explanation to the point. "Kalen was willing to be executed rather than risk bringing harm to his team. There's still hope that he can be saved from Malik's control, so we'll see this through. Anybody disagree?"

No one did. One by one each man, plus their lone female, swore loyalty to the team. And that loyalty included Kalen. As he looked at each of them, he couldn't breathe. *Never* had anyone stood up for him. Stood by him. Not even his own parents, the people who should have sheltered him and loved him the most. The idea that these people who'd come into his life so recently would have his back, even in the wake of him letting them down, overwhelmed him.

He could hardly speak. "I swear I'll do my best not to fail all of you again."

Or he'd die trying. Suddenly the chaos inside him seemed to settle and his purpose became clear—he'd fight Malik with everything in him. And when the time came, he'd make the right choice.

Whatever that proved to be.

"Excuse me," Mackenzie said tightly. "But I think I'm going to be sick."

Spinning around, she dashed to a woman's restroom down the hall from Nick's office and disappeared inside. He would've gone after her, but Nick blocked his way.

"You should probably let her be right now."

It wasn't a suggestion. Frustration rose, along with his anger. Quelling his pissed-off panther again, he nodded and strode in the opposite direction, putting as much distance between himself and everyone else as fast as possible.

Just as he'd done all his life.

"Mac?"

"In here." Bent over the sink, Mac finished rinsing her mouth, then turned off the water. Glancing at Melina, she grabbed some paper towels from the dispenser, dried her face, and tossed them in the trash. "See? I'm fine."

"I don't think so." Melina's sharp scrutiny roamed over Mac's face, and she apparently didn't like what she saw. "To the infirmary with you. I'm going to give you a checkup."

"I don't need—"

"I didn't *ask*. I'm telling you. Doctors make the worst patients," she grumbled. "Let's go."

There was no arguing with her friend when she had a bug up her ass, so Mac relented. Though Melina was slight of frame, and sort of resembled an elf with her short cap of dark hair, she was fully capable of making the toughest Pack member cringe in fear. She was a tough, militant bitch.

And that was when she was in a good mood.

Her friend hadn't always been that way, but that was before her mate, Terry, the Alpha Pack's former commander, had been killed in an ambush several months ago. Accepting Nick as the new leader in her mate's place had been hard on the woman, and she and Nick didn't always see eye to eye. But they'd found some peace between them, based on mutual respect.

Melina led Mac into an exam room and gestured to

the table covered with the hated crinkly white paper. "Sit."

Dutifully, Mac did, and proceeded to subject herself to a complete physical. Melina checked her eyes, ears, nose, and throat. Checked her reflexes. All seemed clear, but the woman still wasn't satisfied.

"I don't like it one bit that you fainted," she said with a frown.

"For God's sake, I thought Nick had killed Kalen! Give me a break."

"How long have you been queasy? Don't think I haven't noticed."

She had? Mac blinked at her friend, hedging. "I don't know. A few days, maybe."

"How often have you been throwing up?"

Mac stared at her, silent. *Shit, shit.*

"O-kay," Melina drawled, brows raised. "Here's what's going to happen. Noah is coming in to take blood for a complete standard workup. Then you're going into the restroom to pee in a cup. Then you'll come back in here, sit down, and wait for me. Got it?"

She sighed. "Yes."

"Good girl."

Melina patted her knee and left. Soon after, Noah came in, swabbed the crook of her elbow, and took three vials of blood. When he was finished, he pressed a cotton ball over the injection site and topped it with a Band-Aid.

Giving her a smile, he pointed in the direction of the restroom. "Go do your thing."

She absolutely hated peeing in a cup. It was a dicey proposition at best, aiming just right. But she managed and in short order was sitting back in the exam room.

Where the clock on the wall ticked by with unbearable sluggishness.

Five minutes passed. Ten. Mac was starting to fidget when Melina walked in, carrying a sheaf of paper. Her friend closed the door and slowly turned to her. The expression on Melina's face sent a bolt of terror all the way to her toes.

"What is it?" she gasped, gripping the edge of the table. "What's wrong?"

"Mac, honey. We have to talk."

Also Available

J.D. Tyler

Black Magic
An Alpha Pack Novella

AN ORIGINAL NOVELLA
AVAILABLE ONLY AS AN eSPECIAL

Recruited by the Alpha Pack, Kalen Black is still very
much a lone wolf. But when a paranormal creature
threatens the life of Dr. Mackenzie Grant, Kalen must
use all of his abilities to rescue her. This brush with death
excites a passion between them, and after a night of
intense pleasure, Kalen leaves Mac with a mysterious
gift that just might save her life again...

"Readers will fall head over heels for the Alpha Pack!"
—*New York Times* bestselling author Angela Knight

**Available wherever books are sold or at
penguin.com**

Also Available

J.D. Tyler

Primal Law
An Alpha Pack Novel

Meet the Alpha Pack, a top-secret military team of wolf-shifters fighting the most dangerous predators in the world, human and nonhuman. After a massacre leaves Jaxon Law crippled, he must relearn how to fight—and battle the anger and guilt threatening to overwhelm him.

But when Jax rescues a beautiful woman who awakens his primal instincts, he is unprepared for the dangers that lie ahead. Soon he must decide if the deep connection he feels with Kira is worth defying the ultimate shifter law...

**Available wherever books are sold or at
penguin.com**